RED STAR 4: VICTORY

RED STAR 4: VICTORY

Dennis J. Barton

iUniverse, Inc.
New York Lincoln Shanghai

Red Star 4: Victory

iUniverse, Inc.

For information address:
iUniverse, Inc.
2021 Pine Lake Road, Suite 100
Lincoln, NE 68512
www.iuniverse.com

ISBN: 0-595-32212-3

Printed in the United States of America

07-09-2112

Thomas woke in a dimly lit space that was rather cold and very hard. He was laying on a concrete floor in a Vigilance holding cell. His head hurt. He had fought Cardinal Api and Father Brown, and he had lost. He had fought them for some time, but they were strong, and fast, stronger and faster than even he was, and, unlike him, they did not seem to tire. This was because they were machines, Thomas reminded himself. Father Brown and Cardinal Api were machines, and the whole of what he had been raised to believe was a lie. The Great CPU, Almighty Harold, the Holy Program, all of it a lie, lie, lie. The sharp shock of this truth had ceased, but the dull ache remained, might always remain, and Thomas could not help but go over it again and again in his mind. It was very much like the feeling he'd had when he'd lost his first tooth, back in the days of his boyhood. There had been a hole, and some blood. The blood had stopped, but the hole had remained for what had seemed a very long time, and it had been nearly impossible to resist the urge to feel that hole with his tongue, to poke absently, or with conscious intent, at the empty space that had once been a wound.

"You fought very well," came a voice from somewhere further back in the cell.

Thomas sat up, and the throbbing in his head came on with much greater strength. He looked back into the gloom and saw a man standing there, a man in an blue jump-suit. "Who are you?" Thomas asked.

"My name is Billy," said the man, stepping forward into the slightly brighter space toward the front of the cell. Dim light from the hallway beyond the bars fell on the front of the man's jump-suit, and Thomas could make out the details on a round patch sewn onto the left breast. A circular swirl of white and gray around a solid black dot. Gold letters at top read "CYGNUS". Thomas looked at the man's face. He'd seen that face before. Far beneath Syrinx. Thomas had seen this very man laying quiet and still on a table, under a clear plexi-glass dome, far beneath the Central Temple at Syrinx.

"I've seen you, at Syrinx," Thomas said, trying to remember everything crazy old Robert had told him about this man. "You're Robert and Michael's brother, right?"

"I am," said Billy. "How are you feeling?"

"I've felt better." Thomas got to his feet. His body ached all over.

"You're doing well, considering the beating you took from the constructs. There isn't another man on this earth who could have survived that fight." Billy smiled a mild little smile. "What are your plans now?"

"My plans? I guess I haven't thought that far ahead yet."

"I don't suppose I blame you, but I came to let you know that time is of the essence. I came to urge you to action sooner rather than later."

Thomas sat down on the hard plastic palette mounted to the near wall. "Alright, what kind of action?"

"Well, you'll want to get out of here, for starters. I suggest you bend the bars and make an escape," said Billy.

Thomas looked over at the bars. "You think it'll be that simple? I just bend the bars and walk out of here?"

Billy nodded. "You know that Father Brown and Cardinal Api are machines. Like all machines, they follow various protocols to perform their assigned functions. What is the standard Vigilance protocol for the handling of prisoners?"

"Well, you search them for weapons, then confine them in a cell until they can be processed."

"Have they taken your weapons?"

Thomas felt his pockets. "Yes."

"Have they confined you in a cell?" Billy asked.

"It would seem so," said Thomas.

"It's that simple then."

"But I'm no ordinary prisoner," Thomas offered.

"Are there, to your knowledge, any rules or regulations regarding extraordinary prisoners?" Billy asked.

"Not to my knowledge, no," Thomas told him.

"I can assure you, there are none."

"But they know about my enhancements, they know what I can do, they've fought me."

"And yet here you are, in an ordinary cell," said Billy. "That's just the way machines think, Thomas. Even very complex machines. That's just the way they are. You know, you could take the most advanced computer in the world and ask it to calculate *pi* to infinity, and it wouldn't know when to stop, it would just run that calculation forever and ever."

"Okay," said Thomas. "What's *pi*?"

"An interesting number, that's all. Used to be part of a basic education, *pi*, circles, all that. A little ironic, really, that *pi* is used to calculate the area of a circle, and can also be used to throw a processor into an eternal loop. Don't worry, children will be taught geometry again, if all goes well. Now I suggest you extricate yourself from your current situation. Find a med-station, and patch yourself up. There is much to be done."

Thomas was about to stand, to go and test Billy's theory, that he could simply bend the bars and walk out of this place, but then he remembered Jon. "They—Harold—still has my friend Jon. Even if I can break out of here, if I do it, they'll kill him."

Billy shrugged. "You mean Harold has your friend? That didn't stop you from fighting with Api and Brown, did it?"

There was no denying Billy's logic. Jon could already be dead. There was no trusting the evil that presented itself as divine, no trusting the Harold who would kidnap and hold Jon against his will. Thomas stood up and walked over to the bars that separated his cell from the hallway beyond. He grabbed a bar in each hand and pulled. The metal groaned and bent, and it felt good to Thomas, after being so soundly defeated by Father Brown and Cardinal Api, to exert his strength and witness such a tangible result. To know that he wasn't so powerless as those two machines had made him feel. He bent the two bars, then applied all his strength to just one until it broke, until it snapped at top and bottom. Then he did the same to the second bar.

He turned around with the second bar in his hands, to show Billy Lifeson just how right he had been, about this being just an ordinary cell, but Billy Lifeson was no longer there. Billy Lifeson had vanished. Thomas dropped the bar and it clattered and bounced against the concrete floor. He searched the corners for secret panels or hidden passageways, but there were none. He was all alone, and there was no sense in hanging around. Thomas snatched up the bar he'd just dropped. It was the best weapon at hand, and would have to do until he could find something better. He had no intention of being so easily defeated again. They would have to kill him to stop him. He would not be defeated again by such walking talking heretical lies.

Thomas walked down the block of empty cells, to the plasteel door that stood between the hallway and the section hub. He looked out the tiny plexi window and saw two Level One Eyes chatting and laughing as they sat before the control console. Each sat with his boots propped up on the counter. Their dark gray Detention Division uniforms were well-pressed, crisp and clean, but each of them needed a haircut, and their lack of attention to detail was horrendous. If they'd been paying any attention to the monitors mounted on the console before them, they would have seen him breaking out of his cell. They would have known he was standing right there, watching them when they should have been watching him, when they should have been calling for back-up. Their light-duty weapons-belts were slung on the backs of their chairs, putting their batons and their pistols out of easy reach. These two were a disgrace to all Vigilance. There had never been an escape, or even a serious attempt at escape from any Vigilance holding facility, but it still pained Thomas to know there were men like this in the service, even while he felt grateful that two such men had been left as his guard.

Thomas stood there watching these lazy men for minutes. He knew he should be going, but their lack of concern for their responsibilities was simply amazing. He had encountered this same level of apathy throughout Vigilance. He had seen much more of it when he'd been a street-level grunt. He'd seen it in his best friend Jon, and here it was again, the complete absence of any sense of duty. Maybe these kinds of men had known more than he had, Thomas thought. Maybe they had known more than he had all along, maybe he had been simply naïve, as his own sense of duty had been built on a foundation of belief in Almighty Harold, and in monsters like Father Brown and Cardinal Api. While these men were sinful in their sloth, maybe he himself had been the worst of sinners, Thomas thought, as he had so diligently believed in and supported a system built on blasphemy and lies.

Thomas had been ready to simply break down the door, but with this strange contemplation, with this unexpected reversal of thought, he altered his plan. These men were just two of the Eyes he'd have to face before he could escape the city. He had no doubts he could defeat these two and all those others of varying dedication and diligence. They would not take him down, but they could slow him down. It would take forever to get out of Megadon if he had to stop and fight a knot of Eyes on every corner. There was an easier way, he thought, a much easier way, a way that might end all the heresy and all the lies more quickly than anything else, and it was worth a try. Thomas raised his fist and knocked on the door, causing both the Eyes in the section hub to swing their heads in his direction, and put their boots on the floor.

They sat there staring at the heavy door, and at Thomas' face in the little window. Thomas waved, and the jailers turned to one another, exchanged a few words, and got up from their chairs. They strapped on their weapons-belts, and walked over to the door. One, the name on his uniform read 'Terabyte', came very close and squinted at Thomas through the window. "What're you doing, sir?" he asked. "You're supposed to be in your cell, sir."

"Let me out," Thomas said, uncertain whether he would be heard through the plexiglass, but quite sure the man would be able to read his lips.

Terabyte stared for a moment, then turned to the other man, whose name was printed on his uniform as 'Steffek'. Thomas couldn't hear exactly what they said to one another, but there was a lot of shrugging between them. He caught a few words and phrases, reading their lips. Words and phrases like "Vice Chancellor" and "orders" and "I don't know".

Terabyte heaved a sigh and turned back to Thomas. Steffek stepped up closer and hit the wall-switch that released the lock. Then Terabyte opened the door a couple of centimeters, and peeked in at Thomas. "You're supposed to be in your cell, Vice Chancellor," he said.

"Things have changed," Thomas told him. "And they're going to change some more." He slowly but firmly pulled the door wide open. Both Terabyte and Steffek pulled against him, but they came along with the door, until they were standing in the hallway with Thomas. "Now," Thomas told them. "Who am I?"

"You're the Vice Chancellor, sir," said Steffek.

"That's right," Thomas said. "And who are you?"

The two straightened up and saluted, barking out their names and ranks almost as if they were top-notch spit-shined and fully dedicated Eyes.

"Where are you two from? Level Two, Four?" Thomas asked.

"That's right sir, LevTwo here, sir," said Terabyte.

"LevThree, sir," said Steffek.

"Do you know where I'm from?" Thomas asked them.

And they both beamed at him. "Oh yes, sir! It's all the talk with the enlisted grunts, sir!" said Steffek.

"Is it true, sir? That you're from LevOne, sir?" Terabyte asked.

"Yes is it," Thomas told them. "I guess that makes the three of us kind of alike, doesn't it?"

The two men looked to one another for the right answer. They smiled, but it was clear they thought they were being lead into some kind of a trap. "Is, is this some kind of a test, sir?" Terabyte asked.

"No test, Terabyte. Just the facts. Do you like living on LevTwo, or LevThree? Do you think it's nice there?"

The men shrugged. "It's home, sir," said Steffek.

"It's dirty, it's dark, it's loud," Thomas told them. "It's a lot better on the upper levels, don't you think?"

"Never been, sir," said Steffek.

"I have," said Terabyte. "I rode through LevFifty once. It's much better, sir."

"Okay, so are you ready to help me change things or not?" Thomas asked, gruffly, with force.

"Yes, sir!" Terabyte snapped. Steffek hesitated, but then followed his partner's lead.

"Alright, where are my things?" Thomas demanded.

"In the locker, sir!" Terabyte trotted back around the console to get Thomas the gear Father Brown and Cardinal Api had taken away.

Steffek stayed where he was, staring at Thomas. "Sir?" he asked.

"Yes?"

"Won't we be in trouble, for letting you go, sir? It was Father Brown, the Chancellor himself who brought you in, sir."

"Is Father Brown from LevOne?" Thomas asked.

"No, sir."

"Has Father Brown ever stopped to talk to you, like I have?"

"No, sir."

"When it comes right down to it, which one of us is going to stand up for you, me or Father Brown?"

Steffek hesitated. "Uh, you, sir?"

Terabyte trotted back with Thomas' pistol and phone, handed them over. "Thank you, Terabyte."

"You're welcome, sir!"

"Terabyte, Steffek and I were just discussing the possibility that Father Brown might return to find me gone, and that this might put you two some trouble. And Steffek's right. If that monster comes back and finds you've let me go, he'll probably kill both of you. Literally kill you. I've seen him do it to other men. But I'm going, whether you try to stop me or not, so I'll give you a couple options. We can stage a struggle, and I can hurt each of you badly enough that no one will doubt that you tried to stop me. I can knock you out, and break your arms, or whatever you think would be enough. That's option one. Option two, you could come with me, help me to change things. This won't be easy either, as there will be stiff opposition. You could be killed. But if we win, I promise things will be different. No more being stuck on the lower levels. No more living in filth for nothing. So, it's up to you. I guess there's the third option, where you both stay here and we *don't* stage a struggle, but, like I said, Father Brown will probably kill you. What's it going to be?"

"You *are* the Vice Chancellor, sir," said Steffek.

"For the moment, yes."

"I'm with you, sir!" snapped Terabyte.

"Me too, sir," said Steffek.

"Alright. I've never worked in Detention, but you have a small weapons-store, correct?"

"Yes, sir!"

"Good, let's take all we can carry."

Terabyte and Steffek opened lockers built into the wall behind their console. Five pistols, five batons, two shotguns. Thomas took a second pistol, and a baton. He had the two men take the rest. Thomas was leading them out of the cell-block when something else occurred to him. He stopped in the doorway and turned to his new followers. "Are there any other prisoners back there?" he asked.

Of twenty-two prisoners on the cell-block, only six left with Thomas. The others were too timid to attempt an escape, even when invited by the Vice Chancellor of Vigilance himself. There was a Level Twenty-Three housewife who had been out past curfew without her husband. She had been robbed of her last solar by a gang of LevOne tough-kids, and had been unable to pay for public transit and unable to make it home on foot before curfew. The Eyes who had arrested her had shown no patience for her excuses. There was a man from LevFour whose arm had been broken when he had dozed off at his job in a soy warehouse and been hit by a speeding forklift. He had then been arrested for failing to meet quotas on his shifts. There was a low-level administrator who had made some kind of minor clerical error while tallying daily tonnages of sewage processed on LevOne. He had been arrested for falsifying official records. There was a seven-year-old boy from Level Eleven who'd forgotten to log on to PrayerNet for his evening prayers. He had been arrested for impiety. These were the kinds of souls locked up in the cell-block, all lost to the world, not bad people but the victims of misfortune, in the wrong place at the wrong time. Thomas opened all the cells, and left them open, giving those who refused to join him the chance to reconsider escape. He ordered Terabyte and Steffek to distribute weapons to the six prisoners who came along. A brief group-lesson in the use of these weapons, little more than point-and-shoot, and Thomas lead his small force of eight out of the cell-block.

"Let's visit the other cell-blocks," he told his followers. "Don't use force, don't even point your weapons at anything but the floor unless I give the order."

The guards in the next cell-block snapped to attention when Thomas strode into their hub. "At ease men," he told them, "but listen, and listen good. You know who I am?"

"Yes sir!" they snapped.

"Good. I'm going to be making some changes. You join me, or you can remain here, the choice is yours." Thomas told them. He paused before proceeding, paused to let his words sink in.

He picked up another four followers in that cell-block, and another seven in the next, and another three in the next. Thomas visited cell-block after cell-block, and by the time he lead his force out onto the streets, there were sixty-four people behind him. They weren't the best, and they weren't the brightest, but they were behind him, and they were all bearing arms. It was no easy task before him, Thomas thought, but he'd made a good start, and there was no backing down. He was the Vice-Chancellor of Vigilance, and it didn't matter if the Chancellor himself was a demon-machine spawned in the darkest regions of Abend. Thomas was the Vice-Chancellor, and it was his job to do what was right, to deliver justice to the people. He would do it alone if he had to, but it warmed his heart to know there were righteous souls ready to join him, these tens behind him and many thousands more who knew what was right, who knew it was time for a change.

David sat on the grass with his back to a tree-trunk, watching Mal trying to hit this woman named Maggie, who used to be David's mother but now was somebody else. Mal had a long padded staff in his hands and was swinging for all he was worth at this *Maggie*, who, back when she had been David's mom, had insisted that everyone call her *Mrs. Lifeson*. Now she was *Maggie*, and not only did she spar with Mal and with Rosella, but she swore almost as badly as Mal swore, and drank hooch almost as much as Uncle Robert drank hooch. She looked like David's mother, but she didn't talk like David's mother, didn't even move like David's mother, and while David had always liked his dad better than his mother because he thought his mother was upset with everything and all uptight all the time, while his mother hadn't been any fun at all, he wanted her back and wanted this *Maggie* to go away.

"Hey, David, you going to give me some fucking help here, or not?!" Mal yelled, taking a swing with his staff. Maggie slipped under the arc of the intended blow and trapped his leg with one of her own, causing him to fall flat onto his back.

"Yeah, dammit! Come on, son, help me burn off some of this fucking fat!" Maggie called. She was wearing a boob-covering top and shorts she'd borrowed from Rosella, both of which were stretched nearly to the point of bursting. Her pale flabby rough-textured gut hung out between the top and the shorts, and her big fat legs ballooned from the legs of the shorts. David had never wanted to see so much of his mother, and he wished she would go find the doctor's robes she'd worn out of Red Star Medical Center. Those robes had been blood-stained, but at least they'd covered her body. The costume she wore now, it wasn't just sinfully indecent, it was just plain gross.

"I have to check on something," David lied, getting up, walking off toward the barn. "You two go ahead without me."

"No problem!" Mal shouted from the ground, swinging fiercely at Maggie's shins with his staff.

David walked off to the barn. He rounded one corner of the big wooden structure, to put the bulk of the building between himself and the creature who claimed to be his mother. He could still hear her teasing and threatening Mal, could still hear the stream of foul language that spouted too frequently from her big mouth. His mother didn't have a big mouth like that. She had a big mouth, but not like that, only about stupid things like Uncle Robert's hooch-drinking or the way Dad used to sometimes not tuck in his shirt just right. David's Mom didn't swear or fight or expose her body the way this weird woman did.

"What's crawled into your underpants, boyo?" Uncle Robert stood just inside the wide entryway where the red Barchetta crouched with its hood propped open by a thin metal rod. Uncle Robert held a small wrench. His hands and forearms were smudged black with grease and dirt. "You in some kind of a trance or something?"

David shook his head. "What're you doing to the car? Is it broken?"

Uncle Robert shook his head. "No, I just like to make sure it's all adjusted right, the belts, mostly. They contract and expand with fluctuations in temperature. Not much, just a little, but, you know, it never hurts to check out under the hood on a regular basis. Like this one time, I had an old two-thousand ten Toyota Suprix, a nice little car, but it had about a million miles on it, and it had developed the smallest oil-leak you ever want to have seen. Well, I went overseas to do a little business, and left the thing in storage to keep it from being stolen, because it was kind of a collector's item, and I was gone for eight months, thinking it'd be okay. I got back, got in the car in this fairly dark garage, without even noticing that little tiny leak over eight months had drained the oil out all over the damned place, and I get in and drive off. It was a good car, because that engine took almost a week to seize up, but then it left me on the highway ten miles from the nearest exit. Just goes to show, you can't look under the hood too often."

"Okay," David said, and moved closer, to look down at the guts of the hot red machine. It looked complex, with tubes and wires and belts and wheels and bottles of different-colored fluids.

"Geez, man, what's your problem, anyway? You alright?" Uncle Robert asked.

"Nothing," David told him.

"Bullshit nothing," said Uncle Robert. "It's your damned mother, isn't it?"

"She's not supposed to be like that."

"Like what?"

"Like a crazy lady!" David said. "Have you heard the language coming out of her mouth? Have you *seen* what she's wearing?"

Uncle Robert peered down into the workings of the car, then stepped back, pushed up the hood with one hand, folded down the metal hood-rod with the other. "Watch your fingers," he said, lowering the hood to within a couple centimeters of the sloping nose of the vehicle. Then he let the hood fall so it latched shut. "You know what you sound like?" Uncle Robert asked. "You sound like she used to sound like, before she got her marbles back. You sound like a Scripture-thumping prude."

"Well, it's not right!"

"Well, is it the swearing? I swear, and your little buddy Huck Finn out there, he swears more than I do. Or is it her general lack of modesty? Your cousin Rosella tramps around in that same kind of outfit on a regular basis, doesn't she?"

"But you're not my mother, and Mal's not my mother, and Rosella is definitely not my mother!" David protested.

"Ah, so your mother isn't allowed to live like other people, is that it? Because she's your mother she can't say what she wants, she can't dress as she likes? She should be checking with you before doing anything, getting your permission?" Uncle Robert placed his wrench in a case of similar wrenches on a small wheeled stand beside the car.

"No, that's not it. She's just never been like this before."

"She's never been herself in front of you, kid, that's all. Why don't you give her a chance? I like Maggie a lot better than I like Magenta, and your father liked Maggie a lot better than he liked Magenta. Harold made Magenta, he took Maggie and fucked her up to make her Magenta, Magenta who was scared of her own fucking shadow, Magenta who thought anything other than prayer had to be a sin. She wasn't right in the head, you know that. You used to complain to me about what an uptight head-case your mother was, or have you forgotten?"

David shook his head. "No, I remember."

"Alright," said Uncle Robert. "So cut her some slack. She's really pretty decent. You know she used to kill people, for a living? That's how she met your dad, you know."

"No, I didn't know that."

"Well, guess what? I knew that you didn't know that. Hardly anybody knows that. Hardly anybody knows anything about the way it was before Harold fucked up your mother and everything else. So your old Uncle Robert, he started writing some of it all down years and years ago. I've been saving it, like I've been saving the car, for you."

David didn't know what to say. He leaned up against the low wide red car.

"Well, you want to read it or not?" Uncle Robert asked. "I'm not going to beg you."

"Yeah," David told him. "Sure, I want to read it."

"Alright, hang on, I'll go get it for you." Uncle Robert headed for the house. He returned some minutes later with a pile of paper, real paper, a stack of it some three or four centimeters thick. He handed it to David, and David flipped through the loose sheets. The paper was white, each piece printed on one side with hundreds of words in neat black sentences that marched on and on throughout the length of the stack. The top sheet was smudged with the black grease and dirt from Uncle Robert's hands, and bore the words "HOW IT ALL HAPPENED".

"Wow, this is a lot," David told his uncle. "Thanks."

"Well, don't thank me yet. I'm no writer, I just tried to tell it like I saw it. Somebody had to." Uncle Robert started back for the house. Halfway there, he called back over his shoulder, "The car's good to go, why don't you take it for a spin, clear your head?" And then he walked on.

David stood there, hefting the weight of words in his hands, wondering just how long it had taken Uncle Robert to write so many pages, and wondering just what each page might contain, what secrets, what revelations, what disappointments and pleasures. He took the pile of words with him into the car, stuffed the stack of paper under the passenger-seat, so the pages might not blow away, then he pushed in the clutch and turned the key. The willing engine responded with a roar. He floored the accelerator and let off the clutch, launching the car out and across the green grass field that lead to the road through the trees.

The wind tugged at David's hair and he was surrounded by the mechanical music of the powerful machine. He threw the car into turns, resisting the urge to go for the brake, and soon his confusion and frustration with his mother had turned into a jittery joy, excitement on the edge of fear as he and the metal beast in which he rode took on the world, took on physics itself, the friction of rubber and the power of fossil-fueled explosions versus inertia and velocity and time. He felt his left leg shaking with adrenaline-driven nerves whenever he let off the clutch, and yet he kept driving, driving as if being chased by all the demons of Legion. He was vibrantly alive as he faced death in every curve and rise, as each massive tree-trunk seemed to lean in toward the car. David felt hyper-aware as he flew along beneath the canopy of branches and leaves, the sunlight intermittently flickering flashing in his eyes, on-again off-again warming his skin from without as the break-neck pace of his heartbeat warmed him from within. The car surged forward with the slightest tweak of the pedal, as if it, too, was thrilled to be racing alone and free, and David gave it more of what it wanted, gave it more gas, gave it more speed, as he left thoughts of his strange mother farther and farther behind.

Anywhere, Anytime (The Fractured Sphere vii)

I began my tenure as the Long-Lost Bringer of Balance, as the deathless god Cygnus, He Who Weighs Reason Against Love, and Love Again Reason, the evening Twilight's father returned from the wilderness and from the mating madness which was endemic to their apparently human species. Twilight insisted on bathing me and drying my feet with her hair and anointing me with olive oil and laying before me the finest breads and cheeses that were to be had in their house. "I'm not a god," I kept telling her, kept telling them both, but the girl would not listen, and her father merely nodded and smiled in a manner so obsequious as to be obnoxious.

"Forgive my earlier ignorance," Twilight said, "and any pretensions of arrogance that may have kept me from seeing your true glory, Lord, but it would indeed be a sin to dismiss your divinity now that it has been presented to me so plainly. I will not be fooled to arrogance again, Lord."

"But, listen, I'm telling the truth," I said. "I am no god! You're being foolish! I'm just a man!"

"Fool me once, and there is no shame," Twilight said. "But fool me twice and pride is my sin."

And so on and so forth, until I realized that it would be fruitless to continue in denial of my perceived godhood. I must admit that the treatments she lavished upon me in the bath were nothing less than heavenly. Her gentle touch and her smell, her nearness brought me to a state of arousal once more, which escaped neither Twilight's notice nor the notice of her newly returned father.

"Is he still in rut?" the father asked.

"Nay!" Twilight scolded the squat older man. "Have you not noticed the clarity of his speech, the clearness of his eye, nor his upright stature?"

"It's his upright stature that concerns me," said the father. "How can we be certain this is not Dionysus, come to deliver us to permanent madness, to reduce us to beasts forever more?

"Father, you seek to be smote by a thunderbolt, speaking thusly of an immortal god, speaking so harshly, especially of the Long-Lost Bringer of Balance! Our people have waited generations on generations for his return, and you, Great Thinker that you are, you fail to recognize the mighty Cygnus when he appears beneath your very roof! Shame on you, father, shame!"

It may have been at this point that Twilight's father began to take seriously the notion that I might be not just any god, but the very god Twilight said I was. He stood silent, and stared at me, then looked suddenly away. "He seems to reason and to speak as does a logical man, and yet he is simultaneously possessed of lust, of passion, and for my daughter at that!" he said. "This could well be Balance Himself, come to deliver us from our curse of two lives! What other wonders has he performed, my daughter? Speak quickly!"

And so, while she continued to rub her hands on my skin, continued to bathe me, Twilight described for her father how I had fallen down the hill outside Apollonia and remained free of injury. She described how I had looked upon his great inventions and dismissed them as toys, as half-steps toward true invention. She described my vanishing and reappearance, though her father had seen me perform this trick with his very eyes. And, as she described these *wonders* to her father, he nodded, and nodded, as if he could not agree more or quickly enough with these supposedly conclusive proofs that my real name might be Cygnus. I kept quiet, waiting for their madness to pass, trying to enjoy to the fullest the feel of Twilight's hands on me, trying to enjoy the scrubbing and rubbing, the soothing worshipful touch.

After the bath, I ate a meal of bread and cheese, the bread as light as air and the cheese made of goat's milk and rich with sharp flavor. Twilight and her father watched my every move while trying not to stare. They knelt on the floor beside the table where I sat, and they watched me while keeping their faces aimed down at the floor. It was an awkward meal to say the least. I told them again that I was not a god, and, when that failed once more, I ordered them, commanded them as a god to sit at the table with me, but they would have none of it. "We are not worthy," Twilight's father said. "We are not worthy, O Lord." And so they continued to grovel but watch while I ate. When I'd had enough, they insisted that I eat more, and insisted and insisted until I finally sat back down and ate a few more mouthfuls to keep them from insisting any further.

I'm certain, brother Robert, that, in your childhood days, you had your fantasies about becoming a god, as I had my own. And these fantasies included the worship of respected elders not unlike Twilight's father, and the entirely different worship and devotion of beautiful young women not unlike Twilight herself. In these fantasies, being a god is, quite literally, everything you imagine it to be. Having such a fantasy become reality on this "earth" on the other side of the black hole of Cygnus X-1, however, I was astonished at how quickly I came to abhor my own perceived divinity. It was bothersome, truly annoying, to have Twilight and her father kneeling and fawning and doing everything they could to avoid engaging me in anything that resembled a normal human exchange. I bore their worship for hours and hours. I allowed Twilight to bathe me, and I over-ate for them, and I even, with momentary joy, accepted Twilight's offer of carnal pleasures when she begged to be the object of my physical lust. It was only once we'd entered her bedchamber that I realized that this, too, was another trap. As Twilight was not in heat, as she had just recently fulfilled her need to mate, she had no idea where to even begin to physically pleasure me, and no real enthusiasm for the task. "That's alright, we don't need to do this," I told her, thinking she would be relieved, but this only made her cry.

"I am a miserable failure!" she cried. "I am a failure!"

And so I allowed her to touch me awkwardly with her little hands, and pretended to be most pleased, then told her that I had finished. In this regard, her conscious ignorance of physical love was to my advantage; as she knew little to nothing of sexuality, she had no reason to believe that I might be lying about having been satisfied.

Returning to the front room of the house, I found that Twilight's father had taken advantage of the time I'd spent in the bedchamber. He had rounded up no less than twenty-seven villagers, crowded them into that front room and onto the front steps of the house, and when I made my entrance, they all knelt and groveled and made sounds of awe.

"Cygnus!"

"The Long-Lost Bringer of Balance!"

"Our redemption!"

"It is He!"

If I had been put off by the worship of two, I was disgusted by the worship of twenty-seven. It was un-nerving, to see almost thirty full-grown adult men and women prostrating themselves before me. "I am not a god!" I told them, but it was of no more use than it had been before. I doubt a single one of them even heard me, they were so wrapped up in their own notions of my divinity. I put up with their bowing and scraping for as long as I could, then sequestered myself in my room, only to hear them outside the door, babbling this and that, babbling out nothing short of prayers. They were *praying* to me, asking me to cure their ailments, to grant them wealth, to bring them happiness, to make them better than their peers.

"Please, O Great Lord of Balance, hear my plea and grant me relief from the pain in my right knee!"

"Cygnus, finally returned to us, please cure my son of his shyness."

"O Long Lost One, I beg of you, just enough gold to let me add two rooms to my house, just two rooms."

"Make me the greatest of Great Thinkers, O Cygnus! I will serve you more truly than any other if only you recognize my true genius and raise me above the others!"

This last one I mention came as barely a whisper, but I recognized it as having come from Twilight's father. It came as barely a whisper, and it took me more than a few moments to realize that such a whisper should not have been audible through the door of my room, let alone over the clearly-spoken and some-times-shouted prayers of the others. It was only once I made this realization that another followed quickly on its heels. I wasn't hearing half of these prayers, not with my ears, at any rate. I was hearing them with my mind. The pleas of these people gathered in the house of Twilight's father, all of these pleas were being broadcast directly into my brain.

It was more than a little disquieting. So disquieting that I found myself simply sitting on the bed, letting the very vocal wills of all these beings wash over and through my own will. I sat and listened, let their voices course through my being. For a brief moment, I wondered at and entertained the thought that I might indeed be some type of god. I was still that human, so human as to grasp at such a prideful explanation, an explanation so directly attached to the ego versus exist-ence itself. Then I began to hear more than prayers. I began to hear other thoughts, thoughts that were obviously not intended for the ears of a god to whom one would pray. I heard the thoughts the people outside my door were having of one another.

"Damn him and his crowding in on me! I was here first! If he bumps into me one more time, I swear I'll knock him down and punch his face in!"

"Great Thinker! Portios is no Great Thinker! I should have his place among them!"

"I wish I could afford to have a robe so fine as the one she wears. She must be stealing from the granary and selling at below cost to afford such a robe."

And these unintentionally intercepted thoughts made me smile, and then made me laugh, because, quite unwittingly, I had begun to reach out for more. I'd actually begun to reach out into each of the heads beyond the door and begun investigate the contents of each. And I'd found that many of these thoughts that my worshippers were having of one another, so many of these thoughts faded in and faded out, so many of these thoughts existed beneath a solid stratum of reason and calm, the very reason and calm with which these people thought they controlled all aspects of their lives outside the rutting season. It was funny, ironic, to look into the minds of such supposedly reasonable beings and find such petty thoughts, all spawned by emotion. Their hearts and minds existed in opposition to one another, not only during neat seasons of lust and control, but during their every waking moment. Heart and mind were joined in battle within each and every one of them, even as they claimed to be in complete control of their feelings by dint of unflappable reason. And so I laughed, laughed at the absurdity of their carefully constrained existence, laughed at their belief in a complete venting of emotion during their season of mating.

Unfortunately, they heard me laughing. They heard me laughing and thought they had somehow pleased me with their prayers. And so, practicing their much-respected reason, they prayed on with even greater aplomb. The majority of them prayed while a few went to summon more adherents to the faith (which, in itself was a defiance of reason). Those new adherents who came and believed and prayed and sent some of their number to bring even more to worship, and within a few hours, the house of Twilight's father was filled with people praying to me, and the street outside was filled with people praying to me, so many supposedly reasonable beings bowing and scraping before some god whom they'd never even seen, a god who was not a god but a man, a man who wasn't even close to godhood. A man foolish enough to get himself sucked into a black hole.

I found I could shut out all their thoughts and prayers, the ones that were being broadcast directly into my mind, not unlike turning off a faucet, that was that, but there were so many voice now, outside the door, outside the window, that it was quite difficult to shut out the real noise that assaulted my ears. It was not a harsh or dissonant sound, but it was still very bothersome to me, that so many should believe I was a god, that they should waste their time and effort worshipping me. I have no doubt that this was an outgrowth of my distaste for religion in general. I, much like you, dear brother, lost the faith our father had helped nurture in us. I lost all faith in the divine when he fell to his death like some kind of cast-out angel. Remember how he used to have us dress up, have us wear ties, and take us to church? Neither of us cared for it, but we believed, or I did, anyhow, until The Caveman plummeted from the mortal coil. To see so many people praying to me, it was too much. I stood on the bed and shouted out the window to those in the street that they should stop, but it only encouraged them. The sight of their so-called god only bolstered their holy spirits. They did not hear a word I said, did not register in the least my most adamant protests.

So I left. I ceased existing within the bedroom and began existing atop the statue of Apollo, at the center of the perfectly round pool in the town square. I stood atop that great marble representation of the thinking man's god and looked down at the still-growing crowd that surrounded Twilight's father's house. I wondered what Twilight's father, Portios, might think of all the damage being inadvertently done to his dwelling, once the fervor had died down.

It had been a mistake, of course, to place myself in such a wide-open position, where I was so clearly visible to anyone who might happen to raise his eyes while passing by. I was spotted by a little toe-headed boy who pointed, and then I was spotted by everyone else. The crowd turned its focus from the house of Portios to the statue of Apollo, and the worship was doubled, and redoubled. Some even waded into the jade-ringed pool, and splashed themselves with the water, applying it as a curative.

I remained where I was for a short while, and then left, this time for the mountains that loomed in the far distance beyond the city. I moved without moving to one of the highest points on this world that the inhabitants called "earth" and I sat on a snow-covered rock, alone, to contemplate my situation, and to wonder at this world, and to wonder at what had become of me, and what I had become.

How It All Happened, Chapter 1

I'm not a writer by training or trade, I'm a coder, a "hacker", a guy who creates and messes with instructions for computers, so if I miss some of the finer points of the writing craft, you'll have to forgive me. Either that or go back in time yourself, and live for yourself all the crap I've been through. Because I'm about the only one who lived through it all and is still alive today and who's going to tell you anything about how it really went down. My name is Robert Lifeson. My brothers Billy and Michael were part of the reason the world turned like it did. I guess I might have played a little part, because I brought Harold's mother to America, but you can't pin all the shit on me, because that's about all I did to make it happen. All the rest of the time, I was fighting against it the best I knew how. It's not my fault that the world got blown all to hell.

The first thing you have to understand, when you look back at how the bombs came down and how the surviving people acted after the nuclear shooting was all done, the first thing you have to understand, if you want to know how little Hitler Harold managed to get everybody behind him and wipe out anybody else, is that it wasn't about guns or technology. It was about people and groups of people and the kinds of groups of people that existed before the atomic slaughter went down. The little bastard understood that, driven by capitalism and its attendant marketing to an unintended level of individualism and personal isolationism, people were adrift and alone.

Basically, when you get down to it, most people, in 2049, were loners. And by this, I don't mean they moped around in dark rooms by themselves or anything like that. I mean it in a relative sense. I mean that they didn't really have any serious allegiances to any groups beyond their immediate families, and even their allegiance to their wives and husbands and kids, even that was questionable, a lot of the time. You had men and women abandoning their families to run off with people they'd met on the internet, people they'd never really met at all. You had women and men breaking up marriages for the sake of personal financial comfort and/or aggression, to take the house or cars or bank-account, or to get alimony-for-life and that kind of thing. Members of extended families were frequently and completely out-of-touch with one another, separated by hundreds or thousands of miles and even greater quantities of apathy or dislike. People had friends, of course, but in a climate where family mattered little, friends, on the whole, meant even less. There were still various old-school religious, business and social organizations, but these groups had fallen largely out of fashion, and were, in their own ways, offshoots of the capitalist economy, existing only to produce "better" consumers, men and women who knew and accepted their assigned roles in the larger economic culture. As such, these groups could not have been relied upon as binding societies following as great a catastrophe as that little bastard Harold had unleashed in 2049.

I'm no social scientist, but let me get into the whole picture in a bit more depth. Let me get down to the level of individual pixels. The world of 2049 was one in which capitalism dominated the world as the primary economic system. And the end-goal and wet-dream of capitalism is the fantasy of sustainable economic growth, which, if one accepts that economics are an abstract representation of real resources, of time and energy and material resources, is a total crock of shit. Sustainable growth would require unlimited resources, and while the earth is a pretty big place, it's not unlimited. But try to explain this to any good capitalist, and they would have told you that sustainable growth really meant a branching out into intellectual capital, which was, in essence, unlimited. Or they'd tell you that, as humanity expanded out into space, humanity would gain access to unlimited physical resources. Well, let's take the intellectual capital idea first, because I like it best, even though it's a crock of shit. The last big boom in purely intellectual capital ended back in the 1990s, with the downfall and devaluing of internet-based companies. There had been some piddling around on the internet since then, but it had been a good fifty years since any capitalist put their money where their mouth was when it came to the "intellectual capital" idea. And the other out, the idea that we'd get unlimited resources from outer space, well, I like that one too, but in 2049, Mars Industry Station had been operating for some years, and had yet to pay for its own existence. It was more of a political show-piece and military post than anything, which I would have had no real problem with, if the government and the press of the time had had the nuts to call it just that, instead of calling it "Mars Industry Station" and giving all the ass-hole capitalists more fuel for their dream of sustainable growth.

But anyway, so you've got the idea of sustainable growth, and without truly unlimited resources, the capitalist machine cranks up its marketing mechanisms to induce each consumer to buy more and more and more. Television, radio, internet, and print-mediums are flooded with well-crafted (and not-so-well-crafted) appeals to buy products and services, ranging from new cars to toe-nail buffing. In order to make these appeals more effective, associations are made with sex and family and friendship and belonging. New cars made men more appealing to women. New make-up made women more appealing to men. Brand X fruit-punch made mothers more appealing to their children. Brand Z toys made children more appealing to other children. And so on and so on, until, impossible as it may sound, the products and services associated with sex and family and friendship and belonging *actually replaced* the sex and family and friendship and belonging. And this worked doubly well for the capitalist machine. Sex and family and friendship and belonging (along with food, clothing and shelter) are what humans need to feel satisfied. In raising capitalist products and services to the level where they replaced these basic socio-emotional needs, the system had managed to deny humanity all but the most short-term measures of satisfaction. People were happy for a little while when they bought their new clothes or their new electronics or their new cars, but when these products failed to bring a sense of belonging, dis-satisfaction returned. And, not knowing any better, most people would attempt to assuage this dis-satisfaction with yet another purchase, which would lead to yet another disappointment, and another and another. This worked out well for capitalism, and it pushed up profits, for a while, even as it dismantled the underpinnings of society, even as it weakened the relationships, weakened the attachments between individuals and groups, cheapened through hollow mimicry the value of human connections. It was a form of economic growth that fed off and diminished the strength of human society itself. It had taken the United States of America, for example, from a country in which one car per household was enough, to a country in which one or *more* cars per person was required; from a country in which one parent working outside the home was enough to cover expenses, to a country in which two parents working outside the home could barely cover the bills. As people bought more, they worked more, to earn more money to buy. It got to the point where parents couldn't be bothered to raise their own children, but hired, at cheap wages, uneducated day-laborers to do so. Parents couldn't be bothered to raise their own children. It had gotten that bad. And not just in The States. Capitalism had spread around the globe, forced in some nations by military interference from the United States and other "free" countries, all in the name of "democracy" of course. North America, Japan, most countries of Western Europe, some of Southeast Asia, portions of India and China, this was where capitalism had its strongest hold, but it was nonetheless prevalent everyplace else, too, and so the world was ripe for the picking by somebody like Harold, somebody who could see not only the big picture, but the underlying image, the unintended personal individualism and isolationism that had befallen nearly everyone on the planet.

How else it could have been, I do not know. I suppose that I, for one, would have liked to have seen a clearer distinction between political and economic systems. Any mention of communal or group effort, or sharing of economic burdens among a people was, even as late as 2049, immediately associated with the communist efforts of the former Soviet Union, which was, in the public mind, an oppressive governmental system, the image of which lead most people to crap on any sharing of economic burden as a political/governmental move versus an economic move. Images of oppressive red-troopers on the march. Similarly, "capitalism" and "democracy" were mated terms, fixed together in the public mind, inseparable. But what, in theory, was to keep a nation or nations from practicing a truly democratic communism, or any other variation of politics and economics? Like I said, I'm no social scientist, and I'm also no political scientist, or economist, so I don't know. By 2049, though, powerful organizations like the World Bank, International Monetary Fund, and the United States military were aligned as part of the capitalist machine, so it wouldn't have mattered if anybody had started doing anything differently; they would have been squashed and squashed quick, kept from playing on the world stage by being denied trade or funding, or being called an "Evil Empire" or a "Terrorist State" and bombed off the map by a U.S. carrier task-force.

Anyway, so little Hitler goes and makes his plays, and the nukes go off, and the majority of people are wiped out. Those who survive the blasts and the radiation are all alone. They owed no allegiance to anyone, to nothing but the capitalist machine, and no one owes any allegiance to them, either. And they come out of their dirty holes to find the capitalist machine has been wrecked, and they're all alone. No community ties, no friends, maybe even no immediate family. Some form small groups, trying to get something together, but for the most part, they're every bit as alone as they had been before, except now they can't buy even temporary satisfaction. Now it just sucks.

And it sucks for everybody but those who followed Harold. Those tens of thousands of truly insane hard-core devotees of his fucked-up religion who knew the nukes were coming, and who not only knew where and how to wait out the destruction, and who knew what to stock up on and how to store it, these frigging fanatics come out of their shelters with their little society more-or-less completely in tact. They are not alone. They are, in many parts of the world, thousands strong, in devastated lands where their rival groups might number in the tens, or in some rare cases, in the hundreds. Harold warned a great variety of his most faithful lunatic followers, from engineers to soldiers to day-laborers. He must have put a whole lot of time into deciding who to choose and why, because the freaks who came out of their specially-prepared shelters wearing their red robes and carrying their fucked-up red-star flags, they were ready to do just about anything. Their knowledge and skills were enough to rebuild the world, if that was what Harold had wanted to do. To give the little prick his due, he'd done a pretty fucking good job of picking his people, of getting the right balance between muscle and brains, of carpenters and communicators, of killers and healers. Too bad they were all such fanatics, such god damned loons.

But I can't say I knew this right away. No, it wasn't like that. To keep this account fair and accurate, I need to let you know where I was when the shit hit the fan. I was hiding out in Houlton Maine. Not a bad place to be when the nukes came down, because nobody, not even the fucking crazed Imperial Japanese, were going to waste a single warhead on a place so far out of the way, so small and insignificant, so nothing and nowhere. Houlton was, at the time, a small agricultural town tucked up near the northeast corner of the state of Maine, which was, in turn, tucked up in the northeast corner of the United States. If you don't know where the United States was, which you may not, given the fact that little Hitler fucking wiped out all knowledge of everything that ever existed before he took over the world, well, if you don't know where the United States was, it was sandwiched between Canada (which had been a fine nation, a very nice place, if you ask me) to the north, and Mexico to the south. This should be enough for you to find it in the appendix with all the maps, so go look it up and let me get on with the story. Houlton was tucked away, way off in the upper right hand corner of the U.S., a town which had as it's claim to fame a relatively small annual crop of potatoes and the fact that it was the administrative seat of Aroostook county, the largest and least populous county in all of the state of Maine. For more on the relationships between municipalities, counties, states, and nations, see the appendix with all the explanations about how fucked up governments used to be. Even to somebody who lived and remembers the time before the little prick's so-called Revolution, it seems crazy, and impossible, that there could have been so many people, and such a complex array of rules and regulations and laws and whatever to keep everybody in line. Such degrees of specialization on specialization, and now all of it gone, it's hard to imagine, even if you don't have to imagine it, if that makes any sense, even if memory saves you the imagining.

Anyway, so I was up in Houlton, with Jimmy, my brother Jimmy, who had shared our mother's womb with another brother, Billy. Billy was the genius, and Jimmy, well, I won't tell it any different than it was, Jimmy was a retard. He wasn't the kind of retard who drooled or had to wear a football helmet or anything like that. He was pretty smart, for a retard. He had a little bit of the Mongoloid about him, and he was built thick, and strong, and he was one bad-ass fighter, even if he was a little short. I think he was such a bad-ass fighter *because* he was a retard. He didn't have a lot of thoughts or mental junk to get in the way of his movement. He knew, in a fight, or in any basic situation like that, what had to be done to win, and he did it, and that was it. He was a fighter from the early days, too, from back when Billy was a geek in school and I was too little to put up a good scrap, and Michael was still in diapers, so he wasn't even in school yet, so I guess it didn't matter what Michael got up to, but back in school, when me and Billy and Jimmy were just kids, and all the other kids knew our father was a professional wrestler, knew our father was The Caveman, those other kids were real dicks, probably because they were jealous. Probably because they thought we were spoiled rich kids. And yeah, our father made good money as The Caveman, but if he meant to spoil us, he wouldn't have sent us to public school like he did, so those fucking asshole kids who picked on us, they didn't know their heads from their asses. Kids were mean, like they've always been mean, and we were their targets. It was Jimmy who took up the slack for Billy and I. It was Jimmy who would take on four or five other boys at a time, and send them off with black eyes and broken noses or lay them out flat on the pavement of the playground. Jimmy was there for us, in the early days, the way Billy would be there later on, after our father was killed in a wrestling stunt. I guess they were two halves of a whole, the way twins are supposed to be, or maybe that's just my old mind trying to find balance in a world that may not know what balance is. I don't know.

Anyway, Houlton. Getting there wasn't easy. Having simply run like hell the night when little Hitler's people surrounded Maggie and Tanabe and me that night when we landed in the gravel pit in Buxton Maine, having run like hell when Tanabe loosed the lightning on Harold's Gestapo, I caught a stray bullet from all the shooting. I don't think it could have been anything but a stray bullet, because it hit me right in the ass, plunged right into my left cheek, which, in retrospect, was a lucky thing for me. It hurt like hell, but I don't think there's anywhere you could be shot and not have it hurt like hell, so there was no getting around that. But the human ass is about as big a chunk of muscle and fat as there is on the whole body, the best part of the body to absorb the tremendous kinetic energy of a bullet. It turned out to be a pistol-slug, nine millimeter, a very common caliber for the time, and fortunately for me, not the most powerful round with which to be hit. A high-velocity rifle-bullet might have turned that half of my ass to red mist and chopped meat, but this bullet simply dug in and stayed put without coming close to any bone. Heroes on old television-programs used to refer to these kinds of injuries as "flesh-wounds" and shrug them off as if they meant nothing at all. I can tell you first-hand that such a wound is far from nothing at all, but I was, on the whole, quite lucky to get out of that scrape with nothing worse of which to complain, at least nothing worse in terms of physical injuries, I should say. Tanabe and Maggie were either killed or captured. It turned out that Tanabe had been gunned down there in the gravel pit, and Maggie, pregnant with Michael's son David, and weak and wounded during action we saw in Imperial Japan, was taken prisoner. I didn't know any of this at the time. I just ran. I realized what Tanabe was doing, sacrificing himself to give Maggie and I the chance to get away. It was a noble act on the part of the old scientist, a very giving act, and I will never forget it, no more than I wished to waste his sacrifice at the time. Maggie wasn't able to move very quickly, and she told me to go, so I went. It was better that I get away and try to find help, try to rescue she and Tanabe should they survive. Better that at least one of us make it away to find Mikey and tell him the real deal, give him the straight scoop, tell him that we'd proven once and for all that Harold was as big a rat-bastard as we'd always thought him to be. Bring Mikey over and put a stop to Harold's machinations before they went any further. In running when I did, that night in the gravel-pit, I was carrying with me the chance to save the entire world.

And so I ran, and I ran. Some of Harold's people chased, but I made it into a cornfield not far from the lip of the gravel-pit, and from there into a wooded stretch cut with streams and creeks. I do not know how long they gave chase, but it wasn't long before I heard sirens growing louder in the distance. Harold was powerful, but not so powerful that his people could go firing off so many hundreds of shots in the quiet countryside without somebody calling the cops. But things were pretty tricky back then, in that you really didn't know who was working for Harold and who wasn't. His half-assed religion was popular, as it made sense to people who felt lost in an increasingly technological world. The cops who arrived on the scene could have been part of his most-trusted cadre, so, while Harold's goons seemed to give up the chase when the sirens began to sound, there was no guarantee that I was out of the woods yet, and that's where I stayed, in the woods, hunkered down and bleeding and feeling my left buttock burn and throb from a fresh new gunshot wound. I knew I would have to move carefully, because, just as the cops could be loyal to Harold, so might a doctor or a nurse, or a cashier in a drug-store or anybody anyplace else. I had to get hold of Mikey, because, so far as I knew, I was the last one who had the true story on Harold's plans. But by that same token, I had to take it slow and easy, because if I was caught or killed, there was no one to take my place.

I stayed in the woods for the rest of the night, and through the next day, until the sun went down again. I took a chance on the water from the nearest stream, and drank until I was no longer thirsty. My ass and my whole left leg was stiff as a board when I set off that second night. I made it to a farm-house where I was going to steal a vehicle. I thought I'd made it to the driveway without being seen, but there was an old man sitting in the dark on an adjacent porch, looking right at me. I must have been weaker than I'd thought, from the gunshot wound, because I hadn't noticed him until he cleared his throat and asked me what I thought I was doing.

He was unarmed, or at least seemed so, and he was very old, the kind of old you've probably never seen, so old his head shook on his neck as he stood up from his rocking chair. "You got something to do with all that shooting in my field the other night?" he asked me.

"Yeah," I told him. "Some of that shooting was shooting at me." I didn't see any sense in lying. I was going to take the car in the driveway if I had to lay the old man out. Not a very nice thing to do to an old man, but the fate of the world was at stake.

"You part of that *communist cult*?" he asked me. "You one of them red star crazies?"

"No," I told him. "They were the ones shooting at me."

"Looks like they got you, don't it?"

"Not too bad," I told him.

"Bad enough so you didn't see me sitting there rocking when you came up to steal my wife's Buick," he said.

I didn't have anything to say to that. If he was going to try to stop me, he was going to have to make his move. It was that simple. I tried the door-handle of his wife's Buick. It was unlocked.

"Don't you think about putting your bloody be-hind on the upholstery of my wife's Buick!" the old man snapped. "She'll have both our be-hinds in a sling!"

I stopped, not because I was afraid of this old man's wife, but because he wasn't so much threatening me as enlisting me in his effort to prevent his being on the receiving end of his wife's wrath. He wasn't addressing me as a car-thief so much as a fellow guy in a guys vs. gals understanding. It was unexpected, and, I have to admit, actually somewhat comforting, to be involved in such a mundane conspiracy, given the severity of the shit that had been going down, and the vast weight of the plots of which I had become aware. It was nice, to be treated like just a plain guy.

"Name's Johnson," the old man said, tottering down off the porch, walking toward the garage. "I'll get something for you to sit on, so you won't mess up the seat, then I'll drive you wherever you need to go. Worked too hard all my life to buy that stupid Buick for that woman just to let you steal it."

And that was that. Johnson drove me to Portland. We talked a little. Mister Johnson was a hard-core Jesus-freak. He didn't say what flavor, but he was no friend of Harold's One True Religion, and that worked for me. I didn't tell him much of what I knew, just agreed with him when he said things like "This bullshit cult's gonna be trouble, more trouble than people'll know what to do with." He didn't ask how I was mixed up in the whole thing, but it seemed more than enough for him to know that I was on the right side.

In Portland, I rang up one safe-house after another until I found a group of my college kids who hadn't gotten bored or been flushed out by Harold's goons. A girl named Molly, her mutton-headed boyfriend Vince, and Vince's half-brother Leon. Not the best or the brightest of the kids I'd organized, but I figured any port in a storm, so I hid out in the back parking lot of a restaurant called *The Village*, down near the old foundry, until Molly and Vince and Leon could pick me up. I couldn't go far with a bullet in my ass. Not only did it hurt, but there was dried blood all over my pants, enough to attract way too much of the wrong kind of attention anywhere I might go.

I hung out in the shadow of a big garbage dumpster. It was November in Maine, and it was cold. No snow yet, but cold, and Portland was cold with the dampness of the sea, so it was an unpleasant cold, but it wasn't all bad because it kept me awake.

When Molly and Vince and Leon showed up, they were too glad to see me. These were three not-so-bright kids who'd always gotten off on playing it cool, playing it low-key, no matter what, and they were all smiles and way too talkative when they pulled up and I got in the car. They wanted me to sit up front, beside Vince, who was at the wheel. This would have put Molly and Leon behind me. I would have been nicely boxed in, an easy target for a bullet to the back of the head. But I wasn't buying it. I told them I needed to drive, and, stupid as they were, and eager to keep up the appearance of friendliness, they let me drive.

I drove like an Egyptian cabbie. Which is to say I drove like a madman with no concern for his own life or for public safety in general. I floored the accelerator from a stand-still and refused to brake for any but the sharpest of turns. "Throw out your weapons," I told them, when they told me to slow down. They didn't want to take me seriously, of course, so I kept on driving fast, cutting it very close when passing other cars, especially once we made it out to the interstate. We got up to just under a hundred before they threw out their pistols.

"All of them!" I told them, scraping the passenger-side of the little car against a metal guard-rail without slowing down, sending up a shower of sparks and making the most god-awful sound you ever want to hear from a vehicle. This really did it. The kids threw out a couple more guns and a couple of knives. "Alright, I'm not even going to ask why you switched sides, but what the hell did the little prick want you to do with me?" I asked them.

They screamed this and that, the three of them, and it was hard to figure out just what they were jabbering, but the long and short of it was that they were supposed to bring me in, and that was it. That was all they knew.

So I had the kids get out, left them out in the November weather on the side of I-95. A lot of other guys would have shot them, but they were just dumb kids, so I just left them out in the cold. Then I drove back into town and ditched their nasty little car. The whole trap was way too easy to avoid, and I should have known better than to think I was in the clear. I could make a whole lot of excuses, about being tired and wounded and hungry, but it was just kind of stupid, the way I let myself be caught.

They had vectored in on where I'd left the car. It had probably been equipped with a GPS tracking device. They must have figured something was wrong when their readings showed the car headed out on the interstate instead of heading straight for Harold's encampment over on Back Bay. Then they must have definitely known something was wrong when the car stopped on I-95 and turned back toward town. Then they vectored in. I ditched the car and had limped about half a block before the first big white van turned the corner in front of me and then screeched to a stop. I turn around and start off in the opposite direction, not half so quick as I would have liked, and it wasn't but a couple seconds before another van comes at me from the other end of the street.

I managed to shoot a couple of the red-robed goons who poured out at me, and they could have shot me down a hundred times, but it was pretty clear they had orders to bring me in alive. This really sucked, because it meant the little prick had some kind of special plans for me, and I was pretty sure these plans were bad. I fought them the best I could, but they ended up taking me down and sedating me, and loading me into one of the vans. Whatever it was they shot me up with, it was a decent little buzz, very relaxing, very soothing. It made the ride go pretty quick.

07-09-2112

Thomas marched out of the Vigilance Detention Center with over two hundred lightly armed men and women behind him. He lead his disorganized force out into the street on Level Five, where they were confronted by a bastion of Vigilance patrol cars drawn up in a line, blocking the way to the upbound ramp, the ramp to Level Six. Twenty or thirty low-level Eyes crouched behind the vehicular barricade, with weapons trained on Thomas' mob. Scatterguns, a few auto-rifles, even. Plenty of firepower to put an end to his march. Thomas knew he had the numbers; it was the training, the discipline that his following truly lacked. If those Eyes opened up on the crowd, it was all over. Some would flee, some would fall, some would stand stock-still in their panic. There would be a few who'd fight back, but they would be disorganized, and their individual efforts would not be enough.

So Thomas held up a hand, ordered his people to stop. He scanned the Eyes arrayed against him, looking for some mark of rank, looking for the leading man on the scene. Not a single officer among them. Most officers, from the Upper Levels, would want to steer clear of such a potential blood-bath. Leave the dirty work to the dirty people, the grunts, the men from down below. This absence of officers, and the fact that these men hadn't yet opened fire, gave Thomas some hope. He stepped out ahead of his disorganized force and waved to a sergeant on the opposing line. "Sergeant, are you in charge here?"

The Eyes on the line fidgeted. Some looked over at the sergeant. "Our orders are to take you alive if possible, sir!" the sergeant called back. "Please have all those people with you return to their cells and their posts, sir!"

"Why have you barricaded only the one end of the street, sergeant? Why have you and your men blocked off only the upward route, the route to the Upper Levels?" Thomas asked.

The sergeant paused, and more of his men looked his way. "Maintain your ready positions!" he barked at them, and they snapped back to their weapons, to their firing positions. Then he called back to Thomas, "Those were my orders, sir! Prevent all access to higher levels, sir! Now will you please return with these people to the detention center, sir?"

Thomas smiled. He didn't feel much like smiling, with so many weapons pointed his way, but he drew up the corners of his mouth in his best fake smile and walked toward the line of patrol cars. "Why not protect the Lower Levels as well as the Upper Levels, sergeant? What happened to the Brotherhood of Man? What has happened to the notion that equality is the stock-in-trade of our society, sergeant?" Thomas paraphrased from Scripture.

The sergeant paused. His men looked at him again. "I'm following orders, sir!"

"And who gave these orders?" Thomas asked.

"Captain Royce, sir!"

"Do I outrank Captain Royce, sergeant?" Thomas asked.

"You do, sir! Except you're a prisoner, sir!"

Thomas took several slow steps nearer the line of patrol cars. He walked toward the sergeant. "I was a prisoner, sergeant, I was a prisoner of falsehood and heresy, but now I am free," he said. "All rank aside, sergeant, what about Scripture? *Look around this world we've made, equality our stock-in-trade, come and join the Brotherhood of Man*...What about Scripture, sergeant?"

"I believe in Holy Scripture," the sergeant said. Thomas was close enough now to see the very real doubt on the man's face, and to make out the name on his uniform. Flashram. Sergeant Flashram. Another of those Lower Level names. The name of some unknown technical something from a vanished time, given by ambitious parents in hopes that it might bestow upon their son some token of rank or class. All it did was mark him as one of the unwashed, the poor. Thomas looked at the man, and saw the generic Vigilance sergeant, a man no longer youthful, a man who, because of his humble origins, had reached the less-than-stellar peak of his career many years ago.

"Then why have you barricaded only the route upward? If I and these people behind me are dangerous, why not protect the Lower Levels as well?" Thomas asked.

"I don't know, sir," Sergeant Flashram.

"Is your loyalty to the orders of Captain Royce, or to Scripture, sergeant? Do you truly believe in equality, the real Brotherhood of Man?"

"I do, sir."

"Then open your eyes to the hypocrisy of the falseness around you!" Thomas shouted at the man. "Your service record is spotless, and you have been a loyal member of Vigilance for decades, and yet you will never be promoted to an officer's rank or pay, because you are from the Lower Levels! The priests preach equality and brotherhood, but they care only for themselves, and for their masters on the Upper Levels! Do not mistake my intent, sergeant, I'm not asking you to join me for matters of personal pride! I'm asking you to join me in the name of Scripture, and for the good of all! You know what is right, and your men know what is right! Even the priests, with their duplicitous ways, could not keep from us the truth of Scripture! Join me, sergeant, in the name of what you know to be right!" Thomas declared. And it felt right, the words that came pouring out of him, they felt right, and true. He had cast off the veils that had blinded him to Holy Truth for so long. It was like something from Scripture, the way he felt. He turned to the men on either side of the sergeant and asked them, too, to join him.

And all but two did. All but two, who simply got into one of the cars and drove away, down the street and up the ramp to Level Six.

Thomas organized his forces with patrol cars on either side of those who would proceed on foot. Of those who would proceed on foot, he put trained Vigilance men at the fore. He assigned two patrol cars to act as a rear guard, and two more to scout in advance of the main party. He gave the orders, and the men and women obeyed. They were glad to receive the guidance. The notion that someone was in control firmed up the determination of those who had begun to feel doubt when they'd been faced with the barrels of Vigilance weapons. And the prominent positions assigned the new Vigilance recruits gave them an added sense of importance. The organization of a working formation was a good use of time and effort in more senses than one.

Thomas was about to lead his people forward, and upward, when his phone began to ring. He answered, and there was the image of the smooth-skinned black-haired man, a screen behind his head flashing images of a man, a woman, and some kind of ancient machine. The light behind the man's head, the glow from the screen, which Thomas had once thought of as something from Scripture, a halo, now looked like nothing more than the light from the fires of Abend. Here was the false prophet, the true evil, the demon who called itself Almighty Harold. "What do you want?" Thomas asked it.

The being on the tiny screen shook it's head. "How you disappoint me, Thomas. I had such hope for you. It pains me to see you turn from the path of righteousness. And it pained your friend Jon even worse." The tiny screen on Thomas' phone flipped to an image of Jon, motionless, his eyes closed. Then back to the black-haired demon. "Eternal death is the bounty of sinfulness," it said. "Stop now, Thomas, so others may be spared the same fate, the same damnation. I have already sent units to the wilderness, to dispose of Robert's settlement there, to finally grind him into the ground, as I should have many years ago."

"I don't know what you're talking about," Thomas told Harold.

"Your friend here is dead, and your friends out there will soon be dead. You should turn from the path of darkness before it is too late, Thomas," said the demon.

Thomas shut down his phone. He closed his eyes and prayed, prayed to the true Great CPU, the true Holiness that had been obscured for so long. He prayed for strength and for guidance, then took his place at the front of his force and lead them onward, and upward.

How It All Happened, Chapter 2

I woke up pretty groggy from whatever it was they shot me up with, so groggy it took me a while to figure out just why I couldn't move my arms or my legs or even my head. I couldn't even move my head, and I could only look straight up, at white ceiling tiles, and I thought it was so very strange, so very odd, that my body was stuck the way it was, before I figured out why. But once I realized I was strapped down, well, let me tell you, the panic that shot through my brain got rid of the grogginess pretty damned quick. There wasn't a whole lot I could do about it, so before long I was wishing I could go back to being groggy, to being out of it. Would have been better than laying there shitting my pants about what was going to happen to me.

The goons came in, and they did some pretty bad things to me. They called me all kinds of names, told me I was a sinner, crap like that, but it was the beating that really hurt, lending credence to that old adage about sticks and stones.

They beat me, and left me there for some time that may have been days, before they finally came back and beat me some more and then gave me some water but no food. After that, they became more inventive, choking me until I nearly passed out, burning my arms and neck with cigarettes, until I wished they would just beat me some more instead. Being tortured is no fun, no fun at all. It's not just the torture itself, which is truly terrible. It's the waiting, the uncertainty. It can make you lose your mind. I'd read about these types of treatments of prisoners, I think most people had read at least some accounts of such horrors, but, as is the case with so many things, you really have no idea just how bad it is until you experience it yourself. There were times when I quite honestly felt I might lose my mind. There is no real describing torture, real torture, to those who have never experienced it. Pain and fear in peaks without any real ebbs in the fear. It was when I was at my weakest that they came to me and told me the torture would end, if only I would declare my allegiance to Harold, and "accept the truth of the Great CPU." Their repeated requests to this effect were, strangely enough, what brought me back to my senses, when I felt I was about to lose my grip on all reality. Their desire to see me join their bullshit religion reminded me where I was, and why I was there, and how much I truly hated that little Hitler Harold and everything he stood for. Their calls for my weakness grounded me and gave me strength. A little ironic, I know, but that was how it worked. I include the account of my torture in this text largely to give the reader an idea of just what kind of person Harold was, and what kinds of people were in his inner circles. I am proud to say that, as bad as things got for me while I was strapped down to that table, for as long as I was there—and it seemed an even longer time than it was—and as nasty as that experience became, I did not break down, I did not give in. I rode out their incredibly harsh treatment and I used it to fuel my resentment and my anger toward them, and that was how I managed to get by. Thinking back on it, if, once the nukes fell, everyone had copied my handling of the tough situation, the world would have probably been a lot better off. If, when things got so very bad that they couldn't possibly get worse, if, when there was no food and no clean water and the survivors of the holocaust were covered with weeping ulcers caused by radiation-poisoning, if those who had survived the nukes had simply endured their own torture, rather than giving in to Harold and Harold's followers, humanity might never have been yoked to that little prick's will. There might never have been the two cities he would call sacred. If people had turned away from Harold and his crazy religion during those toughest of times, the nuclear destruction of society as we knew it might have been the ideal opportunity for humanity to follow a new and better course of its own choosing.

Maybe, without Harold, the survivors would have formed completely new societal and governmental structures. Maybe they would have founded a world based on simple integrity rather than commerce, on generosity instead of capitalism. Maybe, reminded of how fragile the world really was, people would have founded a society based on respect for the environment, and respect for one another, without Harold or his Scripture or his Great CPU.

But the majority of people are sheep. I learned this early on in life, and I suppose I shouldn't have been surprised at what happened after the blasts, or how it happened. I do, however, get ahead of myself in this telling, and so we return to the terrible days of torture, strapped down on a table in Portland Maine.

There did come a time, during my trial-by-pain, that I gave up hope of living. While I was not about to bow to Harold's goons or pay even lip-service to his fucked up religion, I was not disposed to believe that I would survive the ordeal to which I was being subjected. I had no reason to think that anyone knew where I was, or that anyone would think I might have come to harm. Mikey and Jimmy were probably out there somewhere, but I hadn't been in close touch with either of them for some time, nor was it unusual for me to be out-of-touch for months or years at a stretch. I was the malcontent brother. Billy was the brain, Jimmy was the muscle, Mikey was the dutiful one, and I was the rebel. Rebels go off on their own for long periods of time, and nobody thinks much of it. I would eventually return, they probably thought, when they thought of me at all. I could have purchased another boat and gone back into running weed. I could have sequestered myself in some mountain hideaway with a couple of willing young women. For Mikey and Jimmy, there was no telling where I might have gone, and it was probably no big deal.

I did consider that Billy might know where I was. He did, after all, claim to know everything. But Billy had been nothing but helpful to Harold and Harold's cause. Billy was Harold's number-one supporter, the very reason Harold had any power at all in the world, so I had no real reason to think that my elder brother would pull one of his sudden appearing acts and teleport me out of the dire straits into which I had foundered. I cursed Billy, for his apparent apathy or his hatred, or whatever it was that let him leave me there. I cursed him for helping Harold and for abandoning me.

And the torture went on. The goons became even more inventive, moving on from beatings and cigarettes to electricity and razor-blades. They gave me just enough water and eventually a little food, just enough to keep me alive. I was never removed from that damned table, not even to piss or to shit. When I did either, I did it right where I lay. My body ached and burned even when I was left alone. I had no idea how long it would take for me to die this way, but I found myself wishing it would happen sooner rather than later.

It was Jimmy who came for me, Jimmy who busted down the door of the room where I was being held. I guess this probably won't make for the most thrilling reading, but I was so out of it by the time he came to get me that when I heard the door crashing in, I figured it was just Harold's goons coming back to hurt me some more. Even when Jimmy stared down at me, smiling his wide-open stubby-toothed smile, I didn't really get it. I couldn't seem to grasp the concept that yes, there was my brother, and that he was going to get me the hell out of there.

"Robert! Robert! I found you, Robert! I wasn't even looking for you, but I found you!"

I closed my eyes. I remember that much. I may have said Jimmy's name, or maybe I just tried to say his name. I was obviously in pretty lousy shape by this time. Jimmy started loosing the straps that held me to the table, and in some places I could feel those straps coming loose, and in other places, like my legs, I couldn't feel anything at all. Jimmy stood there, waiting for me to get up, but I couldn't.

I couldn't have told you at the time, but I can tell you now that they had held me and hurt me for a month and a half. It had seemed an eternity, but even so, when I later learned that I had been held that long, mistreated for that long, I was surprised. It had been a lot longer than I'd thought. I suppose that's going to happen, when you're trying like hell not to be someplace but there is no route of escape other than the one that leads inward. I was lucky not to be dead.

As it was, Jimmy had to scoop me up off that table. And let me tell you, that hurt, moving, or being moved, after being stuck in that one position for so long. Everything, everything I could feel, anyway, hurt like it was on fire. Throbbing stabbing tearing hurt. "I've got you, Robert," said Jimmy. "Oh wow, you stink! You stink real bad, but I'm really really glad to see you anyway, because Mikey's gone and I can't find Maggie, but I found you, yes I did!"

It turned out that Harold had sent Mikey up into orbit, ostensibly to supervise work on the "defense" platforms under construction up there. But before he left, Mikey told Jimmy to try to find Maggie. Which, to my way of thinking, wasn't such a bad move on Mikey's part, because if Jimmy could have found and rescued Maggie, then Harold wouldn't have had anything on Mikey. Anyway, with Mikey out of the way for the moment, unable to interfere from his post in orbit, Harold went about his nasty business and didn't for one minute consider Jimmy, Jimmy was a retard, and everybody back then was always underestimating

retards. They were occasionally considered cute, but more often useless, a burden, and Harold didn't bother one bit with Jimmy, once Mikey was gone. Good
for me. Good for me, because if Jimmy hadn't come and gotten me out of there,
nobody else would have.

I was in pretty shabby shape as it was. I don't know if I was close to dying or
not. It's not like the human body has a life-gauge on it, like cars used to have
fuel-gauges. It's not like I could look and see that the needle on my life-gauge was
dipping down toward "dead". All I really know is that Jimmy had to carry me,
and Jimmy kept telling me how badly I stunk and how badly I looked. "You stink
worse than when you were just little and made poopie diaper-pants!" he said, lug-
ging me out of the room and into another. All I can remember of this next room
was that the ceiling was tiled with the same white foam acoustic stuff as the last
one. Industrial kind of place, was what I got off it. Then outside, into a cold
night, into a small parking lot bordered by walls of plowed-up snow.

Jimmy had a car out in the parking lot. An old yellow Dodge eaten half away
by rust. Rust used to be a problem for a lot of cars, in places where it snowed,
because they used to use rock salt on the streets, to break up and melt away the
ice. Some car-makers started making cars of more and more plastic, because it
was cheaper and lighter, but a lot of other car-makers stuck with old-fashioned
steel, to save the cost of retooling their manufacturing facilities. "You look real
real sick, real bad sick," he told me, as he laid me down on the back seat. "But I
know how to make you better, I know how to fix you all up! I'm going to fix you
all up Robert!"

The car was so badly rusted that when Jimmy cranked it up and we started
down the road, I could feel freezing wind coming in from all angles. I could hear
the hum of tires all too clearly. But it was better laying on that back seat freezing
my ass off than it had been strapped down to that table, and I wouldn't have
complained about the ride, even if I'd had the strength to do so. I lay there and
Jimmy drove like hell, which is the only way I'd ever known him to drive, at top
speed and with maximum vigor, attacking every turn as he might attack an
enemy assailant. The drive didn't seem long, even if it was cold, and soon we
were stopped again, Jimmy opening the back door to stick his head in and tell me
"Stay right here, I'll be right back, Just stay right here, Robert." Then he closed
the door. I heard him open and close the trunk, and then there were a few
moments of silence, before the shooting began. Muffled shotgun blasts.

Then more silence, and Jimmy was back. He opened the back door again, and
stood there loading shells into a sawed-off pump-action twelve-gauge, looking

back over his shoulder all the while. "It's clear now, all clear," he said. "Now we can make you better, Robert, all better."

He picked me up and draped me over one thick shoulder, carried me across another parking lot. Past three or four other cars, and then up a short series of cement steps, and into a building, an institutional kind of place, with neatly scrubbed and waxed but colorless tile floors, lots of gray and dark green paint, and way too many glass walls. It was the glass walls, and the doors made almost entirely of glass, that made me think it was some kind of research facility, and I was right. I didn't know it as he carried me down the hallway, but Jimmy was taking me to my first rejuvenation.

He stepped over the first body and its spreading pool of blood, just inside the double doors from the parking lot. It was one of Harold's red-robes, laying face down on the floor, his arms and legs splayed out like he might be sleeping. The dead man's pistol lay not far from his right hand. There were two of Mikey's new black-uniformed "Vigilance" men, also dead, a little further down the hall. Their auto-rifles lay cold and useless next to their corpses. And then there was a sci-ence-geek of some kind, his white lab-coat covered with his own gore. "He was going to call the police, so I had to stop him, because he was running away, to call the police," Jimmy explained, as we walked by that one.

"Good job, Jimmy," I managed to croak. I've never been much for killing unarmed people, but it was Jimmy's show, and he could run it as he wanted to run it.

Through one glass door and then another, and another, and Jimmy stopped to knock at the last. Somebody came and unlocked it, somebody I couldn't see until Jimmy laid me down on a table that felt way too much like the one to which I'd been strapped for so many weeks. But Jimmy was there, with a shotgun in hand, and nobody was going to hurt me without going through him first, so I laid there and I looked at the old guy who had opened the door, and there was something familiar about him, like I'd seen his big potato-nose and his gray goatee before. He was wearing a white version of the red robes that Harold's crazy people wore, with a little red star embroidered over one breast. "Jimmy, this is not good, what you have done," he told my brother. "You have *killed* those people, Jimmy, and I can not bring them back! This is very, very bad, Jimmy, very very bad!"

"They tried to stop me, Doctor Hofferman" Jimmy told him. "Fix my brother, or I'll have to kill you too, okay? I don't want to kill you, but you have to fix my brother Robert or I'll get really mad and I'll kill you, if you don't fix him. Sorry."

Hofferman. I knew where I'd seen the guy, and it had been on the cover of *TIME* magazine, just a few years back. Doctor Heinrich Hofferman, who had begun to revolutionize medicine in Third World nations by co-developing a type of remote analytical and surgical apparatus that allowed doctors in places like London and New York to "see" patients in places like Timbuktu and Bangladesh. The sick person just signed in with a semi-skilled attendant and sat down in a chair, and all kinds of probes and sensors kicked in to send blood-pressure and heart-rate and temperature other related information to a volunteer doctor thousands of miles away. Then the attendant could hand out whatever pills the doctor prescribed, or, if surgery was the answer, the attendant got the patient to sign a release, strapped the patient down, and a surgeon could do his or her laser-cutting, also from thousands of miles away. It didn't always work, of course, and some patients died in those Third World countries, just as they died everywhere else. But try explaining that to the patient's friends and family when they think the new invention has just butchered their son or daughter or father or mother or whoever. A lot of the clinics got attacked by mobs, and a lot of the medical machines, which were very expensive to make, got smashed all to bits. Doctor Hofferman couldn't pay to rebuild these machines with his good will alone, but when he went back to the rich people who had been so generous to begin with because such generosity gave them whopping and completely legal tax-breaks, well, the rich folk didn't want to cough up anymore money to "help people who didn't want to help themselves." That's how one wealthy retail king was quoted in that issue of *TIME* that had Hofferman on the cover. And that cover, it was a pretty normal picture of Hofferman, smiling, looking doctorly, in a tie and wearing a white lab-coat, but behind him they put a picture of a mob tearing apart one of the man's clinics. Made him look like he somehow endorsed the destruction of the medical facilities he had helped build. It was this misleading cover, the way the good cause was getting a bad rap, that had made me cut the guy a check for a couple thousand bucks, to help him get the operation going again. A drop in the bucket, a couple thousand bucks, but better than nothing. I'd admired what he was doing.

And now here he was, working for Harold. I say a lot of bad things about the people who joined up with the little Hitler, but I should note here that not everyone who signed up for that shit was mentally deficient. Harold's bullshit religion, like most bullshit religions, was popular because it gave people hope in a time when hope seemed hard to come by. Hofferman never did get his remote-control clinics back on line, and when Billy gave all the "miracles" to Harold, and Harold offered Hofferman a brand-new chance to help a whole lot of people, it wasn't in

Hofferman's nature to turn down such an opportunity. Just as it hadn't been in Tanabe's nature to turn down the opportunity to work with the new Billy-brought technology to create the constructs that would become Cardinal Api and Father Brown. And, as had been the case with Tanabe, Hofferman had no idea that his hard work and talent might be put to evil ends. A lot of very highly skilled, highly intelligent people joined Harold's ranks because they chose to see what they wanted to see. They chose to see hope, and to hear truth in Harold's promises. Harold would tell them whatever they wanted to hear, because he needed them to make a lot of Billy's "miracles" workable. Harold didn't know a damned thing about science, but he did know that people thrived on hope, and he gave them that, he gave them hope and abused their desire to see the brighter side of things. And once Harold had what he needed from the highly skilled highly intelligent ones, he got rid of them, because highly skilled highly intelligent people were less easily controlled than poorly skilled not-so-bright people. But more on that later.

Hofferman looked at Jimmy and shook his head. Then he started examining me. This started him shaking his head again, as he took in my condition, took in my injuries. "How did you come to this?" he asked me. "Who did this to you?"

"Harold," I rasped.

"What?" he said.

"Harold caught him and kept him tied down on a table," Jimmy added, nodding. "I saved him!"

"You're telling me Harold did this?"

"Harold's people," I told him, hoping the question-and-answer session wouldn't go on much longer.

"You can't be serious," he told me. "Harold wouldn't do anything like this. He wouldn't."

I closed my eyes so I wouldn't have to look the fool in the face any longer. He must have turned to Jimmy then, because he repeated himself: "Harold wouldn't do anything like this. He wouldn't."

"You need to fix him," Jimmy said. "Harold hurt him and you need to fix him. You said you could fix anybody unless they were dead, so fix him, or I'll make you dead."

And so Hofferman fixed me. And he fixed me better than I had thought was possible. He wheeled cart after cart of gear up to the table where I lay, and put it on or around me, inserting needles and affixing electrodes here and there, talking to himself all the while, telling himself that Harold couldn't be responsible for my poor state of health, that Harold would never condone such a thing, that

Jimmy and I had to be mistaken. He finally got everything in place, and wired a little control-box to the whole get-up. It was a pretty crude setup, compared to the way med-stations and rejuvenation gear is now, in Megadon and Syrinx. A crude setup, but you have to keep in mind that this was one of the first applications of this kind of technology. This was the cutting edge of medical science. "Now," he said, more to Jimmy than to me, "the process is still experimental. The rejuvenations provided in the Red Star Centers are nowhere near as effective as this, but this process is still under development. You mustn't hold it against me, should anything go awry. We've had some very positive results, but also some failures.

"Fix him," said Jimmy.

Hofferman stepped back and pushed a few buttons. There was no sound, no perceptible movement, and, to those readers who have experienced a rejuvenation, this will come as no surprise. But me, back then, I thought maybe something had come unplugged. We had some pretty nifty gadgets, back in the days before the "revolution", but very few devices operated in such silence. I'd been expecting an electrical hum, or an intermittent hiss, or a gentle pinging, or something, anything. Machines, even electronic machines, without moving parts were, to my way of thinking, supposed to make some kind of noise. These machines assembled and linked together all around me, and tied into my body with their needles and sensors, they didn't make a single sound, even while they began to make their repairs to the ragged and worn-out thing that was me.

Hofferman's machines were of two basic types. I'm no biotechnologist, but let me lay out the basics. Machine type one gathered and processed information about my body, heart-rate, injury-type, injury-location, pathogens, infections, all that. There were several of machine type one, each specialized to pull information about my various fleshly components, heart, lungs, blood, skin, muscle, bone, hair, etc.. Then there was an uber-machine-one, a central processor, which gathered all the information in one place and sent commands to machine type two, of which there were also several sub-types, each a little factory that produced microscopic machines, nanobots. These nanobots were built-to-order based on instructions from the central processor. They were built to trap infectious agents and everyday toxins, or to make other repairs on the cellular level. Some of the nanobots were built to collect better, more detailed information on my physical state, and relay that information back to the central processor, which, based on this latest information, ordered machine type two to send out new and improved nanobots to continue repairs, monitor and report on the process. These miniscule machines were pumped into my bloodstream by the millions, and they did their jobs quite well.

The first improvements to become apparent to me as I lay on that table were to my lungs. After laying there for a good fifteen minutes, waiting for something to happen, I began to breathe more easily. Literally. It was a gradual change, hardly noticeable at first, but then more and more apparent, to the point where each breath seemed deeper and more full than the last. To the point where I thought I could feel a great rush of cold clean oxygen into my body, cleaning and energizing me, making me more aware, filling my limbs with strength even as I lay still, clearing my head and driving the pain from my joints. My breathing must have been very shallow when Jimmy brought me in, because, after I'd laid there for a while with those nanobots doing their work, I felt like my lungs were inflating and inflating, balloons, blimps, zeppelins. It was amazing, how much air I took in and blew out.

It wasn't just my lungs, of course. It was everything. For those of you who have experienced a rejuvenation, you know the feeling, the way you start to feel better all over, until you're so pumped up, so full of life that you don't think you can lay there any longer, but want to get up and run around the room jumping and shouting and laughing. Everything is repaired. Not just the big stuff, the cuts and bruises. All the tiny insults and injuries to the physical self, all the pollutants, all the decay, all the atrophy, it is all reversed by the workings of the millions on millions of tiny machines you will later piss out, once their labors are complete. It is not only a return to normal health; it is a return to mature youth, to your early twenties. I was almost forty when Jimmy brought me to Hofferman's lab. Before Harold's goons fucked me up, I'd thought I was in pretty good shape. I liked to smoke, and I liked to drink, but I'd thought I'd kept it all together pretty well, when I'd been losing it for years and years. People don't get old all at once. You don't wake up one morning to find you've crossed some temporal line to old age. It's a very gradual process, and age accumulates in increments so small as to be unnoticeable. The reversal through rejuvenation of this aging process takes so little time that you're left wondering how the hell you'd gotten so old, become so ruined without even noticing. You wonder how the hell you'd been so completely robbed of vitality without the slightest hint that anything had been lost. You are suddenly new again and the degree of your former decay becomes glaringly obvious as that decay is filled in with lost youth. And that's a normal rejuvenation. As bad off as I was when Jimmy brought me in, I wasn't simply made younger. I was taken from death's door to the pinnacle of my physical strength. If you have never been rejuvenated you may not understand how I felt. I came to a sudden understanding and appreciation of just why that little shit Harold had decided to call Billy's gifts "blessings" and "miracles". My brother had brought back from Cygnus such power and knowledge that humankind may never have achieved without his assistance. I was awestruck. My newly repaired body nearly tingled with new-found vigor and life.

The whole thing took a couple hours. By the end, I felt so damned good that I couldn't stop my mind to make sense of it, to make any kind of conscious realization or rationalization of what had happened. It was unexpected but entirely unquestioned, the way I felt. The crap Harold was selling folks in his Red Star Centers back then was nothing compared to what I'd just got. What I got was a real rejuvenation, just like the rejuvenations you can get today, if you live in the Upper Levels of Megadon.

"Wow!" said Jimmy, as Hofferman wheeled his machines away and I got up off the table. "Wow! Robert, you're all changed! You're fixed up real good!"

I was fixed up, alright. The gray was gone from my hair and I felt I couldn't stand still. Me and Jimmy got the hell out of there. I asked Hofferman if he wanted to come with us, but he wasn't about to leave all that Harold had given him. He couldn't be made to believe that Harold was a total suck-pod, but that was okay. I was young again, and everything was good in the there and the then. Jimmy let me drive his rusted-out shit-box car. Its tapping and rattling was the most beautiful music I'd ever heard. The freezing wind that leaked in through the rust-holes felt like the flickering tongue of a heartless wanton woman, distant while intimate and thrilling.

07-10-2112

It seemed a good idea to David, to teach his mother a lesson by remaining out in the wilderness overnight. He drove the powerful red car through the forest on roads cleared by the labors of his cousin. David drove quickly, he drove fast, until the thrill of speed had spent itself and he began to feel spent himself. Then he drove more slowly, simply enjoying the patterns of sunlight filtered through the canopy of leaves and the sometimes dry pale smells, and the sometimes damp and rich smells of the forest around him, and the feeling of the slowly rolling lowly rumbling car, no longer speed itself but the potential for speed, just as satisfying as had been the racing rushing that had filled the first few hours. David wound his way through the woods on the old roads, feeling the sweat of his earlier excitement dry and tighten on his brow. He wound his way between the great trees, the likes of which he had encountered only in books just weeks before. He wandered, and thought of his father, the way Dad used to cook French toast and tell jokes and sing old songs on those special mornings, when he would send the household staff away and take David to Holy Program Junior High School himself, on his way to Vigilance headquarters. And the way Dad had always been there when Mom had freaked out about some little thing, when Mom used to freak out about sinful this or sinful that. Dad used to step in and Mom would end up freaking out on Dad instead, and later, when Mom was off shopping, Dad used to joke around with David, about how uptight and crazy Mom could be. It was like they were in on something together, not against Mom, but kind of like there were some things only Dad and David could understand, and that Mom never would.

But now Mom was really crazy, swearing, showing her body. And Uncle Robert said that *this* was the Mom that Dad had loved, not the one David had known all his life. Well, it would be a good experiment, to see if she could freak out anymore, to see if she could worry about him anymore, David decided. He drove off across Rosella's bridge, over Deadman's Gorge and on and on through the woods on the other side, kilometers and kilometers further than he'd ridden with Uncle Robert. David followed the road as it wound up the side of a small mountain peaked with bare rock, and then down the other side, slowing down and slowing down for the downward curves, almost afraid he car would slide sideways and toss him down the slope if he took the turns with anything greater than crawling speed. Halfway down the grade, a section of trees had been cleared to afford a stunning view of the next mountain, a long, wide upward protrusion with a sudden jutting peak as bare of green life as was the peak of the mountain David currently traversed. To be driving down a mountain with another in stunningly clear view, it was even more remarkable than the idea of driving through a real forest. There were moments when David felt he might be overwhelmed by the spectacle before him and the memory of his father. He smiled even while he felt like crying, and felt simultaneously empty and full of awe. So much had happened so quickly, and he was glad to have the tricky road out in front of him, the precipitous slope above and below. It gave him something on which to focus his attentions, something very tangible, very real, to keep him from wallowing in the depths of emotion that confronted him. Uncle Robert had alluded to "the feeling of the road" and "time on the road" as good things, had mentioned travel by car with a certain degree of reverence, and David wondered if this was what he had meant, the necessary but only partial focus on the act of driving that such travel required, and the feeling of separation it gave him from himself. The partial focus and the feeling of movement, away from the bad or toward the good in his own mind, and the freedom to make only abstracted decisions while feeling detached from the rest of reality. Only the vehicle, the road, the motion, were real. The focus on driving did not reduce the ability to think, but reduced the clutter of thinking, it busied the worrisome part of the mind with the movement of pedals and wheel, with the monitoring of speedo and tach and the landscape ahead. And what remained of the mind was left unbothered by the need to do something, when there was nothing to be done. David knew his Dad was dead, and there was nothing he could do about it. And his mother had changed, but there was nothing to do about it. Nothing but to move, to continue to drive. It made him feel better.

It was beginning to get dark when he drove down the valley and up the next slope, until he came to another place where the trees had been cleared, and he found a small place to pull-off, a clearing that had been leveled into a short terrace, a brief cut into the uphill side of the grade, and braced against collapse with roughly cut logs. The road went on beyond this parking place, and David wondered just how far it might go, how much road Rosella could possibly maintain. The battle armor allowed her to fly and gave her great strength, but even so, the maintenance of so much road was a feat nothing short of tremendous. Maybe once she got it all cleared, David thought, it wouldn't be so bad, just minor but regular fixes here and there, the clearing of downed trees or limbs, the filling of cracks and holes. There had been a time when he had dreamt about running away and living with wild Uncle Robert, but now David was glad he'd done no such thing. Better to have put up with Mom freaking out every once in a while than have to keep up with such a long stretch of road.

David parked the car and shut down the mighty engine, and the relative quiet of the forest settled in around him and his bright red machine. He got out, stretched, walked up the road, looking out at the mountain he had just driven over. Then he walked back down the road, back past the car and some hundreds of meters down the way he had come. He reconnoitered the area, hiking up and down the mountain, finding his way back to the road, and then to the car. It was nearly true night, and there was no moon. David got back in the car and reclined the driver's seat as far back as it would go. It wasn't going to be the most comfortable night, but it would be worth it, to see if his new Mom would freak out like the old Mom used to freak out, to see if there was anything left of that Mom, and to teach the new one a lesson, to show her that he wouldn't just hang around to take her changing without reason or explanation.

David lay in the car for a long time before finally drifting off to sleep. The forest around him gradually filled with different sounds, with creaking and peeping and buzzing and the occasional distant shrieking of what he hoped were just birds. David lay there and lay there and eventually drifted off.

He was woken by the very distinct and growing sound of turbofans. It was a sound he knew well enough, the whirring of a frontier patrol car. David lay back down, in the seat of his sleek red machine, and closed his eyes, and listened to the great round engines growing louder and louder, nearer and nearer. It was his mother, driven back to her senses by his unexplained absence. His mother, driven to worry and fear, taken to the air in the frontier patrol car they had stolen from the Vigilance hangar in Megadon. His mother, not the crazy woman named Maggie, but his mother, properly dressed and properly serious and uptight, his mother, perfectly beyond all moral reproach and perfectly concerned, his mother out looking for him, combing the forest for any sign of him, her very dear very much beloved son.

David could hear the big air-car cut one way and then the other, back and forth, drawing a wavy line as it approached. Mom was zigging and zagging, sweeping as wide an area as was possible with the onboard sensors, searching for living heat, or the metal bulk of the Barchetta. Mal was probably sitting beside her in the cockpit, wondering who this strange holy-roller woman could be, wondering what had happened to the swearing tearing *Maggie* who had been so fantastically cool. And Uncle Robert might have come along for the ride, Uncle Robert was probably standing behind Mom, telling her which way the valley turned, left, right, telling her to look out for the mountains, telling her to calm down, telling her that David was a big boy, that he was perfectly fine out here, and that they should just head for home and wait for him there. And this would make Mom pretty mad, make her call Uncle Robert a drunk and a sinner, and tell him he was damned.

David couldn't really imagine what Uncle Robert might say to Mom then. He'd never seen Uncle Robert and Mom alone, without Dad between them to protect them from one another. Uncle Robert might swear at her, or he might just grumble something under his breath and retreat aft and downward into the crew compartment to wait out the ride, to keep himself from strangling Mom. Either way, David was glad he wasn't there to see them fight like that. Or maybe not. Maybe it would be good, if he could be up there in that air-car with them, so he could step in like Dad used to step in. Dad would have probably liked something like that, to have seen his son filling his role like that.

The patrol car came closer and closer, until David could see its bulk silhouetted against the starlit sky in the small gaps between the canopy of leaves above. A curved fuselage edge here, a dim glinting of starlight reflected off the chin-turret. Little bits of air-car, viewed intermittently through the leaves made up the picture of the whole. The big ship came in close, moving uphill from the valley below, until it was some hundred meters off, then it slowed, and stopped, and hovered. They had found him. Mom was probably being typical old Mom, getting really really mad, now that she'd found him, now that she knew he was safe. It was her way of being happy, trying not to smile. Uncle Robert was probably telling her that, since David was obviously okay, they should go ahead and leave him alone, that he'd no doubt drive himself back in the morning. But this wouldn't be good enough for Mom, and she'd insist he come back tonight, right now. David knew his mother well enough to know there was no way she'd let him stay out here. No way Uncle Robert was going to win that one. So David brought his seat-back to an upright position, pushed in the clutch and started up the eager engine. Its roar momentarily drowned out the sound of the air-car's turbofans, and then settled down into a low rumble that seemed strangely at odds, in complete conflict with the whirring sound from above. David tapped twice on the horn at the center of the steering wheel, to let his mother know he was ready to go.

The air-car above responded with bullets. Tracers lit the night and tore through the canopy of needles and leaves. A stream of lead lanced out from the chin-turret. Great branches were cut and fell. Trunks were sliced and toppled. Slugs tore threw up earth around David and his sleek red car.

That wasn't Mom. David jammed the car into gear. He worked the clutch and the gas, fishtailing onto the road with tries screaming. That wasn't Mom at all. David slammed the shifter into second and gunned the motor, releasing so much raw power that the car started to slide sideways. The stream of fire from the air-car above followed him, coming so close he could hear and feel the bullets race by his head. He fought the wheel and straightened out the car, going for third before gunning the engine again. The Barchetta surged forward, coming to life with the desire for more and more speed, the love of wild kinetic motion. Loud slamming as bullets punched through a rear fender and the trunk. David could barely see the road before him, but was not about to bring up his headlights. Darker shapes on dark were tree trunks, the road just a fraction more pale than the forest floor on either side. All of it whipped by, seemingly remote, wind in David's hair the only real indication of speed until a curve emerged from the darkness, Then clutch in, ease off. Downshift, accelerate. Inertial forces yanking sideways. Car going flat, hunkering through. Downshift, accelerate. Pushed back against the seat, shot forward down the road. Whirring turbofans behind him, David pushed the car and pushed the car, and it gave and gave, and he knew it would not be the car that failed, if he ended up wrapped around some tree or driving off the edge of the mountain. His death would be his own failure. His own weakness between the power that pursued and the power of the car beneath and around him. His own pride, spending the night in the forest, trying to worry and anger his mother. The thoughts came and were gone as quickly as the tracers that cut the night all around him, as quickly as the curves through which he flew.

David tested his limits within the limits of the sleek red machine. Too slow and he would be killed. Too fast and he would kill himself. The wind tore at his hair and the revving of the roaring engine became a second heartbeat underscoring the thrill and terror compounding second on second. He had returned to a state of removal from all reality but that of himself and his car and the road. He was racing for his life. There was nothing else.

How It All Happened, Chapter 3

I drove for a while, drove fast, just to be moving, drove nowhere really, just this way and that for a while, until Jimmy asked me where we were going. It was a good question. Harold would be looking for us, and so would the law, given the fact that Jimmy had just killed a few guys and briefly held Doctor Hofferman hostage. We had to lay low and we had to get in touch with Mikey somehow. I told him I didn't know where the hell we could go. "I've been out of circulation for a while," I told him. "I don't know who I can trust. You got any ideas?"

"We could go to Vera's," he said.

"Who's Vera?" I asked him.

"She's my girlfriend," he said.

I just about slammed on the brakes, but that would have sent us into the snow-bank on the side of the road, and, even with all the pumped-up feelings of my new-found youth, I wasn't that stupid. But you get the idea. My brother, my retarded brother, had a girlfriend? It was like hearing that the Pope smokes dope. It was like hearing that Santa Claus and the Easter Bunny are into bondage, or that John Wayne liked to wear women's panties. Jimmy had a girlfriend? I guess it showed that I, like everybody else, didn't give Jimmy his due, just because he was retarded. Forget the fact that he was a full-grown man, in his early forties, with all the basic needs of other full-grown men. He was my retarded brother, and he wasn't supposed to have a girlfriend. It made me feel plenty stupid, that I'd made such an unconscious assumption. "Your girlfriend?" I said.

"She's real nice to me," he said.

"Well, that's good. Girlfriends are supposed to be nice, right? Is she, uh, is she kind of like you?"

Jimmy shook his head. "No, she's not a retard. She's real smart. I love her."

And right off, I'm thinking he's hooked up with some whore who's taking advantage of him, some hooker someplace who charges him way too much for whatever tricks she turns. Or, even worse yet, that she's some grifter who was bilking Jimmy without even providing sexual service. Some bitch who accepts his expensive gifts and rewards him with nothing more than a peck on the cheek and a little hand-holding and the promise of eternal love.

Vera didn't turn out to be either of these things, but I had plenty of time to make her into a filthy whore and a grifter, and much worse. I had all the time in the world to make her into a fire-breathing purple-scaled man-eating monster, because the highway north of Portland, once you get out beyond Yarmouth and Freeport, once you start to veer away from the coast and the marshes, that stretch of I-95 north of Portland goes on for a long-ass time. Nothing much to see up there. A few farms near the highway, a scattering of rolling hills, but most of the time you're staring out at trees. Pine trees. Pine trees on pine trees. Some rock, where the earth had been shallowly gouged to ease the construction of the interstate, but mostly pine trees. Exits off the highway are few and far between. Seems like you're rolling on for days before you see another big green sign that tells you it's another thirty-some miles to anyplace with a name. And then there's Bangor, about halfway up on the way to Houlton, Bangor is six or eight exits long. You can see wood-framed houses. You can see a few fast-food joints. And then, north of Bangor, nothing again. Orono, Old Town, these are places that are just names, no proof visible from the road that there are towns attached to the names. Portland to Bangor seems a very long and uneventful haul. Bangor to Houlton is an empty eternity. More pines, pines, pines, and signs that do not mark exits, signs that simply notify you that you're passing through a place called T3-R5. The "T" stands for "township", the "R" stands for "range". Uninhabited blocks of land, surveyed off and cataloged on the map. Somebody once told me that, if you could bring some business or people or just something, anything, to one of these T-Rs, that the state would pretty much give you the land, let you call it whatever you wanted. Robertville. Lifesontown. Driving by these T-R signs, little fantasies of autonomy began to bubble up through my internal vilification of this bitch named Vera who was no doubt taking unfair advantage of my poor helpless retarded brother. I would found a town out here, in the woods of northern Maine, and live off the land, and help others to do the same. I would be the mayor and the police chief and the fire chief, and if this Vera ever came around trying to ever mess with Jimmy again, I'd arrest her and throw her in jail, that stupid heartless whore.

We eventually got to Houlton. We drove through the depressed and fading downtown, through the square, between the little red-brick buildings. If you want to get an idea of what the town of Houlton was like, take some kind of ideal little town: sidewalks, big glass windows in the fronts of stores, a little movie-theatre with a marquee that overhangs the sidewalk before it, a real working bank right there in the heart of this perfect little downtown. Then take this ideal place, which would be fairly thriving with people shopping, going to the movie theatre and the bank, take this ideal place and remove most of those people. Make it look so lifeless that you have to wonder if anybody lives there at all. Then cover everything with a thick layer of what the locals (yes, people really did live there) called "potato dirt". Houlton was an agricultural community, and may yet be one again, and one of the their principal crops was potatoes. The town is dotted with big old wooden barn-like warehouses, some partially underground, called "potato houses", where the tubers were stored in the cool and the dark, to await transport by trailer-truck to far-away markets. When you have the soil for miles around being tilled, it throws up a lot of earth. So, like a lot of farming towns, everything in Houlton was coated in a layer of brown grit. Last but certainly not least, make it cold, sometimes very cold, and cover everything with snow. Even into April and sometimes May, snow falls. Snow falls and snow piles up and snow becomes snow-banks compacted by plows, and the snow-banks go brown and sometimes black from the potato dirt that's thrown up by the tires of cars. Cold and snow for eight or sometimes nine months out of the year, and then, when spring makes its feeble appearance, and that snow melts, and mixes more intimately with all that potato dirt, then what you have is a whole lot of mud, which may or may not dry out before fall rolls around again and everything freezes up and the leaves pour down off the trees and everybody starts making bets about when they'll see the first snow.

That's Houlton. Dreary. Don't get me wrong, I liked the place, I really did. I would, in fact, like to see it resettled, after Harold's little empire is finally pulled down, after people come back to their senses and learn to do a thing or two for themselves again. Houlton would be a good place for people to learn independence from the existing repressive regime. It's fairly remote, and there's no lack of natural resources, for those who know how to make use of them. It took not a single direct hit during the nuclear bombardment, and the closest truly "hot" radioactive site is hundreds of miles away.

Anyway, so we roll off the interstate and over the river and through downtown, then up this big hill toward what was then the Canadian border. Houlton was on the east side of the northern part of the state, right there on the border between the two countries. And Jimmy, who had started driving somewhere in that noplace-zone north of Bangor, took us right up to within a half mile of that border before he turned onto a long dirt road that went downhill, through abandoned and overgrown potato-fields and then over what looked like a frozen and snow-covered stream. There were a couple rotten piles of wood, gray boards and beams in heaps on old foundations, on the one side as we proceeded. "Vera said those used to be houses, farms and stuff," Jimmy told me as we drove by these wrecks. "That's Cook Brook," he said, as we passed over the stream.

Just over that stream, as the road began to run uphill, there was a little trailer-park. Now for those of you who do not know what a trailer-park is, and I suppose that would be most of you who happen to read this, well, a trailer-park is, or was, a place where one could live fairly cheaply. A plot of land scattered with fairly uniform living spaces, each constructed of aluminum and other light-weight materials on a semi-rigid metal frame. These things were built in factories and hauled on wheels to these types of locations, where they were set on concrete blocks or slabs, and people lived in them, as they might have lived in a less portable house. Bedrooms, bathrooms, kitchens, trailers had all of these things, but the fact that they were portable, and the fact that they did not, in general, hold up as well as a normal house, made a lot of people look down upon trailers, and look down on the people who lived in them. It was an economic thing, too, of course. People in houses generally paid more for their dwellings than did people who lived in trailers, and so thought themselves superior to the trailer-living-folk. A strange social phenomenon, looking back on it, but I suppose that was the nature of the capitalist system that controlled or at least dominated common thought and philosophy at the time. In a society where money was valued even more highly than the resources it represented, the monetary worth (or lack of worth) of material possessions was considered more important or noteworthy than the intrinsic or practical worth of those possessions. A trailer could, in general, keep you as warm in the winter and as cool in the summer and as dry in the rain as could any house, and yet, because they cost less and held less monetary value than houses, trailers were seen as "low class" or, in some cases, unfit residences. Most trailers were much more vulnerable than most houses to fire and to heavy weather, but beyond this vulnerability to such catastrophic threats, there was really nothing wrong with them. Usually.

The trailer-park we drove into was a fairly small one, as trailer-parks used to go. Ten units all told, ten little tin cans, white vinyl-sided rectangular living-spaces, shaped like the cardboard boxes in which shoes used to be packaged. Gently sloping stainless steel roofs. A narrow strip of asphalt described a loop about which these trailers were arrayed at regular intervals, and at the center of the little circle of land closed off by that loop, at the very center of the trailer-park itself, there was a flag-pole, on which hung two colorful squares of cloth. One looked very much like an American flag, but for the fact that the little white stars had been replaced by little white skulls. It wasn't something you'd notice from any kind of distance. As Jimmy drove us around the loop, it was the other flag that first caught my eye. This one had a blazing orange sun on a neon lime-green background, with the letters "VIN" in red, in the middle of the sun. At each corner of the lime-green field there was a different cartoon animal: a rabbit, a deer, a trout, a porcupine. Anyway, these two flags flapped in the light but fucking freezing breeze. Skull-stars and VIN, flapping in the breeze, and under these flags, arranged on the circle of snowy ground inside the paved loop, there was a large collection of painted concrete figures. Now these kinds of statues used to be pretty common, back in the times I'm talking about. It wasn't all that strange to drive through an average neighborhood and see a concrete gnome or dwarf on somebody's lawn, or a statue of the Virgin Mary (if you don't know who the Virgin Mary is, think of how your shithead "Almighty" Harold portrays his mother, and that's the Virgin Mary, Harold ripped off the idea) or maybe a concrete deer or two, or maybe a concrete frog. These kinds of things were considered tacky, back in the day, completely senseless things to have, but I always kind of liked them, just because they were a little kooky. You could buy them painted, or you could buy them unpainted, so you could paint them yourself. To match your house, I suppose.

Anyway, I'd never seen such a concrete menagerie, never seen anything like this one that was set up around the flagpole in the middle of that trailer-park. There were no less than twenty-seven gnomes alone, little bearded fat guys made of concrete, wearing pointed concrete hats. Each of these gnomes was painted differently, so this was definitely an inside job, custom work on the part of whatever nut set these things up. Twenty-seven gnomes. Gnomes waving, laughing, toasting one another with concrete beer steins, pointing, sitting, standing, even one gnome with his dick in his hand, standing there smiling as he took an imaginary piss. Twenty-seven gnomes. And then there were the deer, and the chickens, and the gargoyles and a gorilla. Three Virgin Marys, two scallop-shell bird baths complete with concrete birds, a dragon, a handful of frogs and raccoons, a lighthouse that would light up at night, a fake wishing-well. Some of these things were painted their "normal" colors; brown deer, black gorilla. But some others were painted in stripes (a concrete pig, a concrete sunflower and concrete St. John the Baptist) or polka-dots (a concrete Virgin Mary, a concrete Empire State Building) or other disconcerting patterns. The whole thing was kitsch carried to an extreme that probably would have made me laugh if I hadn't been so uptight worrying about this Vera woman who just had to have been taking advantage of Jimmy. Looking at the strange flags and the concrete figures through the red lenses of this self-invented bias, I found them nothing short of threatening, proof that I was entering the treacherous territory of a possibly unstable witch.

Jimmy parked his ratty old car in front of a trailer marked "OFFICE" with a crudely-painted wooden sign. We got out of the car and I just about broke my neck when I slipped on the ice. The pavement didn't seem like it had been plowed all winter. Looked like the residents of the trailer-park had simply flattened out the snow by driving over it a couple million times. This technique kind of works but kind of doesn't. It clears some of the snow to the point where, on warmer days (read "warmer" as just barely freezing) the weak winter sun can melt away the smaller, thinner areas of the snow on the road, exposing the black pavement, which the sun then heats up enough to melt a little more of the snow. But the sun doesn't shine at night, and what you get, when the sun goes down, or when the temperature drops back down so low that the weak winter sun isn't going to melt a damned thing, what you get is a whole lot of ice. Bumpy uneven ice that knuckles into your lower back like a well-aimed fist when you slip on it like I slipped on it when I got out of Jimmy's car.

You can imagine how this affected my mood. I lay there on the lumpy ice for a few seconds, steaming so fucking hard it's a wonder I didn't melt all the snow and ice for miles around. That was one thing, about being suddenly young again. People have always told me I'm a little cantankerous, secure in my opinions and never afraid to act on them, but laying there on that ice, I was simply fuming. I was pissed off like I hadn't been pissed off for years and years. Because I was young again. Because the blood was racing more quickly through my veins, because all the fight or flight chemicals had kicked in and I could have chewed a hole right through Jimmy's rusted-out yellow car. I didn't really figure this out at the time. At the time, I was just pissed. I got up from that ice and saw Jimmy brushing the snow off the back of one of those goddam concrete deer, a purple one, and I just lit into him. "Goddam it, what kind of fucked up fucking goddam fuck-hole kind of fucking place is this?! What the fuck, Jimmy?! What the fuck?!"

Jimmy gave me this blank look then laughed at me. "Your whole head is as purple as Bambi!" he said, petting the purple concrete deer. "Wow, you're really really mad! You should see how purple you are!"

This took a little of the wind out of my sails. I was looking for some kind of fight, and Jimmy wasn't giving it to me, so I stood there and punched the hood of his car and swore and tore and kicked the side of the car so flakes of it fell off.

"Don't, Robert! Don't kick Bessy!" Jimmy yelled.

"Bessy?! You named your fucking car Bessy?! Well, hello, Bessy!" I pulled my boot way back to kick the crap out of Bessy and slipped again.

This time I hit the back of my head on the ice, so hard my vision swam. I'm still all pissed off, but I'm also all clenched up with the crashing that bursts through my skull. And this is how I am, laying flat on my back, paralyzed with anger and self-inflicted pain when Vera makes her appearance.

She's a weird-looking woman, older, in her late forties, very skinny, the kind of skinny that people get from not consuming very much other than cigarettes, one of which is hanging out of the side of her mouth, beneath her big bird-like nose, beneath the gigantic square half-shaded lenses of her faux tortoise-shell glasses. Her frizzy long bottle-blonde hair hung down on either side of her long face as she bent down over me, squinting down at me through those enormous glasses as if I was some strange creature she'd hit with her car. She wore a coffee-stained white tank-top so tight I could see her ribs and her shriveled little missile-tits through the strained cotton. "Well, you must be Robert! Jimmy's told me all about you! What're you doing on your back like that? Aren't you cold, laying on that ice?" A bit of dead gray ash fell from the tip of her cigarette as it bobbed between her lips. The ash landed on my forehead and she swiped it off with a bony hand.

Jimmy came over and helped me up. "Robert, this is Vera, she's my girl-friend!" he told me.

"Welcome to Vera's Independent Nation," she offered. "Let's get inside before my tits freeze off."

And that was how I came to Houlton, and then to VIN, where Jimmy and I would ride out the nuclear storm that loomed on the horizon. This was where we would hole up while the world as we knew it ended and Harold's mad dreams became real.

Anywhere, Anytime (The Fractured Sphere viii)

High on my snow-covered peak, I wondered what had become of me. I sat in hard-driving sub-zero winds without freezing, without even feeling the cold, and I reviewed once more all the possibilities that might account for my newly-found abilities and those strange visions in which I witnessed again and again the destruction of my home world. Was I dead? Or, if I was alive, was I a man, or was

I a god, as the people of Apollonia believed me to be? Was this some afterlife? Or was I, as an earthman, granted superhuman powers by the very nature of this planet on which my *Rocinante* had crash-landed? Ridiculous, every possible explanation seemed so ridiculous. Even more ridiculous was my insistence that there had to be an answer that was comprehensible on human terms, that there had to be an answer that was relatively simple or at least rational to a human way of thinking. I was still clinging to the idea that I was a man, when I had become something much more. What exactly had I become, you ask? Get down to the "goddam nitty gritty" you tell me, my brother? I will try, but you must remember that I am far beyond humanity. You could convey human experiences to a mouse as easily as I could convey my experiences to you. By this I do not mean that you are somehow beneath me. Your human urge to quantify, rank and classify leads you to believe that I have slighted you, but this is not the case. I mean simply to point out the vast differences between the two forms of life. The human tendency to refer to other creatures as "lesser beings" prejudices you against my chosen metaphor, but try to consider the mouse as an equal, in that mice eat, sleep, reproduce. Mice are born and mice die. Mice feel happiness and fear and sadness. You may choose not to believe that mice feel such emotions, but they do. They may feel them differently than do humans, but mice are indeed familiar with most every emotion that humans feel. Try to consider the mouse as an equal even while your mind rebels against the notion with the reflexive thought that mice are very different from humans, and you may see the truth in my chosen metaphor. Even while mice and humans share the same types of lives, eating, sleeping, copulating, and even while they share the same emotions, and even the same basic physical chemistry, there is a tremendous difference between the two species, and it is this tremendous difference that would make it so difficult for you to communicate human experiences to a mouse. This difficulty in communication has nothing to do with one creature being "greater" or "lesser" or better or worse. There is simply a great distance between the two in their modes of communication and cognitive processes. In order for you to communicate effectively with a mouse, you would have to speak mouse. Mice do not, of course, use language in the sense that humans use language, so you would have to transmit signals in the form of scents, sounds, movements, even tastes. Exact translations of human experiences into such a form might very well be impossible, and so you would be forced to make due with half-measures, half-truths, picking and choosing those expressions from mouse-syntax that best fit or come mostly closely to conveying what you wished to convey. You may, for example, express the thrill you feel when you hack into a well-guarded system as "successfully steal cheese from trap". Hacking into a well-guarded system is nothing like stealing cheese from a mousetrap, so while you might convey the feeling of success against highly improbable odds, you've actually miscommunicated nearly everything else. And so it is between you and I. If I am to communicate to you what I have become and how the transformation took place, I can do so only by conveying approximations. A great deal of what I would gladly share will be lost. Applying more time and effort to my explanation only means that more will be lost, the truth made further and further distant with the compounding of approximations and their attendant inaccuracies.

With that caveat in place, here is your explanation. Black holes are, as you know, compression-points in time and space. When I entered the black hole of Cygnus X-1, I was compressed, along with everything else, into a oneness more singular and united than can be described with human language. As time was compressed with me, I knew what it was to *be* time. As light was compressed with me, I knew what it was to *be* light. The same goes for all types of matter and energy, every atom and sub-atomic particle and radiation and everything else that exists in the universe. I became all of these things, and I understood, I understand everything, "from the inside" if you will. It was my humanity that allows me, even now, to use the word "understand" when describing the oneness within Cygnus. Raw matter and raw energy, these things do not understand, they simply exist, but I entered the black hole as human, and it was as a human that I became part of the oneness, less than a single point more full, more dense than anything else in the universe. The compression took no time, for time itself was compressed, and for this same reason, the oneness was eternal and momentary, existing even while it didn't exist. To an external observer who could stand in the very middle, on the very border between the two sections of the universe, which are united and separated by black holes, Cygnus X-1 would look like two funnels attached to one another at their narrow ends. The external observer gazing thusly at Cygnus and both sides thereof would have seen me sail into one end of the black hole and almost immediately out the other side, as time progresses normal outside the black hole, even while it is compressed to the point of elimination, to the oneness within.

Why then, would I emerge from the other side of Cygnus, and why in human form? Because all things that enter Cygnus emerge from Cygnus. Because, as human scientists have somewhat correctly deduced, all matter and energy seeks equilibrium. Matter and energy move from areas of high concentration to areas of low concentration. As the oneness within Cygnus is an area of extremely high concentration, the oneness disperses to the nearest area of low concentration, which is just outside the black hole. Me and my ship were dispersed out into space on the other side of Cygnus, and I retained human form for the same reason my ship retained its form: because I willed it. My panicked humanity wanted out, and used the vast power of all existence to fulfill this terror-driven wish. I had no idea what I was doing at the time, I simply did it; it simply happened. There was no conscious effort or knowing manipulation of my newly expanded being. It was familiar human reflex bound to the power of the universe. My humanity screamed and the oneness responded, and I was out the other side of Cygnus, bringing with me what remained of my Rocinante. I was a fear-crazed man in a ruined spacecraft even while I was the universe itself. You must understand the timeless nature of the interior of the black hole in order to understand how this could be. It will be difficult to couch this in terms that you will readily understand, but the very instant I was compressed into the oneness was the very instant I came to understand everything as I do. As there is no time within Cygnus, everything occurs simultaneously. I was conscious even as I was an unconscious oneness, even as the oneness was me. I was the first conscious sentient being to enter a black hole, and I remained as such, even while I lost all consciousness and all sentience to the oneness. I came to a sudden understanding of the workings of the universe, while simultaneously existing as a panicking human being, while simultaneously being nothing and everything. I was a multiplicity. I am a multiplicity.

My humanity began to understand what the rest of me already understood, as I sat on that windy peak on the other side of Cygnus. I realized that, in a way, the people whom I had left behind in the city far below were very much like myself. Each of them was more than one person. Each of them had an animal side and a completely rational side, while I had a human side and a more-than-human side. Just as the animal actions of the townsfolk seemed brutish and senseless to their rational selves, the fears and wants of my human side seemed inconsequential against the backdrop of my new knowledge. The people in the town below could not do without their animal side, and nor would I do without my humanity. I required both to be whole, for without my humanity, I was simply the universe itself, all-mighty and all-knowing, but unaware, not conscious. Without my humanity, I am all of existence but only existence.

And this, my dear brother, is why I bothered to save humanity from itself. Because I had both lost and become all the more connected to my own humanity. There on that rocky mountain-top, not unlike some Biblical prophet, I made peace with myself, with the one man who was the universe, with the universe who was one man. Me. I knew I would return to earth, our earth, and help guide humanity along the one course among billions and billions that did not lead to its utter destruction. Many would die, and my heart wept for each and every one of them, but my mind knew that this was as it must be. There was no other way.

Couldn't I have used my vast power and knowledge to simply make people different? Make them nicer? Make them more aware of their own fragility? Make them see the error of their ways? Couldn't I have spared all the billions that would die in nuclear fire or radiation or at the hands of Harold's mad mobs or at the hands of Harold's police and paramilitary forces? Couldn't I have spared the three-year-old boy who wailed his hunger and pain to his equally suffering mother as they starved and froze when the power went out and the food stopped coming? Couldn't I have spared the young girl in the electric wheelchair who was caught out in the open far enough from one blast to survive the flash but close enough to be badly burnt over sixty percent of her body? Couldn't I have spared her the three days of lingering agony, the seventy-some hours it took her to die? If it makes any difference, Robert, I did spare many millions the agony of slow deaths. People and animals alike. I was an angel of merciful death for countless multitudes. I did as much as I could to assuage the worst suffering without affecting the course of larger events. I will not detail any one of these quick actions, for you would only be troubled by the scenes I could describe. Understand that I did what I could. Understand that I acted, in every instance, for the greater good of humanity. Understand if you can, if you will.

I do not know how long I remained on the mountain, as the inhabitants of that far-away world also called "earth" tell time. I may have been there, in the shrieking high-altitude winds, for months or mere seconds. I remained there for as long as it took for my humanity to understand what I had become, and then I returned to Apollonia.

The mob that had gathered before the house of Twilight's father had dispersed. I moved without moving to the steps of the house, and entered without knocking. Twilight and her father sat at table, laughing, laughing so hard that tears rolled down their cheeks. Upon seeing me, they both prostrated themselves, and, still chuckling, they barraged me with grateful thanksgiving. "Thank you, O Bringer of Balance, thank you for uniting heart and mind! Thank you for ending the millennia of cold reason and animal madness! Thank you, O Most Cherished of Gods! The prophesy has been fulfilled, and in your returning you have made us whole once again!"

I had made them whole by just showing up. By letting them become excited by my presence. By letting them argue over me. By letting them worship me. A god never had an easier job. I found it curious, that I should have fulfilled their expectations of me with so little effort. It made so little sense, until I heard Twi-light say something neither she nor her father nor any of the other worshippers had said before: "All praise to you, O Creator, Who has returned to make us complete! All praise and all glory to Cygnus, from whom all life on earth does spring!"

"What?" I said. "Hold on, hold on. What? Creator? Why are you calling me Creator?" I asked, reluctant to accept the obvious, even as it unfolded before me, even as it came out from hiding within my own awareness.

Twilight looked up at me from her place on the floor, and in her eyes I saw elements of the animal passion that had burned so brightly when we'd first encountered one another in the wilderness, near the crash-site where I had come down from the heavens. And, along with this animal passion, I saw a very human longing, a guarded questioning, hope suppressed yet nonetheless hopeful. I saw love in Twilight's face, the love a woman can feel for a man. She was feeling this love for me, and dared not truly show it, for she thought me her god. "O Cygnus, be not angry with your humble supplicants, who know not how to address you but in the most simple and functional terms," she said. "Tell us how else you would have us address you who crafted us from the earth and breathed life into our forebears. Tell us how else you would have us address our Creator."

Creator. Do not ask me if it is true. Do not ask me if there exists on the other side of Cygnus X-1 a race of people for whose existence I am responsible. Is it possible that, as I clung to my ignorant and fearful humanity, as I was flung from the black hole, is it possible that, in my longing for safety and familiarity, in my longing for home, I created the world on which I found Twilight and her people? Did I unconsciously craft her and her ancestors so I might not be alone? So I might find physical solace in her body, and comfort in the house of her father and recognition by other humans of my continued existence? Had generations on generations of people lived and died on that world because, in one way or another, I had willed it? It is possible. And are they still there now, awaiting my return? It is possible. I know you find this maddening, dear brother, because humans prefer binary answers, on or off, yes or no; but the universe does not con-form to human expectations on any but the smallest of scales or under any but the strictest of limitations. As humans best understand non-binary topics by means of metaphor, allow me to recall for you this philosophical query: 'If a tree falls in the forest without anyone there to hear it, does it make a sound in falling?' Or, if I created Twilight and her people and her world, do they exist when I am not there to observe them? You are uncomfortable with the very notion of Billy-as-Creator because, if I did indeed create an entire world and all the life thereon, I truly am, so far as human perception is concerned, a god. If I can create life, I am the type of 'supreme being' that many humans refer to as 'God' with a capital 'G'. Moreover, if I, your brother, albeit much-changed, can create life, then how can the people of my homeworld be unique and worth saving? Why have I bothered? And then there will inevitably come other questions: Is there a God? Are there other Gods? How did life begin on earth? Why did life begin on earth? What is the meaning of life? Questions on myriad questions begin to accumulate and behind every possible answer lurks only another question, or questions. This is the way of humanity, to remain busy, so busy with puzzles constructed of and founded on limited perception. And so I will leave it to you, to decide whether or not I created Twilight's world and her people and all the life thereon. You may not choose to believe me, but I must tell you that you will be much happier with your own conclusions than with any answers I could provide. Revel in the questions you can not help but invent, Robert. Revel in your humanity, and understand that unanswered questions are the true lifeblood of the species.

And so I conclude my tale, my explanation, my apology. The rest is known to you. I returned to earth, bringing my ship back to the solar system and leaving it to drift quite near the orbit of Jupiter. I shared some of my knowledge with Harold, so he might capitalize upon it directly as well as commercially. I gave him what he needed to fulfill his mad plans, to initiate a nuclear holocaust. And while he was indeed mad, humanity has been preserved, along with the majority of animal and plant species that recovered and thrived in the wilderness beyond the cities. I assisted in building Harold's cities, providing this or that nudge to his experts, the ones he would order killed after their roles had been played. I bear on my hands their blood, and the blood of many billions, but I have saved humanity from the absolute annihilation that loomed on every other path. I am sorry that salvation had to come at such a high price, but I am not sorry that it has come.

Understand, Robert, if you can, if you will.

07-10-2112

A small cadre of Vigilance officers held positions behind a barricade at the top of the ramp between Levels Ten and Eleven. Their hastily-built fortification was constructed of two garbage trucks and a bus, all the gaps beneath and between these vehicles stuffed with cheap furniture, garbage cans and shipping crates. Every component of the barricade had been commandeered from Level Eleven, the vehicles and garbage cans from the street; the shipping crates from a nearby warehouse; the furniture from people's houses. Thomas had listened to these captains and lieutenants bicker back and forth on their radios, every one of those loyal officers confused and close to panic as they came to realize there were no enlisted men heeding their calls. They were used to giving orders and used to being obeyed. When blank silence had come back as the only response to their demands, their efforts had been momentarily paralyzed, hung up because no one had showed up to do the real work.

Thomas had lead his force to Level Eight, where a sergeant in one of his patrol-cars had alerted him to the situation developing between Levels Ten and Eleven. Thomas had monitored the calls between those officers while he'd ordered his people to hurry. He'd wanted to reach that band of Harold's officers before they'd had a chance to recover and regroup, before they'd had a chance to dig in. And Thomas' people had responded, they'd picked up the pace, and made it to the Level Nine before Harold's officers had reorganized and begun building their barrier. But most of Thomas' people were still on foot, and each level was a huge space to cross. Thomas had considered loading his cars with what men they could carry, and sending those cars ahead to face the rallying officers, but he hadn't wanted to split his force, and hadn't been any too certain that he'd get any more cars, if he lost the ones he had. Harold had sent three large details of enlisted men after the first that had faced Thomas outside the detention center, and the majority of each of these new details had decided to join the impromptu rebellion. After that, Harold had fielded only tentative opposition, two or three enlisted men at a time, all on foot. Every single one of these smaller parties had joined Thomas' force, after hearing what he'd had to say, after hearing his promise of change.

Now here they were, Thomas and some five hundred people behind him, most of them from rank-and-file of Vigilance, all of them armed, all of them determined to better their lives and the lives of others in the name of true righteousness, true holiness, through actions that were truth itself against the false words of the false prophet and the heretical deception of Legion that had so long held sway in the cities of the Great CPU. Thomas felt a quivering lightness inside, in his gut, an excitement at the gigantic step he was taking, the gigantic step they all took, in recognizing sin for sin, even through the false trappings of holiness, the lies of the bishops and the priests, the lies that had kept so many in such darkness for so long. All those millions on the Lower Levels who had toiled and suffered in the belief that they did so for some holy cause, for the glorification of Almighty Harold, scion of the Great CPU, all that toil and suffering had been for nothing, and worse than nothing; it had been for the aggrandizement of a demon and the comfort of his chosen few on the Upper Levels. The city itself was falling apart and rather than fix what was broken, the Uppers had made slaves of those below. Thomas remembered his mother, the way she used to look upon returning late from her job as a maid in an Upper Level house, the way she looked just short of dead. And he remembered being his mother's only joy, the treasure she had hidden and kept and polished and improved upon with the demanding lessons she'd set for him. And he remembered how the Vigilance men had come and taken his mother away. How she had screamed and ineffectually torn at those men as they'd pulled him from her arms. Because she had dared keep something for herself. Because she had wanted her son to be something more, had wanted to spare him from a life stirring the sewage or processing the trash that poured down on the Lower Levels from the overlords above. And then the treachery of the Surgeon General, Wang's manipulation with the promise of his mother's return. Thomas had no doubt, now, that his mother was dead, but she had not failed. She had gotten what she'd wanted, even if she wasn't around to see it. Her son was leading good people in the name of good change, to end the tyranny, to end the heresy and the evil that had brought her and so many others so much pain. Thomas remembered his mother, and all those faceless others who'd had their children torn away for "vocational training"; for training as slaves. This rebellion was for them, and for all those who'd spent their lives sub- sisting in darkness while others lounged in bright light. The very idea that so many were restricted to Megadon, that so many knew nothing of the bounty and beauty of the massive world beyond the levels, the open sky, the feel of true sun- shine, the trembling of a fresh breeze, the calming effect of moonlight, the smell of forest and field. There was no excuse for it, for so many millions imprisoned within the city, entombed within the giant machine, the giant hive, where oppression was the rule. The true heretics, the priests, and their demon Harold, had used Holy Scripture as a shield and noose, to hide their own wickedness and control the people, and it had worked, for a long time, it had worked. But they had been mistaken to use the Holy Word, to try to pervert it to their evil ends, for the lessons of Scripture were more than clear. Heretics were not to be trusted. Heretics were to be driven out or killed. Sinners, the unrighteous, were to be torn down from the high places and trampled, driven back to Abend, to wail and gnash their teeth in the eternal fires of that infernal state of being. Scripture was very clear, more clear than ever, now that Thomas knew who the real heretics were. His duty was clear, and he lead his people in what was right, and they would not be stopped.

This was what he told himself, as he studied the barricade thrown up by the officers on Level Eleven. Thomas scanned the fortification with a set of binoculars and saw at least twenty men manning the crude wall. Officers all, well-armored, some of them wearing partially powered suits; and well-armed, with several heavy guns and medium energy-weapons mounted on tripods atop the barricade. Thomas's force far outnumbered the defenders of that wall, but they would be traveling uphill, up the ramp, against rapid heavy fire so thick that few would survive to storm the ramparts. There was no sense in taking these people up that ramp if it meant only their deaths.

"Get me three patrol cars," Thomas radioed one of his sergeants.

The three cars came, and Thomas ordered them lined up side-by-side. He told the drivers to fix the steering controls so the cars would run straight. "Open up the jets so the cars will accelerate up that ramp, then get out and get out quickly," he ordered.

The men did as they were told, and the cars, three abreast, started up the ramp, speeding up as they went. Without another word to anyone, Thomas crouched low and followed the cars. He walked, then he ran to keep up. He could hear the voices of his men behind him. Some cheered. Some simply shouted their amazement. "What in the name of Almighty Harold is he *doing*?" he heard one man say.

And then he was too far up the ramp to hear much of anything from the men below, and the officers on the barricade above opened up with their heavy weapons. They split their fire more-or-less evenly between the three cars. The one on Thomas' left slowed and stopped first, riddled with holes and smoking from the absorption of fire from the energy-weapons. Then the one on the right stopped dead as its front jets were shot out from beneath it and it nosed down into the plasphalt. The middle car, the one Thomas now followed at a dead run, the middle car then became the focus of every gun on the make-shift wall ahead. Thomas heard its jets falter and then cut out. The last car dropped flat on its belly within three meters of the barricade. That was as close as he was going to get, and it would have to be close enough. Thomas sprinted for the barricade and leapt, and latched on and climbed. He took a grazing hit on his left shoulder as the officers above fired down at him with their side-arms, but then he was up, and he grabbed the nearest man by the leg and swung him at the rest. Thomas heard bones cracking and felt the human club in his hands go limp. He knocked five men off the wall and threw the dead man at another clutch of officers who were swinging a heavy machine-gun his way. He closed on that group and lashed out with his hands and feet, laying them low with deadly strength and speed. Scatter-gun blasts sounded behind him, and Thomas felt slugs digging into his back, pushing him forward. He went with the forward movement and scooped up the machine-gun before him, tripod and all. He spun and heaved it at the officers who fired on him, knocking one down and the other off the wall.

The men he faced were shaken now. They had been ready to withstand any kind of massed charge, but unprepared to take on one man who was seemingly invulnerable. They saw him shot and they saw him throwing their fellows about as if they were made of air. Those officers who remained went for their weapons, but they were slower than they should have been. Some fumbled. And Thomas pressed his attack.

By the time the people on the ramp below rallied to make their noisy charge, Thomas had cleared the barricade of all opposition. His shoulder hurt and his back hurt, and he was bleeding, but not badly. The second skin beneath his skin, the plastaegis, had protected him from any real harm. Some of his followers climbed the wall while others began to tear it down. They salvaged what weapons they could, and mounted these heavier guns to the vehicles in which the opposing officers had earlier arrived.

Thomas found a med-station on Level Ten and patched himself up. The newly-healed skin tingled and itched, but it was whole again.

"That was spectacular, sir!" one sergeant told him. "What now, sir?"

"Now," Thomas said, "we continue. We continue until we reach the Upper Levels and we control the city. Then it's up to you, up to everyone."

And so they continued, better-armed and more mobile than before. They continued their upward march.

How It All Happened, Chapter 4

VIN, Vera's Independent Nation, wasn't a bad place, really, so long as you didn't mind living on a diet consisting primarily of venison, rabbit, pike, trout, and porcupine. Yes, porcupine. For those of you who have no idea what a porcupine is, imagine an animal about half a meter long covered with fur and a thick coating of sharp spikes. Porcupines rely on these spikes as their only means of protection from predators, and, as such, porcupines are some of the slowest and loudest animals in the north woods. You can be out in the woods and hear something crashing slowly through the underbrush and be fairly certain there is a porcupine nearby. While not especially tasty, the little beasts are very easily caught and killed, and were therefore one of the staple foods of Vera's Independent Nation. That's why the porcupine, and the deer, and the trout, and the rabbit appeared on the VIN flag.

Let me make it clear that VIN was not, in any official sense, an independent nation. Vera, and the low-lifers and social outcasts who also resided within that happy little community were just kind of nuts. None of them had very much money. Few of them ever bothered to pay Vera rent in any form except in fruit or vegetables grown during the short summer, or in firewood during the winter months. Vera had inherited the trailer-park from a great uncle named Reardon, as she'd been the old coot's only living relative, and she'd run it as a half-assed business from the get-go, letting just about anybody rent a trailer whether they could or would pay. She struggled on an annual basis just to raise enough cash to cover the property taxes on the place, but always managed, somehow, to get by. Vegetable stand, lemonade stand, breaking and entering, soft porn, selling a little weed, you name it, she and her residents managed to scrape up the five or ten thousand dollars demanded by the county. Are you getting the picture on this place? It was a pocket of resistance against the status quo. As the citizens of Vera's Independent Nation were dirt poor, they held no stake in the capitalist society at large. They were not valued as consumers, because they didn't consume much that they didn't create or hunt down on their own. Nor were they valued as investors, because their only investments were in their trailer-park and their subsistence style of living.

"We ain't pretty, but we do for ourselves," Vera was fond of saying. "Anybody who doesn't like us can just leave us alone, and we'll do just fine."

And they did do just fine. It was a good place. Not especially pretty or overly comfortable in any physical sense, but good for the fact that it was removed, so far as was possible, from the rest of the crazed society, good for the fact that Vera's concerns and the concerns of her residents were real concerns about matters that were essential rather than ephemeral. They didn't care a damn about fashion, or worthless technological toys (the latest television or stereo or video-players) or the corporate-driven media-bathed sexy star or starlet of the month. Vera and her people were concerned with staying warm in the winter, and with hunting up their next meal. Now I've never been one to fall for the supposed allure of simple living, not like a lot of other techies and so-called intellectuals who made it rich and then dropped out to become hair-shirted hermits. You'd never find me living the life of a GreenWarrior, depriving myself of basic creature comforts in order to pursue some 'higher' ideal that wouldn't be any more important, in five or ten years' time, than all the other 'higher' ideals of all the other drop-outs. But VIN wasn't like that. These were people who dropped out, not because they held any notions of superiority or imagined any higher calling, but because they just didn't fit in elsewhere or they just didn't care about all the crap the outside world pushed as important. They cared about their basic needs, and their basic comforts, and that was that. And I found it admirable. I was comfortable enough in my room at the far end of Vera's own trailer. The whole place could have used a bit more sound-proofing, because there were many nights when I could have done without hearing Jimmy and Vera fucking each other's brains out. But other than that, it was very much okay. There was always enough to eat, and drink, and there was good weed and there wasn't a lot of pressure to do much of anything unless it was something you really wanted to do.

I guess if I had to come up with just a couple things that would give you a good picture of what VIN was really like, I'd have to say number one was that the fact that Jimmy got along there as well as he did. You've got to realize that Jimmy had more money than most of those people could ever imagine having. Mostly from stock in the various companies that Billy had established in the years before he took off for Cygnus. Each of us, Billy, Jimmy, Mikey and me, we all had some money. Not insane money like Harold would eventually get when he managed to take over the Gates empire, but we weren't bad off. Jimmy probably had more than any one of us because, unlike Billy, he didn't go blowing a lot of it on an extraterrestrial expedition. And unlike me, Jimmy didn't go buying big sailboats or secret hacker bases in Saint Augustine or high-dollar weed. Jimmy didn't spend much money on anything. Take his car, for example. "Jimmy, what the hell possessed you to buy such a miserable shit-box?" I asked him one day.

"Bessy isn't a shitbox," he said. "Bessy's a good car."

"But why'd you buy it? You could afford something better, something with a lot less rust, maybe?"

"Then what would I do with Bessy? She wouldn't like that, Robert. She wouldn't like that at all."

It was this same kind of reasoning, or lack of reasoning, or inability or unwillingness to overthink, that had brought Jimmy to VIN. He'd been knocking around the state of Maine, looking for Maggie like Mikey had told him to, and he'd run into Vera. She was a skinny kind of dried-up woman who nobody else would have bothered with, but she was good enough for Jimmy, because she was there. And she treated him good. Jimmy made no secret of the fact that he had a little money, but Vera didn't go after that money. She was like Bessy the Shitbox; she wasn't pretty, but she didn't show any inclination to screw Jimmy over, either. She wasn't anything to look at, but she wasn't going to leave my brother stranded anywhere.

"When I met your brother at that gas station down on two-oh-two, outside of Gorham," Vera told me one night, over a couple rounds of home-distilled whiskey and through a thick bank of marijuana haze, "I had no idea just what I'd found, I just figured he looked strong, and was nice enough. I don't really care none that he's a retard, I've dated retards all my damned life. Hell my first three husbands were retards, they just didn't want to admit it."

The way she slung that word around, the way she said 'retard', I didn't like it at first. I didn't like anybody but me calling my retard brother a retard, but then I started to see it differently. It was the fact that Vera wasn't going to pussyfoot around the issue, the fact that she called a spade a spade, that made VIN such a fine place for Jimmy to be. She wasn't saying it to be mean, she was saying it because it was true, and it was that kind of sincerity that made Jimmy's retardation a non-issue. It was out in the open, and not just with Vera. Jimmy started himself this little business, while I was there, harvesting some trees off the back forty of VIN, chopping them into parts small enough so he could drag them out of the woods and into Vera's back yard, where he'd further cut them and split them into firewood. Then he dragged this firewood around on a sled he'd made of two-by-fours, and sold it to the residents of the Independent Nation. And here's the part I'm trying to get at with all this: when Jimmy made his first rounds with that sled full of firewood, and when people decided to buy some from him, they'd ask him if he needed help counting out his product. They'd say something like "I'll take ten. Can you count to ten?" Don't ask me why he sold it by the stick versus by the cord or half-cord or whatever, he just did. But my point here is that, outside of VIN, nobody would have had the balls to ask Jimmy if he could count, because asking if he could count would be more or less telling him that he was retarded, and, back in those days, that kind of thing was a big no-no. It was considered rude at best, to openly recognize differences between people. Racial differences, religious differences, differences in physical or mental ability. That's how it was in the United States. There was this rolling blackout on inequality, this group delusion that, while people were different, they were all equal, which has never ever been the case. All people are not created equal. Some are born rich, some are born poor. Tall, short, genius, retarded, and on and on. And there was this mindset that, if you started openly acknowledging differences between people, if you did that, you weren't far from acknowledging the inequalities between them. People wouldn't dare ask a retard if he could count because that would allow for the possibility that the retard couldn't count, and if you went that far, well, you might as well be lording it over the retard that he or she was stupid. Absolutely ridiculous, but that's how people thought. Their so-called sensitivity made them insensitive.

Not so in VIN. In VIN, it was okay to ask if Jimmy could count. Jimmy told them yeah, he could count, and that was that. No offense intended and none taken. End of story. And, while word got around that Jimmy had a little money, nobody came around to welch off him. "You got to understand," Vera told me one time, as she snuggled up to Jimmy on the threadbare plaid-and-paisley couch that dominated the living-room of her trailer, "They ain't going to go begging money off anybody because it was that kind of dumb-ass move that got them kicked out of the rest of the world to begin with. Most of the folks in here, they're just glad to be away from debt in general. Course, most of them don't count my lot-rent as debt, but that's a whole different ball of wax for them, I guess. They catch up when they can. It'd be different, if I owed any money on this great nation of mine, but it's all paid for, except for that ransom we pay the county every year. Now that, I could do without, but everybody pitches in on that, because they don't want to lose what we got here."

So, that's VIN. Basic, honest. It had its share of problems, like any little community will. Too much drink, some reckless behaviors, a fist-fight or a car crash once in a while, but nothing to write home about.

The other thing that kind of defines what VIN was, for me, anyway, is how they let me bury the place. I buried every single one of those trailers under twelve feet of rock and dirt, and everybody, or almost everybody, was completely okay with it.

Shortly after arriving up there in Houlton, I ran some cable out to the nearest fiber-optic junction-box, so I could hook into the web. Aside from the mile and a half of cable, which wasn't exactly cheap stuff to buy at the time, this gave me free access to what was then called the internet. Jimmy and I ran this cable through the woods to a box where we cleared away the snow and made the physical connection. It was a pretty shoddy job, not exactly covert work, because my cable was there for anyone to see, but most everybody at that point got their internet through satellite or wireless connections. The old fiber-optic network was still there, but it was the realm of fly-by-night third-rate service providers, the kind that sometimes worked and sometimes didn't, the kind that were up and down day in and day out. Nobody was going to notice me tapping into this realm anytime soon. It wasn't the fastest or hippest connection I could have gotten, but I figured it would be the most low-profile, and, once the shit hit the fan, it would be the most stable. The physical networks would be the last things to go, once the nukes flew.

And the nukes were indeed going to fly. Maggie and I had known this when we'd seen what was going down in Japan, but even I had a hard time believing it could really happen. Who the hell wants to believe something like that? Who wants to believe that the end of the world is on its way?

So I hooked in and dug around. I hooked in and hacked like only I could hack. Call me prideful, but I was damned good. I was one of the best. Forget about your firewalls and your black ice and all that shit that was supposed to keep hackers out. None of that shit slows down a real code-monkey any more than a light breeze slows down inter-continental ballistic missile. When code is your element, it's all navigable in equal measure. You see some bad code that's supposed to stop you, you just go around it. It's that simple, when you're very good.

So I dug around. I broke into private networks, and found what I needed. Not what I wanted, mind you, but what I needed. Maggie and that weird-ass weight-lifting macho accountant she'd had flown into Saint Augustine, they'd taught me a thing or two about finance, and how money really moves. I was no accountant, but I could tell that Harold's money was on the move, and not just to Japan. Over the last couple of months, Harold had gradually and very quietly divested himself of almost every piece of stock, every bond and corporate holding he owned. His holding companies sold the investments and moved them into other holding companies, and a whole lot of rather small disbursements had been made, and were still being made, all around the U.S. and the world. A couple hundred dollars here, a couple thousand dollars there, every single one of these disbursements a donation to a localized cell of the little Hitler's crazy cult. Three hundred ninety-six dollars and eleven cents to the One True Religion temple in Boise, Idaho. Two thousand twenty-eight dollars and eighty-nine cents to the One True Religion temple in Tampa, Florida. Nine hundred dollars and zero cents to the One True Religion temple in London, Ontario. Eleven hundred sixty-three dollars and twelve cents to the One True Religion temple in Vallejo, California. And on and on, literally billions of dollars being thrown to the wind. A lot of these relatively small checks went to the One True Religion temple in Portland, Maine, which really came as no surprise. That little shit wasn't about to scatter his money to the four winds without taking very good care of himself in the process.

What I needed to know next was just what his mindless zombie followers were doing with all that money. No way was that little fuckhead just cutting all of these temples loose to preach his ideas however they wanted. No, some kind of plan had been set into motion, and I wanted to know what it was. And this was where I ran into a dead end. Every single one of these 'temples', the ornate free-standing structures like the ones Harold had ordered built in Tokyo and in Portland; the rented warehouse space preferred in most large cities (because it was a lot cheaper than real church or office-space); or make-shift worship-spaces carved out of people's homes; every single one of the 'temples' was wired into the net. And so I went in. I went in and I dug around on their hard-drives. I monitored their internet shopping and their emails. I invaded every bit of virtual space where the little dictator's people worked and lived, but I found nothing. Nothing that gave me the slightest clue just what they might be doing with all these little checks they were receiving from the holding companies.

So, after hacking around for the better part of two months, it became clear to me that I needed to go to the nearest of Harold's temples and snoop around. Believe me, I didn't want to get anywhere near any of Harold's asshole people ever again. The rejuvenation I'd received had done wonders for me, but it wasn't enough to make me forget a month and a half of being strapped down on a table, being tortured almost to death. I had no doubt that Harold had put the word out on Jimmy and me, that he wanted me back and Jimmy along with me, and that he wanted us dead. Just like he'd wanted Maggie dead. I thought at the time that he'd had her killed. Probably would have been better in the short term for Mikey if he had killed her. I know this is stupid talk, because then David wouldn't be around, and he's one damned fine kid, but the hell Harold brought on Mikey by holding Maggie hostage, it was fucking nuts.

But I digress. Somebody's really going to have to go through this manuscript and weed some of this stuff out before it can be released to the people of Megadon and Syrinx as any kind of history. Like I said before, I'm no writer, so forgive my drifting.

Jimmy and I drove down to Old Town, which is about two hours south, maybe an hour and a half, depending how you drive, and we drove nice and easy, because we didn't want to attract any attention. You never knew, back in those days, who was going to turn out to be one of Harold's minions, an adherent of his dumb-ass religion, and even if you knew somebody was an adherent, you didn't know whether or not they were one of the rabid fanatics, the ones who acted as his spies, his cell-leaders, his real henchmen. I'm sure that a lot of people who went in for the little Hitler's bullshit were perfectly nice folks, just stupid and gullible. Or maybe just overly hopeful. People want something to believe in, and most of those many hundreds of millions who bought into the One True Religion didn't know Harold from a hole in the wall. They may have seen him preach in some auditorium or coliseum or civic center, but that's all. To give the little asswipe his due (and believe me, it kills me to admit he was good at anything besides senseless bloodshed), Harold did a pretty good job combining the essentials of the older religions, the ideas of sacrifice and a god and a heaven and a hell, with abstracts of the technological forces that seemed so pervasive and controlling to the common man before the nukes came down and tore the shit out of everything. But okay, that having been said, let me reiterate what an asshole Harold was, and that, driving down to Old Town with Jimmy, I was hoping to find something that would let me ruin his fucked up plans to fuck up the world.

I knew there would be at least one nuclear strike, just because the potential was there, and just because Harold was such a cold crazy bastard that he wouldn't hesitate to make it happen. But how do you take that kind of notion to the world? You can't just run into the offices of the *Portland Press Herald* or the *New York Times* and say you've been hacking around and been to Japan and there are nukes and Harold's out to fuck shit up. Even if I'd bothered to document all the movements of money I'd found online, there wouldn't have been anyone with the patience or any real reason, any drive, to sort through all the connections as Maggie and her accountant and I had. You've got to understand that people, back before the nukes, people were used to having everything handed to them in neat and simple packages. You've got to understand that your average American citizen (The United States was one of the wealthiest nations in the world.) couldn't be bothered to read, neither for the purposes of accruing information nor for recreation. People were used to having information presented to them in sound-bites and video-flashes with transitions every two or three seconds. There was a notion, among the creators of entertainment and informational media, that if something couldn't be stated in thirty seconds or less, it wasn't worth stating at all. This was a function of the capitalist economy, wherein market-share meant everything, and so many businesses were vying for the hearts and minds of consumers, advertisements on advertisements, the whole thing basically reduced to a Technicolor shouting match, a mad race to shove the marketing message (BUY THIS, NOT THAT!) down the throats of the people. This type of communication became so prevalent that when people were presented with more slowly-paced, more comprehensive forms of communication, it was usually way over their heads. It wasn't snappy or sexy or thrilling enough to hold their attention. Facts and details were not sexy. Making your own decisions by gathering, interpreting and judging information was not exciting. Being told by a bikini-clad woman in a convertible hot-rod that Coke was better than Pepsi, case closed, that was both sexy and exciting. This kind of open-and-shut reasoning, or complete lack of reasoning, this constant media bombardment of '*x* is better than *y*' also encouraged black-and-white thinking. There was no gray. Something was either right or wrong, good or bad, as people unconsciously sought to make their realities conform to those they had been force-fed by television and radio and the commercialized internet. So I needed to find something simple, some kind of so-called *smoking gun* that would show the world what a nasty rat Harold really was.

Vera came with us to Old Town, because we took her car, and because I'd shown her all my proof of Harold's weird movements and she believed, as strongly as I did, that the little Hitler was up to no good. And she wanted to help Jimmy any way she could. While Jimmy's old yellow car would no doubt be spotted if Harold had alerted his cell-leaders, Vera's slightly newer Toyota-Saturn, small, gray, as common as snow flakes in the frozen forest, would blend right in with the rest of the dead winter scenery.

We rode through Old Town once, and that once was enough to get the feel of the place. Not a whole lot there. Route Two went right through the more-or-less abandoned downtown. Town hall, funeral home, a gas station, a corner store, and the Old Town Canoe Company, and that was about it. Snow-banks on both sides of the street colored brown and black with sand spread on the pavement and the exhaust of internal combustion engines. Only in the States, folks, did so many cars still run on highly expensive, highly polluting dinosaur juice. Big oil was breathing its last, but it had the U.S. in a death-grip, and was ready to take the whole country down with it when it fell.

Anyway, the place we needed to check out was a big house on the hill just south of town proper, off Stillwater Avenue, almost over in Orono, which was the next town down and the home of Maine's biggest state-run university. It was a big white wood-framed house we were after. Lots of houses like that in Old Town, but this one served as headquarters for the local cell of Harold's One True Religion. And it had a big-ass barn toward the back of the property. It was this big-ass barn that caught my eye as we did our drive-by recon. A group of religious fanatics could store a whole lot of stuff in a barn like that.

I had Jimmy and Vera drop me off down in Orono, where I heisted a little green station wagon from the University of Maine steam plant parking lot. Vera dropped Jimmy off at the Shop-N-Save parking lot between Orono and Old Town, and I picked him up on my way back to the Harold-house. It was about nine-thirty at night, plenty dark, or as dark as it was going to get with all the snow on the ground reflecting the ambient light from the street and the stars. According to the records I hacked into, this Old Town cell had received something on the order of six thousand dollars in small "donations" from Harold's holding companies over the last three or four months. Every single one of those checks had been cashed at the Old Town branch of Key Bank, but not a single dollar had been deposited into the One True Religion account at that same bank. So that money was going someplace. It was either being hoarded or spent, and if it was being spent, there was probably something to show for it. Or at least I hoped there was. Because this cashing of small checks from the holding companies, it wasn't just happening in Old Town, it was going on all over the place. Every single One True Religion cell was pulling the same kind of stunt. I just needed to find out what that stunt really was.

We couldn't have picked a better night for a break-in. Like I said, it was as dark as could be, considering all the snow on the ground. And there was nobody home. The house was listed on the tax rolls as belonging to a Jay Arthur, and it had been my initial assumption that this Jay Arthur guy actually lived in the place. That's why, when we got there, I went up and rang the doorbell. I could hear it ringing inside the house, but nobody came to the door. I rang again and again, but still nobody. So I checked the mailbox. Always check the mailbox when you're about to break into a place. If it's stuffed full of a week's worth of mail, it means the residents are probably on vacation. The mailbox at this place was empty.

"Our tire-marks are the only ones in the driveway," Jimmy told me, and this made me wonder. It hadn't snowed in Old Town for days. No tire-tracks in the driveway meant that no one had been here in days. And yet the mailbox was empty. Not the least little bit of junk-mail. Odd.

I went around back while Jimmy kept watch out front. I forced the lock and let myself in the kitchen. Dead dark. Dead quiet. I closed the door, took a step forward, and tripped over something fairly large and heavy. I fell down onto a whole lot of things that were fairly large and heavy and cold. Large and heavy and cold, with just a little give. I pulled out my little flashlight, expecting maybe to find bodies, but no. What I found were sand-bags. All kinds of frigging sand-bags. Dark green nylon sacks stuffed with dirt and sand and tied shut. Covering the floor two layers thick. Talk about a trippy scene.

It was only as I got up off this floor of sand-bags that I realized how cold it was, inside the house. Too fucking cold for anybody to be living there. I checked the kitchen cabinets, and they were empty. Likewise the fridge (I had to push sand-bags out of the way to open the door) and the freezer. It was pretty clear that nobody was living in this place. And all the sand-bags. I just kept saying "What the fuck?" until I made it down into the basement, and then it became clear to me just what was going on.

The place was a nuclear fallout shelter. Sandbags on top of a brick-and-concrete basement heavily stocked with food-staples. A couple thousand pounds of rice. A couple thousand pounds of dried beans. Then there was a sub-basement, cut in the concrete floor of the basement. Four concrete-lined rooms down there, one simply filled with health and medical supplies, enough vitamins and antibiotics to meet the basic needs of hundreds for years on end. Another room in this sub-basement held weapons and ammunition, and communications gear like radios and batteries and solar-panels. The other two rooms, about ten by fifteen each, were fitted for primitive living. A hand-pumped well beneath the frost-line, where the water would not freeze; a deep pit for wastes; a drum of lime; bunks crammed in three and four high, forty beds in all. And for entertainment, ten copies of Harold's bullshit *Scripture*.

It was pretty clear, what I had to do. There was no calling the news and telling them I'd broken into a house and found a secret fallout shelter. Nor was there any calling the cops. There was nothing illegal about having a fallout shelter in one's home. Unusual for sure, but not illegal. I'd only get myself arrested if I bothered to call anybody.

So I checked out that big-ass barn. More supplies in there. More basic food-stuff, most of this in cans. But there was also a lawn-mower, and that's what I was really looking for. Because, not far from the lawn mower, I knew I would find a can of gas. For once I could honestly say god bless America and the internal combustion engine.

I had Jimmy drive down the street in the green station wagon, and then I used the gas from the gas can to set the house on fire. Things tend to dry out in the winter months, as all the moisture freezes from the air, and that old wood-framed house went up quick. I booked it out across the back yard and down the street to where Jimmy was waiting and we got the hell out of there as the sky lit up all orange and yellow behind us.

We rode south, taking Route Two down along the Penobscot River. There's a decent curve at one point on that road, where it comes closest to the river, and that's where we got out and pushed that little green wagon off the side and watched it roll downhill and bounce over the railroad tracks and onto the slushy ice and into the drink. We hid in the bushes, on the uphill side of the road, until Vera came and picked us up some five minutes later. Then we rode back to Houlton. It was a long, quiet ride during which Vera and I kept checking the rear-views, looking back for blue lights in hot pursuit. Vera and I were nervous, sure we'd fucked up, forgotten some little thing that would cause us to be caught, but Jimmy was all smiles. "That house sure did burn good! It just burnt right up, didn't it? Didn't it?" He made up a stupid little song about a house burning down,

There's a house on fire,
I saw it start to burn!
I know who set the fire,
But you will never learn!

He sang this song over and over until I was about ready to throttle him. I'd tell him to stop, and he'd stop for a while, until he forgot and started singing it again, or humming it, sing-song, over and over. By the time we got back to VIN, I was very glad to be out of that car. So I could stop hearing that song. And because we'd made it. We knew what Harold was up to, and we'd exposed him. The fire trucks would come, and put the fire out, and then there'd be a small-town investigation that would turn up the nuclear fallout shelter. It would make the local news, and with any luck, the national news. People would wonder why little Hitler's One True Religion should bother with a fallout shelter. Then it would come to light that there were more fallout shelters, and then people would start to see the connection between these shelters and Harold's role in the so-called peace missions to Japan. And then he'd be busted. Good guys win, game over for that little shitheel and all his fanatic creep followers.

We made it back to VIN just before eleven, and turned on the tube, looking for a top story about a big house fire in Old Town. We flipped from station to station to station, and saw plenty of weather and sports and cutsie local stories about girl-scouts selling cookies, but not a damned thing about any fire.

"Well, it'll be just a house-fire, until the investigation, and they won't dig through the place until it cools down," said Vera.

"Yeah, until it cools down," said Jimmy.

But I had a bad feeling about it. I knew better. "A house-fire's big news in that neck of the woods," I told them. "I guess we won't be sure for a little while yet, but I think somebody shut us down."

"You mean they put out the fire?" Jimmy asked.

"I mean there's a Harold-fanatic someplace high up in the Old Town Fire Department, or red-robes in the Bangor network television affiliates. The fire should have made the news. That place was really blazing, and it was a big house. It should have made the news."

And sure enough, there was nothing about that house on the news the next day, or the next, or the next. Never. Not word one. Made me feel pretty stupid, to have thought that such a simple trick would actually work. Set fire to the place, and expect the authorities to uncover that little fuckhead's wicked plot? It was a stupid idea, something from the movies, where everything is easy and the bad guys have to lose in the end. For weeks I wanted to kick myself, and what was worse, and made me feel even more stupid, was the fact that I couldn't think of any better plan. I wracked my brain until there wasn't a brain-cell left to wrack, and I couldn't think of any damned way to expose that little prick, or any way to stop him short of going and putting a bullet in his evil little head. And I considered that, considered it long and seriously, but there was no guarantee that killing Harold, this late in the game, would do a damned thing to derail his plans for nuclear apocalypse. We, the good guys, had simply come into this mess way too late. Harold had been working and working on this plan for years on years. Whatever he wanted to happen was going to happen. I wished Mikey was around, or even better, I wished Maggie was around. She might have thought of something. She was used to dealing with high-level intrigues, volatile political situations and shit like that. Me, I was just a computer geek and small-time drug-runner, hiding out in a trailer-park in the far reaches of northern Maine. What the hell was I going to do in the face of such all-pervasive machinations?

My new youth worked against me, during the weeks after our little raid on that house in Old Town, in the weeks after that failure. I was so angry with myself and angry with the world that I couldn't think straight. I smoked too much weed. I drank too much. I wallowed in my frustration. This is what youth does. Not to say I wouldn't have been pretty damned pissed off if I hadn't had that rejuvenation, but I was definitely throwing off more heat than light, if you know what I mean, and it wasn't helping, not one bit.

It was early spring by the time I got my head out of my ass. On April Fool's Day I finally made a decision about what had to be done. There was no stopping Harold's plan. He would blow up the world if he wanted to blow up the world. But damned if I was going to let him and his fanatics be the only ones who survived the fucking nukes. April first, I had dinner with Jimmy and Vera, the three of use sitting around the round glass table in her kitchen, chowing down on deep-fried rabbit-quarters and fiddleheads with vinegar, and I told them what we had to do. "We need to bury the trailer-park," I told them. "We need to buy or rent a couple bulldozers and a dump-truck, and bury this place. I don't think we're in any real danger of a direct hit, but the way the weather-patterns run, we'll be in for all kinds of radiation. We need to bury this place, make it a little underground city, and lay in supplies for a long wait."

Jimmy smiled. "Can I drive a bulldozer? Can I drive a bulldozer?"

Vera just looked down at the rabbit on her plate, flicking the breading off the meat with her fork. She was wearing one of her white tank-tops, with her missile-tits poking at the tight cotton, and the cords in her skinny neck and wiry shoulders were tensed up. The way she was staring down at that plate, with her frizzy hair and her big glasses in the way, I couldn't tell, but I thought she might be crying. I supposed that was natural enough. She called the place Vera's Independent Nation, for god sake, and I could see why she might not want it buried. It could have been that, after finally establishing some place like this, a place that was her own, where she had final say on things, and her only worry was hunting up enough game for food, it could have been that the outside world was at long last intruding on this dream of hers, and that this inevitable misfortune came as a crushing defeat.

"Vera? Vera, are you okay?" Jimmy asked her, putting an arm around her shoulders.

She gave a quick nod, and brought her face up as her body began to quiver. She was laughing. "You want to bury my independent nation?" she asked me.

I nodded. "I figure ten or twelve feet of dirt and rock should do the trick. We can shore up the trailers, and use big concrete drainage pipes as tunnels from one trailer to the next. We'll have to figure out some kind of ventilation system, but that shouldn't be too hard. We're on well-water and septic tanks, so water and waste is pretty much taken care of. It'll be cool in the summer, warm in the winter."

She leaned back in her chair laughing so hard I thought she might shake apart. "You are crazy! I finally get myself a man worth keeping," she said, thumping Jimmy on the back, "and he comes with a loon for a brother!" Vera scooped up her coffee-mug of whiskey and took a swig. Slamming the mug back down on the red-checkered table-cloth, she shouted, "Oh, what the hell! Let's bury the hell out of the place! If the atom bombs come down, we'll be an independent nation for sure! And if they don't, then hell, how many trailer-parks are all underground? We'll be frigging Morlocks! It's not like anybody outside this place doesn't think we're completely nuts already! Let's do it!'

And so we did.

07-10-2112

David drove and was driven before the massive frontier air-car more than twice as wide and four times as long as the screaming red Barchetta that carried him in a streak of twisting speed across the valley. He emerged from beneath the canopy of leaves, engine screaming fierce joy and frightening power. His massive pursuer lumbered after him at tree-top level, trying to sew shut the widening gap between them with a constant stitching of machine-gun fire. David zigged and zagged, holding the accelerator to the floor, the car hunkering down and flattening around and beneath him. The gunner in the ship behind him was a very poor shot, but he had plenty of bullets and odds were in his favor that his near-constant spray would eventually strike some vital part of the car, if not David himself. There was no slowing, there was only random movement and more and more speed, and David kept on.

The sky was lightening in the east when he finally pulled out of range of the guns. Eight hundred meters between the Barchetta and the frontier air-car. If he could keep up this speed, he might get away. David looked back and felt himself smiling. Keep up the speed, and everything would be fine. Keep up the speed, through the turns and the straightaways, and he'd make it back to Uncle Robert's farm and everything would be fine. He'd been so stupid to come out here alone, to have come so far by himself, but it was going to be alright, now.

David brought his eyes back to the road and the cracked old pavement exploded before the car, flew up in chunks as heavy-caliber bullets chewed the roadway to bits. Impossible! He was out of range! He was out of range!

A huge dark shape shrouded in the tearing sounds of turbofans and the chatter of guns bore in from David's left, down the mountainside. Another air-car. This one cut in so close David ducked down and pulled the wheel hard right to avoid colliding with it. The tires shrieked and two wheels fell off the roadway, bleeding off precious speed.

He let off, downshifted, floored it. A fan of dirt sprayed up behind him. He chanced a quick glance back and saw the second air-car trying to slow and turn to give chase, while the first one closed in again. He was back in range of that first car's guns, even as he regained speed. He felt and heard the bullets in the air all around him, a deadly storm that suddenly doubled as the second air-car joined the pursuit.

The eastern sky was glowing pink when the bridge came into sight. David jigged left and right on the roadway, making himself a more difficult target for the fire that rained down from above and behind. He wanted nothing more than to drive straight for the bridge, but they would nail him for sure if he held a straight course. Worse yet, they might open up on the narrow wooden bridge, tear it apart and cut him off from salvation. He drove. He drove and drove fast and wild, weaving with the wind that tore at his hair and the sounds of mechanical music that sent him along. Bit by bit he pulled away and away from the ungainly air-cars, away from their guns and their bulk. He made the bridge and shot onto it without slowing, seeing his own knuckles go white as he aimed for the skinny slot and blazed over the chasm without looking down.

He braked and turned on the far side of the ravine. He slowed, and watched the massive frontier air-cars halt on the far side of the bridge. They nosed left and right, like big stupid brutish beasts, looking for some way across the great divide. The gunners took pot-shots at David and his growling red car, but he was far far out of range.

David brought the Barchetta to a full stop, and stared back at his pursuers. He stopped, but his heart still raced in his chest. His arms and legs were all a-quiver with hot nerves and adrenaline. He knew better than to sit there, knew better than to wait there while the crews of those air-cars called for more help, but the deadly race and the near-sleepless night had exhausted his exuberance, and he wanted just to sit, and know that he had, for the moment, escaped his own foolishness and the malevolence that had come for his very life. Those frontier air-cars were the same evil that had killed his father, and David wanted to enjoy his little victory, take a moment of rest and enjoy his escape.

The sun crept up on the horizon as the air-cars searched the far side of the cut for some way across. They were built to hover, and could do so at significant heights, but they required a surface above which to hover. They could not truly fly. A highly skilled pilot might have coaxed one of those craft across the one-lane bridge, but only at great risk of slipping one way or the other and tumbling off into the void below. And David doubted either pilot on the far side of that gap possessed anything close to that kind of skill. Frontier-duty was given as punishment to the worst and most careless of Vigilance personnel, and David was glad for that; better marksmen would have sawed his car in half with their guns. Better pilots wouldn't have followed him through every curve in the road; they would have taken the tangents and driven him off the road and into a tree.

The sun rose, and the scene on the far side of the chasm was bathed in orange light and long shadows. It was in this odd and somewhat soothing light, with the adrenaline-rush dying down in his veins, that David saw a long thin plume of white smoke lancing out from behind him, from his side of the ravine to the opposite edge, where the frontier air-cars searched for some safe way across. Sharp hissing rushed by with the rapidly lengthening plume as it stretched out and stretched out toward one of the big ships on the far side of the gap. The fluffy soft line of swift smoke reached the air-car, and the air-car exploded. A quick spat of fire flared on its left rear quarter, then a larger burst of black smoke that hung over the ship as it nosed down into the earth and began to burn. The long plume began to break up and fade as new smoke, heavy black and dark gray, boiled up out of the ruined frontier air-car.

David sat there, staring intently, his eyes locked on the scene of sudden, unexpected destruction. He felt no rush of joy at seeing the air-car go down. It fell and it burned and not a single man came out of it. They were dead, blown up or burnt up. They'd tried to kill him, but he took no joy from their deaths. He felt nothing, really, and realized how extremely tired he was, how close to exhaustion after the white-knuckle flight over the mountains and through the forest. He had pushed himself and his machine to the limit, and now fatigue had set in, dulling all else.

He pulled his eyes from the burning wreck across the chasm, and turned around in his seat. His mother was standing there, between the trees some fifteen or twenty meters back. She had a short tube slung over one shoulder. Wisps of white smoke curled up out of the business-end of the rocket-launcher. She smiled at David. "Good morning, kiddo," she said. "Have a nice night?"

David absently shook his head. It was one thing to see his once-holy mother exposing her body in sinful fashion, and to hear profanities from her once-clean mouth, but it quite another thing altogether to see her shooting down frontier air-cars with a shoulder-mounted rocket-launcher. There were benefits, he decided, to having this new Mom, this one who called herself "Maggie" instead of "Magenta". It would take some getting used to, but in this new world where Dad was dead and Vigilance men in deadly machines seemed so intent on taking his life, David guessed he would rather have Maggie as his Mom. She would do something that Magenta had never really been able to do with more than harsh words. This new Mom could and would protect him. And that would be just fine.

Maggie carried the tube with her to the car. "Hey," she said, standing next to David and turning around so her backpack was facing him, "get another rocket from my pack. Reload me and we'll take out that second one before it gets away."

David did as he was told, opening her pack, which contained four little rockets each half a meter in length and no wider than his fist. "Just stuff it in the back of the tube," she told him, and he did. Mom then took a step away from the Barchetta, turned and extended a little telescopic site from the side of the launcher. She peered through the site as she drew a bead on the remaining frontier air-car, which had, by now, turned tail and begun to retreat. David saw her finger begin to tense on the trigger but then she said "Shit," and suddenly let off, and lowered the weapon.

"There goes your cousin," she said.

David looked across the chasm, but didn't see any sign of Rosella, until he scanned the sky. Then he saw a speeding white something plummeting from above. Plummeting toward the fleeing frontier air-car. Rosella in her armor, making a missile of herself. She dove down, into the lumbering air-car, penetrating it and bursting straight out the other side. The air-car staggered, slowed, then stopped, then sank heavily to the ground. David saw two men stumble out of the wreck with rifles or scatterguns; it was impossible to tell which at such a distance. They fired on Rosella, and their shots sounded like small crackling from where David sat. He watched his cousin raise one arm and heard more crackling as the men were cut down by one of the many weapons built into the suit.

"She killed them," David said, as he watched Rosella land and make her way into the second downed air-car.

"Yup," said Mom. "She's a good girl. We'll let her mop up over there, recon for more inbound bogies and meet us back in Xanadu after she's taken out their first wave. We've got a lot of work to do, and it's got to be done quick, so let's go." Mom put her rocket-launcher in the passenger-seat and opened the Barchetta's driver-side door. "Move over, rover. Let me drive my car."

David moved over to the passenger seat, holding the loaded rocket-launcher between his legs. "You might want to aim that out of the car," Mom told him, and he did.

Mom drove more quickly and more dangerously than David had when he'd been driving for his life. She smiled as she took the sharp turns, and sometimes she laughed out loud when the rear tires slipped right or left and she had to counter-steer to bring them back around.

How It All Happened, Chapter 5

We buried Vera's independent nation. Not much to say about that except that we didn't shore up one trailer well enough and it flattened out under the weight of all the dirt and rock we poured and pushed on and around it. Nobody was in it at the time, so that was more-or-less okay. The tenants of the trailer-park, while they'd initially agreed to the idea had decided they didn't like the notion of being buried alive, so they'd said their goodbyes and took off. One of them, this kind of chubby old man named Vincent, who used to be some kind of funeral director, actually paid Vera a couple thousand bucks in back rent before he left. We took that money and put it toward the stocking of supplies.

And god, didn't we lay in some supplies. Cases on cases of canned fruit and meat and vegetables. Thousands of pounds of dry staples like rice and beans. Basic medical necessities, vitamins, antibiotics, antiseptics, you name it. Rifles and ammunition. Clothing for all kinds of conditions, from parkas and heavy boots to shorts and sneakers. Tools, mechanic-type tools for fixing cars and trucks to heavy working tools like axes and sledgehammers and shovels. A couple generators. A few hundred gallons of gasoline and a couple hundred gallons of diesel, in big tanks we buried out on the back forty, away from the trailers. Batteries, little batteries for radios and flashlights and big batteries for cars. Generators, the kind you could crank by hand or pedal-power, and the kind that took fossil-fuel. We stocked and stocked our underground complex. Books and candles by the thousands. Iodine for purifying water. Charcoal filters for the primitive air-exchanging system me and Jimmy rigged up. Knives. Laptops. Dog food. Anything. Everything. You name it, we had it, and plenty of it. The world was going to end, and we wanted to be ready. We built an enclosure over the well, buried it, and equipped it with a hand-pump. We had the septic-tanks emptied, to be sure we had the capacity to wait out the worst of the radiation. We were ready, all ready in Vera's Independent Underground Nation, which we took to calling "VIUN", pronouncing it like "Zion" because here was the land of our salvation. Here was where we would win when everyone else lost, when Armageddon came raging down from the skies. We were ready.

I guess there's something nerve-wracking about being ready for something big before it happens. You work your tail off getting ready and you want the event for which you've been preparing to take place the instant you complete your preparations. But it doesn't work that way. If you're ready for something beforehand, you're often stuck ready and waiting for a while before whatever it is actually happens. You may know the feeling I'm talking about if you've ever prepared for a party and then had to sit around twiddling your thumbs waiting for your guests to arrive. You wonder if anybody's going to ever show up, after you've put yourself through such trouble to put out the snacks and the drinks; after you've hidden all the valuables and picked out just the right music. You sit there, alone, waiting for the people to come to your party, and, until six or eight folks actually show up, you're pretty sure you've gone to all that effort for nothing. Well, preparing for and waiting for a nuclear war is kind of the same thing. You get past the point where you wish the nukes would never come, and you get to this new point where you're resigned to the fact that it's going to happen, and you just want it over. That's how I felt, anyway, when I wasn't just fuming mad at that little prick Harold for setting up the whole nasty situation. When I wasn't dwelling on all the various ways I wanted to kill him. Nope, after we got everything all set up, it was a lot of waiting. Waiting, and hacking, monitoring the emails that slipped back and forth between Harold's HQ in Portland and the various locations of his One True Religion.

Now monitoring people's email may sound like exciting stuff until you've actually done it. Most people, even most people in a fanatic religious organization, send pretty dull emails. Matter-of-fact reports of local happenings, the weather, turn-out at various worship services, drab details on new members, their names, ages, skills and income. And there were plenty of new members every day in every cell. A lot of everyday people, file-clerks, receptionists. Some skilled and semi-skilled workers, plumbers, electricians, carpenters. Some so-called professionals, lawyers, doctors, business managers. All their little electronic dossiers flowed out of the local cells and found their way to Harold's central temple in Portland. Hacking into the databases there, I found all the descriptions of all of the members, all organized, not according to income, but according to gender and skill. Harold was organizing his people, filing them away for use after the apocalypse. Those who could build or repair things, the plumbers and welders and carpenters and electricians, along with the programmers, database administrators, and engineering-types, were designated as "B-T". Those who had no real practical skills, the wage-slaves, the retail help, the unskilled and relatively uneducated, were designated as "R-P". The so-called professionals, the dentists and judges and academics and big-thinkers, were designated as "T-I" or "C-T". Now, I didn't know at the time what these designations meant, but just so you know, here's what they turned out to be:

B-T = Builder, Temporary. These people would help build Harold's sacred cities, but would be killed as soon as they'd played their little part in those constructions.

R-P = Resident, Permanent. These people would stay on in Megadon or Syrinx; their social class to be determined by their level of dedication to "Almighty Harold".

T-I = Terminate, Immediately. These people would be killed right away. These were the well-educated people, most with advanced degrees. Not to say earning an advanced degree was the only way to learn how to think logically, or that every person with an advanced degree was capable of deep or logical thought, but these folks were, in general, the thinkers. And religious fanatics don't have much use for thinkers, because real thinkers tend to ask too many questions. Real thinkers are more likely to challenge commonly held truths, and therefore posed a danger to Harold's new world order.

C-T = Contributor, Temporary. This designation seemed to cover those thinkers whose conceptual knowledge or problem-solving ability made them useful in the construction of the sacred cities or the establishment of the social orders therein. Physicists, chemists, sociologists all fit into this category.

Anyway, I watched the flow of information, and it was all pretty hum-drum. The holding companies kept releasing their little checks. The cells kept reporting to Harold's HQ. I watched this for weeks on weeks on weeks, until April 20. April 20, 2049, Harold himself sent one very brief email to every single one of his cells. This email read: "Prepare to receive my blessing, and the blessing of the Great CPU."

And then all the traffic stopped. No more emails from the cells. Servers in Harold's network went down one by one. Everything just stopped. Dead cold stopped.

Jimmy and Vera and me stayed more-or-less inside from that point forward. I didn't think Houlton would receive any direct hits. I was a lot more worried about fallout that anything else, but I didn't want to take any chances. You get caught outside anywhere within ten or twenty miles of a good sized nuclear explosion, and you're dead. Jimmy and Vera and me, we stayed put. We stayed inside, under the dirt and rock, and we watched the world via TV and radio and the web. We were tuned in when the emergency broadcasts came on, when pan-icked news-anchors told the world it was not a hoax and not a drill.

What I remember most about that last forty-five minutes of good old TV and radio was the fact that here we were, with the world about to end, and who comes on the air but a bunch of pundits. So-called experts called in to share their so-called expert opinions on who might be responsible and what might happen and how it will impact the economy, and/or the careers of various politicians, actors and famous people.

"Now a lot of my colleagues, and a lot of *liberals* want to bury their heads in the sand and give up, but I think this war may give the U.S. economy and American society in general a real shot in the arm. It may be just what we need to up GDP and make a real return to good old fashioned American values." Nukes on the way, and one professor from some private university in South Carolina came on and said these very words. I shit you not.

Then there were the man-in-the-street interviews.

Reporter One: "How do you feel about nuclear weapons?"

Man-In-Street One: "They're a necessary evil, I guess. People don't like them, I don't like them, but the world's kind of like a playground, and if you're not tough, other kids are going to pick on you, like terrorists and stuff like that."

Reporter Two: "How do you feel about the nuclear war?"

Man-In-Street Two: "Uh, the what?"

Reporter Three: "How do you think this is going to change your life, the way you and your family live?"

Man-In-Street Three (this was actually a woman, with a baby in one arm): "Well, my husband and I just got a second mortgage, so I guess I'm glad we got in while the interest-rates were good. Who knows what this will do to the economy, right?"

Madness. Such madness. Nukes in the air and nobody seemed to understand that it was real, that they were going to die, that life would never be the same. It was typical TV, typical radio, but the most fascinating bunch of programming I've ever seen or heard in my entire life. Nuclear holocaust on the way, and we're given pundits and man-in-the-street interviews, and talk of the economy and politics. I'm not sure what else I expected. I was constantly damning society for being oblivious to reality, and yet I was shocked and outraged when the media held its idiotic course right to the end. More concerned with the fantasy of eternally sustainable economic growth than saving their lives. Worried more about ratings than the four horsemen charging through the sky.

MSNBC had some retired Army general manipulating computer-simulated models of nuclear missiles and bombers. "The American people should take heart," was saying, "that our military technology is simply decades more advanced than that of the Japanese and the Chinese, and the Russians, and all the other players in this game. It's going to be a tough game, no mistake about it, but we're going to hunker down and we're going to give it our all, and we're gonna win," he said. Nukes on the way, and he's treating the whole thing like some sort of football game. "These Japanese missiles are old, old stuff, from the commie days of Russia," he said, "and they pack a punch, but we pack a bigger punch, that's all there is to it!"

That's all there is to it. Fitting words; the transmission ended, the TV went to dancing static and loud hissing. The radio stayed on a little longer, and then it, too, was done. My internet connection slowed right down as servers went off-line, and then it, too, went dead. My laptop was fine, but I turned it off, to charge up the battery while the power remained on, which wasn't long. Twenty-one minutes, to be exact. Then we were truly cut off from that thing that used to be called America, that land that was a talking head in every television, a busy voice from every speaker, and blazing light from the grid.

We sat there in the dark for a little while, me and Jimmy and Vera, none of us saying anything. Jimmy broke the silence when he said "Sure is dark," and that started me laughing. An odd thing to do when the world as we'd known it had just come to an end outside, but I laughed. The nuclear war was, in one sense, incredibly anti-climactic. No direct hits anywhere near Houlton, so there were no great explosions to see or to hear. God only knew how the people were freaking out in town, but out here at VIUN, it was still pretty damned quiet. You wouldn't have known that billions were dying all over the globe. Nuclear war had been the biggest boogie-man, the worst nightmare of most all humanity for an entire century. It was horrible, it was unthinkable, it was tremendous and colossal. It was death and destruction on an untold scale. And yet there we were, sitting in the dark and the quiet. I felt almost let down. All the build-up, all the morbid childhood fantasies about being burnt alive or slowly melting down in the shadow of a mushroom-cloud; all the ghastly projections from anti-nuclear activists and pundits of dramatic deaths; all the green-glowing-skull images from the television specials that cropped up every ten or twelve years, when people remembered that, hey yeah, the nukes are still around, and public concern was elevated for six or nine months before the media moved on to some new and more exciting threat; all of that build-up, all of that drama, all the expectation, and here the nuclear war had come and it was so very quiet. It didn't seem right.

Then again, the TV had gone off, the radio had gone off, the power had stopped. It had happened, and it *was* horrible, albeit horrible in a distant and completely removed kind of way. And Jimmy, saying "Sure is dark," well, that about said it. Lights out for civilization. Welcome to the dark ages. Where we you when the lights went out? Dark days ahead. Jimmy said "Sure is dark," and I laughed.

"I think you're brother's finally gone off the deep end," Vera said. I heard her chair scrape across the linoleum of the kitchen floor. "Anybody besides me want some whiskey?" she asked. "Might as well celebrate the rise of our independent nation to super-power status."

"We got super-powers?" asked Jimmy.

"Just joking around, hon," she told him. "You want a snort?"

"Yeah, with ice, please," he said.

"How about you, laughing boy?" she shouted across the pitch-black kitchen.

"Oh yeah," I guffawed. "Double up!"

The clinking of glasses and ice, glasses thunking down on the table in the dark, then sliding across the wood-veneer surface. I found my glass after just a little slow and careful feeling about. Didn't want to knock it onto the floor. I found my glass and took a burning sip. "Should we have toast or something?" I asked.

"Toast! Let's do a toast!" said Jimmy.

"What do you want to toast?" said Vera.

"To surviving this thing and starting a better world, when it's finally safe to go outside," I said, raising my glass into the air above the center of the table.

Jimmy pushed his glass into my wrist. Vera pushed hers into my knuckles. "To surviving," said Jimmy.

"To surviving," said Vera.

"And a better world," I reiterated, but neither of them took me up on that one.

We drank in silence and in the dark until Vera finally found and lit a candle. Then we brought the bottle to the table and drank in silence some more.

07-11-2112

Thomas napped in the back of a captured patrol car on Level Fifteen. He'd not wanted to nap. He'd not wanted to stop, he'd wanted to get it done before more people were hurt. He'd wanted to continue his upward sweep through the levels, but the city was massive, and his people were tired. He'd established a defensive position and set up watches, so his followers might rest in shifts, so they might eat and try to catch a little sleep before they proceeded. Resistance, since they'd broken through that cadre of officers between Levels Ten and Eleven, had been sparse but deadly. A few pot-shots from officers who remained loyal to Harold. Thomas had lost two men to these short-lived sneak-attacks by fanatic members of Vigilance brass. The attackers had each paid with their lives after getting off their first shots, but their deaths made Thomas feel no better about those who had fallen. These officers still loyal to Harold were, after all, only doing what they thought was right. They were following orders in the name of everything they had been taught to consider holy. He couldn't fault them for that. He would have been doing the same thing, just weeks ago. While the majority of down-trodden citizens on these lower levels cheered him on, there were those pockets of the devout who shouted names at Thomas, called him a heretic and a sinner, a blasphemer and an agent of Legion.

But there was none of that, not now, not for the moment, and Thomas napped in the back of a patrol car. He closed his eyes, thinking to do so for just a few seconds, and he fell off into sleep, where he woke into dream.

"You've made some good progress," said dream-Jon, "but don't expect it to last. He still has the satellites, the orbital defense platforms. There's nothing to keep him from turning them on Megadon, once he's run out of alternatives."

Thomas looked around. Sand and sky. Some large reddish rocks in the distance. Sun so bright he thought he might be permanently blinded for chancing a quick glance upward. The air was hot and very dry. "What is this place?" he asked. "Is this Abend?"

Dream-Jon shook his head. "It's called a desert. This is a place that used to be called Arizona, which more-or-less means 'dry land'."

"Did people live here?" Thomas asked.

"Not many, not right around here" dream-Jon told him. "Pretty inhospitable. But there were a lot of desert-areas where people pumped in water from far-away rivers. But not here. This is way out in the desert. You could visit this area even today, after all that's gone on, and it would look pretty much the same."

"Why would I want to?" Thomas asked, pushing some sand around with the tip of his boot. It wasn't just sand, it was sand mixed with a variety of little rounded rocks, pebbles and stones.

Dream-Jon shrugged. "Big world, lots to see," he said. "But first, you'll need to disable those orbital defense platforms."

"So you can come back through Cygnus and help me defeat Harold, or so you can come back through Cygnus and take over the world?"

Dream-John sighed. "Trust me. All we want is to come back home. Harold drove us off the world where we were born, and we want to come back."

"To bring back music and freedom and happiness," Thomas said.

"You sound jaded," dream-Jon told him.

"Why shouldn't I? Everything's turned out to be a lie."

"Come on, chin up! It wasn't long ago you were going to take your guitar to Harold himself and change his way of thinking with your music."

"I didn't get the chance. But what good would it have done? For that matter, you're the one who put the music in me, so why don't you tell me?"

"I didn't put the music in you. I merely taught your mind how to move your fingers on the strings. I only taught you *how* to play. The music, that's all you, your thoughts and feelings flowing out of that guitar. Nobody else is doing that, it's all you."

Thomas crouched down, took up a handful of the hot sand, let it slip slowly between his fingers. "I don't know what to believe any more. I know I'm doing the right thing, but people are getting killed, and it's only going to get harder as we keep going up. The liar calling himself Harold, and all he's done and made, the big sinful lie that is the city, it's all got to go, but people are going to die. People on both sides, people who think they're doing the right thing. I just hope the real Jon's not already dead."

Dream-Jon remained silent. When Thomas looked up, dream-Jon looked away. "He's dead then, isn't he?" Thomas asked. "You know, don't you?"

"Thomas...You know by now you can't trust Harold...."

"So I should trust you instead?" Thomas stood up, flung the remaining sand back to the ground. "I should trust you, and turn off the defense platforms so you and your possibly demonic friends can come back to earth? Why should I trust you any more than I trust the demon calling himself the Almighty?"

Dream-Jon shrugged again. "I don't know. And I'm willing to admit it. I could tell you that you should trust me because I taught you how to play the guitar, but you could argue that Harold's establishment also gave you something of value when they made you so strong and so nearly invincible. So I don't know. I can't give you any unassailable air-tight reasons to trust me, and I'm not going to lie to you about it. But if you don't take out those platforms, more people are going to die, and that's the truth."

Thomas shook his head. "Why didn't you tell me, before, that Jon was dead?"

"Because he wasn't, before."

"But now he is? If you knew he was going to be killed, why didn't you stop it? If you're so powerful, why didn't you stop it?"

"I've told you, we can't risk the defense platforms."

"So you keep yourself safe while they're killing my friend?!" Thomas balled his hands into fists. The ground shook beneath him, the sand and little round rocks visibly vibrating all around. The sky went a deep dark red.

"Calm down, Thomas, you're doing this!" dream-Jon told him. "Please stop it!"

"Why should I? Why should I do anything for you?" Thomas stepped forward and grabbed dream-Jon by the front of his shirt. "Stop looking like my friend who you couldn't bother to save!"

"Alright!" said dream-Jon, instantly becoming Dan, a white man in a white *baseball cap.* Slick black hair stuck out from beneath the edge of the hat around the sides and the back. The gore-stained white jacket he'd worn when he'd last shown himself in this guise was now gone, but the rubber boots remained. Thomas kept hold of the man's shirt, even as it changed in his grip, and he gave Dan a hard shake.

"Don't ever, ever look like Jon again! You hear me?! Never!" Thomas shouted.

"Alright! Look, I'm going to go! Just remember, the defense platforms! You've got to disable them! When you're ready, come see me again, and I'll tell you how!"

And then Dan was gone. Thomas was left holding nothing, and his finger-nails dug into his own palm.

He woke in the back of the patrol car. There was a great clamor outside. His people were grabbing up their weapons, getting up from where they had rested on the sidewalks and streets, and running toward the ramp to Level Sixteen.

Thomas stopped one young man, no more than a boy, really, who'd joined them back on Level Six. Thomas remembered the kid throwing down his soy-stirring paddle and proudly joining the growing crowd as they'd marched for Level Seven. Now the young man held an energy-rifle in his hands and had a fierce glint in his eye. He'd seen people killed over the last handful of hours. He'd participated in the killing.

"What's going on? Where's everyone going?" Thomas asked.

"Father Brown's coming down the ramp," the kid told him. "The Cardinal's with him!"

Thomas didn't say anything. What was there to say? The kid, and all of these people, would learn soon enough that Father Brown and Cardinal Api were no mere men. The kid took Thomas' silence as permission to go, and joined the others in the rush for the ramp.

Thomas followed, and worked his way through the rough lines that had formed up at the bottom of the ramp. Sure enough, there was Father Brown, with Cardinal Api at his side, walking straight down the middle of the causeway. They came on slowly, small and bent, Brown in his black robe, Api in his red, and they dragged something between them. That something was a naked body. Each of the demons held a leg and dragged a body, face-down, behind them.

Thomas didn't need to see the body up close to know who it was. "Fire," he said, to no one in particular.

"What was that, sir?" Steffek knelt in the front line of ready fighters and looked up at Thomas for clarification.

Thomas drew his pistol and took aim at Father Brown. It was a very long shot that would no doubt miss, but that didn't matter. He needed to set the example here, get everyone shooting. "Fire!" he shouted. "Do not let them close! Fire! Fire now!" He pulled his own trigger, and hundreds more joined him. Hot energy bolts and invisible swarms of speeding lead shot out toward the monsters on the ramp and the gristly cargo they dragged between them.

Many of the shots found their targets, and Brown and Api slowed, but kept on, only a little less steady. A number of the fighters in Thomas' line lowered their weapons and stared in disbelief, that two little old men could take such punishment. "What in the name of the Great CPU?" declared one man, and others joined in expressing their astonishment.

"It has nothing to do with the Great CPU!" Thomas shouted. "It has only to do with Legion! You look upon Virus incarnate, Abend given terrible form! If they reach you they will kill you! Keep firing if you value your lives! Fire!"

The men and women on the line renewed their fire, and kept firing. The evil constructs continued down the ramp, absorbing more and more lead and blazing hot bolts as they closed on Thomas' rebellious force. More and more destruction thumped into the gnarled forms and finally Api stumbled and fell, and lay there on the plasphalt, his legs twitching violently as if still trying to carry him forward.

Brown slowed as all the fire was concentrated on him. He slowed, and his steps seemed to falter. There remained only some fifty meters between the demon and the line now, and Brown bent his legs and twisted at his waist, swinging the dead body he'd been dragging, swinging it in an arc and letting go, hurling the once-human thing spinning end-over-end at the line of armed resistance.

A panicked shouting burst out from the line as the body came in. They had been very brave, these men and women who'd never before known real violence. They'd been very brave and fought well, but this, a dead body used as a missile, it was too much for many of them. Scores turned and ran, some dropping their weapons as they went. Those who remained scattered to the left or right of the body, and it landed with a dull thud, and bounced, then rolled, arms and legs trailing the momentum of the torso, bending and flopping to full length again and again. The head lolled loose on the neck, around and forward and back. When the body came to a stop and lay still, the majority Thomas' people stared at it, seeming to forget Father Brown. A handful of men and women kept firing on the demon, but now he charged the ragged line. He became a bony black robe flapping in the wind of his own passage.

Those few who maintained their fire missed as Brown came on as a streak. Between the dead body hurled at them and this unbelievably rapid charge from a man-like thing that could withstand the fire of so many small-arms, Thomas' people were thrown into a full-fledged rout. They truly scattered now, running every which way before Father Brown, but far too slowly to escape his amazing speed.

Thomas shouted for his people to stand, but knew it was up to him now, to be strong when they were weak. He snatched up an auto-rifle dropped by one of the fleeing rebels and ran to intercept Father Brown. He met the monster on the ramp and swung the rifle at Brown's head without slowing. Thomas felt the force of the blow through the plasteel barrel of the weapon. It jarred his wrists and elbows. There was no telling how many hundreds of kilos of kinetic force impacted Father Brown's face but it was enough to knock down the demon, and

Thomas spun to follow through with another blow, and another. The construct began to rise but Thomas knocked it back down, and back down, again and again, until it began to convulse and kick as Cardinal Api still convulsed and kicked, further up the ramp. Thomas kept thumping hard on the black-robed form at his feet, knowing it might not be permanently disabled, knowing that *if it was* permanently disabled by his blows, it was only because it had been weakened by so much fire from so many guns. Thomas bludgeoned Brown until the rifle-barrel bent and then snapped, and then he looked back down the ramp, and saw many hundreds of faces staring up at him. His followers, their panic erased by what he had done.

"Let's get some explosive charges up here," Thomas shouted down at them. "Let's make sure these things are dead."

A voice rose up from the crowd, then another, and in moments, Thomas found himself the focus of loud cheering, joyful hoots and triumphant shouts rang out over and over. Thomas smiled back at the men and women and, when several came up the ramp bearing the explosives he'd asked for, he supervised the placement of the charges on Api and Brown. Everyone retreated to the bottom of the ramp as the timers were set, and when the Father and the Cardinal were blown to bits, the cheering started anew. People reached for Thomas as he passed through the crowd. Hands touched his shoulders, his arms in thanks and congratulation.

The jubilant noise died down some when Thomas went to the body brought by Brown and Api, when he knelt down and rolled it over to look at the broken face.

It was Thomas' most recent adjutant, Lieutenant Serial. Thomas felt a wave of guilty relief. It wasn't Jon. The visitor in his dreams could be wrong. Jon could still be alive, somewhere in the city. Thomas had no idea what the false prophet of Legion thought to accomplish by killing Serial, but at least it wasn't Jon. He scooped up the body and carried it to the sidewalk, where he lay Serial on his back and folded his hands over his chest. There was really nothing else to do for him, or for the people who watched, but to try to make him look peaceful. Someone brought a sheet, and Thomas draped it over the body. He was turning away from the lifeless form when everything went dark.

Uneasy murmuring and calls from the people, a collective sound of soft shock and surprise. The lights had gone out. It was completely dark. That was wrong. The lights never went out in Megadon. They dimmed, at night, but they never went out.

"Stay calm!" Thomas ordered, as his phone began to pip in his pocket.

He unfolded the phone, and there was the face of the one who called himself Almighty Harold. "That wasn't very nice, what you did to Father Brown and Cardinal Api," he said.

"What you did to Serial wasn't very nice, either," Thomas told him. "But don't worry, we'll make amends. Your demons couldn't stop us. Nothing will stop us."

"You'll have a difficult time proceeding, in the dark," said Harold.

"You turned off the lights, then," Thomas said. "We'll turn them back on, once we control the city."

The face on the screen sneered. "You'll never control the city. I *am* the city! I am one with the Great CPU and the Great Computers that control every aspect of Megadon! I hold these millions of lives in my hands! Surrender now and save the lives of these sinners who follow you to the burning fires of Abend!"

Thomas shook his head. "You are nothing. You turned off the lights. That's all. You spread your darkness throughout the city, but you can not stop us. Bring me Jon now, unharmed!"

"He is dead!" said Harold. "He died screaming, as you and all who follow you will die screaming!"

Then the screen went dark. Thomas shut down the phone, put it back in his pocket. He turned on his flashlight and shouted for his sergeants, and they found their way through the dark to him. Together they planned the reorganization of their forces, to minimize confusion in the blackness through which they would travel.

Mom pulled the red barchetta onto the final stretch of the road beneath the trees and gunned the engine again, pushing David back into his seat. David had thought Uncle Robert had driven dangerously, but Mom was nothing short of crazy. They flew out from beneath the canopy of leaves and were halfway across the shrinking field before she braked hard and turned the wheel, sending the car into a sideways skid that blended the acrid smells of burning grass and burning rubber as they plowed across the green space. David closed his eyes and hung on. Again. He was certain they'd slam into the side of the big barn, but they came to a stop right alongside one tall weathered wooden wall, and Mom turned the key, killing the motor and ending this latest of David's ordeals. "Come on, your uncle's in the house," Mom told him.

The dogs bounded through the tall grass and welcomed David by jumping up and trying to lick his face. The furry white-fanged beasts danced and bounced all around him yipping and yowling all the way to the front door of the house.

Inside, David followed his mother to the kitchen, where Uncle Robert and Mal stood by the table, staring down at a map spread out across the wide flat surface. Uncle Robert glanced up at Mom and David as they came in. "About time you got back here. Where's Rosella?"

"She's mopping up," said Mom.

David took a place by the table next to Mal. "What's going on?" he asked.

"Everybody's hauling ass out of this fucking area, hiding out in the woods," Mal told him.

"The shit's hit the fan, boy," said Uncle Robert. "And we're running and ducking to avoid being covered with it. Your friends in those frontier air-cars didn't come out here just to chase you around. They were on their way to Xanadu, with orders to burn the place to the ground, no prisoners."

"Well, Mom and Rosella stopped them, right?"

"There are more on the way. Harold's electronic consciousness has expanded to the point where he'll be in full control of everything, of all systems in Megadon and Syrinx and everyplace else quite fucking soon, if he isn't already."

"Can you hack in and stop it? Him?" David asked.

Uncle Robert shook his head. "Tried. I've tried and I've tried. All I've done is slow it down. We need to take out the primary systems."

"The Great Computer?"

"That's the one. Take that out, and everything else will fold. Game over."

"But that'll stop everything," David said. "Power, water, everything."

"So what?" Mal spat. "Let those frigging pansies come out into the open air, for fuck-sake!"

"The cities are falling apart as it is," Mom added. "Nobody's done any maintenance for decades now."

"That's because the little prick killed anybody who knew anything about anything, back when the cities went up," said Uncle Robert. "There's nobody left who knows a wrench from a screw-driver. A few gear-heads out in orbit or in the interplanetary fleet, but they're self-taught by trial-and-error driven by necessity. When shit breaks in space, you either fix it or end up eating vacuum."

"Alright," said David. "When do we go?"

Uncle Robert tapped the map. "As soon as we get everybody tucked away. We've broken the population of Xanadu into twelve groups, and they're headed out in twelve directions."

"The twelve tribes of Israel," said Mom.

"What?" David asked her.

"I'll explain it later."

"Might as well explain it now, for little Moses," Uncle Robert said. "It's part of the culture of myth I've built for these people, the evacuation plan. Something I took from one of the major religions that people practiced before the little prick blew up the whole frigging world. Myth goes like this. Twelve tribes of this place called Israel get scattered, and then they get put back together when their spiritual leader shows up. In my version, their leader is this mythic figure called Tom Sawyer."

"You want me to lead them? Lead them to what?"

"Depends," said Mom.

"Depends on what?"

"Depends whether we manage to knock out the primary system or not," said Uncle Robert.

"If your uncle and your mother get their asses killed, it's all us, Tom Sawyer," said Mal.

"There are major weapons-caches here, here, and here," Uncle Robert tapped three places on the map. "Minor caches here, here and here. Your best connection into the net is the one here in the farm-house, but secondary tie-ins are available in seven separate locations. Don't give up on hacking and slashing, just because I haven't been able to figure out anything to stop Harold's code from spreading. Could just be you'll come up with something I wouldn't have dreamed of. Then again, you might not, so don't put all your eggs in that particular basket, or any one basket, for that matter. I'll give you a list of people with leadership potential within each of the twelve groups, you should be able to delegate tasks to them, but try not to distance yourself from your people in the field, because you'll need to know what's really going on at any given moment. The situation is not liable to remain static for any long period of time. Never make an attack without a proper diversion, you'll lose fewer lives that way. Don't forget about your Huckleberry Finn, here, either. Mal's your ace-in-the-hole when it comes to working inside Megadon. Count on him for recruiting new talent from the lower levels if you need it, but remember the consciousness in the machine is likely to know about your every move inside the city. There are spy-satellites and the orbital platforms, so Harold has eyes all around the world, but he's got even more in the cities. If everything else goes to shit, and I mean everything, you could try a last-ditch assault with every man, woman and child you have left, because if things get that bad, your people will be dead anyway. Harold's not going to stop until he's hunted down every last living free person on the planet. Okay? Got it?"

"Uh," David stood there staring at Uncle Robert. If Mom and Uncle Robert died trying to destroy the Great Computer, they wanted him to take over. Take over everything. "Uncle Robert, this is a lot...."

"You're damned right it's a lot. And don't expect everybody from Xanadu to accept your orders. There will be those who will challenge you. Not many, but there will be a few who will try to call you out, or lead their own half-assed rebellions. Take them out quick and mean. There's not one of them you can't take in a fight, so take them out at the first sign of trouble. Break an arm or two, it'll work in your favor. These people don't expect their Tom Sawyer to be soft, or to put up with a whole lot of crap. You'll have your work cut out for you, I won't lie to you about that, but you can do it, or I wouldn't put you in such a position. You're a very smart kid. You're a good fighter, and you're the second-best hacker in the world, after me. And there's enough of your father in you that people will trust you, follow you, if you stand up and lead. There's nobody in that whole lot of exiles who can do what you can do, David. They're sheep, most of them. Not to say they're completely helpless, but they need somebody to lead them, and you're the man. Nobody else."

David looked down at the map. "What about Thomas Ryan? He could lead them."

"Everything on the net says he's fighting his way through Megadon, and he's got his own bunch of followers to worry about right now."

"What about Rosella?"

"She's coming with us. She knows how to use that armor better than anybody else, and we'll need her if we're to have any chance of getting through. We need you out here, kiddo."

"But you want *me* to be in charge of all these people out here?"

"That's right," said Uncle Robert. "Get used to it. We'll go over a few more things, but then we've got to suit up and go."

David nodded. Not because he agreed with the plan, but because he knew he had no choice. He nodded and Uncle Robert started reeling off details. Details on details, names and places and contingencies. Tom Sawyer. Twelve tribes. Weapons. Attacks. Retreats. Strategies. Plans. Home-grown myths. Uncle Robert going on and on. David tried to keep up, but he knew he could not. There was too much to know, too much he was missing. He was tired, exhausted by the sleepless night and deadly race. But he was supposed to be the salvation of so many, if Uncle Robert and Mom never came back. If they died. So he listened. David listened, and tried to understand. He wished he was someplace else, but he wasn't, so he did his best to take it all in.

How It All Happened, Chapter 6

You don't know boredom until you've spent nine months inside, a lot of that time just sitting around in the dark. There was plenty of room, at first, because we had the whole underground trailer-park to ourselves, but even that space shrank down to almost nothing, after the first couple of months. Not to say it was all just sitting around, of course. During the first couple of days, more than a few people tried to force their way in to our shelter. We shot them, or drove them off by shooting over their heads. Yes, Jimmy and I killed people, defending VIUN from would-be intruders. I make no apology for it. Such brutality was what the conditions demanded, and damned if I was going to die trying to save people who were already dead. Anybody who spent any real time above ground in the first few weeks after the initial blasts soaked up enough radiation that they would fall apart from the inside. Men, women, children, there wasn't anything you could do for them. They were sick and dying. It sounds so very cold, but we would have been wasting precious resources, trying to keep them alive. Yes, we had more than enough to eat and drink. Jimmy and Vera and I could have survived for a decade, on what we had stored away, but we had to think of the other survivors, the real survivors, who, by dint of their smarts or by plain old dumb luck, managed to live through the first few days, the first few weeks, the first few months. Every meal we wasted on one of the dying was one less meal for those who would survive. It would be some while before those who survived the radiation could produce their own food, and I intended to see them through that lean time. Because it was the right thing to do, and because I wasn't going to let Harold hog all the glory. No way was he going to be the only one handing out candy-bars when the fallout settled and it was safe to go outside.

So we shot people. People who tried to dig their way into our underground complex. People who tried to block up our ventilation system and suffocate us. People who came in small groups demanding we surrender what we had stored up. They came, some exercising the option of force the second they arrived, others making high-blown speeches about morality and their right to this or that. They came, and when they became any kind of threat, Jimmy and I went out and shot them dead. Some of them shot back, some of them did not, but when it was all said and done, we were left standing, after every encounter. We made these little trips outside as brief as possible, one minute, two at the most, and after every trip outside we followed the best decontamination procedures we could come up with. We threw out our clothes. We showered. It was incredibly resource-intensive, incredibly wasteful, but it beat poisoning our warren of trailers and tunnels. It beat bringing the deadly stuff inside and spreading it around.

So, it was boredom punctuated by brief spats of deadly violence. And during the boring stretches, there was a feeling of helplessness. Nothing to do but wait, knowing that Harold's plan to wipe out the world had gone off without a hitch. That little murdering bastard. Big murdering bastard. He'd killed more people than Hitler and all the despots and crackpots who ever lived. He'd probably reduced the population of the world down to less than a billion. Maybe less than five hundred million. Maybe less than that. There was no telling how bad it was out there, no telling how many cities had fallen in flame, and no telling how many stood only as storage-space for millions of millions of rotting irradiated dead. The destruction of the blasts themselves, then the radiation, the fallout, then the diseases and death that would follow from the presence of so many unburied bodies, and the lack of once-basic services like running water and adequate sewage. But there was no telling, sitting around in the dark of VIUN, no telling just how bad it was out in the world, and that was frustrating, knowing you couldn't do anything but wait. I've always hated that.

But, like all things, the waiting passed. Months crawled by. After the first few months, nobody tried to break into our buried compound. It was nice, not having to shoot anybody, but it made the time drag out even worse than before. But still, the time passed, and one winter day, Jimmy and I went outside, and cleared the snow and frozen dirt off a shelter we'd built and buried to hide Jimmy's rusted yellow car.

We drove up Hovey Road and headed down the big hill into downtown Houlton. It didn't look all that different than it had before the nukes came down. No direct hits or near-misses here, so it didn't look all that different, except there were no people, not on the outskirts of downtown. Radiation had seen to that. No living people, but, as Jimmy drove us slowly down the street, something else struck me as rather odd. "Hey, Jimmy," I said. "Where are all the bodies?"

"Maybe under the snow," he said. And there was a good bit of snow on the ground, but I'd expected to see at least a couple corpses, the remains of at least a couple people who'd gone mad from the slow agony of their deaths-by-cellular-deterioration, people who'd stumbled out into the street or into their yards before finally keeling over and moving no more. Not saying I wanted to see more dead people. I'm no ghoul. But they should have been there, and while seeing them would have been creepy, not seeing them was even more creepy.

We rolled on a few more blocks, just crawling along as we looked for any sign of life. Then Jimmy spotted the first red star flag. It was a big rectangle of gray cloth with a big red five-pointed star sewn on the middle. It flapped from the horizontal arm of a brown plastic telephone pole. The light freezing breeze pushed the cloth this way and that, and it was like that goddam flag was taunting me, waving in the open air like that. "Oh, what the fuck?" I groaned. "What the fuck, what the fuck?"

There were more of these flags, the closer we got to the center of town. Red stars on gray fields, all apparently hand-made. By the time we got within ten blocks of the town square, there was one on every telephone pole, and quite a few hanging from the leafless branches of trees. There were also a couple goons with guns who stepped out into the road. They looked like locals, with their worn construction boots and their orange winter hunting-coats. They also looked thin, like they'd only recently recovered from some grave illness. One adjusted his wool stocking-cap as Jimmy slowed the car to a stop, and the hair beneath that cap was quite short and quite thin. A sure sign that the guy had soaked up some radiation during the last couple months. He and his buddy were missing more than a few teeth, too. Each of the goons wore a gray arm-band complete with red star. Their weapons were medium-caliber bolt-action hunting rifles, deer-rifles. Accurate at long ranges, and with plenty of punch. Real decent guns except for their slow rate of fire. The two goons held these rifles cradled in the crooks of their elbows, like mothers might carry babies. Not the best way to hold your rifle when approaching a potential threat.

They split and walked around opposite sides of the car, the guy on Jimmy's side gesturing for Jimmy to roll down the glass.

"Go ahead," I told Jimmy, and he cranked down the window. Our rifles, fully automatic assault-style numbers, were laying across the back seat. The goon on my side of the car looked in through the window, and he must have seen those pieces in the back, but still he held his rifle cradled in his arm, made no move to make it ready. This, and the fact that he stood so close to my door I could proba- bly knock him off-balance by shoving it hard open, made these goons less a threat than a curiosity.

"Hey there," said the goon on Jimmy's side. "Welcome to Houlton. I'm sorry, but we're going to have to ask you to leave your car."

"You want us to get out?" I leaned over to ask him.

"Well, yeah, but you've got to leave it, too. I know a lot's happened, but there's the motor laws now, and you can't keep your car."

"Motor laws?" I asked him. "What motor laws? Buddy, there's been a nuclear war, who's making laws?" I knew the answer, of course, but he didn't know I knew, and I figured it would be better keeping it that way until I was ready to make some kind of move. I wanted him to think that Jimmy and I were just a couple more survivors rolling out of the back woods looking for the remnants of civilization.

The guy sighed. "You're darned right there has been a nuclear war, and that's kind of the point of the motor laws. We don't need things to get like they were before. We're lucky there's anybody still alive after the way society went the way it did."

"And what's our car got to do with anything like that?" I asked him.

"The internal combustion engine is an environmentally destructive mode of transportation," he told me, and I could tell, the way the words fell out of his mouth, that this was something he'd memorized. "The Great CPU brought down nuclear destruction upon the peoples of the earth as he brought flood in earlier times," with this he relaxed back into more natural speech, "so we could start over again, and make it like it should be."

"You always thought that way? Did you have a gasoline-powered car, back before the shit hit the fan?" I asked him.

"I did, but now I've seen the error of my ways. And I'm glad I was spared, and I'm glad things are going to be made like they should be."

"And how's that?" I asked him.

He shrugged. "They haven't told us that yet."

"They *who* haven't told you that yet?"

Another sigh, this one heavy and full of frustration. "God, man, you come down out of the woods just to ask me questions all day? You going to leave your car or not?"

And there it was. I was asking questions and this guy didn't like it. This guy couldn't handle it. This explained why he was assigned to stand sentry, allowed to carry a gun in Harold's new world order. "Sorry," I told him. "I'm curious by nature. How long have the One True Religion folks been in town, anyway?"

"Why don't you just leave your car and go on to City Hall and ask them yourself?" he said.

"City Hall, huh? So much for avoiding the mistakes of the past," I said.

"What was that?"

"Nothing. Thanks for your time. Jimmy, let's turn it around and head back to Woodstock."

"You're going to have to leave your car eventually," said the goon on Jimmy's side of the car. "The motor laws are in effect everywhere you go."

"Okay, thanks. We may be back," I told him, as Jimmy put the yellow rust-bucket into reverse and executed a three-point turn in the middle of the snow-covered road.

I hadn't expected Harold to have gotten so far so soon. The One True Religion cell closest to Houlton had been that one down in Old Town, over a hundred miles away. I'd been ready to kick some ass, back at the check-point going into town, but, talking to the one goon, I decided it wouldn't make much sense to cause a disturbance. Taking out those two guys back there wouldn't have done anything but rile up those newly loyal to Harold's red star bullshit. Then, if Harold had any kind of communications network up and running, word might eventually get out that two guys who looked like me and Jimmy were stirring up trouble in northern Maine, and the little prick would have us hunted down. Not that he wasn't going to try to hunt us down later. He was going to try to kill us with everything he had, especially once we started getting in the way of his plans.

But I'm getting ahead of myself. Let's go back to me and Jimmy in the car in Houlton, driving back out of town. I really didn't know what to do, since Harold's people had already established a foothold in this place where I thought I would begin my own little counter-revolution. My plan had been a pretty simple one: wait until the radiation passed, then come out of the ground with food and medicine and become the savior of those others who'd survived. Not a holy-holy *savior* like Harold was making himself out to be, but just a guy who people would listen to and trust. That's all. Me and Jimmy would save the locals from starvation and disease, and then explain to them just who started the nuclear war and why. I'd figured people would be pissed off enough at the destruction of their lives, and the deaths of their friends and relatives, that they'd want to do something about it, keep Harold from taking over. And this would have been the start of my counter-revolution, my voice of truth versus that little prick's cavalcade of lies and deception. I would guide humanity to some new destiny, I didn't know what, and I didn't know how, beyond simply telling them the truth. I will freely admit that I was more than a naïve, to think that I could have made that big a difference, in so simple a fashion, but at least I was ready to try, ready to at least have a go at making things better instead of worse, and, in my book, there's a real difference between trying and failing and not trying at all.

So we went back to VIUN, so I could think things over. We had dinner outside that night, even though it was freezing cold. It was nice to be out in the open air, after so long a time underground. It was so cold that the food, rice and beans with sardines, began to freeze, but it was good to be out, good to be beneath the open sky, and we hacked away with our knives and forks, kept moving the chow around on our plates to keep it from freezing icy solid.

07-12-2112

The energy-beam that cut through the ceiling and floor of Level Twenty was three meters in diameter and brighter than anything Thomas had ever seen in his life, with the possible exception of the naked sun as seen from space, which he'd looked upon only through the greatly dimmed viewing port of the ships that had carried him to and from Mars. There was nothing between Thomas and this glaring beam, however, but some hundred meters of open air and the bodies of many of those who had joined his cause. This beam had not visibly worked its way down through the dimly-lit ceiling, nor had it taken any consciously appreciable time to burn down through the pavement and supporting structures that made up the floor; the beam had simply appeared, a silently roiling column of blue-red light three meters wide and a hundred meters high.

Thomas turned away from the light, and blobs of wild color floated across his vision. He heard the cries of his followers all around him as they too turned from the searing brilliance.

"What was that?! What was that?!" came the cry.

"It is the wrath of Almighty Harold!" screamed one panicked voice.

"The anger of the Great CPU!" shouted another.

Thomas knew the beam was no manifestation of any will more divine than his own. It was the product of a massive series of lenses and mirrors aboard one of the Orbital Defense Platforms **IS THIS A CONSISTENTLY-USED TERM?** that circled the earth, far beyond above the atmosphere, almost beyond the reach of the planet's massive gravitational pull. It was the demon Harold lashing out with his terrible weapons of last resort, weapons intended by the Great CPU to protect the planet from external threats. Harold had aimed these weapons inward, and now used them to punch holes in a city of millions. The Great CPU alone knew how many lives had been vaporized as that powerful beam cut through all sixty levels of Megadon.

Then it was gone, as quickly as it had appeared, the beam vanished, with no clear beginning or end, it was just gone, before Thomas could explain to his people just what it was. Three seconds. That was the maximum burst possible from a single orbital weapons battery. Then an hour to recharge the system before the weapon could be fired again. There were, of course, multiple Orbital Defense Platforms, but each of these held a geosynchronous orbit, and the angle of deflection between platforms was sufficient to keep Harold from using more than one to target Megadon with any kind of accuracy. The platforms might be moved from their orbits, but that would take some real time, days or weeks. It was possible, and Thomas wasn't about to rule it out, but for the time being, Harold had just the one satellite capable of targeting Megadon. So, an hour. Thomas had an hour before that beam appeared again. He did his best to calm his people as he walked over to get a better look at the hole in the pavement. It was lumpy but smooth around the edges, where the plasphalt had melted. He knelt and held a hand over the hole. It was still warm. Thomas pointed his flashlight down the hole, and gazed down through the circular rift and saw plasteel beams with three-meter-wide sections missing, the metal at the edges still glowing red. Further down, there were heavy bundles of cable and lighter bundles of wiring, sliced and sparking. Pipes, too, had been cut between the levels, and fluids of all sorts surged forth freely, and with some force, pooling up and flowing around in the dark and dusty space. The hole kept on through the ceiling of Level Nineteen below, and straight through some type of warehouse, parts of which were now on fire, and through the floor of Level Nineteen and down through the ceiling of Level Eighteen, where there were more fires, and down and down and down, probably all the way down to the ground, all the way down to Level One and maybe further, down into the dirt and rock upon which the city rested. Thomas had seen massive Megadon from without a number of times, as he'd traveled to and from Syrinx, and as he'd returned from the wilderness, but staring down this gaping hole gave him a new appreciation of the sheer magnitude of the structure, the unbelievable size of the place. It was the single largest structure ever built by mankind, large enough to house millions on millions, to feed them and shelter them and dispose of their waste. The very concept of so many people stuffed into one great tiered edifice was nothing short of astounding.

Thomas wondered how many innocents had been caught by the beam. How many had been simply vaporized? How many had been cut in half? How many had lost limbs or been badly burnt for having committed no crime but for simply having been in the wrong place at the wrong time? Thomas knew that he himself was partially responsible for whatever deaths and injuries had occurred. The demon Harold may have fired that beam, but he'd fired it in response to Thomas' rebellion. Thomas felt the hard cold press of guilt. He knew he was doing the right thing, in challenging the evil that held so many in virtual bondage, the evil that kept millions oppressed in the darkness of a decaying city when the whole wide world beyond was open for the taking and enjoyment and betterment of those millions. He was doing the right thing, in assaulting the system infected by Legion and made foul with Virus. He was doing the will of the Great CPU by fighting the demon that had somehow supplanted the reign of righteousness on earth. Thomas knew he was doing the right thing, but that knowledge did nothing to assuage the guilt he felt when he stared down into the gaping wound that tore through the city.

A few drops of something cold and wet landed on the back of Thomas' neck, and he stepped back from the hole to gaze upward at the circle cut in the ceiling of Level Twenty. Pipes had no doubt been cut above as they'd been cut below. He saw droplets of semi-clear liquid falling from the hole in the ceiling, and watched as the droplets fused into a trickle, and the trickle grew into a small but steady vertical stream, as the fluids that pooled above flowed outward from their points of origin and found the edges of the hole. Considering there were forty levels above, and the beam had cut through everyone, Thomas supposed there would be quite a torrent roaring down to Level One before too very long. Fresh water, sewage, and the Great CPU only knew what else. And then, in another hour, there might be another such torrent, and an hour after that, another, and another, until all the liquid ran down or the demon had destroyed the rebellion.

Thomas wondered how many times he could let the city be stabbed through with such lances of burning light, how many hundreds or thousands or millions of people he could stand to see killed before he surrendered to Harold. He wondered, too, just how much punishment Megadon itself could withstand. One three-meter hole punched from top to bottom of such a tremendous structure would not cause it to collapse or topple, but what about five, or ten, or twenty? He could not imagine anyone surviving the destruction of the city itself. Each level was so massive that it would surely crush the level beneath it. The colossal weight and momentum of such a collapse would build and build as Megadon folded earthward. There might be little but dust and tiny scraps of plasteel, by the time it was done.

He had an hour, slightly less now. Thomas found his sergeants, or they found him, in the barely organized crowd that was his rebellion. He told his sergeants about the Orbital Defense Platforms, about the hour it would take for the weapon to recharge, and then he told them he needed to nap.

The sergeants looked to one another, then back to Thomas. "Keep the people together, and keep them calm," he said, as he headed for one of the captured Vigilance cruisers. "And if I'm not awake in forty minutes, come and get me."

Thomas crawled into the back of the cruiser and tried to make himself comfortable. He had his doubts as to whether he could hurry up and sleep, but he closed his eyes and kept them closed, resisting the urge to check his watch, to watch the time slipping past. He tried to focus his thoughts on anything but the present dilemma, on anywhere but where he was. He thought of Rosella. He hoped she was safe. He imagined her lips on his skin, barely touching, and the warmth of her body against his, and the cabin where they'd coupled, and the forest in which the cabin stood, and the breadth of all the lands beyond the city. He remembered the earth from space, and the feeling of weightlessness he'd experienced in free-fall. And Rosella, and Rosella.

Thoughts and memories gradually merged with the slow deep steady flow of his own breathing, and into the crawl-space between waking and dream, where the thoughts and memories acted of their own will, and from there, Thomas slipped into true sleep, and into the dream.

Dream-Jon was waiting for him atop a craggy mountain, on a spur of jagged rock dusted here and there with powdery snow. The wind howled all around, blowing up white wisps and sending small bunches of snow snaking across the naked rock. "About time you came to your senses," said dream-Jon.

"Nice location," Thomas shouted over the wind. "Where are we now?"

"We're on a planet called earth, on the other side of Cygnus X-1. This is the very spot where Billy Lifeson realized that he was a unique living embodiment of the universe."

"Oh. This is where he became so powerful? His brother, Robert, says Billy Lifeson is like a god. Blasphemy, of course." Thomas shouted.

Dream-Jon shrugged. "Something like that."

"If going through the black hole makes you so powerful, why can't you knock out the Defense Platforms?"

"I've told you and told you: because Billy designed them! You have to take them out! You have to go to Syrinx, and destroy the Great Computer, the real one, way beneath the city!"

Thomas nodded, thinking what a great coward this fellow named Dan must be. Dan and all of his kind, lurking on the other side of Cygnus, but too frightened to come through for fear of being killed. They wanted to regain their home world, wanted to return home, but didn't want it badly enough to fight for it. It didn't make much sense to Thomas, this apparent dichotomy, this supposed true longing for home paired with an unwillingness to stick out their necks. Perhaps this Dan really was a member of the Elder Race, the true Elder Race, banished to Cygnus by the true Harold and the Great CPU. Not that it really made any difference; Thomas had no choice now but to render the Orbital Defense Platforms inoperative, before the demon Harold destroyed Megadon and every single last one of its inhabitants. He would save the millions in Megadon, and then worry about Dan and his fellows. If they presented a threat, he would deal with them as best he could. "And how would you have me destroy the Great Computer?" Thomas asked.

"That's up to you," said dream-Jon. "Explosives, small-arms fire, even your strength-augmented hands, if you're careful to avoid the live wires. And listen, I know you're apprehensive about my motives, *our* motives, but let me assure you, we only wish to return to earth, to come back home. That's not so much to ask, is it?"

Thomas looked away, down the mountain. There was a small, flat city far below, a city on a bay that stretched out to a shining sea. "I should get back, if I'm to make it to Syrinx."

"Good luck," said Dan.

Thomas woke with a start in the back of the cruiser. He checked his watch. Fifteen minutes before the orbital platform could fire again. Not time enough for him to make it to Syrinx. Just barely time enough to pass orders to his sergeants. He got out of the car, rounded them up, gave them their instructions. They were to continue their upward progress, continue to work toward securing the city while he tried to disable the defense platforms. Better to press the attack, to keep the demon on the defensive, than to scatter and hide from the death raining down from the skies.

Thomas took a cruiser and raced down through the levels. He was headed for the Level One maintenance station, where he would commandeer a frontier air-car for the long ride to Syrinx. He wished he could simply drive to the Vigilance flight-deck on Level Sixty and take the Vice Chancellor's orbital shuttle to Syrinx, but, even if he managed to make it unopposed to the flight deck, there was no guarantee he could force the pilot to ferry him to the Holy City, and while Thomas felt comfortable enough piloting a frontier air-car, he had no idea how to fly the orbital shuttle. So he drove down and down, ramp after ramp, to Level One.

The maintenance station had been abandoned when Thomas and his small force had swept through Level One. Most of the Vigilance officers had escaped by fleeing upward, while most of the enlisted men had joined the rebellion. Thomas parked the cruiser, and chose a frontier air-car from one row of such vehicles parked in the hangar. He cranked up the turbofans and eased the bulky ship from its berth, retracting the landing-gear and steering his way through the hangar and into the outbound tube.

How It All Happened, Chapter 7

It was cold, after the nukes came down. Not just cold through the winter, but cold into the spring and summer, and so on and so forth. Massive explosions like those caused by nuclear weapons throw a lot of crap up into the air, you see, dirt, dust, vaporized metal and whatever else happens to be near ground zero. All this particulate matter gets tossed up into the sky, and it stays there, until the wind gets tired of carrying it around. All this crap in the atmosphere cuts down on the amount of sunlight that gets to the earth, leading to a phenomenon that used to be called "nuclear winter". It wasn't as bad as it could have been, I suppose, not nearly as bad as some so-called experts had predicted it would be. But it was bad, bad enough that, during the first year, it was snowing in Virginia at the end of June, when Jimmy and Vera and I made it down that way.

We were driving three big super-duty four-wheel-drive pickups that we'd acquired from an almost-abandoned Ford dealership in Bangor, Maine. Each truck pulled a trailer. We had these trucks and trailers loaded up with all the vital supplies that we could carry, all kinds of foodstuff and medicine, and enough in the way of weapons to protect ourselves from the trouble we found on the road. This trouble usually took the form of red-robed goons with guns. There were a few odd gangs of post-apocalyptic bandits here and there, but fewer of these independent groups than I'd expected. Harold's network of survivors was wide-spread and well-organized, with a palpable presence in most cities and towns, and when they weren't bugging us, I guess the red-robes were doing their best to act as a force for law and order. Harold's law, Harold's order. The red-robes wiped out bandits and the like, wiped out anybody who refused to pledge loyalty to asshole Almighty Harold, his red star and his imaginary Great CPU. It was nothing short of cold-blooded murder in a lot of cases, and it didn't matter how old or young the hold-outs were, nor did it matter why they refused to join up with the new regime. Anybody who said no to the red-robes was killed. And the killings were not always quick. Some were made purposely nasty, to make examples of those who refused to convert. I can't say I was surprised by this, because this is the way of most all religions. It's been the case throughout human history that people have been more than willing to kill and/or torture so-called "infidels". Christians killing Muslims, Muslims killing Christians, Hindus killing Muslims, Muslims killing Sikhs, Romans killing Jews, followers of Isis killing followers of Set, Bear-God Clan killing Wolf-God Clan, and on and on. More blood has been spilled in the name of religion than for any other purpose. So I wasn't surprised. Especially knowing Harold as I did, I was not in the least bit surprised, but my lack of surprise did nothing to mitigate the levels of disgust I felt when we came across the victims of that little prick's bloody crusade.

We were rolling through what used to be upstate New York, up near the crater where Buffalo used to sprawl. It was colder than a bucket of penguin-shit, and snowing like hell. We'd picked up a small following by this point, twenty-five or thirty men women and children who'd been hiding out here and there, people who had no desire to sign up with the red-robes, or people whom we'd simply found first. We'd picked up these folks one or two or three at a time, and they were quite a mixed lot. A couple of them in wheelchairs, rejected from Harold's fold because they were "flawed"; four or five homosexuals of both genders—no need to tell you what the red-robes would have done to these individuals; a sculptor; a poet, both of whom would have been rejected by the red star cult as useless and potential trouble-makers. In addition to these people I mention, there were a variety of others, a diesel-mechanic; a home healthcare worker; a retired drill-press operator; a bunch of people who may have been readily accepted into Harold's new world order had they been willing to join. Some of the people who tagged along with us were devout Christians, so holy-rolly that I myself found them truly irksome. Some of our little group just weren't very personable, and wouldn't have joined Harold's multitudes any more than they would have joined Toastmasters. In any case, by the time we rolled by the remains of Buffalo, we had a little convoy eleven vehicles long, all four-wheel-drive, some trucks, a few Jeeps, and we're working our way through this god-awful snow-storm. I was in the lead vehicle, keeping my eyes peeled for any glimpse of red, red star, red cloth, anything. Now that Harold's little cells were more firmly in control of the regions over which they presided, the red-robes tended to shoot first and ask questions later. Guess they figured they had converted everybody who was going to be converted, and anybody else could go to hell with a bullet. No more polite roadblocks or check-points like the one me and Jimmy ran into outside of Houlton that first day out. Now they were playing for keeps, with an annoying proclivity for shooting holes in radiators. They'd shoot the radiator before taking aim at me or Jimmy or Vera or anybody else. Guess they figured it was a good way to keep us from getting away, and it would have been, if it not for the unnaturally long winter. The cold kept our engines from overheating as rapidly as they would have otherwise. The cold also made wearing body-armor a lot more comfortable. Both Jimmy and I wore full vests with Kevlar sleeves. We had one for Vera, but she wouldn't wear it. Claimed it chafed her boobs.

So I'm driving the lead vehicle, peering out through this driving snow, and I see shapes in the middle of the road. Human shapes. My first thought was that we'd run into some kind of ambush, but as I drove up closer, ready to run down whoever it was at the first sign of trouble, I realized these human shapes were naked.

I'm not sure if there's really any good way to best describe the fucking gruesome scene I drove up on, so forgive me if I write it too gory or don't tell you enough, but here it is: parents, naked, impaled on stakes, with little kids, dressed in winter clothing, handcuffed to the parents. And by impaled, I don't mean somebody drove stakes through the chests of the adults. What I mean is that the points of thick sharp stakes five or six feet long had been driven into the asses of these people. They'd been stabbed in the butt-hole with these stakes, the points driven up into the intestines. And then these thick sharp stakes had been stood on end, so each man and woman was further impaled by the weight of their own body and the motion of their own spastic flailing. Most of these adults were dead when we arrived. The pointed tips of some stakes had worked their way out through the stomach or chest or back; some had come out further up, near the neck; some had been driven straight up, and did not exit at all. Those who still lived were hopelessly maimed, just barely alive, involuntarily convulsing or twitching on the stakes. Their blood and shit and bile had frozen on the stakes and on the ground and had become covered with new snow.

Then there were the kids. Each kid had one wrist handcuffed to the ankle of their mother or father. And we're talking little kids here, some just big enough to stand, but none more than seven years old. They wore coats and hats and boots, to keep them from freezing to death before they could be exposed to the full agony of their parents' gruesome deaths. None of these kids was big enough or strong enough to unimpale their mom or dad, or to knock down one of those stakes, so they would have eventually frozen to death, if we hadn't happened along. Each little boy and girl would have slipped into the big sleep while consumed by the horror and grief of his or her parent's torturous passing.

I stopped the truck, and all the other vehicles stopped behind me. I had Jimmy take some of our folks who weren't scared to handle guns, had him set up a perimeter so me and the others could free those kids and put the remaining parents out of their misery. It was fucking nasty work. Several of our people puked, some several times. Some of the kids were so freaked out they couldn't say a word. Some others went nuts when we sawed off the cuffs and tried to take them from their dead parents. It just wasn't a pretty scene. Now I'd seen some other atrocities committed by the red-robes. I'd seen bodies burnt and strangled and found evidence of vivisections and even quartering. Very nasty very evil stuff, but this was the first time we'd stumbled onto a scene so fresh, such a crime so recently committed. And this was the first time I'd seen one involving kids. Such little fucking kids. Every time in the past, whenever we'd found bodies, well, there wasn't much to do but swear and then keep driving in a silence both eerie and haunted by what-ifs. What if we'd gotten here sooner? What if we could find the shits who did this? Knowing, even as you ask yourself these questions, that it's safer and best to keep rolling on. Knowing that it makes no sense to risk your own life and the lives of everyone else in the party to go seeking revenge for dead strangers. But now, here I was putting bullets into the heads of those impaled parents who still drew breath. Here I was hearing the shrieking of the kids and here I was trying to get these bodies off these stakes. It was too much for me. The kids. There was no excuse for any of it, but to have involved those kids, it was fucking demonic.

I worked with everybody else to get the kids into the vehicles, and to get the bodies down. By the time we were done, I couldn't see anything but red. I got eight other men and women who were equally steamed, and we loaded up with spare weapons and plenty of ammo. I left Jimmy and Vera in charge of the convoy, set a rendezvous-point, and told the main group to go on without me and the others if we weren't there in three hours.

There were some scant tracks in the snow, leading away from the site of the impalements. Foot-prints ninety-percent obscured by new-fallen and drifted flakes, but enough to make a trail, which we followed in three trucks, grinding along across the open country in low low gear.

It was nearly night, by the time we came upon the barn. The snow had let up, and the trail had become more and more easily discernable as we closed in on the murdering bastards and the weather gave up on obscuring the print left by each boot. There was a red star banner flying from the weather-vane atop the great peaked roof, and warm yellow light seeped out the cracks around the two big barn doors.

The tracks indicated a party of twelve. I left two of our group on watch on the hill above the barn, to take out anyone who made a run for it. The remaining seven of us piled into two trucks and hit the barn from opposite sides, ramming our rigs right through the doors on either end.

There were twenty-one red-robes in that barn. Some of them died under the wheels of the trucks. Some died in the brief fire-fight that followed. I remember rolling out the driver-side door of my truck and simply spraying left and right with a machine-pistol in each hand. It didn't matter whether the red-robes had picked up guns or had thrown their hands up in surrender. Anyone on my side of the truck, I mowed down.

We lost one woman to a shotgun blast. She caught it right in the chest and must have died instantly. I took a bullet in my left shoulder, and one other guy had a slug go through his right hand. When the shooting was done, there were sixteen dead red-robes, and we had five prisoners.

I don't know how I managed to keep from immediately killing those prisoners. Some part of my brain was running on auto-pilot, I suppose. I didn't kill them right away. Instead, I lied to them. I stood there in front of the five of them, who knelt with their hands tied behind their backs, and I told them I would let them go, if they gave me useful information.

"Who's going to talk first?" I said.

I took the first red-robe who volunteered, we took him outside, walked him up to the woods, tied him to a tree, asked him what he had to tell us. He told us where the local cell was headquartered, where they had caches of food, weapons, and other supplies.

"That's great, thanks," I told him, then I gagged the guy and stabbed him in the lower gut. A terribly painful and terribly slow way to die, being stabbed in the gut. The guy's red robe went a darker shade of red as his blood flowed out of his body.

This first one was still alive when I brought out the second, and tied him to a neighboring tree.

The first and second were still alive when we brought out the third.

By the time we brought out the fifth prisoner, we'd learned that Harold's cells communicated by radio, and on what frequency. We'd learned that the folks we'd found impaled were the last members of a Pentecostal church-group who'd banded together to survive the nuclear holocaust. We'd learned that the red-robe who'd masterminded their slaughter was already dead, back in the barn. The fifth prisoner, who'd been with the New York State National Guard before the nukes came down and he'd found the One True Religion, told us about U.S. Army special weapons storage facility, a place rumored to be somewhere between Albany and Utica.

"They've got all kinds of advanced stuff up there! We sent a scouting party last month, but they never came back! They've got stuff up there that'd let you take over everything!" he said, then he proceed to beg for his life.

"That's great, thanks," I told him. I didn't bother to gag this one, since he was the last. I just stabbed him in the gut.

I left the five of them to die their slow deaths. Maybe they didn't suffer as long as I would have liked. Maybe they froze first. I don't know. I went back inside and I left Harold a note, telling him that I had survived, and promising that I was going to kill him and kill him slowly.

I later came to realize this probably wasn't the smartest thing I could have done, giving the little prick fair warning like that, but I was following the dictates of my emotion rather than those of my intellect, which had been forced from the forefront of my mind by the rage I felt at what had been done to those parents and kids. I realize now that, in killing those prisoners the way I did, I became a little bit more like Harold, by embracing that type of brutality, but I have no regrets about what I did that day, or any day thereafter. The red-robes who had perpetrated that massacre on the road outside Buffalo had been no better than rabid dogs. Worse than rabid dogs, even, because rabid dogs would never plan so carefully such suffering. I killed those red-robes, some quickly, and some slowly, because they needed killing. I will harbor no regrets at having done what needed to be done.

We took our dead woman, her name was Holly, we took her with us and drove to the rendezvous-point, where we hooked up with the rest of our little convoy. Then we all beat a path roughly east-by-southeast, headed for Utica.

07-12-2112

David watched Mom and Uncle Robert and Rosella gearing up. Rosella had returned from the forest just hours before. "I took out eight of those bimbo boxes," she'd said, when she'd landed on the grass before the old wooden house.

"Good," Uncle Robert had told her. "You didn't blow them all to hell, did you?"

"Only a couple."

Uncle Robert had rolled out a long creaking aluminum cart from the darkened rear of the barn. The cart had been loaded down with two more suits of fully powered armor similar to Rosella's. These new suits were flat gray, with small red-white-and-blue hawk or eagle emblems on the shoulders. There were small black numbers painted on each chest-plate, barely discernable from the lifeless gray.

Uncle Robert had let Rosella get out of her armor, let her eat and rest for two hours, then they'd all headed outside to armor up. David watched as his mother and uncle and cousin transformed themselves, piece-by-piece, from creatures of flesh to monsters of plastaegis and plasteel and ablative plating. Rosella was suited up before either Mom or Uncle Robert, and stood there with her helmet under one massive armored arm, shaking her head, which looked ridiculously small in comparison to the great round shoulders on either side, sighing frustration at the incompetence of her elders and offering unasked-for advice. "The sleeve goes on a lot easier as one piece. Why didn't you assemble it *before* you tried to put it on?"

"Working on it," muttered Uncle Robert, "dammit." He had one armored arm on and the other off, trying to assemble the components of the unworn arm with his single bare hand. "Fucking useless piece of shit."

"Why don't you take off the one arm so you'll have both hands? You're not that good with just one hand," said Rosella.

"Why don't you bite your damned tongue before you drive your dear old dad completely insane?" Uncle Robert quipped back.

"Give him a hand, Rosella," Mom said, as she snapped the arm of her own suit into place. "If you don't, we may be here all day."

"Gladly, Auntie," said Rosella. David didn't like it when Rosella called Mom "Auntie". It sounded like the younger woman was making fun of Mom, like she was calling Mom old or something. Mom didn't seem to mind it, so David didn't say anything, but not saying anything and not liking it were two different things. He watched Rosella walk in her armor over to Uncle Robert, watched her reach out with her big armored hands and take the components from Uncle Robert. She moved as easily in the suit as she would have without it, manipulated the hands and fingers of the powerful system as if they were her own. And she was proud, David could tell how proud she was of herself from the little smirk that took over her face as she held up the assembled arm-piece for Uncle Robert. "There you are, Dad. I always told you I'd be there for you in your old age."

Uncle Robert thrust his arm into the arm-piece, and Rosella snapped it into the shoulder-joint of his armor. "Thanks," he told her. "I'll let you know when I reach old age, smartass." He raised the big armored right hand of his suit and flexed the fingers into a fist. "Been a while since I've been sealed in a tin can like this, but I guess we'll do alright, between the three of us. Let's go dig out the nuke." With this, Uncle Robert slowly picked up the faceless helmet of his suit and turned to lead the rest of them to the storage building attached to the house.

"A nuke?" asked Mal, coming out of the house chewing on a piece of half-raw steak. He ate it with his hands, and blood and fat ran down his forearms. "Like a nuclear bomb? You got a fucking nuclear bomb?"

Uncle Robert paused his slow and ponderous armored steps to turn and nod at Mal. "That's right, kiddo. You didn't think we were going to just fly in there with guns blazing and hope to take out the Great Computer, did you?"

"You mentioned nuking Megadon before," David said, "but I didn't think you were serious." He couldn't imagine anyone actually using such a terrible weapon. They had, of course, been used in the past, but the thought of anyone, especially his own Uncle Robert, unleashing such massive destruction on any kind of populated area ever again was most unsettling.

"Well," said Uncle Robert. "We've got Father Brown and Cardinal Api to contend with, and however many Vigilance goons Harold has over there in Syrinx, and their more advanced weaponry, then there's the city itself. Harold's in direct control of every single system there, which could mean real trouble, some obvious traps, and some not-so-obvious. The less time we spend in Syrinx the better. We get in, drop our egg, and haul ass out before the mushroom cloud blossoms over that shit-hole."

"But all the people," David said. "There are more than Father Brown and Cardinal Api. There are people. Even the Vigilance men are real living people. If you set a nuclear weapon off in Syrinx, you'll be killing hundreds of thousands. I read it, in your How It All Happened, about what a nuke will do. You can't do that to Syrinx."

"Why not? That little prick Harold did it to every other city on the planet! Why not give him a little of what he gave us?" Uncle Robert snapped.

"Because you can't! You can't just kill all those people!" David snapped back.

Mom held up a big gray armored hand. "Hold on. David, if we don't eliminate the Great Computer, Harold wins. He's already fired on Megadon from the orbital defense satellites. We don't have a lot of time, and may not have a second chance to do this. You're right, if we destroy Syrinx, hundreds of thousands will die instantly, and more will die in hours, and more will die in days. But if we *don't* destroy Syrinx, *millions*, maybe *hundreds of millions* will die in Megadon. Do you understand that?"

"She's got a point, David," Mal added.

David felt the sun beat down on his back and shoulders, and tried to imagine that heat magnified a million times, magnified to the point where it burnt him to invisible ashes in an instant. The old Mom would never have advocated nuking anything. But the old Mom was gone, and the one he had made sense with what she said. It was still terrible, disgusting and terrible. Dad would never have gone along with it. "I understand it," he told Mom, "but it's still not right. There has to be another way."

"Okay, I'm all ears," said Mom. "What else can we do?"

David felt himself go red in the face. It wasn't fair, Mom throwing it back on him like this. He looked down at the wild grass around his feet and tried in vain to think of something, anything. "I don't know," he finally told her. "Something."

"Alright," Mom said. "There are times in life, son, when there aren't any good answers, but waiting around for those good answers to appear often causes more damage than taking imperfect alternatives." Then she looked to Uncle Robert. "Let's go," she told him.

They went into the storage building, where Uncle Robert clumsily pushed aside a stack of wooden crates so heavy it left lines of wood-shavings on the concrete floor. There was another, stack of much smaller, dark-green plastic crates behind the stack of wooden crates. "Here we are," said Uncle Robert, as he grabbed the top-most of these dark-green crates, latching onto it with unintended force, cracking the plastic where his armored fingers dug in. David cringed and drew breath, expecting to be vaporized by a flash of light and heat. Uncle Robert winked at him. "I may be a little clumsy, David, but I'm not about to blow us all to kingdom come, not yet anyway. Don't worry, you have to arm a toy like this, before it'll go off on you."

Uncle Robert carried the plastic crate outside. Rosella replaced the stack of wooden crates in the storage building. When they were all back outside again, Uncle Robert set the package down and fumbled with the silvery little latches on the sides of the crate until he was swearing again. Rosella knelt down beside him and flipped open the latches. "You want me to take the lid off?" she asked.

"I think I can manage it," Uncle Robert grumbled, and lifted the top off the crate.

Inside, there was a dark green capsule, the same color as the crate, a flat dark green, absolutely non-reflective. The capsule was no more than one third of a meter long, and maybe half as wide. It sat in a shaped nest of foam padding, also dark green.

"Why's it all green like that?" Mal asked.

"Same reason my armor is flat gray," said Uncle Robert. "Military colors from the old days. Everything was flat gray or flat green, or sometimes flat beige. Boring as hell, huh?"

"I guess," said Mal. "Probably helped blend in, helped you to sneak around, though, right?"

"Sure it did," said Mom. "This one of those Kiesler warheads?"

"Crazy Kiesler, you got it," Uncle Robert told her.

"Who's Crazy Kiesler?" David asked.

"A weapons development researcher. He took some of the principles your Uncle Billy brought back from the black hole, and applied them to tactical and strategic weapons design. This little bomb in the box here is what was known as a *variable yield* warhead. You can set the force of its explosion when you arm it.

There's a little dial inside. It can be set to take out just a couple city blocks, or to flatten an entire metropolitan area."

"And, as you can see, it's just a wee little thing," added Uncle Robert. "A single soldier could carry two or three of these things on his back. Used to be, if you wanted to generate the maximum yield this thing can put out, you'd have a warhead so big you had to carry it around on a small truck. That's why they called Kiesler crazy. Too many bombs like this one, and things could get out of control. Everybody was worried, in those days, about what they called *rogue states*, Arab countries, mostly, getting ahold of a few of these little numbers and blowing up cities in the west. Didn't really matter, of course, rogue states or not, the way Harold played things out."

"Empires fall from within," said Mal, nodding.

Everybody looked at him. "What?" asked Rosella.

Mal shrugged. "It's in all your father's books about history," he said. "the Greek city-states, the Roman Empire, the domain of Napoleon, Hitler's Europe, they all fell to shit and got stomped on because they fucked up somehow, because of stupid mistakes or fighting with themselves or just being too damned proud of themselves. Or at least that's how it looks to me, and it sounds like the United States went down for the same reason."

Uncle Robert laughed. "See, Rosella, I always told you to read more of the history and less of the trash! It's not *just about a bunch of dead people*, as you've so often put it. History is real, and it's the ongoing story of stupid humans repeating the same mistakes again and again. Everybody should know it and understand it, so the species might someday break out of the endless cycle of destructive stupidity."

David enjoyed seeing Rosella's face flush at being lectured. He could see she was searching for some kind of come-back, but Uncle Robert cut her off. "Now, let's get our asses in gear," he said, replacing the top on the crate. "Latch up the crate for me, and we'll high-tail it out to those frontier air-cars, get one in working order so we can take it to Syrinx."

They said their goodbyes, exchanged wishes of luck and urges to caution. David tried to hug his mother, but there was far too much armor in the way, so he stood on the toe of her big armored boot and stretched up to kiss her cheek instead, realizing this might be the last time he ever saw her. Mom seemed surprised and maybe bothered by the kiss, like it was something weird, like he hadn't kissed her cheek a million times before, when he was smaller. She drew back, paused, then leaned forward and kissed his forehead, as if it had only occurred to her as an afterthought. They exchanged awkward smiles, then she locked her faceless round helmet in place, and Uncle Robert and Rosella locked their helmets in place, and then the three of them lifted off, Rosella first, with the crated nuke under one arm, then Mom, Uncle Robert, slightly wobbly at first but steadier as he gained speed and altitude. Within seconds, they were miniatures over the tree-line at the far edge of the field, and a second after that they were gone. Their suits didn't have the range to carry them all the way to Megadon, so they would take a frontier air-car to within easy range of Syrinx, where they would fly in their armor to deliver the warhead.

Then hundreds of thousands would die. David still didn't like it, not one bit. He looked over at Mal. "We shouldn't be using a nuclear weapon," he said. "It makes us just as bad as Harold was."

"It will suck," Mal agreed, "but your mother put it about as right as anybody else. If they don't knock the living shit out of the Great Computer, a lot more folks'll be fucking dead, right?"

David shook his head. "It's not right. It's not fair."

"Life's not fucking fair, David. Just ask the people who got their asses killed in Athens, or in fucking Carthage. Ask the frigging German Jews."

"I don't know who any of those people are," David told him. "But it should be. It should be fair."

"They're people who lost," said Mal. "I don't want to be one of those people."

"I don't either, but you said yourself all the empires fell from within!"

"So?"

"So, if that's how empires really fall, why are we going to go blow up hundreds of thousands?"

Mal sighed. "Because Harold's not going to just fucking give up, and even if he tears his own damned empire apart with lasers from space, millions will get their asses killed! You heard your frigging mother!"

"Alright, we'll just see about that," David said, the beginnings of an idea taking root and growing in his mind. He turned and marched back to the front door of the house, then inside, then into Uncle Robert's bedroom, where he booted up the computer and logged on.

Mal followed him in. "What're you doing now? We're supposed to go meet the twelve tribes or whatever the hell they are."

"Only if my Uncle Robert and my mother don't come back." David tapped away at the keyboard and opened a network mapping utility, which began to list every node in Megadon and Syrinx.

"And Rosella," Mal added. "But what the fuck are you doing?"

"I'm going to find Harold," David told him.

"And what're you going to do, ask him to fucking surrender or some shit?"

"I don't know," said David. And he didn't. All he knew was that he had to try something. If he didn't do anything, if he didn't try to keep those hundreds of thousands from dying, and if he didn't try to keep the millions and millions from dying, then he might as well be killing them himself. David knew his father wouldn't have sat idly by and let Syrinx be nuked, and nor would he.

How It All Happened, Chapter 8

The word about me and Jimmy still being alive spread pretty quick from Buffalo. It must not have taken the local red star cell too long to find the bodies in that barn, and the bodies tied to the trees. They must have figured something was up when those assholes didn't return to base at some appointed time, because we and our group weren't a hundred miles down the road before we started hearing about the slaughter on the radio. We'd been tuned in to the One True Religion frequency since we rejoined the convoy, and we weren't two hours on our way to Utica when we started hearing jaws flapping like mad, red-robes squawking about the slaughter.

"They're dead, oh Almighty Harold bless us, Almighty Harold protect us! They're all dead! They're dead! Somebody's killed them! They're dead!" one guy kept going on.

"Legion! The hand of Legion is apparent in this! The beast stalks the land, hunting the righteous! We must be vigilant! Let all the faithful arm themselves and be vigilant, ready to show their faith by lashing out at the demonic force that roams the land!" another one went off.

It was fun, at first, listening to them freak out. I was concerned, of course, about the fact that these radio-waves were outrunning us, getting ahead of us, letting all the red-robes in New York state and beyond know that we were around, giving them the chance to get ready to attack us. But it wasn't like we hadn't been shot at before by the frigging fanatics, so I figured what the hell, and kept listening to their panicked squawking. I had half a mind to get on the airwaves myself, make some kind of demonic-voice or something, make them shit their pants, but, as much fun as that would have been, I figured it was better that we not tip our hand. Better that they didn't know we were listening in. It was bad enough that the snow had stopped falling and we were leaving a trail of very clear tracks from Buffalo, but there wasn't a whole lot we could do about that, so we just slogged on, guns loaded, eyes peeled.

It took them a while longer to find the note I'd left, then they went off exchanging wild conjectures about where I might have come from, and where I might be going next. From the sounds of these exchanges, they knew who I was, or had heard my name before. It was a little flattering, the infamy.

"Robert is the evil Lifeson, the black sheep among them," came one voice.

"He suckled at the breast of Virus when he was a child, as did his half-wit brother!" came another.

"Has anyone relayed the news to the Almighty?"

Silence on the airwaves. Then six or seven guys talking all at once, trying to get ahold of someplace or someone they called "Central Temple". They chattered like that for a while, before they petered out one by one and there was just one freaked-out voice left trying to tell Central Temple what was going on.

"Robert Lifeson and Jimmy Lifeson have killed twenty-two crusaders outside Buffalo! Repeat, the evil half of the Lifeson brothers have killed twenty-two outside Buffalo! They've left a note threatening the life of the Almighty! Do you read, Central Temple."

A pause. Then a new voice, much more calm, even-toned, in-command. Nobody I recognized, but I hadn't been hanging out in the inner circles like Mikey had been. "We read you loud and clear, and understand most of what's happened from all the uncontrolled exchanges that have taken place. Broadcasting cells, identify yourselves at this time."

A longer pause. Those "broadcasting cells" were no doubt shitting their pants. They'd probably broken some kind of protocol. Knowing that little prick Harold, he'd set up all kinds of rules and regulations on everything. All to control and control, being that kind of freak.

"Varysburg," came one of the voices.

"Elmer."

"Duells Corner."

"Colden."

"Silver Creek."

"Attica."

"Noted," said Central Temple. "Be advised the Great CPU has shared a holy vision with the Almighty. Send crusaders to look for more of Legion's foul work approximately ten miles east-northeast of the slaughter you've found in the barn. Also, it is the wish of the Almighty that you capture Robert and Jimmy Lifeson. I suggest you begin your pursuit immediately, if you haven't done so already. If those two are allowed to escape, the Almighty will be most displeased."

I sat there behind the wheel, driving and wondering what the hell this guy at Central Temple was talking about, then it hit me. Ten miles east-northeast of the slaughter in the barn, that was where we found the grisly scene of the impaled parents and handcuffed kids. That little prick was blaming that massacre on me, and it lit me up like a match held to a bone-dry haystack. That little prick was blaming his own nasty work on me! I should have seen that coming, I really should have. I often wonder how things might have worked out differently if I hadn't been so stupid and proud, if I hadn't left that note in the barn. If I hadn't left that note, they wouldn't have known it was me, and I might have been able to gather a better, stronger following and maybe I could have pushed Harold aside. As it was, I'd given him a damned scape-goat for any rotten things he wanted to do. The impalement of those parents wouldn't be the first atrocity he'd pin on me and mine. No, that little prick would make me out to be a blood-thirsty Satan before it was all done. I should have known.

"Central Temple, this is Varysburg. We're sending skiers north and south to look for a trail."

This made me smile. The fuckers were being hamstrung by their own stupid motor laws. They could have sent out a handful of snowmobiles and picked up our trail pretty damned quick, and then been on us like a pack of wolves, but they'd been forbidden to use internal combustion engines. Their loss. There were electric vehicles around, but four-wheel drive electrics were pretty damned rare, and the snow was deep enough to stop anything that didn't have a minimum of four big wheels spinning at all times.

"Central Temple, this is Attica, we too are deploying skiers."

"Silver Creek here, Central Temple. Ditto on the skiers. We have a couple dog-sleds we'll be sending out as well."

And so they sent out their cross-country skiers and packs of Huskies. No real possibility they'd find our tracks before we were long gone. I listened on, heard all their plans to vector in similar search-parties from communities throughout the state. They gave chase, and we continued to slog our way over unplowed roads, bumping along in four-wheel-drive. We kept our weapons loaded and listened out on the radio, and drove and drove.

It took them a couple hours to figure out where we were going. "All parties be advised Robert and Jimmy Lifeson are most likely en route to Utica. Repeat, they are on their way to Utica. All units coordinate to prevent Lifesons from linking up with the heretics of Utica. Prevent Lifesons from reaching Utica at all costs. Is this understood?"

"Attica, understood loud and clear."

"Ditto that, Central Temple. This is Homer, we copy and will comply."

And the acknowledgements kept rolling in from little communities all over the state. Little pockets of people who'd gone to ground on Harold's order and thereby survived the nukes. Or little pockets of people who'd gone to ground on their own and come out to find that Harold's bunch of freaks were the only ones with food and medicine and other such essentials. I had to really wonder what kinds of numbers we might be up against, how many former citizens of the state of New York had it in for us. There was enough chatter on the radio, that was for sure, as they started talking back and forth, trying to set up some kind of net between us and Utica. And a lot of the voice that came over the airwaves had that flat paramilitary tone common among cops and soldiers, which could have been ordinary folks putting on special radio-voices as they played at being red star troopers. Or it could have been real cops and soldiers, loyal to Harold's new world order. This was a real possibility; it'd been my experience that both soldiers and cops, the guys who like to play tough-man, the guys who like to carry the guns, those kinds of guys never really care too awful much just who's handing out the guns, never really care too awful much about who's handing out the badges or uniforms or marks of authority. Those kinds of guys just want to be cowboys, not the real wild sort of cowboys who make their own rules, but a lesser sort of cowboy, a tough guy sanctioned by whatever forces stand at the head of the dominant society. The cops, the soldiers, they were usually types who needed someone to define for them what was right and what was wrong, and then they needed to know for certain that they were on the side of right. They weren't seekers or experimenters in any sense, just guys who liked to play cowboy so long as someone in power was handing out the white and black hats. I'm no psychologist, nor have I ever had much respect for that field of quackery, but I bet the drive to be a well-tamed pre-fab cowboy blessed by whatever powers-that-be, I'll bet you that drive is linked somehow to getting laid. By making themselves such pre-scripted manly men of right, the cop-types and the soldier-types were basically heightenjng their appeal with the ladies. Oh, yeah, they'd sing "God Bless America" or whistle "Stars and Stripes Forever" until they were blue in the face, but it didn't mean much. When that thing called "America" died beneath the mushroom-clouds and the stars-n-stripes were traded in for banners bearing Harold's red star, a *lot* of cops and soldiers and wannabe cops and wannabe soldiers traded their loyalties just as quickly as so many others. They just weren't the types to risk being seen as outsiders. They wanted into the herd, whatever herd was dominant. You get more pussy that way, which makes me wonder why the hell I never was able to swallow the society-line and get laid as easily as the soldiers and cops, with good decent women who'd been cheerleaders in high school. I was too busy running weed and banging counter-culture chicks and Asian whores to apply for a uniform and a gun. My loss, I guess, but I wouldn't trade my checkered past for all the law-n-order in the world. Nor would I trade it for all the ex-cheerleaders in the world, either. I know my own right from my own wrong, and I don't need Harold or anybody else, no god or government, to define these areas for me, and I never will.

But I digress. We were moving toward Utica. They were trying to stop us. A lot of them sounded, to me, like soldier and/or cops. I figured we had the upper hand because we were mechanized, while they were making do with dog-sleds and cross-country skis. Plus, we knew what they were up to, because we could listen in on their plans.

The long and short of it is that they found us, or we ran into them, just outside a place the old green road-signs called Lairdsville. We knew they were somewhere in that general vicinity, because we'd heard them coordinating their movements, so-and-so go here, such-and-such over there, but by the time we got close to Utica, they'd set up a fairly comprehensive net, and I figured we'd just do our best to wiggle through. I just figured there couldn't be that many of them, or that we could simple outrun them in our trucks. I'd considered saying fuck it and not going to Utica, turning abruptly south and letting Harold's New York militia sit out in the snow waiting for us forever, but their Central Temple placed such importance on preventing me from getting to "the heretics in Utica" that there was no other place I wanted to be. If Harold didn't want me there, I was sure as shit going to get there, hell or high water.

We ran into them, like I said, outside a place called Lairdsville. I couldn't tell you exactly where. You lose track of those kinds of things, your precise exact location, when you're driving far and long. Or I do, anyway. Back before Harold's apocalypse, it wasn't uncommon, in the United States, and in other so-called civilized countries, for people to have their own little GPS. That's Global Positioning System, a tiny computer that asks satellites in space where it is. People had them built into their watches, and they were built into most every car made back in those days. This meant a lot of people could tell you their latitude and longitude, right down to fractions of a second. Crazy. Not that I myself didn't use a GPS when I used to sail, but it was crazy, the whole idea that every man, woman and child needed to know *exactly* where they were on the man-made coordinate-system that divvied the entire world up into neat little squares. What I liked about traveling, especially by car, was the way you could forget, at least temporarily, where you were. You could let your mind wander away from all your cares while your body and the big plastic or metal body around you wandered away from your home. It was good. But I guess a lot of people, before the nukes, didn't think so. They'd lost the pioneering spirit, or the drive to explore, or whatever you want to call it. The unknown was bad. Everything had to be defined, and yet there was no real comfort to be taken from all the definitions. The fast-food drive-through society that dominated much of the world before the nukes, the world where individuals were foolishly sundered from their families and loved ones by the capitalist addiction to sustained economic growth, that society wasn't an easy one in which to feel comfortable. It's tough to feel comfortable when you're basically alone. Humans, in my humble opinion, are very social apes. Probably their loneliness and fear of everything made them ripe for Harold's stupid-ass religion, but I guess I covered a lot of that in the first part of this manuscript, so I digress. I'm good at digressing. I'm stepping way outside my professed field of expertise, but there was some old moldy writer from the way-back days who said something like "The difference between a novel and a short story is meaningful digression." Not saying this is a novel, because it's not. It's a history, but you get the idea. I hope that when I go off on a seeming tangent, it's providing some kind of useful information on how things were. I guess I can always go back and edit out this kind of stuff, if the world ever gets to the point where it'd be worthwhile to go ahead and dig up a printing press and publish this history. Maybe after Harold's regime is knocked down and Megadon and Syrinx are emptied out. It's going to happen someday. I've been waiting too long for it not to happen.

Anyway, where were we when we met Harold's idiot followers outside Lairdsville? There were long sloping hills on either side of the road, the first hundred meters off each side of these hills clear of trees, but big dark stands of pines toward the tops of those hills. We were rolling through kind of a little valley, you could say. The snow on both slopes was undisturbed, not a single track on either side, nor in the middle, in the road, except for our own tracks behind us. I was in the lead truck, slogging along through the snow, and I was thinking that those long hills on each side would make pretty damned decent sledding hills. I was thinking that there probably used to be local kids who used to think the same thing. And I was thinking that a few of those local kids may have actually gone down those hills, in years past, despite warnings from their parents that those slopes were too close to the road. Kids used to do that kind of thing, court danger, especially when their parents told them not to. The kids growing up in Megadon and Syrinx now, though, they're pretty much a bunch of sheep. Yes-men and yes-women just waiting to grow up and make more of their kind. There are some more rebellious kids on the lower levels of Megadon, but they're so poorly educated and usually so poorly malnourished that they're not much good. Not like my nephew David, who's smart as a tack and, thanks to his good old Uncle Robert, not afraid to ask questions, not afraid to challenge authority. Between him and my daughter Rosella, they might get the world back in decent shape, if they're just given a chance somehow.

But there I was, driving the lead truck, and I've got a radio there in the cab with me, and there's all the sudden this hurried squawking: "I've got them! We've got them! Central Temple, we've got them!"

Now I knew it wasn't anybody in our convoy, because we were observing radio silence. It was some red star fanatic. And I knew he was talking about me and mine. I didn't know exactly where this guy was, or how many friends he had with him, but I hunkered down as low as I could in the cab of my truck and gunned that thing for all it was worth.

The window on my left shattered at the same time I heard the first shot. Then more shots, and the metal-drum sound of the fenders being bored through by lead. I swerved this way and that, not sure where the shots were coming from but wanting to make myself as tough a target as possible, and hoping the other drivers behind me would have the sense to do the same. Jimmy was four trucks back, and I knew he'd have his head screwed on straight, but there was no telling with a lot of the others I didn't know so well. It pissed me off that I was getting shot at, but it pissed me off even worse that everybody else was getting shot at. Not trying to paint myself as a saint, but there were plenty of kids in the convoy, including those whose parents had been impaled back outside Buffalo, and those kids had already been through enough. The sheer hateful asshole blind idiocy of the religious fanatics unloading their guns at us. I hated them, and wanted to kill all of them, every single last red star fanatic. It was bad enough they'd nuked everybody, but they couldn't stop at that, they had to make trouble even in the big wide-open world of the post-apocalyptic nuclear winter. Fuckheads.

I kept driving fast, not looking at the snow-covered road, but looking up the hillsides, until I saw the fuckheads, up in the tree-line, leaning on tree-trunks or kneeling down in the snow, blasting away. They were on both sides of the road, on each hill, and there were all kinds of them, so I knew it wasn't going to be easy. I looked both ahead and back, and saw more and more red robes emerging from the tree-line, and it was pretty clear we wouldn't be able to run their gauntlet without taking some pretty fucking terrible losses. So just blowing through wasn't an option. There was no room to put the trucks in a circle like in some kind of old western movie, but there was plenty of room to form the convoy up into two columns, two parallel lines, and I got on the radio, switched over to our own frequency, and told Jimmy to make it happen. I stopped on the left-hand side of the road, and my truck was hit by three times the fire it'd been catching before. Jimmy broke from the pack behind me and pulled up even with me, three meters over to the right. Me and him and Vera got out of our rides, he and she out their driver's side, and me out my passenger's side, putting the trucks between us and the incoming bullets. There was always the chance the red star fuckers had a rocket-launcher or some kind of grenades with which they could wipe us out, but that was the chance we had to take.

Another driver caught on, then another and another, and pretty soon we had our two lines, and we were pouring fire back up at the assholes who were shooting down at us. We lost five trucks from the initial attack, five vehicles steaming or burning back the way we'd come. Some of the drivers and passengers made it to our lines. Some made it out of their trucks only to be shot down. I cursed myself for a complete and utter moron for not predicting this kind of ambush the second we rolled into the little valley. I'd given Harold's goons every advantage. They mustn't have expected any kind of resistance, though. Either that or they were just too stupid to find cover, because we cut down a good ten of them right off the bat. I guess this motivated the rest of them to find tree-trunks behind which to hide, because they dug in and we had ourselves a steady back-and-forth of fire, men falling less frequently on the hills, and men and women falling less frequently on our lines. I say "men" when I mention Harold's goons because, on the red-robe side, there were only men. Harold had brought back the notion that women were the "weaker" and inferior sex, suited only for non-violent pursuits. He'd reached right back into Biblical times and dredged up that foolishness from the days of Jews wandering the desert. It had taken humanity thousands of years to reach the conclusion that men and women were basically equal, but that didn't sit well with the little shithead, no more than it had with other backwards conservatives of the pre-holocaust world, so he had all sorts of rules regarding women and so-called "decency". Women-folk weren't allowed outdoors without a good reason, and they had to wear certain types of clothes that covered their bodies just so, and, if they traveled, they were supposed to travel in the company of custodial men, their husbands or brothers or fathers. We had a few women's women in our little convoy, ladies both young and old who'd fled such gender-based tyranny in their former home-towns, and they almost never stopped talking about it, the way women were treated under the red star.

It was one of these women's women who tapped my shoulder about fifteen minutes into our dug-in fire-fight. Her name was Kelly, and she'd been monitoring one of the radios. "They have reinforcements on the way, lots of them!"

I ducked down, sat on my haunches behind my truck. Kelly ducked down with me. "What's lots? How many is lots?" I asked her.

"I don't know," she said. "A couple hundred, at least!"

"How far out? How long do we have? When will they get here?"

She shook her head. She was wearing a ball-cap, had it on backwards, and it held her hair, which was usually hanging uncombed in front of her face. I'd always assumed she was in her thirties, the way her big hips tested the sides of her jeans, but now she looked much younger, twenty, twenty-one. Her mouth was half-open and her eyes were wide. She was scared. She was scared and I didn't blame her. Sometimes I lost track of how fucked up things really were until I looked somebody else in the face. I spent too much time with Jimmy. Everything was always okay with Jimmy, and with Vera, who'd essentially removed herself from the world-that-was long before Harold had destroyed it. And I was used to living on the edge. Hell, I'd spent years running weed in a sailboat, and years after that running a business called Thailand Express, helping other would-be drug-dealers escape the electronic notice of the U.S. government and military. And before all that, and during all that, I'd been a hacker, a criminal who got his kicks wreaking mischief on information networks all over the world. The long and short of it was, I wasn't the best guy to ask if things were okay, because my idea of okay was a little fucked up. I was the son of a professional wrestler. I'd grown up with a genius and a retard as my older brothers and role-models, and with a boy-scout as a little brother, little Mikey always running around behind me, always asking me why I did this and why I did that, almost like he was morally superior from the get-go, almost like he wasn't questioning my actions so much as my motives. Hell, the only woman I'd ever really fallen for was an under-aged hooker knocked up with some other guy's kid. So yeah, my perspective has never really been one shared by a whole lot of people. So sometimes it hit me, how fucked up things were, sometimes it hit me only when I saw it in somebody else's face. Kelly's face, as she tried to explain to me what she'd heard on the radio, so many red-robes cross-country skiing from one place, so many snow-shoeing from another place, more riding dog-sleds from yet another place, all of these adherents of Harold's fucked up religion converging on this little valley where we were already pinned down by the numbers who'd ambushed us from both sides.

"I don't know," Kelly said again. "I just don't know. There's got to be hundreds of them up there already, and if hundreds more get here, I don't know."

But she did know. And I knew too. I knew we were kind of fucked, and I knew, looking at her, how fucked up it all was. *Nuclear winter*, I thought. The term just jumped into my head. This was *nuclear winter*, and it would be for some time, because there had been a *nuclear war*, but not just any old nuclear war begun by the U.S. and Russia, like they used to tell us would happen. No, this one hadn't even been between the U.S. and *rogue states*. This one had been Harold's nuclear war. In one fell swoop, that little pig-fucker had outdone every other mass-murderer who'd come before. He'd outdone Hitler, and Stalin, and all the Roman Caesars. Harold Gates was the single greatest killer of all time, and yet me and my meager few free-thinkers, we were surrounded by hundreds who were ready to kill even more for the little prick. And there were hundreds more on the way. Maybe even hundreds and hundreds, because people were such weak-willed unquestioning sheep. Harold and Central Temple said I was evil, so that was that, I was evil. I shouldn't have been surprised, because that was how things had been for a long time. That was how these people had been trained to think (or not) by the system that preceded Harold. Capitalism works best when people do not question. When they don't question perceived need and therefore consume and consume whatever it is that's selling. Thinking is hard. Making real connections, intellectually or emotionally with others, is hard. Buying is easy, and leads to more buying, and so on and so forth. I got up and pointed the snout of my weapon up the hill. I sighted in on the exposed red shoulder of a goon behind a tree. I breathed deep, squeezed the trigger, and he fell.

But still there were a hundred or more left, and hundreds more on the way. Hundreds and hundreds, even after a nuclear holocaust. It didn't make the event any less horrific, because billions had been killed, but it made me think of just how many people there must have been before. It made that number of billions on billions that much more real, to know there were still hundreds around in any given area like this one, where we fought for our lives. Amazing. I saw another red-robed body partial exposed behind another tree-trunk and once more took aim.

I was about to fire when Kelly tapped my shoulder again and threw me off. "What?" I asked her.

"Well, what are we going to do?" she whined. Not that I blamed her. This was a sticky situation I'd gotten us into. I shouldn't have left that note back in that barn. I shouldn't have wandered so easily into such an obvious ambush. I shouldn't have stopped and formed these lines. We should have run the gauntlet, because I should have known that, in any kind of entrenched fighting like this, it would come down to a battle of attrition, and that the side with the most people would win. And if Harold's reinforcements showed up with rocket-launchers or enough grenades, it wouldn't even be a battle of attrition. It would be them blow-ing us all to hell and laughing about it. This, all of it, reminded me more than ever that I was no real military mind. I was a better tactician than your average housewife or life insurance salesman, and I'd worked enough against the U.S. military to know a thing or two, but a real military mind wouldn't have gotten this bunch of people into such a sorry jam. Then again, a real military mind might not have bothered shepherding so many women and children through the barren wastes of nuclear winter. Then again, those women and children might have been better off back where they'd come from than they were in this place where I'd brought them.

Kelly was still standing there, waiting for me to tell her what we should do, but I didn't know any more than she did. We could stand and fight, which meant we'd eventually be overwhelmed, or we could get in the trucks and try to make it out, and be cut to pieces as we did so. The red-robe reinforcements were closing in from the back and front, so chances were we wouldn't make it far before being ambushed again, and facing the same situation we faced now. Then there was the question of how many trucks would actually start, now that they'd been used as bullet-stops for a solid twenty-minutes. And if some trucks didn't start, who got left behind? It was a real nasty situation and I didn't have an answer for this girl or anybody else, and it made me feel like shit. I thought about it, and thought about it, the bullets cutting the air all around me, and I finally told her we'd all fire like hell into the hills on both sides, hope to thin out the red-robes or maybe scare them off, then we'd jump in the trucks and go for all we were worth.

She looked at me, continued to stare, scared. "A lot of the trucks are leaking fuel and oil and coolant!" she told me. "What if they won't start?"

"Well," I asked her. "You got any better ideas?"

She didn't, and I sure as hell didn't. So she went off, spread the word about the ingenious plan. It wasn't long before Jimmy came over to me, leaned on my truck and started shooting up at the trees. "That's a stupid Plan, Robert," he said. "You're going to get us all killed, if we break up these lines now."

"I know!" I shouted at him. "Why'd you let me form these goddam lines anyway?!"

"I thought you thought of something better, when you did it," he said, switching out his spent magazine for a fresh one.

"Well I didn't!"

We both shot at whatever stray scraps of red we saw. "We're going to get killed," Jimmy said again. Not angry or resentful. That wouldn't have been Jimmy. He said it like he would have said "It's a nice day." Or "Your shoe is untied." And that was about it. We were going to die, either where we were between those lines, or trying to make a run out of there. We were going to die.

I shot and shot, sometimes at real targets, sometimes at nothing at all. I ran through three magazines and then signaled Jimmy and Vera and Kelly and every-body else, and I yanked open the passenger-side door of my truck.

The red-robed goons on the hillsides saw us loading up and they got brave, coming out from their cover further than they'd dared before. They came out and unloaded on us like they hadn't unloaded on us since they first sprang their ambush.

People died trying to get into their trucks. People died in their trucks before they could try to start them. And when I say people, I mean men and women and even little kids, turned into meat by the impact of high velocity bullets. Then there were those who weren't killed, but merely gutted by a slug, or had a leg shattered. This was worse than the people dying, because those who died just died. The wounded screamed. Men and women and little kids screaming, shriek-ing.

There was nothing I could do. Or at least nothing I knew to do. I yanked open the passenger-side door of my truck and was about to jump up onto and across the seat, ready to get pegged like everybody else who hadn't already been hit. We were going to die, we were all going to die, and it was all my fault.

The hills on both sides erupted in low, puffy white clouds. It was snow, thrown up into the air, all kinds of snow tossed up from the ground, from thick white blanket to fine white powder that obscured all the tree-trunks and all the red-robes on both slopes. There used to be things called snow-globes, little clear plastic or sometimes glass spheres, filled with water and white flakes of plastic, with little dioramas inside, cities or characters molded out of even more plastic. You'd shake the snow-globe, and the white plastic flakes would fly all around inside, making it look as if it was snowing hard inside, partially hiding the diorama. The scene on either slope was like that, a real winter-wonderland, but so thick it looked as if a thousand bags of powdered sugar had been dropped from a height of five thousand meters. There was a sound with all of this flying snow, a sizzling sound, coming from the skies. This sound was my only indication that this latest spectacle was being directed from above.

I looked up, and what I saw were people, flying. Or that's how the suits looked silhouetted against the pale gray sky. Just human figures, hanging there in the air, ten or twelve of them. And this was the first time I ever saw Vulcan Per-sonal Combat Armor live and in-person. I'd seen it on TV, like a lot of other peo-ple, seen it touted on the news as the latest in urban combat armor, seen the brief and usually blurry (probably purposely blurry; specially edited to obscure top secret details) clips of humanoid figures swooping down on hostage situations or against "terrorist" strongholds. I'd heard all the not-secret specs on the thrill-o'clock news, that each one of the "amazing technological marvels" could belt out more firepower than any three old-fashioned tanks; that they could travel at so many hundreds of kilometers per hour, that they could withstand incredible punishment; that weapons-loads could be customized to fit different combat scenarios. All that, and here they were, a whole frigging squadron of Vulcans hanging over the shot-up remains of my little convoy. A whole squadron of flying suits of armor hovering there, hosing down the hills on both sides, slaughtering the red-robes who'd vanished in all the snow thrown up by so much lead, or whatever it was those Vulcans were firing. The spray was so thick and constant that trees fell, their trunks cut clean through. Wood chips and pine-needles and amputated branches thickened the snowy haze, as did a pink stain, blood that made the earth-bound clouds of snow look like cotton candy.

"Look at that!" said Jimmy. "They shot them! They shot them all up good!"

"Hell yes they did," I told him, hoping like hell that we weren't next. We didn't have any weapons capable of knocking out one of those Vulcan suits. No way.

"Hey Vera!" Jimmy called over his shoulder. "Look at them! Look at them shoot them up good! Hey Vera!"

The spray of death from above ended as quickly as it had begun, and the blood-flavored snow began to settle on the hillsides. I stayed low, behind my truck, and kept one eye on the hills, and one eye on the Vulcans. No living thing moved on either slope. In the sky above us, the suits just hung there, hovering, still. It was un-nerving, waiting for them to do whatever it was they were going to do. I was real grateful they'd taken out all those red-robes, but it'd been my experience that there's no such thing as a free lunch. Nobody did nothing for nothing, so even if we weren't next on the Vulcan hit-list, there would certainly be some kind of price to pay for our rescue, and I was loathe to learn just what these flying freaks wanted in exchange for saving all our lives.

So I'm pondering this likely dilemma when I hear Jimmy scream bloody murder, like somebody's jabbed a red-hot poker into his nuts, this fucking animal bellow of pain and rage, like something you'd hear in a horror-flick about demons escaped from hell. I knew it was Jimmy before I turned to look. I'd never in my life heard sounds like that come out of my retard brother, but it was his voice, just twisted, louder and deeper than he'd ever hollered about anything before. It was fucking chilling, and I knew for sure that Jimmy'd been hit by a stray round, hit in the goddam knee-cap or even worse. I turn, and there he is on the ground, by the other line of trucks, beside the rig he and Vera had been driving, he's kneeling there and he's all fucking covered with gore.

He's holding Vera, and he's shaking her while he's screaming. There are tears running down his cheeks. Vera is dead, torn wide open by one of more shots to her midsection. Jimmy's shaking her and then hugging her, shaking her and then hugging her, howling like a madman. Vera's just flopping this way and that, depending on which way he pushes or pulls her. Her head flops forward and blood spills out onto Jimmy's chin and down his chest. Her head flops backward and her guts squish against Jimmy's belly.

I went over to him, and I put my hand on his shoulder, but he lashed out, just swung his arm straight back at me and nailed me in the thigh with his elbow. I gritted my teeth against the pain and tried to be thankful he hadn't nailed me in the balls, and I backed off. I figured I'd let him get his screaming all out before I tried again to lend him any kind of sympathy.

One of the Vulcans picked this time to descend. The suit cut a half-circle around our lines as it came down, and the big heavy boots touched down not three meters from where I stood. The little jets on the back of the armor threw up a small flurry of loose snow before they cut out. And there I was, standing there, looking at this monstrous plastaegis and metal beast. I was looking it in the face, but the helmets on those things don't have any real face. Just a smooth surface and all kinds of hidden sensors, camera, infrared and ultralight sighting systems, sonar, you name it. No need for a see-through face-plate on something like that. The whole suit is painted flat battleship gray, with a little red-white-and-blue eagle insignia on each shoulder. Regiment, battalion, squadron and individual unit numbers in dull black on the chest-plate. And a rank and name: "Col. Mitchell".

Jimmy's still screaming bloody murder behind me. The Vulcan in front of me, the name of which is apparently Colonel Mitchell, it emits this sharp short hissing sound as it depressurizes, and the two big armored hands reach up to pull off the helmet. The guy inside looks like somebody from a military movie, so much the stereotype of the hard-bitten career combat officer that I wonder who's putting me on. Buzz-cut salt-and-pepper hair, hard angular face with a jagged white scar down one cheek, and a sneer on his puss like he'd been weened on a sour pickle. I didn't like him. I didn't know him from a hole in the ground, but I'd been exposed to and opposed by enough of these wind-up G.I. Joe-types to know just what was running through his spit-polished rule-bound walnut-sized mind.

"Colonel Hatch Mitchell," he said. "You must be Lifeson."

"Robert," I nodded. The idea of shaking hands with one of those big mechanical mitts he had on was simply absurd, so I was a little relieved when he kept his hands at his sides.

"Got yourself into quite the mess, didn't you?" he said.

"Yes indeedy," I told him. "Thanks for saving our bacon, chief."

"Verraaaaah!" Jimmy screamed, once, twice, three times, shaking her body more violently than before.

"My brother Jimmy," I told the Colonel.

He gave a curt nod. "I suggest you get your people moving," he said, chewing off each word with that abrupt military-speak that just oozes asshole machismo. "There are more red star militia convening on this location. We'll escort you to our base, where we can discuss your status." It was pretty clear this wasn't so much an offer as an order, the way he snapped on his helmet without another word and went skyward again, to take his place in formation where the other Vulcans hovered, waiting. They waited for us to get our shit together, and we picked up our wounded and dead and piled into those trucks that would start. We had to leave some stuff behind, luxury items mostly; I myself had to abandon a couple cases of Scotch whisky, for example. Then, when we were ready to roll out, the Vulcans switched up their formation, three leading the way, three above and behind our torn-up convoy. The remaining Vulcans roamed on either side. I drove the lead truck, and followed the three suits that were out in front.

I shared the cab with Jimmy and Vera. He'd refused to get in the truck without her.

"Jimmy, I'm sorry," I'd told him, "but she's gone."

"She's not gone! She's right here! She's right here and I'm not going anywhere without her!"

So she sat propped up on the seat between us. Most of the blood had run out of her, so she didn't make too bad a mess, sitting there. I realize I may come off as sounding rather cold, talking about Vera like this, so let me put it straight: I was sad and angry, downright pissed-off, that she'd been potted by one of those red-robed morons. It wasn't right, that she'd get it like that, in the last few minutes of the fire-fight, before the flying cavalry showed up on the scene. I would have given my left nut to bring her back, not just for her own sake, but for Jimmy. I'd never seen him such a wreck. Jimmy wasn't supposed to be sad and angry. Those emotions were for me. Jimmy was supposed to be the happy retard who never let anything bother him. Jimmy was supposed to be a constant, an emotional and physical constant, always strong, always there. The Jimmy who'd protected Mikey and me from the bullies at school, the Jimmy who'd rescued my ass from that table where Harold's goons had been torturing me to death. Seeing Jimmy all torn up like he was, the way he kept rocking back and forth on the seat of that truck, the way he kept groaning, the tears running down his face as he held Vera's lifeless hand. The way he reached over with his other hand and kept stroking her hair. Seeing Jimmy like that, it was proof that the world real had gone completely fucking insane. Harold had unleashed the nukes, and okay, civilization as we knew it had come to an end, yeah, sure, but that *and* Jimmy breaking up, it was almost too much. I knew how the others felt, the other survivors in the convoy. I understood that look of fear that I'd seen on Kelly's face, and on so many other faces, but now I understood it from the inside. Nothing was right, and it probably wouldn't be right ever again. I felt far away, worlds distant from even the steering wheel I held in my hands, like everything was about to start slipping sideways.

So I did what everybody else in the convoy had been doing for a while now. I drove. I drove the lead truck after the Vulcans and I tried to ignore the corpse on the seat beside me, tried to ignore my brother so lovingly petting death. Sounds dramatic, I know, but that was about it, that about describes the crystallization of the moment, like when the nukes were in the air and that retired Army general on MSNBC was going on about the superiority of the American nukes, and he said "…that's all there is to it." And then the world ended. Maybe there really is no telling how it felt, to live through those times, except to relate it as a series of crystallized moments like that. I'm probably rambling far too much, old man that I am, but only because I'm trying to bring it real for you. I'm probably just trying too hard.

We let the Vulcans escort us to what appeared, at first glance, to be a massive multi-tiered warehouse, the kind of nameless and windowless place you used to see when driving on the interstate through a seemingly unpopulated countryside. The kind of big concrete box that would emerge from the trees and then get tucked away again as you sped past at one hundred or one hundred twenty kilometers per hour. It was what used to be an eminently forgettable building, bigness its primary feature. The kind of place you'd define without reason or knowing as a shipping depot or a storage facility, when it could just as well have been home to a three-ring circus or a post-modern sculpture that challenged the notion of scale. Big, gray, concrete box.

There were red-robes, dead ones, littered all around as we approached the big box. Some frozen stiff, partially covered in snow. Some more recently dead, their blood still as red as their robes, rather than rust-colored and old. Hundreds of dead red-robes, some simply gun-shot, some torn apart as if by explosions. Harold had wanted into the big gray box, but he hadn't succeeded, not yet anyway. It was a welcome distraction from my own gloomy outlook, seeing those bodies. It gave me more hope that we might have found allies in these folks who had saved us from the ambush in the little valley. Maybe it was going to be alright. Maybe we could team up and take out Harold and all his fanatic followers, make a new and improved world from the ashes of the last. I was riding with a corpse, but maybe this was as bad as it would get.

Chain-link fence surrounded the massive building. This fence was topped by rolls of nasty-looking razor-wire, on which hung three or four red-robes who must have been caught while trying to get over the top. The fence was breached here and there, ripped open as if by blasts in some places, and snipped open as if by wire-cutters in other places. It was beyond me, how Harold's forces could have gotten so close to the place, that they could have made it as far as the fence, with so many sets of Vulcan Personal Combat Armor to protect perimeter. But they'd gotten pretty close, close enough to damage the fence, close enough to die draped over the razor-wire.

A double-gate opened before us, and we drove through. All but one of the Vulcans descended out of sight onto or into the roof of the big building. The one that remained guided us to a large heavily-armored roll-up door built into the side of the big gray box, at the top of a concrete ramp. The door eased up and open, and we followed the last Vulcan into one end of a big hangar-like place, where six big ungainly-looking troop-transport hovercraft sat parked in a neat row at the far end of the gigantic chamber. They were painted a flat battleship gray, and their front ends were complete with chin-blisters packing twin machine-guns. Each one of these hovercraft looked like a big dark gray toad, a line of six big dark gray toads staring at my little convoy as we pulled in and the roll-up door rolled down behind us, shutting us in. These were the types of hovercraft destined to become frontier air-cars in the dark years that would follow. Faster than any troop-transport equipped with wheels or tracks, the hovercraft were cheaper and easier to operate than helicopters, and they'd been commonly used by the U.S. Navy, Army and Marines for at least a decade. The common soldier-slang name for the things was "fan" or "fan-box" because of the large turbo-fans attached to the sides for forward-motion, and the even large turbo-fans affixed to the underbelly for lift.

I parked my truck where I was told, and the drivers behind me followed suit. We'd obviously been brought to some kind of military-base, probably the U.S.

Army special-weapons storage facility we'd learned of back at that barn where I'd left Harold that stupid note.

I turned off my engine and made to get out of my truck, but the Vulcan left to babysit us told me, through his suit's loud-speaker, to "remain in your vehicle!" And so I waited, with Jimmy and Vera. It wasn't so cold in the hangar as it had been outside. Certainly at least some ten degrees above freezing. I'd refrained from turning the heat on in the truck during our drive, keeping it chilly for Vera's sake, but there wasn't much I could do about the temperature in the ware-house. I knew it would be a while, before she started to smell, but I had no idea how long I'd have to share the cab with her. It was time to try talking to Jimmy again.

"Uh, Jimmy?"

He just kept rocking in his seat, hold Vera's hand and stroking her hair.

"Jimmy, listen to me. I think Vera wants a rest."

He turned his head and glared at me. "No she doesn't!"

"Jimmy, you remember when Dad had his accident, and he wanted to rest. This is like that."

"I know she's dead, Robert! I'm not stupid!"

"Okay, well, you can't keep her around forever! She'll start falling apart!"

"Don't say that!"

"You know it's true!"

"Don't say it!"

"Okay, I won't, but you know it's true! You want to see her falling all apart?"

"Shut up! You shut up Robert!"

"I think she'd rather rest than fall all apart, Jimmy."

He faced forward, then stared at Vera, squeezed her hand, put his other arm around her shoulder. "Not yet," he whispered. "Not yet."

I nodded, looked away, looked out at the hovercraft, giving my brother as much space and privacy as I could for his mourning. I looked away and thought of all the different ways I wanted to kill Harold. Then, as I'm sitting there think-ing black death for the little prick, this kind of dread comes over me, almost like a claustrophobia. I look back at the armored roll-up door, now closed tight, and I look at the too-solid concrete walls all around and, despite the size of the gigantic hangar I'm in, I feel trapped. Because I am trapped. The lone Vulcan here in the hangar with me, he's got enough firepower to wipe out me and all of mine. He, and Colonel Hatch Mitchell, and the rest of them, they are our captors. My cap-tors. The presence of their force is the threat of their force, and it is with this threat that they're holding us here. I couldn't get out of the hangar if I wanted to.

And it bugged me. It more than bugged me. It was driving me a little nuts, my mind racing around in my skull like a gerbil on a wheel, looking for some way out before these people did whatever they planned to do to me. I was literally sweating, sitting there behind the wheel of my silent truck. I was sweating and my hands had started to shake, just a little, but they were shaking and I couldn't make them stop. I realized I was biting the inside of my bottom lip. I tasted blood in my mouth. I sat there for a while, maybe an hour, just quietly freaking out. It wasn't until Jimmy sniffed and wiped his nose on his sleeve and said "Vera wants to rest," that I snapped out of it, came back to myself and realized just what a nut-case I'd become.

"We'll find her a good place to rest," I told Jimmy, the words coming out with a slight quiver I hoped he wouldn't notice. I sat there wondering what the hell was wrong with me, why I was losing it so badly for no good reason, and it finally occurred to me that I was freaking out because I didn't want to be tortured again like I'd been tortured by Harold's goons back in Portland. Being held against my will was my new and until-now unsuspected number-one fear. Capturophobia. The rejuvenation I'd gotten from Doctor Hofferman had fixed up my body, made me young and restored my vim and vigor to the point where I'd been able to tuck most of the negative experience into the darker recesses of my mind. But now, having been made more-or-less a prisoner again, it was all coming back. Or that's my best assessment, my best amateur psychological diagnosis of what was going on. Alright, I thought, you know what the problem is, so get over it, I told myself, but it wasn't that easy. I couldn't just get over it, not by just sitting there anyway. I needed to do something, or I was going to spontaneously combust, sitting there behind the wheel of that truck.

I reached down to my belt and unlatched the holster of my revolver, the big stainless steel three-fifty-seven, one of the four that we Lifeson brothers treated like family heirlooms. I wrapped my hand around the grip and eased that heavy pistol free of its holster. Then, with my gun in my lap, I opened the door of my truck, all the way open, letting it swung wide.

"Remain in your vehicle!" came the voice from the loud-speaker on the Vulcan, who took a couple steps in my direction, his massive boots thudding down with each stride.

"I'm tired of *remaining in my vehicle*!" I told him, lowering myself from the cab of the truck to the concrete floor, holding the three-fifty-seven aimed at my side, barrel aimed down at the floor.

"My orders are to keep you all in your vehicles!" said the Vulcan.

"I don't care about your orders, I'm tired of sitting. We're not your prisoners."

He must have noticed the pistol then. "Put the weapon away! It won't do you any good against this armor! Put the weapon away and return to your vehicle!"

"I'd rather not," I told him.

"This is your last warning! Return to your vehicle!"

"Or what?" I shouted back at him. I raised the pistol and pressed the business-end to my temple. "Or what?" I shouted again. "You'll kill me?"

Silence from the Vulcan. A collection of muted exclamations from the remains of my convoy.

"What're you doing, Robert?" shouted Jimmy, leaning out the passenger window of my truck. "Don't shoot yourself in the head, Robert! You'd die if you did that! It'd kill you dead!"

"It's under control Jimmy, you stay with Vera," I told him. "Hey, tin-man!" I yelled at the Vulcan. "Why don't you get your Colonel Mitchell out here so we can all have a nice chat? Get him up here or I'll blow my own goddam brains out all over your hangar!"

Nothing from the suit of armor. I figured he was already talking to somebody on his comm-link. Either that or he was sighting in some kind of weapon, sighting in on my pistol, or sighting in on my forehead. Or maybe he'd fallen asleep in there. There was no way to tell. He could have been dead inside that suit, for all I knew. But I stood my ground, holding myself hostage, waiting for my demands to be met. It was a crazy-ass thing to do, to point that gun at my own head, but it was all I had at the moment. And it eased the madness I felt at being taken captive. I was in charge again. Even if it meant killing myself, I was in charge. Better to take myself captive than let somebody else do the same. I figured they wanted me alive for something, or they wouldn't have saved us from that ambush, and this made my life a decent stake with which to gamble.

The Vulcan in the hangar remained silent and still. Everybody was pretty much silent and still, until Mitchell showed up. He came through a steel interior door on one side of the hangar. He was a compact man, without his Personal Combat Armor, a rather short guy, really, but taut, the way he held himself in his dark blue fatigues, the way he clipped across the hangar toward me with quick even strides. It was like he was a little machine, driven by a carefully controlled collection of mechanical tensions. Behind him came two other guys, big beefy military buzz-cut types with their chests all puffed out and their shoulders thrown back. None of these three seemed to be armed. I figured they didn't see the need, with the one Vulcan still there in the hangar.

Mitchell was smiling and shaking his head when he snapped to a stop about a meter in front of me. "So, everything I've heard about Robert Lifeson is true," he chuckled. "I was beginning to wonder, after you walked right into that ambush out there, but I suppose we all have our lesser moments."

"English, please," I told him, still holding the gun to my head.

"You're a wild one, an unconventional thinker, a real rebel," he said. "I think we'll get along just fine, once you stand down and put that pistol back in its holster."

"We're not your prisoners," I told him.

He shook his head. "I didn't mean to give you that impression. We just didn't need your people wandering around our little base here before we'd had a chance to talk."

"Well," I said, "we're talking."

He sighed. "It'd be easier if you put the weapon down, don't you think?"

I lowered my gun. "Alright, what do you want to talk about?"

He nodded, smiled. "Joining forces. Against Harold Gates and all his miserable ilk."

I nodded back. "Ilk. It's been a while since I've heard anybody use that word in conversation."

"A man's conversation is only as good as his vocabulary," he told me. "Will you join me in my conference room, where we can further discuss our mutual enemy and develop a plan for achieving our mutual goal?" He gestured back toward the door from which he'd come. And there was something atypical in his gesture. It was far too fluid a movement from such a tense military-man. Same with the way he talked, different from the way he'd talked during our brief exchange outside. Too fancy, like he was putting on airs or something.

"What about my people?" I asked him. "We've got dead to take care of, and wounded."

"Forgive me. I should have considered these factors earlier, but after the excitement of combat, I sometimes do not think so clearly as I should. I will send corpsmen to assist the wounded, and will dispatch others to help cut graves in the frozen ground for your dead."

Sounded fair enough, except again, the way he talked. No military man I'd ever run into would have said "the excitement of combat". They would have said "the rush of combat" or "the heat of battle". "Excitement of combat" just didn't sound right. But it was no big deal. I put Jimmy in charge of the others, telling him that if I wasn't back in an hour, he was to take everybody and try to get the hell away. Then I followed Mitchell through that interior door.

A short hallway, then another door, and a set of steps, a long set of steps, down and down and down until I was certain we had to be beneath the surface. "Most of our compound is underground," Mitchell said without turning. His voice echoed off the bare concrete and steel. "Not a bad place to be, considering how everything's turned out."

"Not a bad place at all," I told him. "We held out underground too. The way we've been attacked lately, I wonder if we shouldn't have stayed there. We're pretty popular with the One True Religion folks right now."

"I know. We've been monitoring their transmissions for some time now. You're a person of great interest to them. They raided your buried trailer-park not one week after you'd abandoned it."

"You caught radio signal from clear up in Houlton?" I asked.

He chuckled. "You'd be surprised what we can pick up. We still have active connections with satellites."

"I figured the pulse of all the explosions would have fucked up most of that."

"Some of it." We stepped down onto a landing that had to be ten stories underground. The steps kept on descending, but Mitchell stopped and pressed his hand to a reader next to one of two heavy doors. The reader made a polite beep, and the door unlocked with a click. "But there were enough redundant systems to keep us in pretty decent shape. So we followed the ongoing saga of Robert Lifeson and his brother Jimmy as they scoured the country-side looking for people to save."

He lead us into a dimly-lit conference-room. Two lieutenants in blue fatigues stood up from their chairs on opposite sides of a long black table and snapped to attention. "Colonel," they both said.

"Gentlemen," said Mitchell, "this is Robert Lifeson, star of the little drama we've been following. His people are in the hangar upstairs and require medical attention, as well as some assistance burying their dead. Please send up men to fulfill these needs, and find Captain Halsey, send him here."

The lieutenants nodded in my direction. "Honored, sir," said one, while the other scooped up a handful of printed charts and diagrams. I nodded back, and those two left through another door at the far end of the room.

"Won't you have seat?" Mitchell said, taking the place at the head of the table.

I took a chair on one side of the table, so we were sitting at right angles. "Quite the place you have here. Is this typical of how the military's survived the nuclear assaults?" I asked him.

He shook his head. "I'm afraid not. We're a little unique. We've always been a little unique, here at Camp Gladiator."

Mitchell looked at me, as if searching for some sign that I might recognize the name and significance of his installation, but I'd never heard of a Camp Gladiator. Didn't surprise me, really. So far as I knew, the Vulcan Personal Combat Armor was some of the latest and greatest military technology going, developed using some of the arcane knowledge Billy had brought back from Cygnus X-1. It was to be expected that the government would have kept a place like this under pretty tight wraps, hidden so far out in the country beneath such a featureless box of a building. I gave Mitchell my best blank look, shrugged. "You telling me you survived because you're so far underground?" I asked him. "I thought there were a lot of underground bases, like that big Air Force place under the mountain in Colorado."

"There are, or there were," Mitchell nodded. "But you must understand that the military mind exists to serve. There's a certain degree of the sado-masochist in every soldier. He, or she, wants to dominate others, while being dominated himself, or herself."

"Following orders," I said, "orders that, in time of conflict, are orders to kill people."

"That's right." He paused, drummed the fingers of his right hand on the table. "Now, with the dissolution, or destruction of the United States Federal Government, there was, of course, a break-down in the larger chain-of-command. The president and certain key politicians in the line of succession to the presidency, they were supposed to have been spirited off to airborne or underground shelters."

"But it didn't work that way?" I guessed.

Again, he nodded. "It didn't work that way. A number of politicians and senior military staffers seem to have cut secret deals with one another, as the possibility of a nuclear conflict raced closer and closer to becoming a reality. Republicans and democrats vied for positions in shelters, making generous promises to senior military officials, who, in turn, made promises to their fellows, all of it under the table, all these high-level conspiracies for one group or another to survive the coming conflict."

"So when it came time to spirit the president and the key people away to shelter, things went to shit?" I guessed.

"Something like that. As all those high-level deals were made in secret, there was, of course, some confusion, when the missiles were in the air. Twenty minutes should have been plenty of time to get the key people airborne and moving at mach three, but it didn't work out that way. The telecommunications traffic we picked up, in those last few minutes, revealed just what a twisted web had been woven by all those rich and powerful men and women. Senators and congress-people waiting in vain for their rescues, while the generals and admirals who'd promised to put them first waited in vain for their own rescues. Pilots fueled up and ready on the runways waiting for cars that would never arrive, or receiving orders to be in ten or twelve places at once."

"Sounds like a real cluster-fuck," I told him. "Any government or big brass make it out?"

He pursed his lips, drummed his fingers on the table again. "Yes. An elected official named Keegan." Again, Mitchell looked at me, the same way he'd looked at me when he'd said *Camp Gladiator*. He was searching for some hint of recognition on my face.

And he got it. I must have looked like I'd just sucked on a lemon. "That fucking asshole," I grumbled.

Mitchell smiled. "I thought we might share the same feelings about Mister Keegan."

"If the feeling you're talking about is hatred, or loathing, or a combination of the two, you're right on," I told him.

"Then I'm right on," said Mitchell. "Keegan has been in league with Harold Gates for some time now, you know."

"I know."

"Alright, then. Shall we combine our efforts to put an end to this terrible game Mister Gates and Mister Keegan have been playing with all of humanity?" he asked.

"I don't know," I told him. "You still haven't explained about the whole military situation. What about the other underground bases?" I was hoping he'd come out and tell me something like he was the ranking officer in all of what remained of the U.S. military, that he had at his disposal whatever we needed to take out Harold and all his goons.

"Some bases survived relatively unscathed, as this one did," he said. "But let me return to the nature of the military mind."

"The need to serve?" I reminded him.

"Yes, the need to serve while being authorized to subjugate others—"

"The surviving military units signed up under Harold's banner, as he and his outfit are the only authority left."

"Correct. You're quick."

I shrugged. "I'd thought about it before. Cops will be cops, soldiers will be soldiers, they just want their guns and the permission to use them. If they were free-thinkers, they wouldn't be cops, they wouldn't be soldiers. So what's your story?"

Mitchell paused. "We are...an *elite* corp, a bit *different* from others. As I said, *unique*. I hand-picked every man and woman in my specialized force. We handled *unique* situations, counter-terrorism, counter-intelligence, high-firepower micro-duration covert forays into what used to be allied, neutral, and enemy territories. We were the *special* Special Forces, a step beyond. Expendable, non-existent, but extremely potent, extremely effective."

"So your *esprit d'corps* is what held you together when all the other surviving military folks went over to the red star?" I asked him.

He coughed. "You could say that."

The door at the far end of the room opened. Another man in blue fatigues, another compact man, a black guy whose movements were as quick and tense as those of Colonel Mitchell. This new guy wore captain's bars and carried a laptop under one arm. He nodded at Mitchell, then smiled at me. "So you must be Robert Lifeson," he said, pacing over to shake my hand.

"That's me," I told him.

"Robert," said Mitchell, "this is Captain Halsey, my second in command, and most trusted advisor."

"Alright," I said.

Halsey leaned over Mitchell to put the laptop down on the table. He opened it, turned it on, then put a hand on Mitchell's shoulder. "I loaded up the maps you wanted him to see," Halsey told Mitchell.

"Thanks," said Mitchell. Then he reached up and put his hand on top of Halsey's. It was a weird gesture, one I hadn't expected, and my first thought was that the two were about to put on a display of some kind of hand-to-hand combat, some kind of fierce judo. But that wasn't it. Mitchell put his hand on top of Halsey's and let it rest there, then gently pet the other man's fingers. Then Mitchell gave me that look again, searching for some hint of recognition.

I looked away, first at the table, then at the wall. I'd never been a homophobe, but damned if I can say I was comfortable sharing a room ten stories underground and a million miles from nowhere with two guys holding hands.

"I think Mister Lifeson may have caught on to what makes us unique," said Halsey.

"I hope this won't pose a problem, Robert," said Mitchell. "We don't force ourselves on others, but we thought it would be wrong to keep it from you, if we're to form an alliance based on trust."

I took a breath, nodded, looked back at Mitchell. "So, you're *all* gay?" I asked him.

"Don't ask, don't tell," chuckled Halsey.

"Just the men," said Mitchell. "The women are lesbians."

"Yeah, yeah," I told him. "Spare me the semantics. But that's why *Camp Gladiator*" now that I had a better understanding of Mitchell and his men, the name made more sense, "hasn't gone over to Harold? Because he wouldn't take you?"

Mitchell shook his head. "We wouldn't want anything to do with him if we did. Men like him have despised and degraded, tortured and killed our kind throughout all of history. Religious fanatics have hated homosexuals almost as long as homosexuals have been great warriors. The Greeks, the Romans, the greatest ancient civilizations had elite units composed only of gay men, you know."

"I know," I told him. "And I'm alright with it." And I was. Then I thought about Jimmy. "Just don't be surprised if my brother asks a lot of what seem like stupid or rude questions. He means well, but he's retarded."

"We know," smiled Mitchell. "And we're alright with it."

"Okay, so why do you need me?" I asked, leaning back in my chair.

"Because not everybody knows what you know about us," said Halsey.

"Nor should they," said Mitchell. "It's none of their business, but word gets out, it always does. And we're not naïve enough to believe that even the survivors of a nuclear holocaust will accept the leadership of a fag Colonel. You, though, you they might follow, if you don't push their limits to much, don't ask them to change too much too quickly. Harold Gates certainly seems to think you pose a threat. Could be that if we remove him and Keegan, you could lead us all to a bright new world, a better tomorrow."

"While you control things from behind the scenes?" I asked, wary of what they seemed to be offering.

"Nope. Remember what we'd discussed about the military mind. All I and my people want is to be an elite corps of ass-kicking bad-asses, like we always have been. You give the orders, we'll carry them out."

I sat there and thought about it, and found myself smiling and nodding, thinking that things could have turned out a lot worse. A whole lot worse. An elite corps of ass-kicking bad-asses wanted to join my cause against Harold? Did it matter if they were all queer? Nope, not one bit. You weren't going to hear me complaining about such a windfall of extremely good fortune. "Alright," I told Mitchell, "you got a deal."

Things got better for a while, with the addition of Mitchell's forces. He brought not only a couple squadrons of Vulcan Personal Combat Armor troops, but a half battalion of multi-disciplined storm-troopers, the elite of the elite, each man and woman trained by U.S. Marine Corps Special Ops., U.S. Army Rangers and Special Forces *and* U.S. Navy Seals. This was one mean bunch, capable of exploiting enemy weaknesses from the air, the land, the sea, you name it. These were the soldiers you used to hear about on the news, the ones without names, ranks or insignia. The ones the reporters used to refer to simply as "unidentified U.S. forces." As in: "Unidentified U.S. forces eliminated a terrorist training camp in the mountains of Pakistan earlier this afternoon." You always had to take the word "terrorist" with a grain of salt, back then, because the U.S. government had this bad habit of naming anybody it didn't like as a "terrorist" but the "unidentified U.S. forces," those were Mitchell's people, his horrible homos, his fighting fairies. How many flag-waving ultra-conservative U.S. citizens would have choked on their gum if they'd known a bunch of gays and lesbians was out there putting it on the line to achieve government objectives? Mitchell called his Vulcans and his storm-troopers the "Phantom Legion" and the name fit. The U.S. government and the U.S. military kept the force secret, and thereby ensured the secrecy of the operations they carried out; the Phantom Legion stayed out of sight and enjoyed the anonymity, the invisibility, to freely but quietly exercise amorous preferences that would have been frowned upon by Mr. And Mrs. Wholesome American. *Don't ask, don't tell,* that was the line favored by the old military establishment. In the case of the Phantom Legion, they really meant it.

Aside from the fact that they were all homos, which was not to say they were either soft or light, because they were not, the members of the Phantom Legion reminded me of Mikey's Maggie. They were people who knew what they were doing when it came to accomplishing dangerous tasks. They were no-nonsense killing-machines with good minds for strategy and tactics, the kinds of people who could probably kill you with a flick of a finger while figuring out how to storm an impregnable mountain-top fortress. Proud, but not too proud to do whatever it took to get the job done, to get through the blood and the mud and the snow and the shit to kill the enemy.

Not everybody who'd hooked up with Jimmy and me, not everybody in the old convoy really dug the whole notion of joining forces with Mitchell's group. Some few who'd been okay with the presence of a few homos in the convoy couldn't stand the thought of working with so many more. Some few who'd been willing to tote guns for self-defense couldn't stand the idea of joining forces with so militant a group of purposely deadly allies. Some in the convoy, though, mainly the homosexuals, some thought the alliance was just groovy. Their enthusiasm helped lessen the disappointment I felt in those few who up and quit the Free-Thought Movement, which was what we eventually came to call ourselves.

It didn't surprise me too awful much, that some would just walk off into the nuclear winter wilderness rather than compromise whatever principles made gays and lesbians or killers so objectionable to them. It was in the nature of all true idealists to put their ideals before all else, and a good part of our convoy was, as I've already said, composed of idealists of one sort or another, people who couldn't stand the thought of conforming to Harold's One True Religion. So, we lost a few. Not to Harold, but lost just the same. But, for the most part, it was a decent alliance, everybody getting along, at least enough so they cooperated when they needed to, when it was time to throw in against the red robes. That first night we were there, Mitchell and his people threw a big celebration to welcome our ragged bunch. It was a drunken affair in the big hangar where we'd first been brought in, and he climbed up on top of one of the parked hovercraft to make a speech.

"We're fortunate to have found you when we did!" he began. The terseness of his posture somehow translated into something that most of the crowd, the old convoy and the Phantom Legion alike, took for real excitement. Maybe it was genuine enthusiasm flowing out of him, but I couldn't really see him as the kind to ever really cut loose and let himself be caught up in the moment. Seemed to me he was working the crowd, giving them a necessary pep-talk. Better him than me, I thought. "We're fortunate," he went on, "because now we share the same great leader, the one who has brought you together from all throughout the devastated landscape! The one man who has always stood up against the red star! The one man who has always spat in the face of the so-called *One True Religion*, the religion of lies and death! The one man who will lead us to defeat Harold Gates! The one man who will help us rebuild a new and more perfect world!"

I hid my face in my cup. I knew where he was going with his little tirade, and I didn't feel like making as big a spectacle of myself as he already had. But there was no stopping him. "This one man is Robert Lifeson! And he will lead us to victory!" With this, he extended a hand toward me in a palms-up gesture, presenting me and inviting me up to his impromptu platform. I shook my head, waved him off, demurred, but he waved at me to climb up there with him, and the crowd joined him, shouting out for me to get up there and make my own little speech. I didn't have anything to say, really, but climbing up onto the hovercraft was better than standing around having hundreds yelling at me, so up I went.

Mitchell clapped me on the back and retreated a step, to put me in front. It was like something you used to see on TV, a political rally, a Republican or Democratic national convention, Mitchell playing the firebrand who gets the masses all worked up only to step aside and let the real candidate become the focus of the energy he's summoned. And he'd done a good job. He'd hit all the right buttons, reminded these people of how much they hated Harold and set me up as Harold's mortal enemy, and their infallible savior. It was a total crock of shit, of course. I hated Harold, and yeah, I was going to do my best to bring him down, but as for me being *the one man* who could do that, as for me being the one who would help them rebuild a world that would be anything close to *perfect*, that was complete horseshit. I'd realized it was horseshit when those red-robes had ambushed us in the little valley. I had no idea what the fuck I was doing. I hated Harold, and I was glad to have Mitchell's help against that little prick, but I still had no idea what to do, no good plan, no better idea than to go out and kick some ass.

So that's what I gave them. "Thank you," I said. "I don't deserve it, but thank you. I do truly hate Harold, and I want nothing more than to bring him down, to make him pay for the billions on billions of lives he's taken with his nuclear holocaust! I'm not going to let him get away with what he's done, and I'm not going to let him remake the world in his fucked-up image! With the help of Colonel Mitchell and his highly trained professionals, his little army of bad-asses, I say we find Harold and simply kick some ass!" That's all I had. The words sounded stupid, coming out of my mouth. But the crowd ate it up. They roared. They jumped and clapped.

And there it was. Our plan for victory, no plan at all. I often think things could have different if somebody smarter had been in charge. Maybe even somebody dumber. I just didn't have any real good idea what to do. Beat Harold. Win over the survivors of the holocaust. Build a better world. Big concepts, simple enough when held at arm's length, but useless when it comes down to actually getting something done. It would seem to work for a while, going out and simply kicking some ass, and, like I said, things did get better, with the addition of Mitchell's Phantom Legion, because when it came to kicking ass, they were the best. But in terms of affecting real change, in terms of realizing how human minds worked individually and en masse and developing a course of action that would take into account those workings, well, I was just plain empty-handed. As much as I hate to say it, Harold understood humanity a lot better than I did. He understood that people are creatures who live in packs, creatures who work cooperatively to survive. Creatures who work like that are called *social predators*. Wolves are social predators. Apes are social predators. Not sure about ants, but they might be social predators too. And humans are social predators. As such, the average human, whether he or she knows it or not, thrives on acting as part of a structured society, thrives on being assigned a definite station and role. Thrives on believing in *right* and *wrong* as defined by those within the society who make laws and dictate religious practices. The average human *likes* being a little cog in the big pointless machine that is society. Harold understood that, and he offered the survivors places in the new machine he'd created. He offered them relief from the sorrow and loss and alienation brought on by the destruction of the old society. He took the survivors in as if they were beaten dogs found by the side of the road, and they indulged him by playing the part, by acting like beaten dogs, happy as hell to adhere to whatever rules he laid down, just so long as they could eat on a regular basis and enjoy a feeling of belonging.

I guess I knew people were this way, but I figured something like a nuclear war would point up the wrongness of the pack mentality, the wrongness of *fitting in* and *obeying the rules*. The wrongness of acting as a mindless cog when the entire machine was bent on madness, belching oil and poisonous smoke while running at top speed toward the edge of a cliff. I thought maybe people would think, and there was my problem. I *thought*. And I thought for myself. Like most of the people in my convoy, I was a thinker, and an idealist of sorts, and idealism blinds as much as it enlightens. Idealism blinds the idealist to other ways of thinking, to non-thinking. It's ironic, really, the way idealism makes one so sure that he or she is right that it causes him or her to miss the point altogether. Just like I missed the point in missing, or at least forgetting, or not wanting to believe in the true nature of humanity. I was an idealist, and a thinker, so it made sense to me that all the other survivors would also be thinkers. It made sense to me that if we just went out and destroyed Harold's establishment, the survivors would think for themselves, would become idealists like me and Kelly and everybody else in my convoy of free-thinkers. I thought it was the system keeping the people down. I thought the old pre-nuke system had forced them to be cogs, and I thought Harold's new system was continuing that shameful tradition. I thought it was the idiot system keeping the people down, but, truth be told, it was the idiot people upholding the system. I know this might come off as arrogant, it might come off like I'm sitting in some ivory tower I've built on the rock of some colossal ego, but a system is no better than it's components, and your average American just wasn't that bright, just wasn't that questioning, just wasn't that concerned. People used to like to blame it on society, just like I had, but it seems to me, after having tried to free the survivors of the holocaust from Harold's tyrannical yoke, it seems to me that you can't blame it on society. You can't blame it on the system. It's up to the individual to make the decision to think for himself or herself. Societies can help and societies can hinder, but they can not truly control the mind of any individual who has decided to make his or her own decisions. Everybody has the same choice to make, and that choice is whether to rely on your own senses and your own logic to determine rightness and truth and fact, or to simply accept what is dictated, handed down by others who may or may not have your best interests at heart. It's often a choice between walking alone or joining the crowd, and most people would rather join the crowd, for the warmth, for the safety, for the belonging. For the assurance that they are right, because one person, alone, is more likely to be wrong than are ten or twenty, or a thousand, or a million. And that's how most people think, or fail to think.

My own failure was in giving the survivors too much credit, in assuming they'd rather fly high and free than huddle in the herd. There's a big part of me that thinks humanity got what it deserved. I just wish it hadn't fucked up everything so badly for the rest of us. Even back then, in that hangar, giving that stupid meaningless speech I gave, I might have been just as happy to go off and start a little commune somewhere. But I knew that little prick Harold would never leave me alone. It is in the basic nature of all societies to wipe out other societies, societies that are different, because the existence of such difference means, in the black-and-white mind of the average human, that one society or the other must be wrong. And just as nobody's going to see the gray and think the difference is okay, nobody's going to want to think it's *their* society that's wrong. It's got to be the other guys. So, even if Harold hadn't been such a diabolical murdering ass-wipe, it would have eventually come down to a fight. Such is the way of humanity. Maybe someday it can be different. Or maybe that's the idealist in me doing some wishful thinking.

Anyway, so yeah, we made war on Harold, and for a while it was good. For a while we won, went virtually unopposed, at least in a military sense. But it didn't matter what we did militarily; we—I—couldn't win over the hearts or the feeble minds of the survivors.

Our first big fight took place the day after the big party in the hangar, when a relatively large force of red robes attacked Mitchell's base. I was asleep, down in the underground quarters that I'd picked out. There was all kinds of room in Mitchell's complex, no lack of space for me and my original group, but not a single scenic view. Just concrete over steel, and plenty of it. I was asleep and I was woken up by a god-awful noise coming out of the little red claxon mounted on one wall. It was a call to arms, and I got dressed in a hurry, got my rifle and headed up topside. No need, really. Once I made it out into the freezing cold air, I just joined the rest of the folks who'd come with me. Joined them in standing back and staring as a couple squads of the Phantom Legion defended their turf.

Mitchell waved me and the rest of the greenhorns back from the front. "We have the situation well in hand," he assured us, as no more than twenty or thirty of his men and women took up positions against the horde that charged the barbed wire. The body-count later revealed the attack had consisted of some two-hundred fifty-nine red-robes. A considerable number in the post-apocalyptic world. A considerable number when you stopped to consider how far these guys must have come on skis or by dog-sled or however it was they got there without using any kind of internal combustion motors. This many red-robes rallied so quickly after the battle in the little valley, it told me that Harold was pretty pissed off. It told me that little prick didn't want me to join forces with Mitchell's group. It told me Harold was scared and desperate and making hurried decisions. No number of men on foot bearing nothing more than small arms could have taken out the Vulcan suits of the Phantom Legion, but Harold could have waited, could have gathered more men for the attack, could have had a larger number of much better-organized and much better-armed men to throw at the compound. But no, here he was, wasting the lives of those men who trusted him with the future of all humanity.

Mitchell didn't even send out the Vulcans. He merely dispatched two squads of his elite fighting force, and set them loose on Harold's fanatics. "No sense in loosing the lightning on a lemming," he told me later. "Keeps my people sharp, to let them take on a larger force like that."

To say that the Phantom Legion was sharp was to say that a nuclear warhead was dangerous. The men and women who took to the field that day made minced meat of Harold's red-robes. And not a single person lost or wounded on our side. It was really something to see. Exciting, at first. Then inspiring, filling me with the feeling that we could take on Harold whenever or wherever he might choose. Then it was kind of sickening, the slaughter, seeing red-robes getting hung up on the barbed wire, watching them tear themselves again and again as they tried to get loose from the razor-edges, watching as their fellows came on behind them, running over their entangled comrades, using their bodies as bridges across short sections of the blood-thirsty barrier. It was really nothing short of a massacre, the red-robes driven on by their fanaticism, which faltered as they saw their pals being torn apart. Two minutes into the fight, most of them had lost their nerves, and it was easier to see them as the former school-teachers or software salesmen or maintenance men that they were. They had no military training. Just guns and red robes and orders, and the poor schmucks didn't stand a chance against the handful of Mitchell's people who fired and fired and fired again, killing and killing and killing again and again and again. The red-robes faltered in their charge, some few stopping to return fire from where they stood exposed on the snowy plain inside or outside the wire. Some others just stood there, not firing back. Some ran in seemingly random patterns until they were shot dead. A bunch ran back the way they'd come, but the Phantom Legion got up and chased them down. No prisoners. No mercy.

And that's how it was. I don't mean to oversimplify, and I sure don't want to paint myself as any kind of butcher, but that's pretty much how we did business with those who opposed us when we swept into areas where Harold had set up shop. We rode in on Phantom Legion hovercraft to let survivors know that they didn't have to take Harold's shit anymore, to let them know that we would protect them if they wanted to say fuck the red star. We came in bearing food and medicine to show our good intentions and we were usually shot at. Harold had spread the word far and wide that Robert Lifeson and the Phantom Legion were a bunch of no good marauders. It wasn't true, but in the post-nuke world, those people who survived were ready to believe the worst of their fellow human beings. So, when Harold told his people that me and mine were responsible for the impaling of so many innocents outside Buffalo, well, people didn't bother to ask if it was true or not. They knew that it was Harold and Harold's new order that kept them alive, kept them fed, helped them to band together against the cold of the nuclear winter, and that was enough, for most people. If Harold said we were bad guys, we were bad guys. So they shot at us, and the Phantom Legion shot back, with extreme prejudice, as they used to say, and we wiped out all kinds of red-robes. I made a point of never killing any non-combatants, any women, children, or unarmed men, but that didn't seem to matter one bit, oh hell no. Every time we defended ourselves from attack, there was one more "massacre," further proof of my "bloodthirsty evil". I'm giving you the Reader's Digest version of how things went here because they didn't go well, and there's no need to go into all the frustrating little details, how this or that fight went, or how many got killed here or there. That would be pointless. It's enough to say that we won every battle, but we were losing the war. We looked more and more like wolves, so those who followed Harold acted more and more like sheep, wanting nothing to do with us, even in those few places where they didn't open fire before I had a chance to make my pitch. In these places, where the people actually heard me out, they just didn't care to hear my message. They didn't give a damn about freedom, or anything but their next meal. They were average people who didn't want to think too hard, and Harold provided their food and that was good enough. Me, with my talk of a brave new world, with my talk of free-thought and communal rebuilding, I must have come off as nothing short of a crazy man. A

crazy man they knew to be dangerous. And so I failed, and Harold won. And that
was that. It sucked, very badly, but that was that.

There was this one time, outside what used to be Saint Augustine, in what
used to be Florida. We kept our central base in Utica, but we roamed as far as
Florida to the south, and even further than that when we wandered west. We
were always testing the limits of Harold's control, looking for areas where he
might not have spread his idiot network. He was all over, of course, him and his
One True Religion, and his fucking red star, and the fucking red-robes. But anyway, this one time, outside Saint Augustine, I was leading an expedition of Phantom Legionnaires, twenty of us in all, fifteen in two hovercraft and five more
flying shotgun in Vulcan Personal Combat Armor. I'd lead us down there thinking to look around by the old airport, poke around near the old safe-house down
there, see the old sights, see what had become of the Ancient City. Turned out
the airport, with its military manufacturing facility, had taken a direct hit, so we
didn't get so close to the old safe-house or the city after all, but veered south and
west.

We ran across a new population center some fifteen miles west of Saint Augustine proper, about twenty miles from ground-zero at the old airport, a little too
close for anybody to be living, in my opinion, but there were, nonetheless, a
bunch of survivors making a go of it in an old trailer-park. Fifty-some folks,
young ones mostly, the oldest man in his early thirties, the eldest woman in her
late twenties. A lot of the survivors, wherever we found them, were young like
that. Young people handled the radiation and the subsistence living a lot better
than did the older people. And this no doubt helped Harold's cause. Younger
folks tend to have minds that are much more malleable than those of their elders.
As an old fart and dedicated stick-in-the-mud I can testify to that fact as truth.

Anyway, this trailer-park, it wasn't anything like VIN had been. Didn't have
any panache whatsoever. It was dreary and relatively lifeless, kids standing around
barefoot on the pavement, open ditches along the sides of the road barely facili-
tating the conveyance (note that I do not say *removal*) of piss and shit and all
manner of organic waste. Women peering out from trailer windows, most of
which lacked screens in that mosquito-haven of a climate. Men sitting around in
front of their trailers in groups of two or three, eating food out of tin cans, their
red robes soaked with sweat, their rifles nearby. I don't know whether it was the
incredibly heavy humid and hot weather or the fact that we'd approached slowly,
on foot, that kept the men in that place from picking up their weapons and
shooting at us, but in any case, this turned out to be one of those places where
they actually let me say my piece before telling us to get lost. One of our Vulcans,

flying tree-top high out in front of the rest of our group, scouting the territory, had eyeballed the settlement without being spotted, so we'd landed the hovercraft a couple miles down the road and fifteen of us had hiked in, leaving the five Vulcans behind, to guard the ships and act as an airborne cavalry reserve. Seeing those big menacing suits never did anything to calm the people we met, so I figured it was just as well to leave them behind anyway.

Well, me and fourteen Phantom Legion regulars just walked right into that stinking cesspit of a settlement, with our rifles slung over our shoulders, trying our best not to look threatening. For me, this meant trying to smile my best fake smile and waving gentle little waves at everybody I saw. For the men and women with me, this meant keeping their fingers off their triggers. I realized it didn't make such a great impression, to go waltzing in with such a bunch of rough guys and gals behind me, but damned if I was going to walk into any red star settlement all alone.

We walked by two red star banners, the poles of which framed the main entrance to the trailer park. A couple little boys who'd been sailing little plastic toy boats in the sewage-filled drainage-ditch abandoned their vessels and ran on ahead of us, shouting "Strangers! Strangers!" It felt like a scene out of some kind of cheesy old wild west movie, me and the Phantom Legion the band of banditos come to tear up the peaceful frontier town. Come to rape the women and steal the horses and piss on the bar.

We'd walked on past ten or twelve trailers, all apparently empty, before the welcoming committee came down the street toward us. Five men, in red robes, with automatic rifles. They all had rough beards, which wasn't uncommon in such settlements. Shaving had declined in popularity with the absence of running water. And regular washing had gone the way of shaving, so the five who came around the corner and stood looking at us probably stunk to high heaven, but they didn't come close enough for us to find out. They stood there and looked at us, then they turned tail and ran like hell, back the way they came. I waited a couple minutes, then got on my comm-link, and called back to the Vulcans, to see if they heard anything on the radio, on the One True Religion frequency, but they said no, which was slightly promising, if also a little strange. In situations like this, when confronted with armed strangers, most of Harold's people called for reinforcements and then started shooting at us. But not here. Here five armed guys just ran away and the street before us remained quiet and still. I figured it could have been an ambush, the five guys the bait in the trap, so we abandoned the street, broke into two groups, got our rifles ready and started moving through the narrow yards between the trailers. Everything was clear, and we regrouped, near the center of the settlement, where our Vulcan scout had seen the most activity.

There at the center of the trailer-park were the barefoot kids, and the men sitting around in small groups, their red robes soaked with sweat, their rifles nearby. Just as our scout had reported. They all looked at us, just sat there or stood there picking their teeth or scratching their heads, staring at us or through us as if they couldn't give a damn whether we came or went. As hot as it was, I didn't really blame them. But me and the Phantom Legion, we were there for a reason, so I went ahead and threw my pitch.

"Hey there," I said, raising one hand and taking a couple steps toward the biggest knot of men, a group of five who sat around on up-turned five-gallon plastic buckets in front of one old trailer sloppily painted with a big red star. "I am Robert Lifeson," I announced.

One man with a big gut and alligator-tan skin, he was sitting there with his red robe open, wearing nothing else but a pair of green-and-orange swimming trunks and a pair of plastic flip-flops, his round belly and thick legs covered with dense black hair, a big guy, but then again, the leaders of these local bands usually were big guys; Harold had probably singled them out for leadership roles before the holocaust, knowing there would be heads to be bashed, if his new world order was to survive; anyway, this big guy with his big gut and his flip-flops, he kind of snorts and says, "Figured that. What do you want?"

"I want to help you and your people here," I told him. "I want to help you to live better by rejecting the red star and Harold Gates and everything he stands for."

A couple red-robes snatched up their rifles at that. It might have turned real ugly real quick, but gut-man waved his people down. "We don't want any trouble," he said. "We've heard about how you and yours operate, what you do to people like us. We don't want any trouble."

"Nor do I," I told him. "I just want to bring you the truth."

"And what truth is that, Robert Lifeson?"

"Don't you think you could be living better than this? Do you like living like this?" I asked him.

He shrugged. "Beats the alternative." And his cronies all chuckled. He waved them down again, and they shut up. "Considering everything that's happened, I'd say we're lucky to be alive at all."

"I agree," I told him. "But how do you think all that went down? I mean, how do you think it came to a full-on nuclear conflict?"

Another shrug. "The world was full of sin. What did you think would happen? Even the old-fashioned backwards religions predicted a day of judgment, and the coming of a true holy kingdom on the earth."

Yeah, it was clear to me at this point that this guy was one of Harold's original goons, one of those who'd known the holocaust was coming, one of those who'd hoarded supplies and known when to go to ground. Either that or he was a real loon, a guy who'd been a loser in the pre-nuke world, a guy who now gloried in his leadership position, saw everything that happened as proof that the entire world had been wrong, that he had been right. Lots of that going around in those days. I guess people had to deal with the whole thing somehow, but any way you cut it, weighing eight billion deaths against your own survival and using it to justify or validate your own worth, well, it's just kind of sick.

I shook my head at gut-man. "What if I told you that Harold Gates himself started the nuclear war? What if I told you he destroyed the world?"

Dark stares from the men around the leader, but he just laughed it off. "Then I would say all praise Almighty Harold, for he has delivered us from the days of darkness and sin! All praise Almighty Harold, for he has shown us the Holy Program and set us as shining bits in the sequence of code that runs shimmering through the Great CPU! All praise Almighty Harold, for he has delivered us from Virus and Abend and will shield us from the forces of Legion who walk the earth and preach lies and deception and bring only death!" He stood up and spread his arms wide and tilted his head back to laugh up at the sky. "All praise Almighty Harold!"

"All praise Almighty Harold," said his men.

"All praise Almighty Harold," said the shoeless kids who hung around.

"I can see my efforts are wasted on you," I told gut-man. But I wasn't ready to give up. I searched the faces of the other men, looking for some sign of openness, for some willingness to listen. "But the rest of you, those of you who didn't see this coming, like your chief here, the rest of you, what about your families, what about the lives you had before everything went to shit? Don't you want that back? Or don't you want something better? Do you like living in a shit-hole trailer-park with open sewers and your kids running around without shoes catching god-knows-what diseases might be festering around here?! Do you like being thrown back to the fucking stone-age, living without clean water or electricity, forcing your women to cower indoors all the time because some religious fanatic who doesn't know you from Adam tells you that's the way you have to live? Do you think that's right? He's killed billions and he's having you live like this?!

Don't you want to think for yourselves?! Don't you want to make the world the way *you* want it to be?!"

Nothing. Nothing from any of the faces but those same dark stares. Not a single word from a single mouth. Just silence, me demanding change, demanding they think for themselves; them staring at me wondering where the hell I got off criticizing this way of life they'd so whole-heartedly embraced.

"Are you finished?" asked gut-man, a coy smirk on his face. "And if so, what now? Will you kill us, as you have killed so many who have rejected your evil heretical speeches? Will you gun down the true faithful, or will you tear our lives more slowly from our bodies, by impaling us on sharp stakes while forcing our children to watch? What now, deceiver? Will you show your true nature, now that we have proven our righteousness and turned from the sinful temptations you dangle before us? What will you do, now that we have rejected you along with the sinful world that Almighty Harold brought to an end?"

"Don't be ridiculous," I told him. "I've never killed anybody who hasn't shot at me first!"

"Liar! Heretic! Blasphemer! Spawn of Virus! Leader of Legion! Go! Be gone from this community of the faithful! Go! I cast you out!"

"Oh, fuck you!" I shouted back at him. Not that I thought it would do any good, but it was the only magic I had left, the only response I could muster in the face of such willful deception and ignorance. Like I said, things might have been different, Harold might have been defeated in the years immediately following the holocaust, if I hadn't been at the helm of the opposition. I just wasn't that good at dealing with so many god damned stupid people.

And that was that. We marched back out of that settlement, while the men of the place chanted "All praise Almighty Harold!" behind us and the barefoot kids skirted our ranks calling us devils and demons and murderers and scum.

And that was one of the more successful encounters. At least nobody got killed. Not that the Phantom Legionnaires with me didn't want to spill some blood; I just didn't let them. The more people we killed, the harder it would be to sell our cause. Not that our cause wasn't doomed anyway, because it certainly was. Just how doomed, I had no idea at the time, but I was to find out soon enough.

We went and regrouped with the Vulcans I'd held in reserve. Me and the infantry boarded the hovercraft and our whole group flew north, to scout out a few more locations and then return to headquarters outside Utica.

The next day, outside the remains of Athens, Georgia, we came across a group of former academics and free-thinkers besieged by a small army of red-robes from

Cornelia. We swooped in and played the cavalry, saving the day for the good guys in much the same way Colonel Mitchell and his Vulcans had saved the day for me and my convoy that day in the valley. We picked up two former University of Georgia professors that day, a Russian scholar and a physicist; an animal-rights activist and her Great Dane; and a fellow named Dan, who had sailed with Tiger Lily right up until the day she'd been killed. Dan Garrard, and with him were four former GreenWarriors who'd helped wreak havoc on the open seas in the name of the Tiger Queen. I took some heart in this, that we had, against all odds, found these guys, just stumbled across them in the woods of northeast Georgia. I figured if Dan Garrard and a small band of GreenWarriors had survived, there had to be others out there. It made me think maybe we stood a chance against Harold, no matter how bad things looked at the time.

"Well, if it isn't a Lifeson, riding in to rescue us just in the nick of time!" said Dan. "I never thought I'd see another Lifeson brother in all my life!"

"You're welcome," I told him. And then I got his story, how he and his small group, all of whom had survived the sinking of the *Bristling Maiden* had hung out in New Imperial Japan, ready to support Harold.

"And we waited and we waited, but that little prick turned his back on every-thing his mother had started," Dan told me. "It was like he was too damned good for us, and then he started recruiting all kinds of real freaks, so we decided to get the hell out while the getting was good. We kicked around Southeast Asia for a few years, trying to round up other GreenWarriors, trying to get something started up again, but with Tiger Lily gone, it just wasn't happening. It was like she was the soul of the whole operation."

It struck me as odd, to hear him mention Tiger Lily like that. Tiger Lily was, to me, a naïve little girl who'd gone and lost herself in a big world, after she left me. I never thought much of the bullshit she got up to after she left. It had pissed me off that Mikey had gone and joined her, and I figured everybody else who'd joined her were a lot of real scum, and that everything she'd done was just plain stupid and violently pointless. But hearing Dan talk about her and what she'd done, I kind of realized that she had grown up, and that she'd accomplished something, or at least died trying. "Well, she was really something, alright," I told him. "So how'd you get clear out here to the woods of Georgia?"

Dan shook his head at me. "It was pretty clear that something was going on, man," he said. "The Japanese nuclear missile crisis, the fact that Harold and Kee-gan went there on a supposed peace mission. The writing was on the wall in big bright red letters ten feet high. Anybody who didn't see this shit coming was going through life with their eyes wide shut. Me and my buddies here, we got back to the States and headed for the hills. Like in that old old Iron Maiden song, *Run for the hills, run for your life*, man. We were doing alright, hooked up with some big brains from the university and some other folks who avoided being nuked. We were doing alright, until the holy-rollers found us. They killed a couple of the professors when we weren't expecting it, then we kicked their asses a couple times, wiped out the first couple patrols they sent out, but then they just mobbed us, then you came along. Nice equipment you guys have got. What'd you do, raid the secret vaults at the Pentagon or something?"

"Something," I told him. "What're your plans now? You and yours going to stay here, or you want to team up with us?"

"Stay here?" Dan said. "Fuck that. In three or four days, there'll be so many red-robes swarming this area that it'll look like the place was painted in blood. If you'll have us, we'll come with you. Your brother Michael was a real decent guy, a good leader. If you're half the man he was, we'll follow you to hell and back. I see you've got Jimmy with you, but I don't see the Mike-man. He didn't make it, did he?"

The bit about leadership, I let go. I might have been as much a man as Mikey, but I wasn't even close to being half so good a leader. Mikey had that boring but rock-solid boy-scout core that made people trust him, even with their lives. Sub-culture types, rebels and outcasts would follow me, but anybody would follow Mikey. That's just how he was. "No," I told Dan, "Mikey's alive, so far as we know. Harold's got him trapped in high earth orbit."

"What?"

"The little prick's holding Mikey's wife and unborn kid hostage someplace, and he's got Mikey himself locked up in a tin can out in space," I said.

"Have you tried to rescue him?"

I shook my head. "Cape Canaveral took two or more direct hits. So did Houston. I wouldn't know of anyplace else in this hemisphere to find a launch vehicle. I'm sure Harold's got something somewhere, but damned if I know where. You?"

Dan grimaced. "Shit, that's tough, man. What about Michael's wife? Any idea where she is?"

"None. We've kept our eyes open, but honestly, our real efforts have been directed toward overthrowing Harold. I figure if we win the war, we get Mikey back, and Maggie too." And that was how I had been figuring things. There were nights, of course, when I felt like a real heel for not trying to build some kind of rocket so I could go and free Mikey, and some nights when I felt pretty bad for not making more of an effort to find Maggie, but you have to understand how things were. Every single day was a struggle, a struggle not to get killed, a struggle trying to make sure we had adequate supplies, a struggle trying to believe anything we did was going to matter. Besides which, building a rocket was beyond me and beyond anybody who we'd yet found. People these days really have no idea how tough it used to be, to design and then build any kind of a launch-vehicle at all, let alone a launch-vehicle capable of docking with a space-station and then re-entering the atmosphere without burning up into a crispy cinder. It was true that we had a few aerospace engineers on our side, but we had no access to the types of advanced manufacturing facilities necessary to build a spaceship. It used to be that groups of thousands, even tens of thousands worked for years, or even a decade, to build all the components necessary to cobble together an orbiter or a Mars-ship. All I had were a couple aerospace engineers, a few welders, and no materials much more advanced than wood or scrap-metal. I had to believe that Mikey was going to be fine where he was for the time being. Life in orbit would take its toll; he'd lose muscle-mass and bone density like any astronaut, but I figured if Harold had wanted him dead, he would have simply killed him. Likewise, Maggie and her unborn kid would be safe so long as Harold wanted to control Mikey. These were my self-justifications for not trying to mount rescues, anyway. There wasn't anything I could do, so I had to believe that they'd be okay.

And in the meantime, the madness went on. Dan joined us, and he became popular among our people. He was a capable guy, and he became my second-in-command. And he and I kept trying to win people over with nothing but promises of freedom and promises of a better world, and it never came to anything. People kept trickling in to join us, but not in number significant enough to make a difference. We held out, and held out, pestering Harold's efforts as a horsefly might pester a big brainless lumbering bull. We couldn't really stop him, all we could do was annoy him, and annoy him. We won what fights we got into, but we couldn't really stop him.

The cities went up with a rapidity that betrayed Billy's hand in their creation. I was sitting around in the Phantom Legion base, going over plans with Dan and Colonel Mitchell, trying to come up with some kind of strategy that would be worth a damn in the face of Harold's seemingly all-pervasive influence, when Halsey came in and said "They're building, and whatever it is, it's huge."

Megadon went up roughly in the middle of the North American land mass. As the name indicates, and as can be seen today, assuming I haven't yet blown up the place, Megadon looked like a gigantic tooth. It was and remains the single largest structure ever created on the face of the earth. As most readers of this volume are probably from Megadon, and are probably familiar enough with the city,

I won't go into a lot of detail about it, save to mention that it was shockingly massive. Earlier buildings had gone up one hundred, two hundred stories, but Megadon was much higher by far, and wider. It could not have been constructed without Billy Lifeson's help. I say "help" because there were human engineers involved, plenty of them. Thousands and thousands of them. Harold had plenty of highly educated and highly skilled sheep in his flock, and he used them as he might have used paper napkins. They served their purposes and then he threw them away.

We found our first pile of dead engineers on a reconnaissance run around the beginnings of Megadon. Dan and I and Colonel Mitchell had taken a hovercraft out to get a look at the big tooth bursting up through the ground, and spotted a small force of red-robes marching through the woods. The idiots were always so easy to spot through the leafless branches of the hibernating trees, and yet they never took off their signature red robes, not even when they broke into full retreat, not even when they tried to run and hide for their lives. Just goes to show that fanaticism dulls thought. Anyway, we saw this bunch of red-robes and circled them a couple times, buzzing the naked tree-tops to put some fear into them, to let them know that we hadn't given up, would never give up. They scattered, running, and we cut wider and wider circles above them, herding them the way ranchers sometimes used to herd cattle by helicopter. Well, on about our ninth or tenth circling, that's when Jimmy, who was down in the chin-turret, calls up "There's more of them! There's more of them just laying on top of each other!"

"What do you mean, laying on top of each other? They fucking or something?" I called back.

Dan had gone back to the midsection of the ship and was peering out the port on the hatch. "He means they're dead! There's a pile of bodies down there!"

I leveled us out, and Mitchell called in our escort of Vulcans, ordered them to set up a cordon and blast anybody who came close. Then I found a clearing and put the ship down.

Each of the bodies had a neat little hole in the back of the head. The size of the hole, and the lack of an exit wound indicated that each man had been killed with a twenty-two caliber rifle. Chafing about the wrists indicated their hands had been tied with some type of rope, and that they may have struggled a little, but not too much, because there were no bruises or other marks. It was, in general, some neat, clean and workmanlike killing. Cold and efficient. "There are others," Mitchell said. "Or there will be more."

I nodded. There were maybe thirty bodies in the pile, but I had no doubt there would be more piles. "Probably going to be a regular assembly-line. Wonder what these guys did to piss off the little prick?"

Dan was going over the bodies, kneeling down in the snow and going through the red robes and the pockets in the clothing underneath. "Well, I've found three I-triple-E membership cards already," he said, holding up a few little cards as he started searching the next body.

IEEE stood for Institute of Electrical and Electronics Engineers. Used to be a non-profit geek-club for computer engineers, bio-med and telecommunications specialists. I recalled what I'd learned of Harold's system for classifying his followers. "These are probably C-Ts," I said, as I went to start searching the bodies on the other side of the pile.

"What's a C-T?" Mitchell asked.

"Contributor, Temporary. The little prick had files on every single one of his followers, before the nukes. I hacked in, saw them. R-P was resident, permanent. T-I was terminate immediately. There was a B-T, too, builder, temporary, and these might be B-Ts, but I had the distinct impression anybody with an education was a C-T. I could be wrong."

"It would be like him, wouldn't it?" Dan said. "Maybe he needed them to help build his fucking monster of a city, but he sure wouldn't want them hanging around afterwards. Anybody with any technical savvy would be a threat to his authority."

I found all kinds of odds and ends on the bodies. Interesting, what people hang onto, when they've lost just about everything else. A lot of pictures of kids, and of whole families. Folded-up college degrees, most of which were from well-known technical colleges of schools that used to have good reputations: MIT, Stanford and the like. Union cards, cards declaring allegiance with IEEE and similar organizations. Worthless loose change. Wedding rings of gold as worthless, in Harold's new world order, as the worthless loose change. Last letters to loved ones. Last letters from loved ones. Nail-files. Pocket-knives. The red-robes who'd done the killing had probably conducted their own searches, and had taken any items of practical value. But they'd left us enough to guess that this pile of dead guys used to be engineers. Dan's theory seemed to make sense, as did Mitchell's conjecture that we'd be finding more and more bodies. Both ideas were borne out by what we found over the weeks to come: more bodies, and further proof that the dead had been technically skilled in one way or another. We'd find a pile of plumbers, a pile of structural engineers, a pile of medical practitioners, you name it, Harold was getting his use from them and then killing them off. You can probably guess who got blamed for the killings. Harold had it all figured out, alright. We were perfect scapegoats. The harder we fought him, the more it ruthless and violent it made us seem.

We came up with all sorts of plans to simply kill Harold. Fight our way in with Vulcans and hovercraft to wipe out the little prick. Get a tactical nuke close enough to fry him. Send in a special strike-team disguised as supplicants from the wilderness. Any one of these plans might have worked. Or maybe not. We'll never know, because we never launched any of them. I've already told you that idealism can be its own curse, and it was idealism that hamstrung us when it came to taking decisive action against Harold. There were those in our number who were strictly non-violent and wouldn't kill Harold to save their own lives. There were those who had no problem killing Harold but didn't want to run the risk of harming anyone else. There were those who didn't want Harold killed, but had no problem putting him in a permanent coma or lobotomizing him. There were those who wanted to kill Harold and every single one of his followers. Even separating out the non-violent types, excluding them from the action committees, there were endless discussions about how best to assassinate the little prick, and further debates about whether or not my god-like brother Billy would allow such an assassination to take place.

It was this last point that worried me the most. The idealists and academics discussed it ad nauseum, as they discussed everything ad nauseum. But there were nights when even I couldn't stop wondering about the Billy-factor. If he really was so god-like, then to what degree might he be controlling not only the rapid growth of Megadon, but the fate of every single living being left on the planet earth? It was ridiculous, circular thinking, and I knew it, but I, like so many others, couldn't help but run through the cycles of illogic trying to figure it out. If Billy was controlling all of us, then would it really matter what we did? Was he controlling us as a puppeteer steers his lifeless creations, or was he controlling us by controlling our perceptions, and was there a difference? If I scratched my nose, was it because Billy moved my arm and my hand by some force of his will, or because he put the thought in my head that I should scratch my nose, or was it because Billy made my nose itch? Was our resistance to Harold's new world order simply a part that had to be played in the script drawn up by Billy in some timeless time of eternity that we could never perceive? Mental masturbation, all of it, but difficult to resist just the same.

And while we discussed and debated and argued, Megadon grew, and grew. Until one day our recon parties came back to report that they'd found no new piles of bodies, and that there was no one outside the city. Everyone had gone inside. No one came back out. Aerospace planes launched and landed now and again from a hangar-deck at the top-most level of the gargantuan structure, and refugees still trickled in from the countryside, but that was it. Megadon was a closed system. There were no more dead bodies because Harold had done away with all his builders. He'd done away with everyone for whom he no longer had any use, and I should have caught on that we were next, but I didn't. I didn't catch on until Billy showed up and spelled it out for me.

It was early evening. Jimmy and me and Dan were out on a mission, looking for survivors who'd not yet been brain-washed to believe in the One True Religion. I'd grown weary of all the rejection, all the failure, and I'd elected to remain with the hovercraft while Dan and Jimmy and a handful of Phantom Legionnaires went into the local settlement. They'd yet to return from their little foray, but they weren't late enough to make me worry. Time, after the nukes came down, had become more plastic and relative than it ever had been in the days of timers and clocks and daylight savings. I was alone in the hovercraft. A squad of Mitchell's Vulcans stood guard outside. I was laying back in the pilot's seat, just staring at the ceiling, thinking about taking a nap, when Billy spoke to me.

"Hear me, Moses, for I am an angel of the Lord!" he shouted.

I bolted up in my seat and drew my revolver, trying to spin around while getting to my feet. I fell off the seat and onto the floor.

Billy was standing there in the hatchway that lead back into the cargo area. He was wearing what seemed to be a brand-new blue Lifesoncorp Mission Cygnus coverall. He was laughing. "Sorry, Robert, I couldn't resist," he guffawed. "I know how irreligious you are, I thought you might enjoy the irreverence."

I just about shot him right there and then, for all the good it would have done. "What do you want?" I asked him.

"That's no way to greet your long lost brother," he said. "But you are perceptive. This is more than a social call. I came to warn you that your base, outside Utica, will be attacked soon."

"So what? Harold's been throwing goons at that place since before I even got there," I said.

"He's launching a nuclear strike, multiple warheads, enough to dig down deep."

"When?" I asked. "And why are you telling me this?"

"Soon. And I'm telling you this so you can warn your people there, give them a chance to get away. But listen, Robert, Harold will not stop with a single strike. Wherever you establish any kind of base, he will drop warheads."

"Well, thanks a fucking bundle," I told him. "Why don't you do a little more than give us a goddam warning? Why don't you give us some actual help? Why don't you stop the missiles, or, better yet, why don't you go make Harold's fucking head explode? Why'd you let him get away with all this shit he's pulled? You know how many millions—billions—have died?! Do you, you stupid arrogant fuck?!"

Billy gently shook his head. "I knew you would be angry. But do not allow your anger to blind you to the larger scheme of things. Only Harold can ensure the survival of the human race. I have foreseen it. Please believe me that there is no other way."

"Please believe that I say fuck you and fuck your fucked up notions of fate, you asshole!"

"Please, Robert. Control yourself. There is still time, if you act now, to warn your people at the Phantom Legion base. They must flee. But they will never be safe on earth. There is only one place where Harold and his forces will not pursue them, and that is through the black hole of Cygnus X-1. Do you understand?"

"I understand you're as responsible for all this fucking chaos and death as Harold is! I understand you're a murderer!" I shouted, stepping closer and reversing my grip on my revolver. I gripped it like a little club, and I swung it at Billy's nose for all I was worth.

I connected with only the stale air of the cabin. Billy was gone.

I walked the length of the ship, looking for him. Yeah, I'd seen his disappearing act before, but I wanted to be sure I was alone, to think. And so I looked, and when I failed to find him, I sat down again, and thought about what he'd said, and why he might have said it. He'd never lied to me, so far as I knew, but he was sure as shit on Harold's side of things, so I didn't think I could trust him. Could be he was lying about a nuke strike, to flush out the Phantom Legion, get them out into the open where the red robes might stand a better chance of wiping them out. And that bit about the only safe place to hide being Cygnus X-1, well, how better to get rid of the opposition than to have them fly into a fucking black hole, where they would be crushed by the gravitational equivalent of a thousand thousand suns?

Then again, if Harold was indeed launching a nuke against the Phantom Legion base, they needed to be warned.

I got on the radio and signaling Phantom Legion base. I told Mitchell what I'd heard, and from whom, and left the decision to him. The Colonel decided to get everyone out, and it was a good thing, too, because that whole base was reduced to a glow-in-the-dark crater less than twenty-four hours later.

And so the end had begun for the full-scale resistance movement on earth. Just as Harold had disposed of his builders and engineers, once they'd served their purposes, so he tried to dispose of those who opposed him. We'd served our purpose, which had been to unify his people against a fearsome common enemy. He called us "Legion" and "The Elder Race" and blamed the nuclear holocaust on us, and painted us as everything vile and evil that had existed in the world before the nukes had come down. He painted us Satanic and blamed his own mass-murders, his pogroms, on us. We had served our purpose, and now he tried to wipe us out.

We established another base in Florida, because it was warmer, and because we figured the further we moved, the fewer Harold's chances of finding us again. But the little prick did find us, and he tried nuking us there. Then he tried nuking us in Arizona then in Texas and then back up northeast, in Vermont. We moved, Harold found us, Harold launched nukes. This is how it went for some years. He kept us hustling, kept us on the defensive, never let us settle in one place for too long. What was ironic about these repeated nuclear attacks was the fact that Mikey was coordinating them, from inside Megadon. Harold had brought my little brother back down from orbit, and shown him the brand new world. Harold had lied to Mikey, told him that I was dead, that Jimmy was dead, and Mikey, still held hostage by his duty to Maggie and to his unborn son, Mikey had decided to do what good he could by working within Harold's new world order. He tried his best to make the oppressive society a bit less oppressive. He tried his best to bring a little justice where Harold wanted only Vigilance. Mikey did his best, and when Harold ordered him to launch nukes here or there, Mikey delayed, or did his best to fudge the coordinates so the missiles went slightly off-course or detonated after they'd hit the ground rather than in the air, where they would have done a lot more damage. Mikey did his best in a terrible situation.

I didn't know this at the time, of course. If I'd known Mikey was in Megadon, I would have found some way to contact him sooner than I eventually did, or I would have discovered the secret tunnels behind the waterfalls a lot sooner than I eventually did.

07-13-2112

David had never hacked so hard in all his life. Every string he sent out toward Megadon either dissolved into nothing, simply disappeared against or into the massive systems of the city, or was transmuted and reflected back as a nasty little worm that attacked Uncle Robert's firewall. The disappearing strings of code that brought no response were frustrating, but the counter-attacks were especially disturbing; they were unlike anything David had ever encountered. Uncle Robert had shown him the ins and outs of the network, the nervous-system that was the unconscious intelligence of Megadon and of Syrinx. Uncle Robert had taken him on virtual tours of the pipes and paths, the gates and doorways that made up the network, from the smallest relay nodes in Megadon to the subsystems of the Great Computer itself. There had always been defenses, a couple firewalls, a maze of tricks and traps and counter-measures, but Uncle Robert had shown David the way, shown him where not to step, or how to tread lightly, and none of those defenses had done so much as slow David down on any of his thousands of previous virtual travels through the bits and bytes that made up the whole thing. One type of code would open one portal, another type of code would open another. This or that string of characters would act as a key for this or that gate. It had been like a game for David, as he'd learned the language of symbols, the short-hand of computing, the unthinking thought-patterns of machines. It had been a game, to go here and there, to nose around in places he was not supposed to go, to access records he wasn't supposed to access. And it had always been exciting, to know that, of all the people in the entire world, only he and his Uncle Robert could move around in the information-space as they did. But now, not only was he being denied access, but this network that had been his playground was actually lashing back at him. Things were different, very different in the system now. The firewalls were suddenly substantial, the tricks and traps—those few he actually got a glimpse of, before they shut him down—were wickedly intricate. It might have been an entirely different network, for all the changes that had apparently taken place.

So David began building new strings of code to send out, trying to find the right places, the right gates for these new keys that he forged from best-guesses and remembered lessons in the principles of coding logic that Uncle Robert had given him. He sent these new keys out, and most of them disappeared, but some came back, changed. Changed in ways that made them keys to Uncle Robert's own system, changed in ways that left David scrambling to catch these strings of code, scrambling to get in front of them and change the targeted portions of Uncle Robert's system so these attack-keys wouldn't work. It was as if whoever or whatever received David's strings in the Megadon/Syrinx network could interpret the incoming strings, could read them as guides to Uncle Robert's system, could glean insight on how to best hack into Uncle Robert's machine. And when David finally caught on to this, he began writing his code a bit differently, began trying to write code in a manner that he or Uncle Robert might not. He tried to write code that Uncle Robert would have called "sloppy-ass shit". Lengthy, convoluted code in which one section might call another for no good reason but to cycle through a loop ten or a hundred times and then return to the original stream of logic. David wrote code that included calls to non-existent classes, and included paths for handling these intentional errors. Then he sent out these new strings, which were really strings on strings looped through strings, knots and knots of strings, and sure enough, when the Megadon/Syrinx system transmuted these hacks and sent them back, they came back as knots and knots of strings, and Uncle Robert's own system defenses knocked them down, destroyed each attack as it came back down the pipe.

This freed David from having to defend Uncle Robert's systems from the counter-attacks, and allowed him to dedicate more time to his outgoing code. He started weaving more devious keys into the knotted messes he was sending out. He began to veil his own attacks in the loops and false calls and error-handling routines, and these new, more complicated methods, each more lengthy and detailed than the last, eventually wore holes in the outer-most firewall. Then, through these holes, David began sending complex little bombs of recursion, clumps of puzzle-box code that turned ever in and in on itself. These bombs were immediately seized upon by the anti-intrusion agents that swarmed beyond the first firewall, but that was exactly what David wanted; the recursive bombs were sticky, and when the anti-intrusion agents latched on and tried to tear apart the globs of code, they themselves were caught in the round-and-round logic, the infinite loops contained in the bombs. Having finally made it in, and having finally, finally made some progress against the newly-evolved systems surrounding the Great Computer, David leaned back and watched the havoc wreaked by his own code. He sat back against a pillow on Uncle Robert's bed and watched his little wind-up toys at work and laughed.

"You finally got somewhere?" Mal asked. He was leaning against the doorway, his hair a mess, nearly as tangled as David's more intricate code. As if he'd just woken up.

Looking at Mal, David realized how badly his own eyes burned from staring at the screen, how difficult it was to focus. "Yeah, I think I'm in." He blinked. The lamp-light that had filled the room when evening had come had been supplanted and overwhelmed by bright sunlight pouring in through the window. The green world outside was alive with yellow-white light, when last he'd looked it had been nothing but black.

"Took you long enough," said Mal. "Thought you said that shit was easy."

"It used to be. But now it's different, I don't know why."

"Your uncle said Harold was fucking alive in the damned machine. Think that might have something to do with it?"

David looked back at the screen. "I don't know. Maybe."

"Well, did you find the shithead?"

"I just got in!"

"Alright, don't get your underpants in a bunch! I was just asking, you grumpy fuck."

"I'm not grumpy," David said, knowing he probably sounded more than a little gruff. It had been a long night.

"Alright," said Mal. "Well, let me know when you find him. I found a few books in your uncle's library that have some stuff that might fuck him up."

"What? What are you talking about?"

"I'm talking about fucking books! You know, with pages and shit written all over them."

David sighed. "I know what a book is! I just don't know how you think a book, or books, or whatever you've found, are going to hurt an artificial intelligence that thinks it's Almighty Harold."

"Well, alright, you just go ahead and do whatever the fuck you were going to do and I'll go eat my breakfast and play with the dogs or some shit like that, and when you find him, you call me in, and we'll kick his ass."

"You think it's going to be that simple?!" David could hear the irritation in his own voice. He'd been up all night working harder than he'd ever worked at coding in his whole entire life, and all that work had just now gotten him into the system. Now Mal was going to go eat breakfast and play with the dogs, and he expected him to stay and continue to slave over the keyboard? "You think it's going to be that simple, just to find the AI, and then you're going to read to it or whatever you think you're going to do, and that the Great Computer's going to change it's mind about everything and surrender or something?! What are you, crazy?!"

"I'm not going to read to it," said Mal.

"Alright! Alright, then, what exactly *are* you going to do with a book?!"

"Well, a computer is more or less a thinking machine, right?"

"That's how they used to explain it to little kids, yeah," David told him.

"But it's still a machine, and all machines have limits. In the case of a computer, a processor can only process so much information at once, so we're just going to overload the processor."

David coughed up a mean laugh. "You're going *overload* the Great Computer? You know what my Uncle Robert would say about that? He'd say *you might as well fart in a wind-storm.* That's what he'd say! You have just about as much chance of overloading the Great Computer as you do of flapping your arms and flying to the sun! You're talking about *the Great Computer* here, not some minor processor that might route packets through a node!"

Mal shrugged. "I don't give a fuck if it's the Great Computer or the Great Shitpile. It's still a computer, and your uncle's books say that the difference between real and just fucking simulated intelligence is that there's limits on simulated intelligence. I think maybe you got too much of the holy-holy dog-shit pushed into your brain, like every other Upper! I think you really believe in your damned Almighty Harold and the dumbass Great CPU! You think there's no way to stop your Great Computer, so why don't you go to that shit-hole Syrinx with everybody else and beat your meat at it!" Then Mal turned and walked out.

David closed his eyes, listened to Mal rattling pans in the kitchen. He closed his eyes and slipped into sleep.

He woke up when Mal started kicking the bed. Mal stood there with a plate in his hand. He thrust the plate at David. "Don't say I never did anything for you, even if you are a brain-washed Harold-fucker."

David took the plate. Steak. Mal never seemed to tire of cooking steak. But it looked good and smelled good, better than soy-textured pseudo-steak had ever looked or tasted in Megadon. It hadn't taken David too long to get over the initial revulsion he'd felt toward eating real animal-parts, and now he dug in with gusto.

Mal went back to lean on the door-sill again. "Alright, genius, what's pi?"

David cut himself a piece of rare meat, stabbed it with his fork. "What? You mean the pi used in geometry? I know about that. Uncle Robert told me about that. It's a value used to determine the area of a circle."

"Yeah, that one."

"Pi is a figure used to determine the area of a circle, roughly equivalent to three-point-one-four," David told him.

"Roughly, right," said Mal, and left the room again.

He came back with a thick hard-bound book that he threw onto the bed beside David. "That's pi carried out across two hundred and eighty-seven fucking pages! And that's not even all of the fucking thing! It says right in the front of the frigging book that pi could go on forever!"

David ate his steak, leafed through the book, which contained nothing but twenty pages of text explaining the historical origins of pi as well as some kind of overview of accompanying theory. Then following these twenty pages of text were, just as Mal had said, two hundred eighty-seven pages of numbers, beginning on page twenty-one with "3.14..." and carrying on and on across page after page.

"That's a pretty fucking long number," Mal said, proud of himself.

"Okay," David told him. "So?"

"So, all kinds of people who wrote this book and the others about pi think that there may be no end to it, that the number could go on and on forever."

"Alright."

"So, in other books, they talk about things called supercomputers, and that sounds a whole fucking lot like the Great Computer, if you ask me. And they used to have these supercomputers work out so many digits of this pi and it would take them days and days to get to trillions of digits, and that's if the supercomputer didn't have anything else to do. Figuring pi took fucking days! And that's if they put a limit on how much of it the computer had to figure out! Like trillions of digits!"

David looked down at the book about pi. "There's not a single book in my uncle's library that isn't at least fifty-five or sixty years old."

"So? It's not like anything's changed in all that frigging time! Nobody's been inventing anything new, and sure as shit nobody's been doing anything to the fucking Great Computer!"

David thought about this. Mal had a point. Uncle Robert and David himself were the only two people on earth who knew anything about code. Scripture forbid any but the most cursory education or exploration of any kind of engineering, electrical or otherwise. If Harold, in his desperation to preserve his power for all eternity, had made his AI-self vulnerable by putting an end to all technological advancement, that would be nothing short of incredibly ironic. Choking the processors of the Great CPU by asking it to calculate pi to infinity? It would be perfect. Even Uncle Robert, who so badly wanted to blow the Great Computer to bits, even Uncle Robert would appreciate the approach. The thought made David smile. "I guess it's worth a try," he said.

"Fuck yes, it's worth a try! You know how many computer-books your uncle has, and how many can put you to sleep going on and on for fucking forever about computing theories, and how many of them talk about figuring out pi? And if figuring out pi doesn't do it, then there's a lot of other problems that are supposed to keep a computer so busy it might break down or catch on fire or some shit, or whatever they're supposed to do when they freak out."

"Okay, okay, I'll try to write some kind of equation, and sneak it in some operational sequence someplace."

"There's all kinds of fucking math in the other books about computers and pi. You want me to bring you some of those?"

"That would probably help," David told him, then returned to his steak as Mal went off for the books. When Mal came back, David set aside his empty plate and dug into the new texts.

Mal took the empty plate, but on his way out stopped and turned in the doorway. "Don't get used to this shit," he said.

"Don't get used to what?"

"I'm not going to be your fucking butler," Mal said.

David shook his head. "Of course not. Butlers don't cook."

Mal gave David a blank look then scowled. "Very funny, fuckhead!" He stomped off to the kitchen and David began examining solutions for pi.

How It All Happened Chapter 9

You might say it was inevitable that Harold won the way he won against me and mine in the decades following the holocaust. As I've stated again and again, we fought and fought well, but that little rat-bastard held all the cards and that's all there was to it. The biggest card he held was knowledge of the fact that people are basically herd-animals who like to conform to group behaviors. He got all the conformers, and I got all the free-thinkers, all the independents, and, when you get right down to it, it's just a hell of a lot harder to form independents into a cohesive group than it is to form sheep into a flock. Believe me, I know, because I've had experience with both. The exiles who make up my little village of Xanadu, they're ninety-nine percent sheep, and they're a lot easier to manage. Spin them a little myth, tell them somebody named Tom Sawyer is going to come and unite them, lead them to victory or salvation or whatever it is they want to hear, and they'll line up to listen, to conform.

But it wasn't just the individual and social dynamics vs. those of Harold's following. It was numbers; there were a hell of a lot more people with him than there ever were with me. And it was the fact that little Hitler had been planning his new world order for years on years, before the nukes ever flew, before Maggie and me made that ill-fated trip to Japan, before Harold ever left Japan to start touring around in the States, so many years back. Harold had built his "Orbital Defense Platforms" and once Megadon and Syrinx (not that I knew Syrinx, clear on the other side of the world, even existed, not until Mikey told me) were finished, and those death-satellites came online, there was really nowhere left for my people to hide. Wherever we went, the eyes in the skies were sure to find us. Mikey wasn't privy to the actual pictures. All he knew was that there was a small army of murderers loose in the world, and that we had to be stopped. He had his doubts about anything and everything Harold told him, of course, so he fucked up when and where he could, like I said. Sent the nukes a little bit off course or whatever, but Mikey was under some pretty tight supervision, and his choice was between the known good and unknown-but-possibly-good. The known good was keeping his wife and child alive and trying to help the people of Megadon and Syrinx, even if they were a bunch of lunkheads blindly following a mass-murdering maniac. The unknown-but-possibly-good was standing up against Harold for the sake of a small army of people (us) who may or may not have been murderers, who may or may not have impaled all those people outside the smoking crater that used to be Buffalo, who may or may not have killed all those red-robes in that barn, who may or may not have been responsible for the piles of dead bodies that lay outside Megadon. Harold knew Mikey well enough to know that Mikey wasn't going to risk the known good for the unknown-but-possibly-good. Mikey always was a dutiful boy, and didn't have enough dreamer in him to abandon one duty for the possibility of a greater duty. Not that it's my place to decide that the greater duty would have been to help me instead of protect his wife and child. Whatever. I don't fault him for it, not most of the time anyway. All he would have done in standing up to Harold at that point in time was get himself killed, so that's that.

As the nukes kept coming down wherever we'd settle, and those nukes became occasionally complimented by energy-beams from those frigging death-sats, it became apparent that Billy had told me the truth, that there really was no place on earth where we'd be safe from Harold.

I could probably write a whole book about our attempts to get off-planet. The abortive trips to Cape Kennedy, to Houston, the nukes and the on-the-ground opposition Harold sent to meet us in both places. The adventure up to Toronto, where we had hoped to find but failed to find some useful left-overs of the Independent Canadian Space Agency. All the plans that were drawn up to build a spacecraft of our own. All the scale models thrown against the walls when the academics went at it with the engineers and it sometimes even came to blows. Then the realization that it would probably be easier to try to steal some of Harold's ships than to salvage or build anything ourselves. When you got down to it, our forced nomadic existence didn't really afford us any opportunity to set up the kinds of facilities necessary to construct a launch vehicle, let alone an interplanetary vessel. And even then, once we'd decided we'd simply steal what we needed from Harold, even then there were so many arguments and fights about how best to steal those ships, and where they should be piloted once they were stolen. Mars was the favorite, because of the existence of the Mars Industry Station, that warren of livable tunnels and poisonous factories that had been championed by the old U.S. government and sponsored by a handful of multi-national (U.S.-lead) corporate conglomerates. They'd founded the place in the name of exploration and expansion, but, like most large-scale human endeavors, the venture had been driven by greed. All the sponsoring companies had wanted a leg up on all the non-sponsoring companies. They'd wanted to snatch the rights to Martian resources from minerals to real estate to polar ice. Things had really gotten that crazy, in the world that had buzzed and hummed and fed on itself before Harold blew up everything and almost everyone. Corporations were projecting future profits decades ahead of time in order to keep up the belief in sustainable growth. As such, it only made sense to some of them that, while they took interest from and in future profits, they should also invest in future resources. Didn't matter that it cost more to move those resources back to earth than those resources were worth; it made sense in the world-on-paper, the world-on-spreadsheets that was reality to the corporate mind. So there was Mars Industry Station. A small colony where people worked for no real reason on projects that didn't matter. But people meant resources, at least enough to get us started, which beat the hell out of going to some barren moon of Jupiter and knowing we were completely on our own.

So we argued, and kept moving to keep from being nuked, and eventually we had a plan. It involved me setting up enough of a network, restoring enough of the internet, that I could access the systems of Megadon, hack in and fuck shit up long enough for a few thousand of us to fight our way to Harold's hangar deck way at the top of the city. Then we'd steal as many aerospace planes as we needed, and be off. If there weren't enough planes, we'd have to hold the area long enough to make multiple trips. I'll admit it wasn't such a great plan, but there are times when you have to balance the need to act against the inherent risks, and I wasn't sure how much longer we could keep dodging nukes and energy-beams. I guess I haven't made it apparent, but we were losing people with every attack Harold made. We would accidentally leave people behind, or lose track of small groups that would wander the wrong way at the wrong time, and there were even some folks who just got their fill of running and decided they'd stay in one place and take their chances, and their chances were terrible. Staying in one place was certain death.

And so I, along with a team of other code-monkeys and network geeks, pieced together this and that bit of what used to be commonly referred to as "the internet". We found generators and powered up nodes after replacing parts that had been cooked by the EMPs of all the nuclear explosions. We got it together, then came the tough part, or what we thought would be the tough part, which was linking up to the systems of Megadon. We needed a way in, wire or wireless, didn't really matter, any way in.

I was sipping a can of beer from a case I'd found in an abandoned grocery store, watching my fellow hackers and geeks argue about hacking Megadon, like they argued about everything, when Billy showed up. Same Billy as last time, in what appeared to be the same spotless blue jumpsuit. He just appeared, and my guys went for their guns. A couple even fired, filling the garage in which we stood with deafening sound but producing no apparent harm to my supernatural brother, not a scratch or any other mark on him.

"No one's impressed by the sudden appearing act anymore," I told Billy. "You could simply knock."

"Sorry," he said. "But I heard you arguing, been listening to you arguing, actually, and I wanted to set your minds at ease. Wireless and hard-wired connections into the Red Star network are already available."

"He's been listening! He's been listening to us!" one hacker named Garrard went off. Not the same Garrard who used to work for me back in St. Augustine when I teamed up with Maggie, but equally slovenly, equally lazy. How many computer-geeks like him, how many Garrards must there have been before the nukes came down? I'll never know how someone like him survived the holocaust, but that's besides the point.

"Shut up, Garrard!" I said. Then to Billy, "Connections available, huh? And I suppose you're just going to give us IP addresses and everything?"

"I already have," he said, gesturing toward our laptops, which were arranged on a table in one corner of the garage.

"Check it out," I told Garrard and the others, and they got down to it.

"I've got a link-up!" one called.

"Wireless signal is strong! Connected at ten megs!" called another.

"Some kind of firewall, definitely protected, whatever it is!" called Garrard. "But we're definitely in contact with something!"

I nodded at Billy. "Alright, so what's the trick? You connect us just so Harold's systems can burn ours?"

"No," said Billy. "It's for David, really." Then he disappeared. And despite what I'd told him about not being impressed, it wasn't anything I ever really got used to, his being there one second and not being there the next. It was like he ran off while I blinked, minus the blinking. No special-effects, no smoke or explosions. I think it would have been easier to handle with at least a sound-effect, but no. He just disappeared.

But we had our connection into Megadon, and into Syrinx, although the two ran as a single big network and there was no knowing they were two cities without digging for that kind of information, which wasn't our goal at that point in time. I had no idea who this "David" was that Billy had mentioned, but nor did I care. I had my work cut out for me, putting up our own firewall and intrusion counter-measures against possible attack from Megadon, and then I knew it would be up to me to hack through whatever defenses Billy had built for Harold.

I did my work, and I did it well. Not that it would really matter. It turned out Billy was burning the candle at both ends, that he was playing both me and Harold with equal ease and effect.

I hacked and built defenses, and I ended up shutting down surveillance and automated defense systems throughout Megadon. We'd discovered schematics for the massive city, and in those schematics, we'd discovered the secret route up and through the towering structure, the paths between levels, the caves behind the waterfalls that turned and churned, crystalline or polluted, at the center of each square on each and every level. It was through this secret system that we infiltrated the city and made our climb, up and up and up for what seemed like forever. Thousands of us, well-armed and ready for the worst fight we'd ever faced. We climbed and climbed through the levels, peering out through the curtains of falling water at the new world Billy and Harold had made, wondering at the closed system they'd created. We must have looked like a colony of ants, the way we proceeded in a long line up through Megadon, so many individuals focused on a singular purpose, following a singular path. It was hard work, all that climbing. Easier for the fact that we had the Vulcans with us, and they simply flew up the spaces between the levels, carrying two or three people, the tired or sick, in their arms. The hard work was also made easier by the fact that we were moving unopposed through the interstices of the city. We'd come loaded for bear, expecting to fight tooth-and-nail for every inch, expecting heavy losses despite our superior armaments, but nothing, nada. We climbed in relative silence.

And I thought it was because I was clever. I thought I'd pulled some perfect hacks, completely disabled the entire place, shut down the red-robes so fucking completely that they were sitting around with their thumbs up their asses, unaware that we were even there.

I was wrong about this. My hacks were good. I *had* done a good job, but when we sent that first Vulcan out through the waterfall on Level Sixty, clear at the top of Megadon, and that first Vulcan radios back that there's a welcoming party out there beyond the wall of water, well, we started to shit our pants and I figured I'd been out-hacked somehow. It didn't seem fucking likely, but I couldn't figure how else Harold and his asshole followers might have known we were there.

It was Billy's doing, of course. My brother the master puppeteer playing us all.

"They're standing under a flag of truce," the Vulcan reported back. "Shall I open fire?"

I looked at Colonel Mitchell, he looked back at me. "*Who* is standing under a flag of truce?" I radioed back.

"I—I think it may be him, sir—I think it's Harold Gates himself!"

"No fucking way," I mumbled to Mitchell. "It's some kind of a fucking trap."

"Take him out?" Mitchell asked.

"What's the tactical situation?" I radioed our Vulcan. "Can you take him out?"

"Possible sir. Heavy guard all around, some armored. Target is flanked by two old men."

"The constructs," I told Mitchell. "What do you think?"

Mitchell shrugged. "Your call, but I highly doubt Harold has left himself vulnerable out there. He's not that stupid."

Dan had come up to the front to join us behind the waterfall. "Could be he's testing his own faith," he grinned.

I sighed. "Well, we know damned well we can't trust him."

"Uh, sir?" our Vulcan radioed back.

"Go ahead," I told him.

"There's someone out here who says he's your brother sir."

Now I figured this was Billy again, appearing on the scene, deus ex machina, to ensure that everyone read their lines just as he wrote them. "Solider," I responded. "Please tell my brother Billy to go fuck himself. Do you copy?"

A pause. Then, "Sir, he says his name is Michael, Michael Lifeson."

Mikey? I crouched there in that cave behind the waterfall, forgetting the gun in my hands, feeling all the eyes on me, Mitchell and Dan and the eight or nine others all armed to the teeth and waiting, their lives on the line. It's one thing to be a daredevil, a rebel and a risk-taker when it's your own life at risk, but being responsible for the lives of so many others, it just plain sucks. Now here I was, confronted by the possibility that Mikey might actually be out there, that my long-lost little brother might be alive, and this possibility was impacting my ability to lead. I knew the whole thing was some kind of trick, a trap devised by Harold and/or Billy, but what if Mikey was really out there?

I did the right thing and went out to have a look for myself. I left Dan in command, with orders that he and Mitchell should follow the original plan if anything bad happened to me, that their primary objective was to get our people off-planet. If they had a chance to take out Harold, well, that was good too, but they weren't to take any big risks trying to make that secondary goal.

So I stepped out through the curtain of chilly water. Our Vulcan was there, standing there like a less translucent variant of the crystalline statues that surrounded Level Sixty Revolution Square. Arrayed in a semi-circle facing the Vulcan were two squads of faceless armored goons, half of them in red armor, half of them in black armor: Cardinal Api's acolytes and Father Brown's acolytes. Behind these armored cadres were at least a battalion of black-uniformed vigilance regulars. Front and center of the assembly was Harold himself, in the most ridiculously ornate and overblown red robes chased with gold filigree and diamond-like stones. Beside Harold stood Keegan, in an outfit just slightly less outlandish. Harold and Keegan were bracketed by Professor Tanabe's constructs, Cardinal Api and Father Brown, those deadly fighting machines made to look like ancient and wizened men. And to the right of Father Brown stood Mikey, in a plain black Vigilance uniform.

Mikey wore a smile so big I thought his head might break in half. He left his place beside Father Brown and strode toward me in his big black boots, looking like some merry villain from a bad sci-fi movie. I kept waiting for somebody from Harold's side to shoot Mikey in the back, but he had apparently been okayed to walk over and see me. "Robert," he said, and grabbed me in a big hug that I returned. We stepped back and looked at each other.

"You look healthy," I told him.

"You too. I just now learned you weren't dead!"

"Same here. You're working for the wrong side, you know."

"Up until just a few minutes ago, I thought it was the only side. Sorry."

"Don't be. So, what's the deal here?" I looked back over Mikey's shoulder, and the whole evil assembly was eyeing us, watching our every move.

"The old men, Father Brown and Cardinal Api, they can hear us. Probably recording," Mikey said. "The constructs?"

"Yeah," said Mikey. "So I couldn't tell you much, even if I knew anything. But Harold says he'll let you and your people go into space, if that's what you want."

"Well, Mikey, it's not what I want, but it seems it's that or stay here and get nuked. Hell of a decision. I'd ask you if I can trust the little prick, but I know I can't."

"He's tricky alright. He's got Maggie, and my son."

"That's a tough one," I said. I didn't know what else to say. I was thinking he should have said to hell with Maggie and his son and saved the world instead by taking out Harold, but I wasn't about to tell him that. It wasn't my wife or my son Harold was holding hostage. "We've got a strong force in the city. We can try to kill the little prick, put an end to it all right here and now."

But Mikey shook his head. "I gave him my word, on Maggie's life, that I wouldn't betray him."

I kind of lost it then. "Jesus Fucking Christ, Mikey! The fucking asshole's betrayed you enough times! He's betrayed the whole fucking world! What the fuck?!"

He wouldn't even look at me then, he just shook his head again and looked down at the pavement. "I can't," he said.

I toned it down a bit, put a hand on his shoulder. Something about the scene, about me and him standing there like that, reminded me of that time me and him were in Great Silicon Lawrence Town and I had to sucker-punch him so he wouldn't run off and get himself killed trying to save Maggie. It was the same deal now, with me telling him to forget about the bitch and do what had to be done, and he was the same Mikey, putting some notions of honor before his own life, except this time it was bigger, it was more than his life he was laying down, it was the lives of the billions killed by Harold, he was putting his personal notions of honor before all those poor fuckers, and before any larger sense of justice. He was being Mikey all the way, and while it used to be admirable, his foolish prom- ise-keeping, his word-as-bond, his boy scout mentality, there was just too much at stake this time. An entire world needed him to break his word, billions on bil- lions of innocent souls needed him to break his word, I needed him to break his word. But he wouldn't do it, and it disgusted me. His strength was his weakness as never before, and it made me sick, to see him so fucking useless, so willfully handicapped, so purposely self-neutered.

"Well, fuck you then," I told him. And I was so let down that I radioed Mitchell to send out another five Vulcans, and when they came out I walked with them right up to Harold. Mikey stayed where he was, hanging his head like a beaten dog, but I walked right up to Harold with my armored killing machines. "Why don't you just kill yourself and save us the trouble?" I asked him.

Harold smiled what I guess he probably figured was a saintly smile, no teeth, just his lips going up at the corners. "You won't kill me," he said. "It has been foreseen."

I laughed at him. "You can't stop me. Do you realize how much firepower I have in just these six suits behind me?"

Harold gently nodded. He might have thought he was playing the saint, but he just looked like a frigging jackass. "Weapons are useless unless one has the will to wield them," he said. "You are no more willing to order your armored monstrosities to kill me than the nations of the world had been willing to unleash their nuclear arsenals. You haven't the will to kill me while I am under your brother's protection. You would not want to be responsible for the deaths of his dear wife and unborn son."

"What's a couple more lives, compared to what you've already done?" I asked him.

"You try my patience," he smiled. "I stand under a flag of truce in order to offer you the opportunity to leave this world. You may take your collection of sinners and sexual deviants and all of space may be yours, so long as you leave the earth to the Great CPU and the truth of the Holy Program."

I'd had enough of his shit. I saw no reason to retreat into space when I could just take him out right there and then and rid the world of his fucking tyranny and bullshit. I nodded to the Vulcans. "Kill him."

What happened next happened fast, so I may not recount it just like it went down, but I can give you the basics. I dropped to the ground the second I gave the order for the Vulcans to kill Harold. This kept me from having my head taken off my Father Brown, who had taken a chop at my neck. That fucking construct was so god damned quick that it was still a close thing. His arm was just about invisible, but his palm grazed the top of my skull as I went down and skittered back. Four of the six Vulcans opened up with their mini-guns on Father Brown instead of on Harold. The two that did open up on Harold ended up hitting Cardinal Api's back as that construct threw himself in front of Harold and grabbed the little prick and leapt back into the press of acolytes and Vigilance regulars that charged forward. Father Brown followed Api, also escaping behind the armored acolytes and black-uniformed goons. And Keegan, asshole Keegan was probably the only one who got what he really deserved. I really can't say whether it was fire from our Vulcans or shots from Harold's forces or both, but Keegan got cut to fucking ribbons even as he screamed for Harold to come back and save him. "Lord, do not forsake me!" he screamed, or something like that. There was a lot of shooting going on, so it's really hard to say.

And there went my best chance at ever killing Harold Gates. The Vulcans were mowing down the red and black forces that came at them, and another squad of Vulcans burst out of the waterfall to help with the slaughter. There was no chasing after Harold and the constructs without getting caught in the cross-fire that ensued between our guys as they poured out of the waterfall and

Harold's guys as they poured out of nearby buildings. The armor of the acolytes was proof against the rapid-fire but small-caliber bullets that Vulcans spewed from their mini-guns, so things got messier than they should have, within the first minute. Black and red armored figures hanging onto and trying to drag down the big gray Vulcans, the Vulcans wrestling around to shake free or fling the acolytes into the Vigilance regulars. Phantom Legion stromtroopers emerging from the waterfall blasting away at the Vigilance guys. There was no clear line of battle, the way things had erupted, it was just a fucking free-for-all, which was probably better for the Vigilance forces, as they were less disciplined and a lot less skilled than Colonel Mitchell's men and women. I played my part, shooting, punching, kicking, scared shitless and madder than hell and just trying to stay alive. I caught a glimpse of Mikey at one point. He was staying out of it, sitting down at the base of one of the crystalline statues on the far side of the square. From the quick look I got, he wasn't even watching the fighting, he was just sitting on the pavement staring down at his own hands.

I unloaded clip after clip into black uniform after black uniform. Most if not all of the action was happening at extremely close range. I used my machine-pistol as a club as often as I used it was a firearm. At some point I lost the machine-pistol, dropped it or had it pulled out of my hands, then I was down to my revolver. There was no time to reload the revolver in the close fighting, so I somehow managed to get it holstered and unsheath my knife, which was really the best weapon once things got tight like that.

It was the kind of fighting I used to read about as a kid, full-on melee combat, just a mob of men (and on our side some women) going at it tooth and nail trying to kill each other. You might be fighting with an enemy or an ally at your back. I read about this kind of fighting in *The Iliad* and *The Gallic Wars* and I always wondered how the hell anybody could come out of a battle like that without being killed or at least badly wounded. So many people all around shooting or striking out with more primitive weapons, it's like dancing around in a meat-grinder, no matter where you step, there's something deadly. How I came out of this fight alive, I'll never know. I've never been the best fighter. I'm a coder, a hacker, not a warrior. I'm not particularly big or strong or quick. But I knew that I didn't want to die, and so I kept fighting, kept fighting as hard as I could and as ruthlessly and as mean as I could, every single fraction of every second, lashing out and lashing out again and again and again, trying my best to dodge whatever harm came my way. My head might as well have been on a well-oiled pivot, the way I kept looking all around for the next target or the next incoming attack. The whole battle lasted only about twelve minutes, and I know this is going to sound stupid and not mean much to most readers, but it seemed like it lasted forever. Every moment as packed with more fear and anger than I would have thought possible. We won, of course, or I wouldn't be here to write all this shit down. Or we thought we won, anyway. The Vulcans made a real difference, of course, and the fact that the rest of the Phantom Legion were such a bunch of badass motherfuckers. Mitchell's men and women had taken some pretty heavy losses, one out of every five Phantom Legionnaires killed or badly wounded. There were bodies all over the street and the square. Twelve minutes of fierce fighting and what remained of the Vigilance forces turned tail and hauled ass.

I hadn't gotten another look at Mikey during all the fighting, but when it was done and I looked for him, he was right where I'd last seen him. Except now Jimmy was sitting down next to him. Jimmy sat there beside Mikey with his knees drawn up. Jimmy was hugging his own belly and Mikey had an arm around him. I stood there looking at the two of them not wanting to understand what I saw. Jimmy was always excited after a fight, always pumped up, babbling about what he'd done and how he'd done it. Jimmy didn't just sit down after a fight. Jimmy didn't sit down and fold all in on himself like that.

I went over and looked at Mikey and Mikey looked at me then looked away, looked off down the street at nothing in particular. Jimmy was pale in the face and the hands. The front of his shirt, and the shirt-sleeves over his belly, and his pants, they were all black with blood. He was shivering, his jaw quivering. "We really kicked ass," he said, smiling up at me with a weak version of his goofy retard smile.

"Yes we did, and you, as usual, were the chief ass-kicker," I told him.

"I got shot," he said. "I got shot good, right in my belly."

"I see that." I sat down on the other side of him, put arm around him, just below Mikey's arm. Jimmy's shivering made him feel smaller, weaker than I'd ever known. Jimmy who defended me and Mikey from the asshole bullies at school. Jimmy who'd saved my bacon any number of times when we used to run weed. Jimmy who saved me when Harold was torturing me to death. Jimmy, trustworthy stalwart honest Jimmy. He was shrinking right there under my arm.

"I got shot all up," he said.

I looked over at Mikey, who was still staring off into space. "Don't you have some kind of medical shit going in this place?" I asked him.

"The med-stations aren't online yet," he told me without sparing me a glance.

"Well there's got to be something," I told him.

"I'm all ears," he said. "But if we move him, he'll die for sure. He'll die because of all this stupid shit, for this stupid little fight in this stupid little city because some people can't talk without showing their asses and getting into stupid fights. What just happened here? What did it accomplish?"

I could have choked the life out of Mikey then, but that wasn't going to help the fact that Jimmy's guts were all torn to shit or that Harold had gotten away. "You think you can get up?" I asked Jimmy.

"I got shot real good," he said.

"But can you get up?"

"I got shot real good, just like he said. I can't feel my legs any more. I can't feel my legs, it's like they're not there, but I can see them, they're right here, my legs."

"He can't get up," said Mikey.

"We could carry him," I said.

"Carry him *where*? For *what*? Come on, Robert, *where the hell* do you want to take him?!"

I told him to shut up.

"You're fighting," said Jimmy. "You're fighting like when you were just little. Just like when you were little and Billy used to tell me to separate you. Remember that, when Billy used to tell me to separate you? And then I separated you and you said Billy sucked all the brains out of my head when we were in Mom's belly. You used said Billy sucked out all my brains and kept them for himself. When you were just little."

I wanted to break out bawling, but managed to pull off a snort that was kind of like laughter. "We remember, don't we Mikey?"

Tears were running down Mikey's face. "Yeah," he said.

"Billy got my brains," said Jimmy, his teeth chattering. "Billy got my brains, and that's why he's so smart."

"Come on, Jimmy, you're smart, you're just smart in different ways," I told him.

"No, Billy says that's why he's so smart. He tells me."

"He tells you? You mean he told you, back when we were kids."

Jimmy shook his head. "No! Billy tells me. When he comes to see me he tells me. He tells me all kinds of things. He told me I was going to get shot all up, and I got shot all up. And he said I was going to get shot all up and you were going to fight and I got shot all up and you two started fighting, just like when you were little."

Mikey looked over at me. I looked back at him. *What the fuck?* Was written all over Mikey's face, and probably mine too. "Jimmy? What else did Billy tell you?" I asked.

"I can't tell you what he tells me. He made me promise. He says that's why he comes to see me when there's nobody else around, so it's our secret. Just our secret, nobody else's."

"Well, come on, Jimmy, you already told us that he said you were going to get shot. So it's not like it's a secret anymore."

"He says I can tell you about that, but not about the other stuff. That's secret."

"What's secret?" I asked quick, trying to fool it out of him.

"Secret," he said.

Colonel Mitchell strode up to us then. "We've secured the hangar-deck and are currently searching the ships for booby-traps. We should be ready to go in fifteen," he told me.

I nodded my understanding and Mitchell went back to supervising the transportation of our wounded to the hangar-deck. The Phantom Legion were taking their dead as well. Our thousands of others, the non-combatants, the academics and intelligencia other idealists and freaks and outcasts, they were emerging from the waterfall and being directed to the hangar-deck. It really looked like we'd won the day and were going to make it away to start new lives on the outer worlds.

"He should be here soon," said Jimmy. "I hope he gets here soon. Getting shot all up sucks."

"Who's going to be here soon?" Mikey asked. "Billy?"

And there he was, right on cue, making the entrance he'd no doubt written for himself in this little drama we played out for his asshole amusement or to prove his godhood or whatever bullshit he was up to. "Hi guys," he said. "Nice to see the family in one place again."

I was about to give Billy a piece of my mind, but Mikey spoke first. "Christ, Billy, what the fuck are you doing? None of this had to happen. Not the nuclear war, not all these dead, not Maggie and not Jimmy, what the fuck do you think you're doing?"

Billy sighed. "But it does have to happen. Believe me, it does. Ready Jimmy?"

"Yeah," said Jimmy. "I told them about the getting shot all up part, but not anything else."

"Good man," Billy told him. "You should probably tell them goodbye now."

"Bye Robert, bye Mikey," Jimmy said, looking at each of us in turn.

"Hold on, Jimmy," I said. "Billy, you arrogant fuck, what're you doing with Jimmy?"

"I'm going to heaven," Jimmy said. "Just like Mom and Dad."

"You're going to heaven?" I asked. But Jimmy was gone. Jimmy was gone and Billy was gone, and me and Mikey were left alone falling into each other on the pavement. We got off each other and stood up in a hurry.

"Well," said Mikey.

"Yeah, well," I said. "That fucker."

"Billy?"

"Yeah, Billy."

"Do you believe him?" Mikey asked.

"That Jimmy's going to heaven? You know as well as I do there's no such fucking thing as heaven!"

"No, about everything else. That this is the only way."

"Of course I don't fucking believe him! Do *you* want to fucking believe that so many people had to get killed? I never liked the old systems, the fucking governments and everything else, but I wouldn't have fucking killed everybody!" I told him.

"No," said Mikey. There were a few seconds of silence between us, then he said "I'm surprised the Vigilance forces didn't put up a better fight."

"You mean *your* forces? You're in charge of them, aren't you?"

"Nominally. They're calling me the Vice Chancellor. Father Brown's always looking over my shoulder. I didn't plan any of this today, I was just told to show up. Be careful, Robert, I don't know what Harold's up to."

"Alright, Vice Chancellor. Are you willing to throw in with me against him or not?"

"I told you I can't. Not openly. Not while he's got Maggie. I'll help when I can, though. This whole thing, it's wrong."

"Alright, that's a start. I'll be in touch," I told him.

I'd started toward the hangar-deck when Mikey said "Sorry."

I stopped, looked back at him. "For what?"

"Jimmy. Everything."

"Me too," I told him. "We'll figure something out."

I went to the hangar-deck. I got onboard one of the ships, ready to leave the earth, regroup somewhere on Mars with everybody else. It was only once we'd made low orbit that I told the pilot to bring me back. He asked me where, and I told him any place in North America. I wasn't going to run from Harold like that. I wasn't going to let him off that easy. I left Dan and Colonel Mitchell in command of everything. I had no idea what I was going to do, alone, back on earth, but I wasn't going to take off and abandon Mikey to what ever black plans that little prick Harold may have had for him.

07-14-2112

The image on the screen before David was one of a long hallway dimly lit by flickering monitors mounted in big black brackets on the walls. It had been another long day and night of cutting code, of digging into the systems of Syrinx and Megadon, trying to find a route that would bring him to the Great Computer. Trying to find his way to the disembodied spirit of Almighty Harold himself. A program, a simulation, that was all he was seeking, but David had to remind himself of this fact, remind himself again and again as he worked his way through interior firewalls and logic-gates and probed his way through the nodes on nodes that made up the colossal network. Uncle Robert had once told him that the networks of Syrinx and Megadon were really a single network as large if not larger than the entire world wide web that had existed before the Revolution. But it was easier for David to compartmentalize the portions of that huge system, to think of them as an arrangement of smaller networks, which, in a way, they were. It was sort of like what Uncle Robert said about chaos and order in the universe, that it was all a matter of perspective, that what might seem chaotic from far away may seem orderly close-up, and vice-versa. A lot of the things Uncle Robert had taught him and told him came to mind while David was hacking his way to the Great Computer. And, counter-balanced and tugging against Uncle Robert's wisdom was the frightening notion that Almighty Harold was lurking somewhere in the system. The same Almighty Harold who smote Virus and Legion and drove evil from the face of the earth and cast the wicked down into the eternally fiery furnace of Abend. Almighty Harold without whom there would be no life but only agony and the torment of sin. That Almighty Harold. Just a simulation, just another collection of symbols, just more code, just a complex program, a set of routines. David knew this, but still, he felt edgy. Knowledge and belief were two different things, it seemed. He hated Almighty Harold for killing his Dad, and he knew that there once was a man named Harold, who was not-so-Almighty. But all those years of hearing it, all the lectures, the constant presence of the belief, the Holy Faith, such immersion, it had somehow seeped in, become part of him even as he'd scoffed and denied it. David felt tense as he worked the keyboard. What if the monitor exploded in bright white light, the kind of "Pure Holy Essence" mentioned in Scripture, and what if Almighty Harold was real and cast him into Abend? Thinking about it in such terms, trying to visualize it as anything near real made it seem ridiculous, a childhood fantasy or nightmare, but still the tension remained, the belief lurked in David's brain as the simulation lurked somewhere in the Great Computer: Almighty Harold was in there somewhere, and Almighty or not, simulation or not, he was, to some degree, real.

So David worked, through the day and into the night. Mal brought him food and bothered him by asking for reports on his progress. And David worked.

It was almost two in the morning when the screen switched from gray-white characters, raw code at a prompt, to the image of the long hallway lined with flickering monitors. Okay. It looked like a settings for one of the many morality plays on TempleVision. It had that old but not-quite-real look. Like things were too clean, or the lights or the shadows weren't quite right. David never really knew what it was that made those TempleVision shows look so weird, so fake, but the image on the screen before him reminded him of nothing else. A fake setting for a boring drama written long ago for the sole purpose of pushing Scripture, ramming it down the throats of the idiot viewers. David expected a horribly made-up personification of Legion to come running onto the scene, spewing fake fire and raging against all that was Holy. But there was no such appearance, by Legion or anyone else. Just the hallway, the flickering monitors.

"Mal!" David shouted. "Hey, get in here, I think I've got it! Mal!"

"What?" Mal shouted back from the living-room. He sounded groggy, had probably been asleep on the couch. He came into the room with his hair alternately flattened to one side of his head and sticking straight up on the other.

"Have a nice nap?" David asked him.

"Yeah, well, it's late, so fuck you. What the hell you want?"

David pointed at the screen. "I've never seen anything like this outside of TempleVision. I think I've found him."

Mal rubbed his eyes and peered at the screen. "That's it?"

As if in response to Mal's disappointed question, the on-screen perspective began to shift, making it look as if the hallway was moving forward, or they were moving down the hallway. "I guess so," said David. "Not very realistic, is it?"

"Looks like shit, looks wrong somehow," said Mal.

The on-screen perspective continued to move, and the end of the dimly-lit hallway became visible. At the end, there stood some kind of throne, with a series of flickering monitors behind it. As the throne drew nearer, the flickering of the monitors behind it resolved into rotating images of a veiled woman, and a man wearing spectacles, and the ancient god Jesus Christ on a cross made of light. The images flipped and flipped and flipped above and behind the head of a figure who stood silhouetted before the throne. It was supposed to look like a halo, but it looked cheap and stupid instead.

"Is that him?" asked Mal.

"I don't know," said David. "I guess so. Kind of a let-down."

"Kind of fucking stupid, if you ask me. Go ahead and ask him to compute pi so we can shut his ass down."

"How am I supposed to do that? It's not like the image on the screen can hear me. This may be some kind of video-loop built into the system's defenses, for all we know. Could be the end of the line for my hack."

Mal shook his head. "You'd be pissed off if it was. You wouldn't be sitting there just watching this shit. You'd be all pissed off."

"Yeah," David admitted. He sat and watched the on-screen perspective close in and tighten on the figure before the throne, watched as the perspective zoomed in on the head of that figure. Soft blue light came up on the face, revealing it to be rounder, softer than David had expected. Younger, and certainly less grave than should have been the face of the one and only Scion of the Great CPU, less grave than should have been the face of the Savior of All Humanity, less grave than should have been the face of anyone called "Almighty". The eyes were dark brown or black, it was difficult to tell. The hair that lay on the forehead was certainly black, where it poked out from beneath the intricate red-and-gold head-piece encrusted with jewels. David stared at what was evidently supposed to be the face of Almighty Harold, and tried to find some of the might and majesty always attributed to the mythic figure, but it just wasn't there. Harold's face was as big a let-down as the rest of the flimsy presentation. David felt a mixture of relief and disappointment. There was no way the entity represented by this image would ever cast him into the fiery torment of Abend. Here was yet another reminder that much of what he'd been taught as "eternal truth" was completely false, more lies on lies.

David saw, now that the light was up on the face, that Harold's mouth was moving. Harold was saying something. "Turn on the speakers," David told Mal. "The button on the front of the left speaker."

Mal pressed the button, and one tiny green light lit up on each of the speakers that bracketed the monitor.

"—for with my holy grace, would be but a cinder, a shiveled remnant of sin, devoid of all that could be remembered as good, the memory itself unbearable torment," said Harold, finishing with a slow blink and a long, solemn nod.

"What the fuck's he babbling about?" Mal asked.

"Something from Scripture, or something that sounds like it, anyway," David told him.

"Well, do we talk back to him or what the fuck do we do now?"

"I don't know," David said, getting up and checking Uncle Robert's setup for some kind of microphone. "I know it's possible, but I don't know if we can."

Harold's face stared serenely out of the screen at the opposite wall. "He can't see us, can he?" Mal asked.

"No," David told him. "At least not anyway I would know of." He found a dusty old wire jacked into what looked like an audio input. The wire hung down behind the heavy cabinet._David gave it a light tug, and felt a little resistance. He pulled the wire up and found a tiny microphone dangling from the loose end. "Well, we've got a mic," he told Mal.

"So we can talk into it and that fucker can hear us?"

"If I can get it working." David returned to the keyboard, tapped in a sequence that brought a text-based utilities-menu up in front of Harold's staring face. He set the audio input to ON and dismissed the menu. "Can you hear me?"

"I hear you, Lifeson, son of Lifeson," said Harold.

Mal looked to David. David held up one finger, for silence. "Praise the Almighty," said David. "Praise the Almighty who sees all and knows all."

"Your rote response to my palpable presence does nothing to disguise your thinly veiled contempt for the Holy Program, David," said Harold. "It is only my infinite mercy and holy love for you that restrains me from smiting you from the heavens."

David waved to get Mal's attention, then mimed writing with an invisible pen on an invisible piece of paper. Mal nodded, and padded quickly out of the room. "Praise the Almighty for His infinite mercy," said David.

"Yes, as well you should praise me, as all of humanity should praise me," said Harold. "And yet, your father and your uncle and your mother and now so many misguided others seek to sow again the seeds of sin and corruption that brought this world so near to ruin just decades ago. I know you have heard their lies, David, and I know that you have been tempted by the evil that has been let loose by those who would worship Virus and Legion and all the forces of darkness and the sickness and death that serve as their handmaidens."

"Please forgive my family," David said. "They do not understand your power, your wisdom."

"Indeed they do not," huffed Harold. "I have transcended mortality, and have risen to be as one with the Great CPU. I have given my human life to spare them from the consequences of their sins, and yet they persist in their wicked behaviors."

Mal came back in with a pen and a pad of paper, handed them to David, who hastily wrote *He/it recognizes the patterns of my key-strokes from Prayernet. Unique, like fingerprints.* "Why must they be so blind?" David spoke into the microphone.

Mal read David's note, made a show of wiping his forehead in relief, then took back the pen and pad. *He can't see us?* Mal wrote back in his slow, careful hand, to which David shook his head no.

"Because they are proud, and foolish," said Harold. "Because they are part of the corrupt world that existed before the revolution, before the cleansing fire destroyed the kingdoms of the wicked on earth, before I smote Legion on the outer worlds and drove the Elder Race from the blessed haven provided us by the Great CPU. Tell me, David, where is your uncle now? And where is your mother? To what wicked works have they set their hands?"

"I do not know, Almighty," said David. "They have left me here alone, and I am afraid. I was certain that you, in your all-seeing wisdom, would know, and so I sought you out."

"Do not assume such an insolent tone with me, David," said Harold. "For I could destroy you with but a stray thought. I see all and I know all, but my infinite knowledge is not for mortal minds, which are made imperfect and flawed by sin!"

He doesn't know where they are, David wrote on the pad. "I'm sorry, Almighty!" he said into the microphone. "Forgive me!"

Thought he had satellites and shit, Mal wrote back.

David looked at Mal and shrugged.

"My forgiveness knows no bounds!" Harold barked. "Do you believe I could mistake innocence for insolence?"

Fucking crazy, wrote Mal.

"No, of course not, Almighty," said David.

"Very well," said Harold. "I merely wish you to find your own path through the dilemma your family has presented you. The Great CPU helps those who help themselves."

"Thank you, O Merciful One," said David. "I have been searching my uncle's files, but he is, as you know, a clever and devious man, expert in the proscribed arts of computing. There is one file containing a code I can not decipher, no matter how hard I try. And I have tried, Almighty, I have tried and tried, but I fear the sinful nature of computing and code itself keeps me from solving the riddle my uncle has left. I feel certain that if I could but puzzle out this code he has left behind, I might know where he and my mother have gone, and I might intercede with them, and keep them from whatever foolish plan they have devised."

Pretty fucking smooth, wrote Mal.

"It would be like your uncle, in his pride, to leave his plans guarded only by some simple puzzle," said Harold, smiling. "Your heart is good, David, and I see the goodness in you, and know it is not too late for your soul to be saved. Allow me to share with you my infinite love by helping you to solve your uncle's paltry code. Show me your willingness to embrace the Holy Program by lowering the firewalls on your uncle's system and revealing to me the file containing your uncle's devious code."

"Praise the Almighty," David said. "Thank you, O Lord, thank you, Savior!" David went to work on the keyboard, lowering the firewalls on those portions of Uncle Robert's system that he had prepared for just this purpose. It was a great chunk of hard-drive space filled with cloned files, enough data to simulate the entire system while the original copies and essential workings remained protected behind more intricate intrusion counter-measures that mocked the boundaries of a virtual space large enough and complex enough to be mistaken for a system set up by an expert hacker like Uncle Robert. David had no idea whether or not his work would suffice to fool an artificial intelligence of the magnitude he now faced, but it was now or never, and so he unveiled his false little world, he let Harold in.

"Excellent," said Harold. "And to think that, in teaching you the dark arts of computing, your uncle sought to make you an agent of his evil! How foolish he was, to think that his impertinent mortal teachings could overcome the spark of the Holy Program that burns so brightly within you, young David. Which file contains the puzzle, your uncle's childish code?"

"It is the one named The Weapon, Almighty," said David.

A moment passed, then another, and Harold's smile grew wider. "This is but simple mathematical formula. I can process the solution for this paltry code in but a fraction of a moment! Your uncle may burn in the eternal fires of Abend, David, but you shall sit at my right hand in the Kingdom of the Great CPU!"

"Praise the Almighty," said David. "What are my uncle's plans? Where has he gone?"

"It is a…simple enough formula…so simple," said Harold.

"Almighty? What disturbs you, Almighty?"

"I require but a moment…" said Harold. "It is a much…longer sequence than I had anticipated…."

"Are you alright, Almighty?" David asked.

"Do not be foolish! No mere mathematical puzzle will…."

David took the pen and pad back from Mal. *He's slowing down.*

Fucking quick, wrote Mal.

I set no limit to how many places pi should be calculated. He could go on forever, David wrote back.

Can he hear us? Male wrote.

I don't know. Let's wait.

So they waited, silently. David sat and Mal stood and they watched Harold staring into the room as the Great Computer beneath Syrinx calculated *pi*. Five minutes, and Harold remained still, the only movement in the image the steady flicker of the torches mounted on the walls. Then, another five minutes, and the flickering flames slowed their random dance, became less regular, jumpy. The shadows cast in contrast to the dim orange light ceased to react, ceased to move with the choppy movement of the flame, and sometimes appeared to be crudely-drawn cross-hatchings, just the framework of shadows. Another five minutes, and the flames had stopped, just froze on the end of the torches, the light they cast no longer apparent, the shadows completely gone.

Another five minutes and there were no flames, then there were no torches.

Another five minutes, and the throne and monitor behind Harold was also gone, just blinked out of existence.

Another five minutes, and the walls, the hallway itself went away, leaving Harold's face against a black background.

The system is trying to conserve resources, David wrote on the pad.

Meaning?

Meaning the calculation of pi is taking up more and more processing power with each iteration, as there are more and more numbers to crunch each time the processors make a pass. The Great Computer is really starting to slow down.

We did it? Mal wrote.

Don't know. Maybe, but we have no way of knowing how many other processes it's managing to maintain while it calculates pi. It could be shutting down only those processes that aren't important, David wrote back.

Well when the fuck will we know? Mal wrote.

I don't know David wrote back.

Harold turned his head, just a handful of degrees, very slowly opened his mouth, as if to speak, but the sound that came from the speakers was a rapid series of clicks followed by a long low groan. Harold blinked and the image on the screen began to stutter, became a series of stills that each conveyed a different degree of distress on Harold's soft round face, the confident pseudo-smile becoming a pinched grimace, the brow going from smooth to furrowed. The stills slowed and slowed, and finally stopped, leaving David and Mal staring at a still of an angry dark-haired dark-eyed young man wearing a ridiculous hat.

David got up and unplugged the microphone from Uncle Robert's system. "It's okay to talk. He can't hear us, even if he is still functioning."

"That's it?" Mal asked.

"I don't know."

Mal walked up, tapped on the monitor-screen. "You fucking guess so? That's fucking great. So, for all we fucking know, he maybe never started figuring *pi*. It's a pretty damn simple trick. It could be he knew what the fuck we were up to, and the whole show we just saw was a trick, to make us think we won!"

David shrugged. "I'd hate to think that was the case, but it could be."

"Well, can't you hack in there and find out?"

David thought about this one. "Well, I doubt it."

"Why the hell not?"

"Think about it. If our trick really did work, there will be no system into which I can hack. If it didn't work because the Great Computer and the Harold AI caught on, well, they could make it seem like there was no system into which to hack. Right?"

Mal rolled his eyes. "I don't fucking know! You're Mister Fucking Computer!"

"Okay, then, take my word for it."

"Take your word for if the shit worked or not?" Mal asked.

"Yes," David chuckled.

"Yes fucking *what*?!" Mal shouted.

"Yes, I don't know if the *shit* worked or not."

"Very fucking funny!" Mal stomped out of the room.

David glanced at the clock on Uncle Robert's bedside stand. Two forty-five. He lay on the bed and stared up at the ceiling, wondering whether or not he had indeed put an end to the AI that had called itself Harold. There was no knowing, not at the moment, but he considered and considered, sent logic chasing logic, until he fell asleep.

He was woken an hour later when the whole farmhouse was shaken by two great slamming sounds, and the night outside the window was violated by a torrent of blue flame from the sky.

"What the fuck?" Mal shouted, as he came running into the bedroom.

David raced to the window and peered up at the raging short columns of blue fire. They were so bright in contrast to everything else that it took him a few moments to make out the familiar shape of the black ship that descended to rapidly toward the field beyond the barn. "It's my father's orbital shuttle, from Megadon," he told Mal.

"You said your father was dead!"

"Alright then, it's the Vice Chancellor's shuttle, okay?"

The heat from the VTOL engines evoked smoldering flames from the green grass outside. A scorched black circle was painted beneath the ship as it settled down on its gear.

"So it's Thomas?" Mal asked. "Is it fucking Thomas or who the fuck is it?"

"I don't know. Let's not wait to find out. Let's go."

"Fuck yes!" Mal was out the bedroom door in front of David, and they ran through the farmhouse to the garage, where Uncle Robert's pack of half-wild guard-dogs were growling and barking and clawing at the outside door.

David opened that outside door and released the pack. The dogs surged out into the night, hunkered down and growling as a single being, intent on sinking in fangs, intent on tearing the flesh of whatever waited in the darkness.

"That's not so fucking good," whispered Mal, as he and David stood still in the pitch-black garage.

"No," David whispered back. "Let's go." He lead the way out of the garage, not sure which way to go. He wanted more than anything to get behind the wheel of the red Barchetta, to use the deadly speed of the car to fling himself away through the woods. The shuttle had landed close to the barn, but if they could just make it to the car, they might get away. The orbital shuttle was built to transport people thousands of kilometers at a time by cutting a huge arc into and out of orbit; it was not designed for close pursuit, and would be of no use in chasing that powerful beast of a car.

David lead Mal around behind the garage, then toward the barn.

"You're taking us right fucking toward it!" Mal hissed.

"Got to get the car," David hissed back.

They rounded the corner of the farmhouse and there, in the field between the shuttle and barn, were the dogs, a snarling mass of fur and fangs, leaping at swarming over a single gleaming dark figure. The dogs leapt and tried to latch on and tried to shake, tried to tear with their teeth, but their jaws found no purchase, and the beasts were thrown back ten, twenty meters across the field, sometimes landing with terrible whining cries to limp or drag themselves away into the night; sometimes rolling and regaining their feet to renew the attack; sometimes landing with nothing but a dull thud and laying silent and still. David hesitated. "We need to go," he whispered to Mal, even as he stopped and stared at the pitched battle before him. The dark figure wore a full-faced helmet, and the gleaming surfaces of its arms and legs must have been some type of metal, some type of armor. Not bulky jointed armor like that worn by Cousin Rosella, but a light, flexible protective coating that allowed the figure to move with incredible natural grace. Rosella was graceful enough in her suit, but it was a forced grace, the manipulation of a complex machine. This figure did not move so much as flow. It was a deadly flowing, and David found it familiar. He had seen these quick, naturally lethal movements before. "We need to go," he said again, feeling his skin turn cold, feeling his legs turn stiff and heavy.

"Well, fucking go!" Mal pushed him from behind, and David stumbled forward, trying to will down his fear, trying to fight through the animal urge to remain still, to simply freeze where he was.

They ran, exposed, across the open space between the farmhouse and the barn. "It's coming after us!" Mal shouted behind him.

David looked back. The dark figure was walking after them, brushing the remaining dogs aside, dismissing their snarls and cries as if the beasts were tiny insects existing only to be swatted and squashed.

David ran. Mal ran. They made it to the barn, then inside. David leapt into the waiting car, Mal followed. David reached and reached for the keys, and the dashboard seemed kilometers wide but he found the cold metal with his hand. He grabbed and turned. The car choked and bucked. He'd forgotten the clutch. Left foot on the pedal then down. "Let's fucking go, David!" Mal shouted. "Let's fucking go now!" Turn the keys again. Familiar hot roar. Gas, clutch. The car leapt forward and fell silent. Mal yelling again. Clutch, keys: roar. Gradual gas, gradual clutch. He'd done it a million times why was it so hard now? The car screamed. The engine screamed. The tires screamed. Pressed back against the seat. Barn door lunging. Barn door splintering. Red line red line. Clutch, shift, gas. Back end swaying, slipping sideways. Counter-steer. Back end slipping the other way. Counter-steer. Red line. Clutch, shift, gas.

The Barchetta hunkered down and ripped a straight line across the field. David felt his left leg quivering as he glanced into the rear-view. No sign of the dark figure. The tree-line loomed large and larger dead ahead, and then the road, the kilometers and kilometers of road. Red line. Clutch, shift, gas. Speedometer needle climbing past ninety. They were away. They were away. Uncle Robert would have been proud. Steady hand on the wheel. No sense in escaping only to hit a tree. David reached down and turned on the headlights as they entered the forest.

And it was as if flipping the headlight switch produced two dark gleaming legs on the hood of the car. No, they'd come from above, come down on the hood from the sky. Mal's shouts of exuberant joy became a stream of panicked swearing. Gleaming black hands locking down on the top edge of the windshield. Smooth metallic black head atop gleaming black neck and gleaming black shoulders and David saw, in the clarity of his adrenaline-fueled fear, that there were small round lumps at regular intervals beneath the seamless armor.

The figure reached for Mal as David cranked the wheel one way and the other, but it was no good. There was no shaking him. Mal was thrown out with one swift flick of the gleaming black arm, then David found himself hanging in the air as the car raced off the road and into the trunk of some massive tree.

David hit the ground hard, and his momentum caused him to bounce, then roll. He felt and heard the bones of one arm snap, and it was all abstraction after that, the rolling, new pain piling on that of the existing fracture, all of it very real but distant. Then stillness and throbbing screaming agony as he lay face-down on fallen leaves, the smell of the rotting foliage blending with the over-riding high-pitched internal alarms of his own nervous system on fire.

The pain did not fade but became more regular, no more bearable but more regular, not better but regular, until he was rolled over and dragged over the forest floor back toward the field, every bump and tug a new mixture of screams. It faded, along with everything else, as they neared the orbital shuttle. David himself faded, was gone.

He woke strapped down to one of the plush chairs in the passenger compartment of the shuttle. There was no more pain. Directly across from him, the dark gleaming figure was also strapped down, in a similar chair. A light-haired man in the white robes of the medical priesthood leaned in over David and stared into his eyes. He held in his right hand one piece of what looked like a portable med-station. "Feeling better, David?" he asked.

David flexed his arms and legs against the straps that held him down. He had been healed.

"I am Surgeon General Packard-Dell," said the medicine-man. "And I believe you already know the former Bishop Compaq," he added, gesturing toward the silent and perfectly still figure strapped down in the other chair. "Although I suppose he might be a bit difficult to recognize, given the nature of the extensive modifications we've implemented by the Holy Will of Almighty Harold. It was good of you to leave him for us, right there in the Red Star Medical Center."

David closed his eyes. He'd heard this kind of man give this kind of speech before. He could hear the man capitalizing phrases like *Holy Will.* A proud high administrator flaunting his accomplishments. He'd heard it whenever he and Dad had encountered other high administrators in public or in private. He'd heard it and didn't want to hear it any more. The very fact that such a high administrator existed, together with the fact that such a high administrator held him captive told him he'd failed to bring Harold down by asking him to calculate *pi* to infinity.

"Why so downcast?" asked Packard-Dell. "Why do you close your eyes, boy, when a physical manifestation of Almighty Harold's holy glory sits in the chair before you? I opened your file, when I received the order to visit the wilderness, when the Almighty Himself appeared to me on the view-screen of my telephone and told me to do His holy bidding. Your file told me you were such a bright boy, and I should think a bright boy would want to gaze upon a Miracle wrought by knowledge handed down by the Almighty Himself. It was just after your mother so cruelly murdered Surgeon General Wang, after she had taken you into the wilderness, that the Almighty first appeared to me and named me Surgeon General, and shared his Holy Wisdom and Holy Will with me. It was then that He made me His tool and shared with me the Holy Knowledge necessary to restore and improve the fallen Bishop Compaq. Have you not noted the beauty of this creation of the Almighty? Have you not noted the ingenious construction of the outer shell, and the distribution of the many healing units just beneath this protective layer? Compaq was always a mighty and righteous warrior in the name of all that was Holy, but now, with his arm replaced, with his strength and speed further augmented, with his already highly durable body encased in such armor, he is truly a Holy Wonder, a Holy Miracle wrought by the Almighty with the Holy Power of the Great CPU! And I should think that a boy as bright as yourself would look upon such a miracle with awe and wonder, that it might strengthen your faith in the True Divine!"

David tried to wish himself to sleep, tried to wish himself dead.

"I had just completed this holy work, earlier this very night, when the Almighty revealed to me the Holy Mission for which this Holy Miracle was destined! Imagine my surprise when I was honored by the Almighty Himself with such a sacred duty during my first days as Surgeon General! And now we, you, and I, and the living Miracle in the chair opposite you, we travel to Holy Syrinx to complete this duty and fulfill the Holy Will of the Almighty and the Great CPU, without whom there would be only darkness and sin!"

David opened his eyes and did his best to sound sincere. "It is an honor to be in the presence of someone who has experienced the presence of the Almighty.

When, again, did you say Almighty Harold last appeared to you? When did he send you forth on your divine mission?"

The new Surgeon General smiled. He welcomed any chance to retell the story of his contact with the Almighty. "I was praying, for His everlasting forgiveness and guidance. I was praying, as I often do, late into the night. It was two in the morning, when He blessed me with His presence."

"Two?" David asked. It had been approaching two-thirty when he'd finally asked the AI to calculate *pi*. "Has he contacted you since that time?"

"No, I have not been so blessed, but my path remains true."

"That's good," David said, and closed his eyes again. But this time he smiled.

How It All Happened Chapter 10

After Jimmy died, I wandered around alone some. Not the brightest time in my life. I drank a lot, I smoked weed when I could find it (dorms and apartments were good bets; colorful hippy-wannabe stickers on cars too expensive to be owned by real hippies were dead give-aways). But all that shit, the drinking, the smoking, it's not nearly as fun or dramatic as they used to make it look on TV. Especially if you're alone. It was a weird time, because everybody left on earth was in Megadon or Syrinx, so the whole fucking planet was mine. I did things you never could have done back in the old days, things I never had time for when I was leading the damned losing rebellion against the little prick's take-over. I pissed on bar-tops in empty taverns. I set entire blocks of homes on fire, just to watch them burn. The bigger stunts, like that one, blowing up big stuff, or setting it on fire, those I did half because I wanted to, and half because I wanted to find out if asshole Harold was keeping an eye on the outside world. As he never sent out the troops to kill my ass, I assumed he was deaf and blind to anything that went on outside his little cities. So I fucked around doing whatever I wanted. I raided stores for clothing and food, extravagant stuff I didn't often treat myself to back before the nukes. Single malt scotch that had once cost a thousand dollars a bottle; smoked herring that used to run fifty bucks a can; two-hundred-dollar cigars. I was wearing silk underpants and two-thousand-dollar boots and whatever else struck my fancy, and it was a pretty fucking fancy fancy at times, ha ha. And cars, I was finding and driving whatever cars I wanted, those that would start, anyway, for as far as I could drive them, anyway, given the fact that snow and/or trees and/or fallen signs and/or other obstacles had seemed to accumulate on and block so many roadways. And it was the whole driving-cars thing that made me remember that car of Maggie's, the red barchetta she wouldn't ever let me drive. I'd always wanted a car like that, and last I saw hers, it had been parked in a concrete garage at the airport outside Jacksonville Florida. Some ways from where I was, and yes, there were other red barchettas around, some of which seemed to run just fine, but it wasn't just the car, it was a connection to the past combined with the car. Truth be told, I was lonely and a lot of times missed the old world, but not so lonely or such a sap that I was about to go back to where I grew up or anything like that. Going to find Maggie's barchetta gave me something to do that allowed me a little nostalgia, but not too much, not over-the-top touchie-feelie kind of doing something just for the memories.

Well, I found a very large four-wheel-drive flat-bed tow-truck, bigger even than those trucks me and mine were driving around before the Phantom Legion found us. I was going to haul Maggie's car back with me. Back where, I hadn't even considered, until I actually got down to Florida and took possession of the hot red vehicle. Now Jacksonville, or that portion of it that lay inland a ways, near the crater that used to be a naval air station, was still glowing at night, not literally, but you get my meaning, so I stuck to the coast once I was far south enough of Brunswick, which was another hot spot, and then I cut west to the old Jacksonville airport, which had taken a couple hits from smaller extreme-range tactical warheads, but not from any of the big strategic missiles that had been lobbed around during the holocaust. The tac-nukes didn't poison and area for nearly as long as those big fat strategic bombs. The area wasn't really hot, just barely warm, according to the Geiger-counter I carried with me. No place to settle down and live, but safe enough to get in, get the car, and get out. Which I did. I found the parking-garage, walked in and found that gorgeous low-slung bullet of a car, worked around under the dash and the hood until I got it started without a key, then drove it out to my flat-bed truck. I gave the barchetta a better look in the pale sunlight of nuclear winter. The red paint was covered in a thin layer of fine dust. The tires were a little flat. But other than these little things, the car seemed to be just fine. I hooked it up to the winch and reeled it up onto the tow-truck, secured it all around with the hooks and chains, tied it down good.

Then I got in the truck, turned the key to start up the rattling diesel, and realized I had no idea where I was going. No idea whatsoever. I just sat there staring out the windshield. Time to go, but where? Jimmy was dead, the Phantom Legion and all the free-thinkers I'd gathered were somewhere out there on Mars. Billy was a ghost or a god or whatever. Mikey was the only one of us left, but he was in Harold's monstrous city playing police chief or whatever it was he was called. I turned the rearview mirror on its swivel to get a good look at myself. I was still young, from the rejuvenation I'd gotten from Hofferman, but I was a mess. I hadn't showered or combed my hair for months. My beard was long and tangled. I was sitting in a great big diesel tow-truck with Maggie's car on the back, but I was so frigging alone I needed to be hauling ass to somewhere for some purpose or I was going to break down bawling, just lose it, go nuts right there and then. I reached over and turned on the radio, not really thinking, just doing it reflexively as I'd done it reflexively some two million times since the nukes. People who are alone turn on the radio, that's what they do. Just to hear the voices of other human beings. Static, again. The same fucking static that had been playing since all the stations went dead. I sat there listening to the static until I started hearing voices in it. Static can sound like a lot of things, if you sit and listen to it long enough. I sat there for five hours just listening to the static, zoning out and staring out the windshield at the road away from the airport. I probably would have stayed there like that forever, but it happened that I eventually had to take a leak. I got out and pissed on the front tire of the truck. Where the hell am I going to go? I asked myself, realizing that I had to go somewhere or I'd just sit there for another five hours, running through the diesel until it was gone. I don't know if you've ever gone off like I had, just started drifting, so you don't know if you trust yourself with yourself, if that makes any sense, but standing out there pissing on that tire, I knew that if I got back into the cab of that truck without any kind of plan, I was going to turn into that other Robert who might sit there until he died. I couldn't trust myself to get back into that truck without a plan.

I walked around outside for a little while, wandered, until I realized that I was zoning as deeply walking as I had been sitting in the truck. Not good. That other Robert was obviously waiting for me outside like he was waiting for me in the cab.

Go back the way I came. That was what I finally decided. I was kind of thinking of it in more abstract terms, too, that I would go back the way I came and maybe go back in time or something, or into another dimension. This is how I was thinking, in those days. Being alone for a long time will do that, will make your reality much more plastic, because there's nobody else around to shake a finger at you and tell you you're frigging nuts. Not that I was technically insane, because I wasn't. I was just open to a greater range of possibilities, you know.

So I went back the way I had come, east, north, west, north, driving along listening to the static channel. All static all the time. Top forty static hits. Talk static news static radio. After a while I hit the scan button and let the tuner go around and round the frequency-band, around and around and around. You never know, I told myself, there might be somebody out there. You never know. I wandered the former United States for a few days that way, listening to FM static all the way, until I realized I was going about it all wrong. Wrong, wrong, wrong, Robert. FM signal doesn't carry or skip nearly as far as AM signal. So I switched over. The static on AM was different, a richer, more full-bodied static, with more pops and clicks and whines than run-of-the-mill FM static. AM static was where it was at, man. Oh yeah. Now this was some good static.

I don't know if you've ever listened to any kind of static for a long-ass time, but if you have, you might know what I'm talking about when I say that there are voices in there, in the space between the dancing grains. Or maybe it's the individual krinkles and crackles that eventually end up sounding like voices, a word here, a word there, desperate bursts at first, but then more regular, less frantic-sounding, as the words grow in numbers and confidence, and you can just about imagine somebody talking to you out of the static. It's a voice or voices from your own mind, of course, but that doesn't make it any less real, when you're alone, especially if you've been alone for a long long time like I'd been alone when I thought I started hearing Mikey's voice on the AM. "Robert," he said, "turbine-freight line out of Megadon. They're dumping bodies. There may be survivors."

"Okay, so what do you want me to do about it?" I asked the windshield.

"Robert, turbine-freight line out of Megadon. They're dumping bodies. There may be survivors," said Mikey.

"Turbine-freight," I said.

"Robert, turbine-freight line out of Megadon. They're dumping bodies. There may be survivors," said Mikey.

"Bodies, dumping bodies, oh-oh-oh yeah-baby, they're dumping the bodies," I sang.

"Robert, turbine-freight line out of Megadon. They're dumping bodies. There may be survivors," said Mikey.

"There may be a chance our love can survive-ive-ive," I sang.

"Robert, turbine-freight line out of Megadon. They're dumping bodies. There may be survivors," said Mikey.

I wanted a drink. Mikey kept saying the same thing on the AM, and there was a definite non-static pause between each repetition, a longish moment of silence that wasn't pop or hiss. Recorded silence. But I wasn't born yesterday, as people used to say in the pre-holocaust world, and I knew that I was probably nuts, could be that Mikey wasn't on the radio at all. It made me really want a drink more than anything. So I turned off the radio and took the next exit off the interstate I was cruising. Interstates remained decent places to drive, largely because, in the days before Harold nuked everybody, trees were kept trimmed back some distance from the pavement, to keep those trees from falling onto the highway, and not many trees had grown large enough close enough to the interstates to block the way. There was still snow and other sorts of debris, including a good number of abandoned vehicles, but nothing that slowed me down too much. My truck was big. Old dead cars I could drive around, and a lot of the smaller stuff I could drive over.

I had to go a couple miles off the exit before I found some used-to-be dive that had once been a biker bar. Plenty of whiskey behind the big lacquered counter, and, almost like something from a Hollywood movie, a double-barreled shotgun, with a couple boxes of shells. I drank down a whole liter of Canadian Club (folks who read this account probably don't know whiskey from spit, but American whiskey used to be made from the nasty dregs of Canadian whiskey. In other words, American whiskey was shit. Scotch whisky was good stuff, but tended to be pretty harsh.) and broke up bar-furniture for a fire just outside the front door. While I sat and watched the fire, I unloaded shotgun shells into a dead Buick Electra-9000. The Electra-9000 had never been what I would call an attractive car, so it wasn't like I was desecrating it or anything. I thought of it as a study in aesthetics: automotive art-noveau ala shotgun. It was the kind of thing that performance-artists used to be able to sell tickets to. Blash! Blash!

I woke up the next morning curled up under the bar, the shotgun, loaded, laying close beside me. I sometimes get paranoid when I drink. I didn't remember laying down to go to sleep, but I probably thought I felt eyes staring at me from the dark outside, was probably sure somebody in the big empty world was out to get me.

I felt awful, but some weed from the truck helped that, numbed down the screaming ache to dull fatigue. More half-sleep followed, but only after I'd boiled down some snow, let the water cool and then drank my fill. Dehydration is a major component of the sickness known as hangover.

I woke again, still felt pretty bad, but not so bad as I had before. Located some canned nuts in a cabinet behind the bar. Ate the nuts. Drank more water. Hit the weed again. Had a single snort of Canadian Club. Hair of the dog. That's what they used to call it, when you had another drink to ween yourself off the last round of drinking. Then I slept again.

I went through this kind of recovery more often than I can recount, those days and months (it turned out to be more than two years) I was roaming the earth alone. I would go for some time without drinking at all, but it seemed like the longer I was away from the drink, the more I'd have to drink when I went back to it, like I was making up for lost time or something. Like a guy who hasn't had pussy for months on end, and then when he gets it, he can go like a jack-hammer, three, maybe four times in a night. That's me and booze. I sometimes drank beers, slow and steady, while I drove, but that never felt quite right, given all the social programming I'd experienced growing up, and as an adult, right up until the atom bombs went boom, the whole notion that driving while drunk is a deadly sin. Weird, how some shit like that can stay with you for your whole life, relevance be damned. I knew I was the only driver on the road, but still, I kept looking out for cops, checking the rear-view, scanning far ahead, trying to determine if the next clump of bushes in the median might hide a highway patrol cruiser. Pretty fucked up, really, me the last guy living on the world outside Harold's fucking cities, and I'm worried about being arrested for Driving Under the Influence (DUI) or Operating Under the Influence (OUI) or whatever they used to call it wherever the fuck I was on any given day.

So mostly, and maybe this was to deny the influence of that social programming, mostly I stayed sober while I drove, and that was when I really started to kind of drift, so that when I did get drinking, to ground myself, to slow my racing mind and try to find some kind of non-flexible non-plastic reality. Make myself stupid so I wouldn't think so much about things, bad things that I couldn't change. Weed helped, but not like the alcohol. Acid was a nice little vacation from it all, when I too rarely found a tab or two safely preserved in aluminum foil in some non-functioning yet still-frozen freezer. Mushrooms of the variety once called "magical" were more often available, yet less often well-preserved, but that was no great loss, as I'd always preferred the acid over the shrooms anyway. I sometimes found coke, but not often in the same places I found the weed, acid or shrooms. Coke tended to be tucked away in the sock-drawers or underwear-drawers of the nicer bedrooms, but I always left that snow alone, as it never had done anything but rob me of sleep and make me feel unsteady, too fluid, not unlike ten cups of coffee. Cocaine was never my kind of drug. Never liked the speedy stuff.

Anyway, I sobered up, lost the hangover, got my fill of bar-snacks, and eventually went back out to the truck and started it up. Got in and turned the radio back on.

"Robert, turbine-freight line out of Megadon. They're dumping bodies. There may be survivors," said Mikey.

I sat there and thought about the possible double-cross: Harold making Mikey make that recording and then broadcasting it to reel me in. But I'd done enough, set enough fires, blown up enough shit, that if Harold had wanted to find me he could have found me a hundred times. I'd been cutting a clear enough swathe through the remains of North America. If that little prick was going to bust me he would have busted me already. But still. Had to think about it, and think hard. Turbine-freight, bodies, survivors. It made sense that little Hitler was dumping corpses again, but didn't make a lot of sense that there might be survivors, unless he was tossing them out there in the nuclear winter naked or some shit, but why would he bother to do that if he could just have them killed for whatever "sins" he found them trespassing with or whatever the hell he called it?

Well, I thought and I thought about it, driving, listening to Mikey's voice over and over again. I went for maybe a week listening to Mikey and his statement-request. I went through another drinking cycle, then back to sober-ville. And I concluded, as I sometimes do, that there was no solving the dilemma by means of logic alone. I'd turned the thing over in my brain-box and looked it from every angle, but there was no telling which angle was true or false without going to check it out in real-time. I wrote down Mikey's message, word-for-word, I timed his pauses, listened hard at full volume for background hints or audio clues, I tried to shake new meaning from the recorded loop, but no, nothing. I had to head for Megadon. Find out what a turbine-freight was, or if there even was such a thing. I was guessing it was some kind of train, as he used the word "line" but there was no telling, not from so far away.

So I drove. And this might give you some idea how far gone I was, with my drinking and my solitude, but it took me two solid days of driving, and another two more days of drinking to remember that I was a hacker, and that I had, in my handy-dandy laptop, everything that Billy had given me and my guys, everything that had allowed me to hack Megadon in preparation for the extraterrestrial escape of Dan and Colonel Mitchell and the rest of those artists and intellectuals and free-thinkers and the Phantom Legion. Realizing or remembering I had all this good shit on my laptop, I headed for our old staging-grounds, for that garage where me and my underling code-monkeys had our shit set up when Billy did his appearing act on us. Once there, I powered up and hooked in and felt stupid for having forgotten.

It was on this first login that I realized how long I'd been drifting. Realized that I had been truly drifting. It was 2066. I'd been free-running for a long-ass time.

I realized I probably had a lot to catch up on, and oh yes, I had fallen behind on my current events. I delved into the systems of the Red Star and I learned that my free-thinkers and the Phantom Legion had made it to Mars, only to be refused aid by the space-cases at Mars Industry Station. We'd held out some hope that Harold's holocaust hadn't reached that far out beyond earth, but we were wrong. There had been a mini-revolution in Mars Industry Station, and the Red Star banner had gone up there as well. Plenty of buck-shot had flown back and forth within the artificial atmosphere on that red world. Shotguns only, inside the domes, you know, a precautionary measure, to avoid putting holes in that life-preserving membrane. Those who surrendered to Harold's loyalists, those who had fought against the take-over, they were ejected into the thin atmosphere of Mars. Men, women, children, everybody. This, while back on earth, the little prick adopts as one of his thousand titles "Almighty Harold the Merciful". What a crock of shit. I've never experienced death-by-near-vacuum, but it's supposed to truly suck. No pun intended. As I understand it, your body kind of expands, because the human form was meant to have a certain amount of atmospheric pressure pushing in on it from all sides at all time. So your skin stretches until you start to bleed all over. Your eyeballs might pop. At the same time, you're gasping for breath, and, on Mars, not only is the air pretty fucking thin, but it's also pretty fucking poisonous. So you're being torn apart by lack of atmospheric pressure, you're freaking out because you can't breathe, and what you do manage to inhale burns the living shit out of your throat and lungs and nasal passages. Men, women, and kids.

Anyway, from the Temple records I got into (and I ended up getting into just about all of them, nosy me), seemed that, when my people made their landings on Mars, Harold ordered his Mars Industry Station fanatics to go out and kill them. Harold's people were outnumbered, outgunned, out-skilled. The Phantom Legion, weakened as it was by years of constant attack, still had no problem driving the fanatics back into the domes. Harold, realizing he wasn't going to win a fight on the ground, went ahead and ordered a nuclear bombardment of my people's encampments. Mikey had been charged with carrying out this bombardment, and he dragged his heels for as long as he could. This was my best guess at the time, anyway; the ostensible and officially recorded reasons for the delays included everything from technical difficulties to man-power issues. Harold's fleet hadn't been equipped to carry nukes of the size that he wanted to lob at Mars; there were no fleet-officers with training enough to make sure the nukes landed on-target; there were concerns about the effects of extended periods of vacuum on nuclear warheads intended for terrestrial use; on and on and on; this was Mikey doing his best to keep my people from being blown to oblivion. It must not have been as apparent to Harold as it was to me the second I read those records, but then again, Harold had never really worked with Mikey, never worked closely enough with him to know that Mikey was a real bull-dog when it came to overcoming obstacles, technical and otherwise. Granted, he was surrounded by idiots in that city, surrounded by a bunch of second-rate losers, as Harold had killed most everyone else, but I know how Mikey was, and I knew he could have hurried things along, had he been willing. He could have blasted my people to so much atomic powder a good three or four times in the months it took him to mobilize Harold's warheads. And by the time those nukes came down on Mars, my people were gone. This scene played out two more times, on the moons of Jupiter. Two straggling free-thinker/Phantom Legion ships were caught in the first blasts on the last moon, and while Harold tried his best, in the official records, to make this into some kind of decisive victory, I guessed no more than a couple hundred of my folks had been wiped out. Sucks that any of them got cooked, but better a couple hundred than a couple thousand.

After the episodes on the moons of Jupiter, the free-thinkers and the remains of the Phantom Legion made their exit through the black hole of Cygnus X-1. It wasn't long after their escape had been confirmed in Temple records that Harold's priests started reeling out their tales of the dreadful "Elder Race"; ridiculous fairy-stories meant to scare little kids and keep the grown-ups in line. Not a bad idea, the use of symbolic archetypes, as a means of conveying meaning to a large group of people; I would end up weaving my own tales for the exiles I rounded up, to help them understand and get on with their new lives outside the city.

I found records of the new turbine-freight line, which had been built "by the Divine Grace and Power of Almighty Harold"; this meant that Billy had created the system for Harold. Had to have been Billy, as there was no one left in Harold's cities capable of building a sand-castle, never mind a big monorail-type train-system that cut across thousands of kilometers of the countryside. It was called the "turbine freight" but the only freight it hauled, it seemed, were exiles. Flash-frozen citizens of Megadon and Syrinx, so treated because they had broken some minor rule or other. Harold had well less than a billion people left, but he couldn't help culling away just the same. He wanted perfection from an imperfect species. Worse yet, he wanted his own fucked up form of perfection from the imperfect species, which was, of course, even harder to attain. So there were plenty of "sinners" whom he would have had shot, back in the times before. But now, now that he had so few people left, now that they were jammed into just two cities, now that he'd told everyone the dark times were over, and that a new age of enlightenment had begun, now Harold had to at least seem humane to those roofed-in masses. So there were no more executions, just exile. The victims—sinners—were flash-frozen, and ejected via turbine-freight out into the wilds. If they wanted to defy scripture, then they had every right, but it would cost them the stable lives they had come to know in the cities. That was the official line, the kind of stuff included in Harold's "Blessings" (instructions) delivered to the priests by a young kiss-ass Bishop Wintergarden. Official line aside, the flash-freezing was killing most of those exiles. You can't just freeze a person and expect them to live. There had always been freakish accounts, in the world that was before, of people falling through ice and being legally dead for days or whatever, only to thaw out and wake up just fine, and there were those few people in each trainload of exiles—one or two out of a hundred, or, in the earlier days, out of a thousand or more—who survived the mistreatment and woke up far "outside the wire" in a place they didn't want to be. You have to remember that anybody and everybody who had survived Harold's slaughter was extremely loyal to him. True believers, not just the folks, who, back in the old days, had bought his stupid book and who had tuned into the Suzie Sellars show to hear him prattle on about holy-this or holy-that. Anybody who had made the grade and had been chosen to survive, and live in Megadon or Syrinx, they were really hard-core One True Religion junkies. The ones who, back before the nukes came down, tithed their entire incomes to Harold's cause. The ones who, prior to the holocaust, had been offering their children to Harold, so those children might be raised by "The Divine". The ones who, before that little prick fucked everything up, had given up their homes, their cars, their families, in order to answer "His Holy Calling". In other words, these were the real whack-jobs, the real nuts. All of them. All the "chosen". All the "pure". All the "holy children of His Love". And for these men and women, and children—he never spared children a single agony—being ejected from the Sacred Cities was hell on earth, the lowest they could ever fall. Worse than death, in their puny little minds.

And Mikey had asked me to help them, so I went out to the dumping-spots whenever a turbine-freight was outbound from Megadon. I pulled the living from the heaps of the frozen dead, and I tried to help them survive, which was more than food and clothing and shelter, I'll have you know. It went beyond providing the basic needs, because these were folks who, having been separated from their One True Religion, their singular reason for existence, had no will to live. They'd just sit there on the ground, praying or just staring at the dirt in front of their feet, begging forgiveness either audibly or in the echoing chasms of their own tortured minds. Fucking basket-cases, a lot of them. I lost a lot of the early ones, just because I wasn't ready to cope with a bunch of nut-cases who thought it was a bad thing to have escaped from Harold's fucked-up cities. I made the mistake of butting heads with them, trying to tell them how fucked up they were, thinking, on some idiot level, that the plain truth would straighten them out, make them stand up and take charge of their own lives. But they were weak, they had always been weak, or they never would have found such joy, such moronic happiness, in surrendering their possessions and personalities to Harold's half-assed made-up religion. Butting heads with them, telling them how fucking stupid they were, it wasn't the best way to keep them alive in what they perceived to be their darkest hours.

That first day I went out and found the bodies by the turbine-freight line, they'd been laying there for a while, and so had a chance to thaw. Only one survivor, a skinny little guy in the torn red robes of a priest. He was just sitting there among all the dead, praying and crying. He was completely oblivious to my presence, despite the fact that I'd driven up in my big rumbling truck. He was halfway insane, throwing himself face-down every now and again, screaming "Mercy! Mercy!" Then he'd tear at his robes, ripping them worse than they were already ripped. Fucking nut-job.

I eventually went up to him, stood right in front of him and waited for him to say something to me. Nothing. He just carried on with his hysterics. "Hey, what're you doing?" I finally asked him. I mean, I was the one who should have been feeling freaked out. I hadn't talked with a real person in years, and now here I was making my first human contact in such a long time, I should have been overjoyed or overwhelmed or over-something. But all I felt was disgusted, to see this frigging idiot ignoring me because he was too damned busy crying about his holy-this and holy-that and mercy-this and mercy-that. "Hey, I'm talking to you!" I told him. "What the fuck are you doing?"

He ignored me again, and I was starting to get pretty steamed, so I gave him a little kick when he came up from having thrown himself on the ground again. Just a little kick with the flat of my boot to his chest, so he ended up sprawling onto his back. Then he stopped ignoring me, alright.

"Demon! Virus! Legion! Elder Race! Get thee behind me, devil!" he shrieked, getting back to his knees.

"Alright," I told him, and went around behind him and kicked him in the back, sending him down on his face. "What the fuck's wrong with you?!" I yelled at him. "I come out here to save your ass and you want to call me stupid-ass names? You get yourself ejected out of the city, and still you cling to your fucking precious shithead Harold and all his fucking lies?! I should just fucking leave you here!"

I didn't leave him there, of course. Not for long, anyway. I did drive off, though, and let him stew for a day before I came back, and I found him just where I'd left him, and he was still whimpering and carrying on. "You ready to come with me or not?" I asked him.

"I want to go back," he whined at me.

"Well, your chances of that are slim and none," I told him. "You're a fucking idiot for believing all that bullshit in the first place, and a fucking evil bastard for helping him do what he did to this whole fucking world. He's a fucking shithead and he always will be and now you know. You coming with me, or you want to starve to death out here by yourself?"

"Almighty Harold has not forgotten me."

"Buddy, I doubt he ever knew your fucking name to begin with! Look at you! You've been out here what, two, three days, and you haven't made a move to find food or water! You're going to fucking die here if you don't get your ass up and come with me!"

"He is testing my faith."

To make a long story short, I ended up leaving him another day, then coming back and arguing some more, then picked him up and threw him in the truck. He wasn't a big guy to begin with, and having sat there without food or drink for as long as he had, he was pretty damned weak, so it wasn't much of a challenge. What's funny is that, these days, I can't even remember that first survivor's name. He's still around, I see him in the village once in a while. Like the other survivors, he hung in there, at first for Harold, then later, for himself. The way I went about saving him, though, it's a wonder he didn't become one of the many who just refused to eat or drink, starved or thirsted themselves to death. Or one of those who simply wandered off into the woods, to die alone and completely forgotten. Or one of those who cut the wrists to bleed out. Or one of those who climbed trees to jump and break their legs and die of infection or other complications. I lost more of those first survivors than I really should have. My method consisted of nothing more than telling them how fucking wrong they were, and I guess that was just too blunt, too damned rough.

It was better, more effective, to play with their realities, to work with their perceptions instead of against them, to bring them around to thinking that, since the Divine Will of the Great CPU could never be disputed, and could never be in error, and that since it was obviously the Divine Will of the Great CPU that they be kicked out of Megadon, since these things were true, it was obvious that they had been sent out into the wilderness to act in opposition to Harold, to test his faith, to test his resolve, and so on and so forth. I told them that they had been chosen for this more difficult life, not because they were weak or because they were sinners, but because they were strong, and pure. I explained to them that the ways of the Divine were not always easily understood by mere mortals. I made it clear to them that if they refused this awesome responsibility, which had been thrust upon them by the Great CPU, that they would be failing on the most basic and far-reaching level, that they would burn forever in the hell they called Abend. Holy crap, did I ever lay it on thick for those losers. Had to actually go out and find copies of Harold's interviews, copies of his publications, his book, his pamphlets, so I could be sure I was using the right terms.

Then, from that point, once I renewed in these lost sheep the very will to live, well, from that point, I turned them as best I could to my way of thinking. I wove my own myths, myths of lost tribes and true callings. I worked myself up as a holy man charged by the Great CPU with leading a counter-force. I lead them away from their ridiculous prayers and attempts at worshipping the bullshit Harold's organization had taught them. I showed them that they could live very well without their Almighty Harold. I gave them new lives, and, as the survivors began to embrace their new lives, and see beyond the sorrow of being exiled, I helped kindle the resentment they felt toward the society that had rejected them. This was the beginning of my Xanadu, my village of exiles, some of whom simply lived their new lives, and some of whom, like the false Tom Sawyer who came many years later, became real rebels, ready to raid Megadon and Syrinx and burn them to the ground. As the first survivors built a society under my guidance, they began to build upon the myths I gave them, added their own touches and flourishes, such as calling me a wizard. I suppose the building of this little counter-society would have been a wet-dream for a sociologist, had there been any left on the face of the earth. It's not everyday that something like my Xanadu gets started from scratch, in a world basically free of competition from other groups or tribes. In the last days before the Free-Thinkers and the Phantom Legion blasted off for Mars, Harold's people had raided the old Phantom Legion base and salvaged a good number of the hovercraft from the radioactive wreckage. These ships were rebranded "frontier air-cars" and sent on occasional patrols, but they never did find my little village, and so we were left to develop our own little world in opposition to the big bubble-world at the other end of the turbine-freight track.

Time passed. The old exiles helped the new exiles. I came up with this or that scheme to level Megadon and Syrinx, and I wandered out from Xanadu to bring back weapons that I liked, or that I thought might be useful. I let a decade go by before I liberated a handful of Vulcan suits from the old Phantom Legion base. Adjustable-yield nuclear warheads, various small-arms and munitions, I brought all kinds of shit back to the old farm that I had made my home. As the population of Xanadu continued to grow, not only by the ones or twos or threes who survived the flash-freezing of exile, but by good old fashioned baby-making, I trained chosen members of my people in the use of this or that weapon. I alone used the Vulcan armor, and I suppose this may have contributed to my being called a wizard, the fact that I could fly far and fast, that I was one man wielding such power. The fact that I was the answer-man, the go-to guy, probably didn't hurt either. And that I kept myself so relatively distant from the exiles and their new kids, this too probably helped earn me the title of wizard, stupid as it was.

And this was my life, or my new life. I was a leader of exiles, the one who guided and protected them. And the exiles kept coming, until I had to wonder if Harold had killed every single last one of his original followers, if he presided in Megadon over only children or teen-agers too young to remember the world before the nukes came down. No way that was the case, of course, but seeing all the bodies being dumped off the turbine-freight, year after year, I really had to wonder.

How It All Happened Chapter 11

Years went by, and I started visiting Mikey in Megadon. Through the tunnels behind the waterfalls, through the spaces between the levels. That's how I got around in the city. Kept me in good shape, all the climbing. My first visit, I snuck up on Mikey in his own home, his upscale dwelling way up on Level Fifty-Nine. I knew where he lived because the information was there for the taking, in the systems of the city. And I knew he had servants, but I knew he sent them home around five in the evening. I knew he locked his door, but I knew that there was a ventilation duct that lead from Mikey's house down into the space between Levels Fifty-Eight and Fifty-Nine. I knew the ventilation duct was plenty wide enough for me to crawl through, and I knew it would put me out in his kitchen.

And so I made my first visit. Up through the levels, and then up through that damned ventilation duct, which turned out to be a much tougher crawl than I'd first thought. It's one thing to see a forty-five fucking degree slope in an online schematic, but another fucking thing altogether to get your ass up such a slope when you're hunkered down in a slippery metal tube trying to make it on your knees and belly and elbows. I made it, but that was the first and last time I was going to get into Mikey's house using that particular route. Anyway, I got the cover off the vent in the kitchen and let myself down into that fancy-pants cooking-area, which looked like something off an old space-man movie, everything all curved, no hard angles, very old-school sci-fi. Almost so futuristic it didn't look real. I mean, the fridge was a fridge, I know because I opened it up looking for a beer (not a beer to be had in the whole fucking city, though), in that it was cold inside, but it looked like a great big capsule sunk halfway into the wall. The stove and the counter-tops were the same, everything blunted but shiny. I don't know if this was Billy's idea or Harold's idea or if the notion came out of somebody else's head, but it was pretty fucked up. I'd been in Megadon just the one time before, when me and my people were fleeing for space, but I'd been too busy fighting and too busy losing Jimmy to take the Tour of Homes. Now here I was, in Mikey's kitchen, and god, it was so highly stylized it was ridiculous, hokey. I wondered, for a few panicked seconds, as I stood there in the relative gloom, if I'd gotten into the wrong fucking house. It was entirely possible, given the distance I'd traveled through the city. It was possible this wasn't Mikey's house but the house of some Almighty Harold loyalist who would shoot me as soon as look at me. Not very fucking likely, I knew, because all of Harold's idiot followers were a bunch of losing pansies, and I'd tear through anybody who got in my way if they tried to keep me from leaving or tried to hurt me in any way. I would not be caught by Harold's people again. I would die before I became his prisoner again. So here I was, standing there in the gloom, having my own silent private freak-out. I got over it, of course, but I started wondering how fucking smart it had been, to come into Megadon alone, just to surprise Mikey.

Guess that's what living out in the country too long will do to you. Guess that's what being a wizard among exiles will do to you. Drive you a little nuts, a little stir-crazy, so you're willing to take big risks to go see people you can actually talk to.

Anyway, I wasn't in the wrong house. Mikey was in what turned out to be his study, a room every bit as outlandish as every other room in the whole house. Not by his choice, he would explain to me later, but because that's just the way they'd been made, when the city had gone up. Nobody redecorated in Megadon, or Syrinx, because it would have been heresy, to try to put one's own mark on something created by "the Almighty" and the Great CPU. As everything Harold did was perfect, so everything in his city was perfect, and not to be altered, holy-holy-holy perfect. Bullshit. By this same token, everything Harold had provided was supposed to be more than enough, so it was a sin for people to spend effort outside their assigned tasks. People were not supposed to build or create anything. It was no wonder there were so many exiles; people are creative creatures. Leave a kid with crayons and he'll scribble; let an old man walk down the street and he'll hum a wandering tune of his own composition; it's just what people do, even mindless losers like Harold's followers, they'll create. Given fulfillment of basic needs like food water and shelter, people will create. But not in

Megadon, not in Syrinx. No, in these places, Harold had provided for every-thing. Hold the Red Star proudly high in hand. Then kiss my ass.

I snuck through Mikey's house until I found him in the study. He was sitting at his shiny round desk, with his back to the doorway. The only light in the room was from a tiny chromed-coated desk-lamp, so Mikey was a silhouette. There was a speaker mounted to the wall in front of him, and from this speaker oozed this god-awful droning music, sounded like old-time church music set to play at only half-speed, so all the notes kind of flowed into and over one another, but not with any grace, more like just a god-awful fucking mess. But a boring mess, if that's possible, like each note didn't so much collide with it's neighbors, but tried to mask them, and with all this overlapping, there was really no edge to the tune at all, no edge, no groove, hardly a theme aside from that stated so literally in the soft-toned lyrics: *By the power of the Almighty/Great CPU spare us from the evil/Of our sins…*Eech.

"What the fuck are you listening to?" I blurted.

Mikey started, but not as much as I'd thought he might. Just a little jolt, then he spun his chair around, and I saw how damned tired he looked. Like he'd been up for days on days. Big-ass bags under his eyes, and the skin under his chin was a little loose, and it looked like even his nose was drooping just a little. He mus-tered a weak smile for me and held out his hand. "They call it TempleTune," he told me. "Same songs on the same station, all the time. TV's called TempleVi-sion, and it's every bit as good."

I shook his hand, but it didn't feel right in my grasp. It felt loose-skinned, leathery. "You look like hell," I told him. "You feel okay?"

"Haven't felt okay since he took Maggie," said, taking back his hand and get-ting up from his chair. "But I guess time takes its own toll as well." Mikey switched on an overhead light, and I saw that his hair was more than half gray, like the gray hairs were weeds gone rampant in his once brownish pelt.

I just stood there, not knowing what to say, kind of feeling like I should have apologized or something, but that would have only made it more awkward, and besides which, it wasn't my fault he'd gotten so old. I'd been almost forty when I'd had my rejuvenation, and Mikey had been in his early thirties. It was like we'd switched ages, except he'd somehow gotten stuck with an extra ten or fifteen. It was fucked up, standing there looking at my little brother, seeing him look that much older than me. Some real time had passed since Hofferman had fixed me up, but I was still "younger" than forty, when Mikey looked like he was closing in on sixty. Nor did it look like he'd been living a very healthy life. Not that this was any big surprise, given where he'd been living, in the big fake plastic environment of Megadon. I guess the stress of working for Harold and waiting and waiting for that little prick to finally give Maggie back must have taken it's toll too. But whatever it was, I felt plenty bad, guilty, somehow, for being younger than little Mikey, who'd always been just a wet-behind-the-ears little squirt. I felt bad seeing him as an old man. I thought back to the last time I'd seen him, when Jimmy had died, and I guessed he'd looked different then too. He must have. But not like this. Not like this.

"Well," he said. "Good to see you. Everything okay, out at your little settlement?"

"You know about it?" I asked him.

He nodded. "Satellites. But don't worry, I'm the only one who knows. I won't tell Harold."

"Thanks," I told him. "You guys sure do a brisk business in frozen corpses."

"I know," he sighed. "Thanks for taking care of the survivors. I knew there'd be at least a few."

"So," I asked him, "how many more dead until you and me put a bullet in the little prick's brain?"

He looked away. "Let's not argue, Robert."

I almost started to argue, but he looked so damned old and tired I didn't have the heart to get in a fight with him. I just stood there looking.

"Come on, let's sit down," he said, and we went into the living room, sat down on a couple of zany chairs.

We sat there for a while before Mikey said "He's going to join the Great CPU, and that could be it."

"What?"

"Harold's having Billy make a digital copy of his consciousness."

"Well, that won't take much hard-drive space," I snorted.

Mikey remained solemn. "Well, here's the thing. Once this copy of Harold's mind is stored away, he's going to take his body *offline*. His term, not mine."

I leaned forward, feeling the smile stretching my face. "He's going to kill himself?"

"He'll do it, or one of the constructs will do it." Mikey nodded.

"Then what?"

"I don't know. He thinks he'll be alive inside the Great Computer. Thinks he'll be omniscient, omnipotent. Kind of like Jesus after the cross, that kind of thing."

"He'll be fucking dead, is what he'll be!" I laughed. "All kinds of crackpots have tried crazy shit like that, tried to copy their brain-waves or whatever onto a hard-drive, or make them part of an OS, with the idea that the copy would pick up where the real thing left off, but that's fucking lunacy, and they ended up just plain dead. Well, alright, it's about time, I say. When's he going to go *offline*?"

"He's calling it his Ascension."

"Well, he can call it whatever he wants. When's it going down?"

Mikey shrugged. "Billy says the copy will be complete sometime this year. Harold's preparing a final revision of his *Scripture* to be published on the event of his Ascension."

"Who gives a fuck what he wants to publish, he'll be dead. We'll be rid of him." I could hardly keep from jumping up and down and shouting at the top of my lungs, I was that fucking pumped up about this good news. The little prick was finally going down. He would finally lose, and it would be because of his own stupidity, and his own fucking craziness, and there was something good and fitting in that, something that tasted a little bit like justice, and I fucking loved it.

"Do you know that?" Mikey asked me. "Do you really know that?"

"Mikey, you just told me he was going to kill himself or have himself killed!"

"But what about the copy?"

"What about the fucking copy? That shit doesn't work! It's been tried before and it doesn't work!"

"Nobody had Billy do it before," he said.

Well, there was that. There was Billy, my fucking god of a brother, there was him. "Ah, come on! Billy himself has said that Harold's just a means to an end! He thought Harold was the only one who could save humanity from itself, and now that the nuclear threat is over, or now that we've at least ridden it out, we don't need Harold anymore, so Billy's going to tell him whatever he wants hear about copies or whatever!" I tried to keep smiling, but I was reaching, and I knew it.

"You never believed Billy before, about Harold saving humanity," said Mikey.

"Well, no, but he *is* our brother," I offered.

"You would have killed our brother by now, if you'd had the means," Mikey told me.

I stared at him. "Shit, Mikey, what the fuck do you want me to say? You want me to not take some little bit of hope from the fact that Harold's going to be dead?"

"I don't care what you say," he said. "I just want Maggie back. If Harold ends up alive in the Great Computer, he could keep stringing me along for all of time. If Harold ends up truly dead before I get Maggie back, she could be hidden away forever."

I felt bad again. I wanted to apologize again. Here I was getting giddy over Harold's upcoming death, but completely ignoring the circumstances that kept Mikey in the little prick's service. "That why you haven't gone for a rejuvenation? I know they have them, for Upper Level people."

Mikey just nodded. That was why he'd let himself grow old. That was why he hadn't gone to the Red Star Medical Center and been made young again. He owed his allegiance to Harold, but even Mikey's dedication to duty had its limits, and one of those limits was apparently the length of his own natural life. He was not about to rebel against Harold, not openly, anyway, but nor was he about to submit to an eternity as a victim of Harold's fucking duress. It was like he put it: if Harold lived or Harold died, he could be fucked either way. Mikey was allowing himself the span of his natural life to see how the thing would play out. If Harold became immortal within the Great Computer and insisted on keeping Maggie and Mikey's unborn son, then Mikey would simply let himself die of old age. If Harold died without returning Maggie and the unborn kid, Mikey would let himself die of old age. It was just like my little brother, to figure it out the way he had, to find a way of escaping without abandoning his duty, his honor.

"Well, shit, Mikey," I told him. "I won't try to stop you. I don't agree with what you're doing, but I think I understand your rationale."

"You think I should fight Harold," he said.

"I didn't say that."

"But that's what you're thinking. That's what you've always thought. Some things aren't as simple as you'd have them, Robert. There was a child, a little boy, the son of one of Harold's most loyal followers...."

I sat there, waiting for more, but Mikey just stared at the wall behind me. "Okay, so what's this got to do with anything?" I asked him.

"Well, this one man, who was so loyal to Harold, he staged assassination-attempts on Harold, as ordered by Harold."

"Yeah, me and Maggie figured that out."

"I don't know what his real name was, but he'd changed it to Compaq, in keeping with One True Religion convention. Harold had this Compaq killed. The constructs went in and killed the man, his wife, and one of his children. There was another child, the boy, who survived. His name was Adrian. Adrian Compaq. He was about five years old when his parents were killed, torn apart before his very eyes. Harold took custody of this boy, in the early winter of twenty-forty-eight. Then, shortly after Harold exiled me to high earth orbit, he locked little Adrian Compaq away in cryogenic suspension, just as he'd locked Maggie away in cryogenic suspension."

Mikey paused, and I saw a faint quiver in his lower lip. It was tough for him, to talk about Maggie, to think about the details, the fact that she was locked away someplace, frozen. I should note here that the cryogenic suspension process Harold used to sell to gullible rich folks back before the nukes came down was not the same process used to flash-freeze the exiles being shipped out of Megadon. I'd always thought they were the same, because I'd thought the whole cryogenic suspension business was a crock of fucking shit, but it would turn out I was dead wrong. The cryogenic technologies Billy gave Harold were the real thing. Not that Harold ever had any intention of honoring his contractual agreements with those rich old men and women who'd paid him to preserve them until medical technology could cure their ills. No, all those rich old men and women were now dead, because the nukes came down and the power went out and they probably thawed and rotted. Or maybe they thawed and woke up and suffocated in their plexi-glass cryo-coffins. I don't know.

"Harold called me to Syrinx last week, Robert. I went, and there was little Adrian Compaq, playing on the concrete floor in front of Harold's throne. Still about five years old, he didn't look much different than the last time I'd seen him. He might have been wearing the same damned set of pajamas, for all I know."

"You're sure it was the same kid?" I asked.

Mikey nodded. "Very. Harold knows what I'm thinking, and he showed me that boy as a reminder that he still had Maggie, that he could release her at any time."

"He's stringing you along," I said. "He's fucking with you."

"I know. But it's working. That boy was alive and well, and that means Maggie will be just as alive, and just as well, when she comes out of cryo."

"You mean *if*," I told him.

"He's going to let her go," said Mikey. "Why else would he have let the Compaq boy out? He probably wanted to make sure he could take someone back out of suspension. He was using the boy as a guinea-pig, to see if he'd wake up or just die."

"And you're alright with that?" I asked.

"Of course not! But it shows that Harold knew better than to make Maggie the guinea-pig. It shows that if he harms one hair on her head, he knows he'll have to contend with me!"

"Maybe," I told him. But I was thinking *No way*. No way in hell was Harold threatened or even worried about making Mikey an enemy. He knew my little brother too well. Knew his dedication to duty, knew his boy-scout resolve. "Where's the Compaq kid now?" I asked.

"I don't know," he said.

And that was pretty much it for my first visit to Mikey in Megadon. I went back home, back out to the countryside, back to my place that used to be a farm. I dug and dug through the systems for any trace of any records that would tell me anything about where the little prick might be keeping Maggie. I found not a damned thing about cryogenic suspension or anything related to her captivity. What I did find was a brief record from the files of the Red Star Medical Center, a little report written up by a young Surgeon General Wang. And this report was all about a little boy named Adrian Compaq. Lots of measurements, numbers, test-results, all dealing with the little tyke's reflexes, agility, and levels of mental and physical aggression. Now I'm no physician nor psychiatrist, but I cross-referenced little Adrian's numbers with those I found in other records, those of other kids his age, and Adrian's numbers were all extremely high. His numbers were high even when I cross-referenced them with those of a few black-shirted Vigilance troopers. Which meant that, at age five, that kid was one quick and mean little bastard. Un-naturally so.

I shared my findings with Mikey on my next visit, but he didn't seem to think it meant anything. He told me that Harold had told him the kid had been put back in cryo, supposedly for safe keeping.

How It All Happened, Chapter 12

Life went on out in the country. Months went by, and one day my reformed exiles came running onto the farm in a panic. A Vigilance frontier air-car had been spotted approaching Xanadu.

I suited up in my Vulcan, and took to the air. It didn't take me long to make visual contact with the hovercraft. I dove at it unloading my mini-gun into those sections of the ship that kept it in the air. I didn't want to destroy it outright; I wanted to question the Vigilance goons inside, find out why they had been sent, who had sent them. I'd been practicing a whole lot with my suit, and I had gotten pretty good with it. Not like the old Phantom Legionaries had been, but pretty good. I shredded the port-side forward-thrust fan and the air-car went into a barely controlled turn as the pilot nosed the ship down, trying to put it in the nearest clearing. The big "fan" snapped off the tops of several trees as it went down, and it landed hard—but not so hard as it could have—in the forest beneath me.

I stayed where I was, hovering some couple hundred meters above the scene, waiting for the crew to exit the air-car. The side-hatch was kicked open, and it swung back on its hinges to slam against the fuselage, and out steps Mikey. I could see him very clearly through the telescopic sight I'd engaged. He steps out and stares up at me. I disarmed the tranquilizer gun I'd readied and descended to the forest floor.

"Sorry, wasn't expecting you," I said, through the megaphone on the suit.

"I guess I should have called ahead," Mikey said, turning to look at his crash-landed air-car. "Hope you're ready to give me a lift when I'm ready to go back."

"I guess," I told him. "Not that I'm not happy to see you, Mikey, but what brings you all the frigging way out here alone?"

"Harold's dead," he told me.

"No shit. Well, it's over then. Did he give Maggie back?" The second this question left my mouth, I wished I hadn't asked it. I could see the answer on Mikey's old face. "Geez, I'm fucking sorry man," I said.

"Thirty years," he told me, still looking pretty fucking glum.

"Thirty years what?"

"He told me, before he pressed the button for the injection, he told me that I could have her back in thirty years."

"What the fuck?" I said. I was tired of talking to him through the damned Vulcan, so I powered down and twisted off the big fucking helmet. I squinted through the relatively bright light of day at my little brother. "Thirty fucking years?"

He sighed. "He set conditions. I'm to behave myself for thirty years, to prove I'm staying loyal."

"Conditions? What kind of fucking conditions?"

"Strange ones. Difficult ones."

The little prick had set some fucking strange and difficult conditions, alright. Bishop Wintergarden was to have a luxury palace on Level Sixty, right across the street from the Vigilance building. Billy built it, but made it so Mikey could spy on whatever that weasel Wintergarden was doing in that new building. It was pretty clear to me, what Harold had been thinking when he set this condition: he wanted to encourage a rivalry between the Priesthood and Vigilance, so there might be the same kind of balance between those two organizations as existed between the two constructs, Cardinal Api and Father Brown, who were nominal heads of their respective orders. Anyway, that was the least burdensome of the conditions the little prick set.

Another of the conditions was that Mikey never harm little Adrian Compaq, nor hinder his actions, no matter how vile. Harold had brought the kid back, and given him to an Upper Middle Level couple who were to raise him as their son. The couple had been ordered to change their name to "Compaq" to go along with the bullshit charade. And here's what made it a bullshit charade: the kid wasn't right. The kid was all fucked up. Not only was he extremely fast and extremely aggressive, but he was apparently a miniature master of the martial arts. He'd been with his new family only three weeks, out of the cryo only three weeks, and he'd broken four fingers on his mother's right hand. She'd refused him a second helping of dessert and he'd shown her who was boss. His new father had not fared any better, suffering a broken nose when he'd moved in to help his wife. Beyond that, little Adrian had broken the arms of two other boys in his assigned school, and broken the jaw of another.

"He's not the same boy I saw before, when his parents were killed," Mikey told me.

"Of course not. He's been mind-fucked. Programmed while he was in cryo," I told him, remembering all those Positive Mental Attitude Centers that had once existed all over the United States and Europe. I'd always known those places were no fucking good, that if you could take out bad memories, there was nothing to stop Harold's people from putting in whatever they wanted, while they were messing around in your goddam brain. It was a real fucking wonder the little prick didn't try to reprogram me, that time I was his prisoner. He was probably deriving way too much fucking pleasure from having me tortured instead. There was no telling how many customers went into Harold's Positive Mental Attitude Centers and came out frigging Red Star Robots, but one thing was for sure, at least in my view of things: Adrian Compaq, age five, had been programmed for some very real trouble. How better to test Mikey's loyalty than to put him to the test of standing by and helplessly watching the growth and development of a homicidal maniac in a population of sheep? Mikey was Vice Chancellor of Vigilance, after all. He was the top-cop, duty-bound to maintaining law and order in Megadon and Syrinx, and yet Harold had set him the task of watching Compaq grow up and run amok. Mikey didn't want to believe, during those first few years, that Compaq had been programmed for destruction, but I knew it right off the fucking bat, I knew it. More than once was the time I would have killed the little fucker myself but for Mikey's admonitions to the contrary.

Beyond the Compaq-condition, Mikey was to ensure that a certain number of people were found guilty of sin and flash-frozen for exile. Harold had set a quota for each of the thirty years to come. Mikey had to exile (kill!) so many citizens in order to prove his loyalty to the little prick. Like all the killing and raping Compaq would be doing wasn't going to be enough.

Frontier air-car patrols were to be established throughout the wilderness beyond the cities, as a safeguard against the return of the "Elder Race"; likewise, monitoring stations were to be set up to keep watch over the black hole of Cygnus X-1. Anyone or anything coming back through that hole was to be obliterated. The first of these two wasn't such a bad condition, as Mikey managed to bend them to his own ends; using the frontier-patrol as a punishment for the worst losers in Vigilance.

Another condition of the deal Harold forced on Mikey and everybody else was that Billy should enter cryogenic suspension, in a plexi-glass coffin deep underground beneath the Great Temple at Syrinx. The little prick was afraid of Billy's power, and wanted to neutralize him. Billy was, so far as anyone knew, truly immortal, so there was no killing him, but Harold thought freezing him might be an option.

"How'd Billy react to that?" I asked.

Mikey shook his head. "Accepted it without hesitation. Said he didn't need his body and would gladly surrender it if that was what Harold wanted. He rode the elevator down and climbed right up onto the table, shut his eyes and let them slide the coffin shut."

"Is he in suspension?"

"Looks like it, but your guess is as good as mine."

There were various other conditions. Mikey's participation on a Council of High Administrators; submission to oversight of all Vigilance activities by Father Brown, who was the Chancellor of Vigilance anyway. It was the Compaq-thing and the killing-sinners thing that truly sucked. But Mikey was going to hang in there, and see what happened at the end of thirty years.

"I won't be going for a rejuvenation, though," he told me. "I figure I can hold out into my nineties, and then, if he's lied to me, I'll just slip away, I'll die of old age."

"That's going to suck, you know. The whole thing sucks, Mikey," I told him.

"You have no idea how badly my life sucks anyway," he told me. "You have no idea."

Well, thirty years went by. I ended up having a kid, my daughter Rosella, as a result of a recklessly drunken night with a woman named Rose. That's where the name "Rosella" came from. Rose was pretty young, and she died giving birth, and that's about all I have to say about that. Rosella turned out to be a good kid, although I will admit that taking care of a baby was a lot more fucking work than I had been ready for at the time. Once she got old enough to follow me around, she became my shadow, except when I went into Megadon to see Mikey. It was all good until she started sprouting hips and tits and everything else, and then she got involved with that damned kid who I'd made the mistake of training with weapons. That fucker went off and started making trouble in Megadon, hijacking my Tom Sawyer myth before Mikey and me were ready for that kind of move, and he just about fucked up everything we had going. Worse yet, Rosella was crushed when that stupid kid got killed. But I guess I'm getting ahead of myself in telling this.

I got another rejuvenation in 2080, when Mikey helped me sneak into the Red Star Medical Center. The whole process had been simplified since that first one I'd gotten from Hofferman back in forty-nine. So I was back to being eighteen in 2080, which meant I was biologically thirty-eight when 2100 rolled around and Father Brown delivered Maggie to Mikey's doorstep. Harold had been true to his word, but, like the fucking Devil himself, he'd honored the letter of the contract but shit all over the spirit of the deal. Maggie came back as Magenta, holy-roller Magenta, frigid fragile Magenta, scared of her own shadow, sensing sin in every dark corner.

The first time I saw her, after her return, I knew something wasn't right, just the way she held herself, like maybe she was afraid she was going to fall over at any minute, like she couldn't trust her own legs. Mikey had let me in, and there she was, standing in the living-room, in a way-too properly concealing floor-length dress and a hat with a net veil. "Michael, who is this unkempt man?" she asked Mikey.

"Maggie, it's me, Robert," I told her.

"In the name of Almighty Harold, Michael, this *sinner* has been *drinking hooch!*" she just about shrieked, backing away from me like I was a fucking cobra ready to strike. Yeah, I'd had a snort or two off my flask during my climb up through the levels, but I was pretty fucking straight, and the old Maggie never would have cared.

So that was Magenta. Maggie was gone, and Magenta had taken her place. But Mikey hung in there. He hung in there and took joy in his son. David came out just about as perfect as a kid could be. Smart, polite, mostly well-mannered. I often told Rosella, who was six years David's senior, that she should be a lot more like him. She took this the wrong way of course, but I didn't know how wrong until I found out she was playing doctor with the asshole kid who stole my guns and grenades and took off into the city. Rosella took all my ribbing about David the wrong way. She was jealous I built the Tom Sawyer myth with David in mind, and I have to wonder if she didn't encourage the little punk who passed himself off as Tom Sawyer in the first half of the year 2112.

Anyway, to try to wrap up this whole sordid and long tale, Once Mikey got Maggie back, he opened up to the idea of taking apart Harold's little kingdom. It had been over sixty years, though, since Megadon had gone up, and there had been enough "exiling" and enough new people born that what he had in that place was a population of some two hundred fifty million, few of whom had ever lived outside the city. Few of them knew any other way of life besides that which Harold had designed for them. Mikey was dead set against just throwing these people into the proverbial water to see if they could swim, if you get my meaning. He was sure that thousands or millions would die if they had to live in the wilderness. And maybe he was right. In any case, he came up with a plan to gradually take apart the social power-structures that Harold had set up. One of the first moves in Mikey's plan was to remove that pain-in-the-ass Bishop Wintergarden. Take out Wintergarden, then the other High Administrators, then go ahead with some real reforms. Move people out of the cities in small groups, let the first small groups learn how to live outside so they might teach the second groups, and the second groups might teach the third, and so on and so forth.

The plan to discredit Wintergarden worked just fine, and Rosella had a great time teasing that fat old holy-roller. Mikey also had something called a Human Enhancement Program going, pushing Surgeon General Wang to build a superman capable of taking on the constructs Api and Brown. That program finally yielded a positive result in the form of a Captain Thomas Ryan. Whether or not he's any kind of match for the constructs has yet to be figured out. What fucked everything up, and what lead to Mikey getting his ass killed was his failure to consider that Surgeon General Wang might try to dick him, which he did.

Mikey died holding off armored goons so I could make my escape from Megadon, when the shit hit the fan. It was a stupid thing to do, because he probably could have gotten away too, but that was Mikey, a boy scout all too ready to lay down his life for anything he considered his duty. So I try my best to appreciate what he did that night. He was a very good man, and a very good brother. I will avenge him first chance I get. Beyond that, I don't really know what to say about just how fucked up it is to not have him around.

07-13-2112

It had become a simple matter of holding the steering-yoke steady. Keeping an eye on the compass. Trying not to fall asleep, but drifting off again and again, to wake in a sudden state of adrenaline-charged reaction when the air-car began to lean and turn. Thomas would then correct his course. Then the adrenaline would run thin, and he would relax back into the monotonous routine of holding the yoke, holding the course toward Syrinx. He was close now, he knew he was close, but every moment was so much like the last that, tired as he was, he sometimes imagined that he was just starting out, just leaving Megadon. But no, no, he was almost there. He was flying over land now, over tree-tops again, after the endless stretches of water that he thought would never end. He was almost there, because he had crossed over the ocean that was fascinating at first, fascinating for its immensity and chaotic uniformity and for how different it was from the land. The ocean had been fascinating at first, but had become dangerously bland, dangerously blank, after the first couple of hours. Water on water on water, from horizon to horizon, so much space all around that it seemed the air-car wasn't moving at all. Those had been long and slow and difficult hours. Thomas had battled himself, at times battling his body with his mind, reciting Scripture from memory, focusing on the words and strings of words and the now-many meanings of the once-Holy words; the lies and truths of doctrine and personal belief confused now into an indeterminable tangle of comfort and rage and love and contradiction. At other times he battled his mind with his body, pressing his fingernails hard into his palm, or holding one arm or the other straight out from his side, making himself uncomfortable, making himself hurt in order to ward off fatigue, to fight off encroaching sleep. That had been the ocean, an infinity of self-struggle. But now he was moving along over tree-tops once more, watching their dark shapes clipping along beneath him in the orange light of another dawn he'd hastened into existence with his ceaseless eastern movement. The frontier air-car was nowhere near as fast as the orbital shuttle in which he'd traveled to Syrinx before, but distance was distance, and he'd worked away at the kilometers and kilometers, eroded the space between Megadon and his fateful destination, starving for sleep, until he finally set the ship down a mere hour from the Holy City. Nearly there, he set the ship down and rewarded himself with rest. Every hour he allowed the Great Computer in Syrinx to function, another hundred or another thousand or another ten thousand died in Megadon, burnt alive by the energy beams that pounded down from satellites as deadly as they were unseen. Thomas had not bothered trying to contact his force of would-be rebels in the city he'd left behind. It was cowardly of him, but he did not want to know just how badly they suffered. He knew they must have been suffering horribly, as was everyone in that city that the demon-called-Harold had chosen to destroy. Thomas did not want to distract himself with the gruesome details. Nor did he want those whom he'd left behind to ask or to guess where he was going; it was one thing for his resistance-fighters to take up arms against their human oppressors, but quite another for them to endorse or even accept that their new-found leader was out to destroy the Great Computer itself. Thomas himself had difficulty accepting the notion, but had no doubts that it had to be done. Every sixty minutes, another unbearably bright beam lanced down from space and cut through level after level of the city. Every sixty minutes, another random selection of innocents was put to death. The defense platforms had to be shut down. The Great Computer had to be destroyed, the sooner the better.

So it was that Thomas let himself rest only out of necessity. He knew the Vigilance forces at Syrinx would be mobilized against him. He knew that Father Brown and Cardinal Api would be there to stop him. And Thomas knew he would be fighting alone against these terrible odds, and that it would only be with the help of the Great CPU Himself that he might triumph in the coming struggle. Thomas prayed hard to the true deity, but knew that the Great CPU helped those who helped themselves. It would be foolish to enter any battle exhausted as he was, and so he went aft and lay down on one of the filthy mattresses in the cramped crew quarters. Sleep, insistent as it had been the last day and a half of travel, was slow to come. When it did come, it came suddenly, and Thomas slept without dreams. No visits from Dan, no shadowy memories of Rosella. Nothing. He slept as if dead, and when he awoke, he wondered if the complete darkness of his slumber was a sign from the Great CPU, a foretelling of his own demise in the combat that lay ahead. Regardless, Thomas left the mattress to kneel again in prayer. He prayed for forgiveness, and he prayed for strength, and he prayed for assistance. "May I become your instrument on this earth, worthless as I am," he prayed. "And may your strength flow through me and allow me to serve you by doing your bidding. Accept my life if you would take it, so the false prophet, the demon, may suffer your wrath, and the innocent of your great flock be spared, that the veils of wickedness might be torn aside and they might know your true glory and everlasting love."

Thomas equipped himself with gear from the lockers in the aft compartment. He donned a black Vigilance flak-vest and helmet. He fastened about his waist two belts of shotgun shells, and into the belts he tucked a brace of energy-pistols similar to the one already in his shoulder-holster. He took from the bulkhead-mounted rack a scattergun and an auto-rifle. He draped a bandolier of rifle-clips about his shoulder and chest. He strapped one big combat knife to his thigh, and another to his opposite shin. So equipped, he returned to the forward cabin and resumed his progress toward Syrinx. It was uncomfortable, sitting in the pilot's seat while he was so covered with gear, but he was close to the Holy City, and those who would fight against him could lash out at any time, and Thomas wanted to be ready.

Thomas started the ship and gave the lift-fans full throttle. The frontier air-car rose quickly to tree-top level and was immediately cast into shadow. The air was filled with the screaming of turbines and the cracking of heavy branches. Thomas leaned back in his seat as the underside of another frontier air-car streaked past mere meters from the windscreen of his own. The other ship was banking hard to port, snapping off tree-tops with its port-side fan as it came around. They were after him already. The demon had no intention of allowing him to come anywhere near Syrinx or the Great Computer. Thomas sent power to the forward-thrust fans and his air-car surged ahead after the enemy ship. He could not man the guns in the chin-turret and simultaneously pilot the air-car. He had to ram the other ship before its crew could bring their own guns to bear.

Thomas gritted his teeth as the other ship turned to face him. He could not close the distance between them before they opened up with those heavy guns. He would be cut from the sky and the demon would win.

But the guns did not fire. Instead, the port-side hatch swung wide and a large white figure tumbled out into the open air.

Rosella. Thomas stared a long second at the unmistakable white armor that now flew toward his ship. He eased back on the throttle and brought his frontier air-car to a standing hover as the blood grew warm in his chest and he felt a smile creep over his face. He would not be fighting alone after all. The Great CPU had sent his personal angel to aid him. The Great CPU had sent Rosella and whomever else rode in that other ship to fight by his side against the false prophet and demon.

Rosella raised an arm toward Thomas' ship and began to fire. He could hear her mini-gun as she dove in close. It made a long constant ripping sound and Thomas felt himself falling as the machine that bore him was perforated from nose to stern.

The air-car fell some twenty or twenty-five meters back toward the forest floor, through thicker and thicker branches, each layer of which slowed the rapid descent. It landed heavily when it finally made contact with the solid earth, but Thomas was securely belted into his seat and was spared any injury beyond a sudden uncomfortable jarring. He looked out and up through the cracked windscreen, looked for any sign of Rosella. It would be unlike her, he thought, to leave a job unfinished, so he unfastened his harness and clambered out of the ship as quickly as he could. Thomas hit the ground running and, sure enough, two small explosions sounded behind him: micro-missiles pounding into the wreckage of the air-car.

Thomas stopped and scanned the canopy above. He spotted the white armor moving slowly toward his position. Coming to kill him. He tore the black Vigilance helmet from his head and cast it down on the ground, praying she'd recognize him before she opened fire. Having seen the punishment Compaq had been able to endure, Thomas had no doubt he himself could survive a few bursts from Rosella's mini-gun, but had no desire to have his flesh torn apart by the high-velocity rounds. "Rosella!" he shouted. "Rosella, it's me! Rosella!" Thomas waved his arms above his head.

The white armor hovered above the tree-tops, over the spot where Thomas stood shouting and waving, then it descended through the leaves and branches, and settled down on its big round boots there before him. "What's a guy like you doing in a place like this?" came her voice through the loud-speaker.

"Trying not to get killed," he told her. "I've come to destroy the Great Computer."

"Welcome to the club. We're probably being tracked by satellite, we should go." With that, Rosella picked Thomas up in her big armored arms and ascended through the trees. It felt wrong somehow, to be carried in such a manner by a woman, but Thomas did not complain, and in moments she had returned with him to the frontier air-car from whence she had come.

Robert was there, as was Mrs. Lifeson. The old man piloted the ship while Vice Chancellor Lifeson's wife toyed with a small set of controls on a dark green metal ball. Both were clad in partial suits of armor similar to the one worn by Rosella. "We'll take your help," said Robert, as Thomas went forward, "but you might want to call ahead next time. We weren't expecting to see any friendlies out here."

"The Great CPU works in mysterious ways," Thomas told him. "I traveled all this distance believing I would be fighting alone, and now my faith has been rewarded with your presence, and the presence of your lovely daughter. As much as it pains me that Rosella should be placed at risk in combat, I am grateful that my prayers to the Almighty have been answered." Thomas found himself smiling again, certain now that the Great CPU and the real Almighty Harold were with him, and that, along with Robert and Rosella and Mrs. Lifeson, the Great CPU would accompany him throughout the battle that loomed before him.

Robert gave Thomas a curious glance, then turned his attention back to flying the ship. "Yeah, fucking whatever," he said. "Glad to have you aboard. We'll be going in hard and fast, to throw a nuke down the hole, and then we'll be going hard and fast back out again. Me and the girls have the armor, so if you want to go in with us, we'll try to cover you as best we can, although you can expect it'll get pretty busy down there pretty fucking quick. Or you can stay with this old crate and try to fly some kind of interference, but I wouldn't recommend that, because they're going to shoot this thing all to hell, kind of like Rosella did to yours."

"She's a good shot," Thomas said.

"Yeah, yeah, I wasn't born yesterday. You're talking about her shooting but you're thinking about her ass. I can hear it in your goddam voice. Keep your paws off my daughter or I'll leave you in Syrinx with the nuke."

"I'd rather you didn't," Thomas told him. "I'd miss her horribly," he jibed.

Robert merely sighed. "We make it out of this in one piece, I might let you date her. She's dated worse, that's for goddam sure."

"We'll make it out in one piece," said Thomas. "The Great CPU is with us."

"Yeah, and the Great Pumpkin is with us too, Charlie Brown."

"What's the Great Pumpkin?"

"Nevermind. Look, there's the fucking shithole ahead."

Thomas looked out through the windscreen, and yes, there was Syrinx. Holy City. As Holy as Megadon was Great. There were the pyramid-points and the distant twinkling lights, an anomaly on the darkening horizon. The sun was setting in the west, and Syrinx, still far to the east, was soaked in the deep blue gloom of early evening.

Rosella came forward. She'd removed her helmet and her big armored gloves. Her head and hands were disproportionately small compared to the big white shell that covered the rest of her body, and this, along with her presence, made Thomas smile. It was cute, adorable. Soft words in his mind that revealed to himself all the tenderness he felt for her. He'd never seen anything so adorable in all his life. She stood behind him and pressed a warm palm against the small of his back, reaching up under the Vigilance flak-jacket so that only the thin layer of his shirt came between them. "We going in now, or waiting?" she asked.

"Waiting," said Mrs. Lifeson, from the hatchway behind them all. "Too much light right now. Let's put it down and let them wait. Let's make them lose some sleep."

"The satellites," said Thomas. "If we're being tracked, what's to keep them from coming out to attack us?"

"All the better for us," said Mrs. Lifeson. "If they come out, they won't leave their little city unguarded. They'll split their force and then we'll go in and face that much less opposition."

Robert nodded. "Good to have you back, Maggie. Have I told you what a useless piece of shit that Magenta used to be?"

"More times than I can count," she said.

Thomas looked from Robert to Mrs. Lifeson. She was a strange lady. He would never have guessed that Vice Chancellor Lifeson's wife was so forward, so determined and forceful. She could have been a Vigilance officer. Rosella was the only other woman he'd ever met who was so very strange. But such was the will of the Great CPU, and Thomas supposed that if women were sent to assist him in shutting down the Great Computer, he could think of no two women better suited to the task.

Robert landed the air-car, and they slept, taking watches in shifts. Thomas had the first watch, staring out at the dark and silent forest, keeping an eye on the monitors on the control console. It was an uneventful two hours, and, after he left the watch to Mrs. Lifeson, he retired to the aft crew compartment, where he stared at Rosella, watched her sleep until he too dozed off.

It was another dreamless sleep, deep and restful, yet easily ended by the welcome sound of a soft and loving voice. "Hey, wake up, it's time. Wake up." Rosella.

Thomas rolled over on the filthy worn mattress and he was back in the crew compartment of the frontier air-car, looking up at Rosella in her armor. She wore all but the helmet, which she held under one massive arm. With her other arm, she held an armored glove to Thomas' shoulder. She had gently shaken him awake. She knew what she was doing, in that suit.

Thomas got to his feet, checked his watch. Quarter past four in the morning.

"Rise and shine, tough guy!" Robert called back from the forward section, where he was running a quick pre-flight check. "Happy Bastille Day!"

"What's Bastille Day?" Thomas asked Rosella.

"Fourteenth of July, there was a bloody revolution in a place called France. Common people overthrew their kings and queens. Long, long time ago," she told him.

"Was your father part of that?"

"Fuck no, I'm not that fucking old!" Robert called back. "But it's fitting, that we're here to kill Harold once and for all on this very day! Almost wish the little pud-knocker was still around, so we could march his ass to the guillotine!"

Rosella saw the question on Thomas' face and answered before he could ask: "Machine used to cut people's heads off. Used in the French—that's in France—Revolution."

"Sounds terrible."

"Supposed to be pretty gruesome."

"Yeah," Robert called back. "They say you'd still see out your eyes, hear with your own ears, feel your head falling down into the basket, before you lost consciousness. Bet you didn't feel much, though, not really, because the fucking pain of having your neck cut clean through would send you straight into goddam shock, if that term even applies to somebody who's just a head. But enough bullshitting, everybody ready to kick some ass?" He started the vertical lift fans, and the ship began to hum with a slight yet constant shudder.

"Ready," said Mrs. Lifeson, latching the helmet to her armor.

"Ready," said Rosella. She leaned over to give Thomas a quick kiss before fixing her own helmet in place.

Mrs. Lifeson opened the aft hatch, letting in the cool early-morning air. She did not bother to lower the steps, but simply leapt out and activated the jets on her suit to launch herself into the blue-black sky. Rosella followed. One-two heavy thumping steps and the hiss of jet-nozzles thrusting against gravity, and she too was gone.

"Shut the door already!" Robert shouted from the forward cabin.

Thomas pulled the hatch shut, secured it in place, and joined the old man at the control console.

"They'll be flying high cover for us as we go in," said Robert. "I used to be pretty damned good in a Vulcan, but it's been a long time, and I'm a little rusty. We'll take the fan in as far as we can, then we'll bail. I'll carry you while the girls provide cover."

Thomas nodded. He did not say anything, because there was nothing, really, to say. Nothing that would mean much of anything. Thomas realized that he may have seen the last of Rosella, that she could die or he could die or they both could die in the next few minutes. He realized that they could die, that they could fail, and if they failed, the false prophet and demon might forever rule the world and make it more and more a hellish Abend for all those who remained. Generations on generations would continue to worship the demon, and conditions in Megadon would grow worse and worse, until Level Fifty-Nine became as Level One was now, and Level One was nothing but darkness. Little children would be pushed and beaten onto the buses, and mothers would be pulled, screaming, from their daughters and sons, as Thomas' own mother had been taken that horrible night. There would be no end to it, and there was really nothing left to say, in the face of such daunting prospects. It was very basic, from where Thomas sat in the cockpit of the frontier air-car. Very basic: they would win and a new day would dawn on a new world; or they would lose, they would die, and the rest of the world would slowly and painfully follow them into a death far worse. Not much to say in the face of the current circumstances. Words would be weightless compared to what would or would not occur in the next few hours.

Robert pulled worked the throttles and the ship eased its way up from the forest floor, past the many-crossed network of branches that seemed to reach for the fuselage. They cleared the trees and hovered there. Robert pulled on a radio-headset. "We're up," he said into the tiny microphone.

"Roger that. One has visual," came Mrs. Lifeson's voice over the console-speaker.

"Ditto for Two," called Rosella.

Thomas stared out the windscreen. The sky was still dark, but so was the horizon. It took him a moment to realize that something was missing, and that something was Syrinx. "It's dark," he said.

Robert stared out. "Yes, it is, isn't it? Girls copy?"

"Roger. Been dark since we launched," said Rosella.

"Repeat? You mean it went dark *when* you launched?" asked Robert.

"Negative. It was dark when we cleared the trees," said Mrs. Lifeson.

"Well, thanks for letting us know." Robert drummed the fingers of his left hand against his heavily-armored thigh and sighed.

"Figured you'd see it for yourself," Mrs. Lifeson came back. "No way you would have sat there on the ground and taken our word for it."

"They can't think to hide the city from us," Thomas told him.

"No, but it probably means they know we're on the way. And this would be a little easier if they had left the lights on."

Thomas felt a sudden impatience with the old man. Lights on or lights off, they still had to shut down the Great Computer and destroy the demon that resided within. And he wanted it done, whatever was going to happen, life or death, he wanted to do it, to have it resolved. Sitting there hovering above the tree-tops was nothing but a waste of time. "Well, are we going in or not?" he asked.

"Yeah, shit, yeah." Robert gave the forward-thrust fans some throttle and they eased gradually forward. "Still, have to wonder what they're up to."

"It's just darkness," Thomas told him. "You have infrared and ultravision in your suits, and I'll make my way as best I can."

"Of course," said Robert, but it was clear to Thomas that he wasn't listening, that he was busy thinking, busy trying to determine just what the demon was doing in Syrinx.

Thomas sat back in his seat, stared forward at the darkness ahead. They rode for minutes in silence, Robert easing the forward throttle open until they were rushing along at well over a hundred knots. A few minutes more, and the darkness ahead was sullied by a bright burning spark high in the sky. Something glowing yellow-orange, plummeting downward toward the invisible horizon. It fell and fell but eventually slowed, and the yellow-orange went orange, then the orange went a dull and barely visible red, and the red faded to be replaced by a steady blue glow. Then it disappeared from the sky.

"Now what do you think that was?" Robert asked, easing off the throttle, slowing the air-car.

"Orbital shuttle," Thomas told him. "Maybe mine."

"I know *that*," said the old man. "But why the hell and who the hell and what the fuck are they up to? Girls, any input?"

"Nada," said Rosella.

"One of the constructs, Api, or Brown, sent to help defend Syrinx," said Mrs. Lifeson. "Who else could it be? Those shuttles can't carry many passengers."

"I thought the copies of the Cardinal and Father Brown were kept here at Syrinx," Thomas told Robert.

"Yeah, so?"

"Well, we destroyed two of them in Megadon before I left."

"Two more could have been sent to Megadon while you were on your way here," Robert said.

Thomas's felt his frustration return. "Alright. Let's go then."

Robert gave him a long look. "Alright," he said. Then, into the microphone, "I'm going to floor it, let's go!"

"One roger," said Mrs. Lifeson.

"Two roger," said Rosella.

Thomas was pressed gently back into his seat as the old man brought them up to full speed. Thomas kept his eyes closed because, just as there was no sense in wasting words, just as there was no sense in wasting time, there was no sense in his bothering to look out any longer at the featureless early morning. There was no sense in fueling pointless speculation with imagined shapes from the darkness all around. There was no sense in his being on the ship in which he rode but for the fact that it would deliver him to Syrinx, and to the fight there, and to the Great Computer. The old man was doing all the flying, and there was nothing for Thomas to do until they closed the gap between themselves and the city.

And so he sat there, trying to think of nothing but what had to be done. Trying to see only the objective ahead. He sat there, eyes closed, until Robert said "Ten kilometers and closing."

Then Thomas opened his eyes, and left his seat. He opened the small hatch between the two seats and lowered himself into the chin-turret, and loaded the guns. All was still dark. The forest zipped by beneath the clear plexi bubble, but it was only a vague repetition of shadows on shadows.

"Five kilometers and closing," said Robert.

Thomas wrapped his hands about the grips of the guns, rested his thumb lightly on the firing button. He wasn't sure there would be any targets for him to shoot. He wasn't sure he was doing anything in that turret but making himself a more readily accessible target, but it felt better to be sitting there with those guns in his hands than sitting above feeling completely useless.

"Four kilometers and closing," said Robert.

Thomas felt he should pray, and tried to focus on the might and majesty of the Great CPU, but it was no good. He tried to focus on the Holy, but felt only the cold grips in his hands, felt only the forward rush of the ship, felt only the press of the action that was just barely pending.

"Three kilometers and closing," said Robert.

Thomas saw great dark shapes against the darkness ahead. The pyramids of Syrinx, an indefinite yet massive bulk looming. Syrinx was nowhere near the size of Megadon, yet still it seemed large, with the trees the only indicators of scale. And so dark, as if the sky was dark only for the presence of the city, which Thomas had once thought of as Holy. Still, Holy, perhaps, somewhere beneath the layers of foul deception heaped on by the demon called Harold.

"Two kilometers and closing," said Robert.

Two kilometers was close enough for the opposition to have opened fire. Thomas had expected a barrage of shoulder-fired missiles, followed by concentrated fire from the energy-rifles with which the acolytes of both Cardinal Api and Father Brown were equipped. That was how he would have done it. The Vigilance garrison at Syrinx possessed twenty single-use shoulder-mounted ground-to-air missile-launchers. Thomas would have deployed those as a first line of defense, knowing that the incoming frontier air-car was too slow and ungainly to dodge them all. Then he would have assembled the acolytes, both the red and the black, as a second line of defense. Their energy-weapons were powerful at long ranges and highly accurate. It would be nothing for the acolytes to stitch the ship from nose to stern. The two armored women, that would have been another matter altogether. It would be better to set some kind of trap for them, lure them in close and contain them somehow, or simply overwhelm them with numbers. Maybe that was why the city was so dark, so seemingly lifeless. Thomas had no doubt they were flying straight into some type of trap.

"One kilometer and closing," said Robert. "Ladies, you got anything out there?"

Thomas flipped on the intercom in the chin-turret. "Two groups of fifty each, standing in review formation before the Great Pyramid," came Rosella's voice. "Temple and Vigilance acolytes, but it looks like they're just standing there, weapons at port-arms. They're standing facing the orbital shuttle that came in. One man standing at-ease near the shuttle, probably the pilot."

"Anybody in the shuttle?" Robert asked.

"Unknown. It's still hot enough so I can't tell."

"Well did you get a look at anybody getting off the damned thing when it landed?" Robert asked.

"Negative. Out of range. Too many buildings in the way."

"Maybe they've sent someone to surrender," came Mrs. Lifeson's voice. Thomas could hear her smiling.

"Fat fucking chance," said Robert. "Let's go." With that, he must have pushed the steering yoke hard forward; Thomas felt a moment of near weightlessness, then had to let go of the guns before him and grab the lip of the overhead hatch to keep himself from being pulled by gravity into the nose of the turret. The ship was in a sharper dive than any for which it had been built, and the entire air-car began to rattle and vibrate as it took on speed.

They were inside the city now, the taller buildings moving by as bulks of black on either side, lesser pyramids recognizable only for the steep rake of their silhouettes against the backdrop of the less sacred structures. Thomas stared out the turret, scanning this way and that for any sign of danger, any hint of the trap that he knew would be waiting. He kept a wary eye as Robert piloted the ship through the maze of the Holy City, and, as Thomas kept looking, he thought he saw more; either his eyes had adjusted to the gloom of pre-morning or the sun had its climb, far off beneath the horizon. It was dark, but slightly less dark than before.

"Approaching target zone," Robert's voice came over the intercom. "Let's get ready to kick some ass. Copy?"

"Rog," came Mrs. Lifeson's voice.

"Yup," said Rosella.

Thomas keyed the intercom. "Ready."

Robert banked the ship hard about the corner of a lesser pyrmid, nosing up to climb then diving again, almost to street, level, as they cleared the hurdle. They were in the great courtyard before the Great Pyramid. There in the middle of the plain before them was the Vice Chancellor's orbital shuttle, a black spike resting on its stalk-like landing gear. And beyond that shuttle there stood two distinct formations of men. Temple and Vigilance Acolytes, ordered there as if for review, just as Rosella and Mrs. Lifeson had reported. And beyond these formations of zealous men was the eternally stout and steadfast center of all that had been sacred, the Great Pyramid, which had once anchored the Holy City to the rest of the world by the presence of the Almighty Harold within its sacred meters-thick walls. Wider than it was tall, it still looked stronger than any structure not built on faith, yet Thomas knew better. The Temple of Temples had become home to evil, to deception, a hive of heresy, lair of Virus and Abend and Legion, beacon for the return of the Elder Race. Robert may have given Thomas the truth behind those tales of the wicked race cast from earth by the might of the Great CPU, but Thomas still had his doubts, still harbored fears he knew were primitive and beyond reason. It was enough that the demon called Harold should be destroyed; he could sort out the rest after this great labor was complete.

They raced across the plain. Robert kept the orbital shuttle between the air-car and the acolytes assembled ahead, but they must have seen the ship closing on them, must have seen it and heard it and yet they remained where they were, their weapons at port-arms. Because this was what they had been ordered to do. Thomas knew the men in that armor were as faithful as faithful could be, beyond the point of being rabid fanatics. If told to put their energy-rifles to their own heads and take their own lives, they would do so, with maximum speed and zero hesitation. If told to stand at review on the plain before the Great Pyramid, if told to remain there no matter what came, they would do so.

And they did. Thomas saw acolytes begin to fall as Rosella dove in on their formations, firing micro-missiles and launching grenades as she went. Small and instantly-disappearing bursts of light broke out among the ranks of black armor as Rosella's munitions found their targets. Vigilance acolytes fell where they stood, or were blown forward or back or sideways into their comrades, who stumbled but then returned to stand with their weapons at port-arms. Similar destruction was wrought among the ranks of those armored in red when Mrs. Lifeson made her dive on their formation, yet the remaining Temple acolytes remained arrayed for review, as if the attack was not taking place, as if their fellows were not falling all around them. Thomas wondered what might be going through the heads of those faceless men on the ground. Something to do with faith, no doubt. Something to do with holiness, duty, sacred honor. Thomas himself had endured enough during his days in Vigilance, and accepted all that he had endured as a series of tests on his faith. The loss of his mother, the desperate poverty of Level One, the brutality he'd seen as an enlisted man, the injustice he'd seen as an officer. All tests of faith, as mentioned in Scripture. Thomas had never considered a future as an acolyte, but he could guess what they might be thinking. He knew those men were second to none when it came to self-sacrificing self-discipline; they would stand there because they had been ordered to stand there. It was the will of the Almighty; it was the will of the Great CPU.

What Thomas could not understand was how the slaughter of those men fit into the plan, the trap set by the demon called Harold. It made little sense to let those most dedicated troopers be cut down, unless their deaths were intended to lull Thomas and Robert and Rosella and Mrs. Lifeson into states of overconfidence. But how could even the demon perceive such a terrible loss as any kind of gain? It made no sense, no sense at all.

"Grab those guns, Ryan," came Robert's voice over the intercom. "Cut us a path." With that, Robert swung the ship around the resting orbital shuttle and sped the air-car directly at the decimated formation of Vigilance acolytes. Such senseless slaughter, Thomas knew that this must have been just what the demon wanted, knew they were flying right into a trap, but he swiveled the guns forward and opened up on the armored men just the same. The grips bucked in his hands as the guns spewed forth a steady stream of lead and more and more acolytes fell. Robert cut a zig-zag pattern through the standing assembly, and those whom Thomas did not shoot down were run over by the low-flying air-car, a steady series of thumping sounds against the hull.

Robert brought the ship back around and repeated the attack on the acolytes armored in red. Rosella and Mrs. Lifeson swooped down and killed those few stragglers who remained, those fanatic fools who still stood, their weapons at port-arms. One hundred men lay dead on the plain before the Great Pyramid. They had not put up any kind of fight. Thomas sat in the chin-turret looking out at all the fallen, and pieces of the fallen. Where was the trap? Where was the terrible opposition they'd expected?

"Pilot's gone into the shuttle, he's started the engines," came Mrs. Lifeson's voice over the intercom.

"Got him," said Rosella. Thomas had to crane his neck to look back through the narrow section of the chin-turret, but he watched Rosella in her white armor launch herself at the solid black orbital shuttle. Its engines were glowing blue in preparation for take-off, but she cut an arc down through the air and straight through one set of the shuttle's landing gear. The ship stood there a moment, then tipped slowly to the one side, as if unwilling to accept its immanent fall. It tipped and then toppled, and came smashing down on its side.

"Round one for the good guys," said Robert. "Let's do what we came here to do. Let's finally end this shit."

Thomas wanted to key his intercom, wanted to suggest the fight had gone too well, that it had been all too easy, that something was wrong. But Rosella's voice came over the speaker before Thomas could bring himself to protest.

"Hey, I've got something weird here. Looks like Cardinal Api and Father Brown."

"Say again," Robert told her.

"Cardinal Api and Father Brown, right here. They're just laying there."

Robert swung the air-car around to face Rosella, who hovered over the space between the fallen orbital shuttle and the fallen formations of acolytes. Robert eased the air-car forward and there on the red-paved surface at the edge of the landing-pad lay a lump of red robes and a lump of black robes. Pale bald heads and pale skinny arms protruded from both lumps. Cardinal Api and Father Brown.

"Hit them with something," Robert ordered, as he eased the air-car back away from the apparently figures. Thomas sighted his guns in on Father Brown. He knew, just knew that black-robed bastard was about to leap up into the air, leap up impossibly high, and with all the force of Legion grab Rosella by the ankle and pull her down to the ground where both wicked old men or machines or demons or whatever they really were would tear her to bits.

Rosella fired a barrage of micro-missiles at the figures, and they were tumbled by the tiny but powerful explosions. Tumbled as if lifeless, tumbled as they were nothing more than chunks of dead flesh.

"Hit them again," Robert ordered. "Everybody."

Mrs. Lifeson joined Rosella in raining down more destruction, and Thomas opened up with his guns. The bodies on the ground were pushed back and forth as the robes were torn to shreds, yet neither the Cardinal nor Father Brown made a single move of their own.

"Guess that's that," said Robert. "Let's not lose track of the constructs, but let's move on." He turned the air-car around and flew on toward the Great Pyramid, over the red-paved path and straight through the fountains toward the massive double doors. "Let's knock down those doors," he said, and Rosella and Mrs. Lifeson launched more explosives to tear the great doors from their hinges.

"Three heat-signatures inside the first chamber," called Mrs. Lifeson, as she climbed back into the sky.

Robert banked away from the open doorway and put the ship down hard and fast beside the Great Pyramid. He landed so abruptly that Thomas' teeth were jarred as the landing gear slammed down. "Let's go, let's go!" Robert called from above.

Thomas crawled out of the turret to find Robert pulling on the gloves of his armor. "Hand me that frigging helmet," he said.

Thomas passed the old man the helmet that lay on the deck. Robert lowered it onto his head and snapped it in place, then took a dark-green metal ball from an overhead bin, and tucked it under his left arm.

"What's that?" Thomas asked.

"It's a nuke," said the old man, through the loudspeaker on his suit. Then he lead the way out of the ship. Thomas grabbed his scattergun and auto-rifle and followed.

Rosella hovered on one side of the open doorway, Mrs. Lifeson on the other. When Robert walked slowly into the darkness of that first chamber, the two women took up positions on his left and his right, hovering forward above and behind him. Thomas held his scattergun in one hand, auto-rifle in the other, and walked along beside Robert, ready to blast whatever might reveal itself in the gloom.

The darkness was pierced by a bright red spark, and the three in armor stopped. Thomas went down on one knee, closing one eye to keep from being blinded by the sudden onslaught of bright light.

It was a flare, a bright red emergency flare, thrown to the floor at the opposite end of the long narrow chamber. Its rapidly flickering light revealed a man in the white robes of the medical priesthood. Behind him, a gleaming dark figure, a man tightly wrapped in some kind of metal. This metal man held a smaller figure that Thomas recognized as young David, Mrs. Lifeson's son. The gleaming dark figure had one hand wrapped about David's arm; the other hand rested on David's throat.

"Greetings, infidels!" shouted the one in white robes. "Surrender now and the boy will not be harmed!"

"It's over!" called David. "We won! The Great Computer is down!"

"Shut up!" the white-robed man shouted at the boy. Thomas recognized the man then, recognized him from his visits to the Red Star Medical Center.

"Packard-Dell!" Thomas shouted. "Who are you to threaten the son of the former Vice Chancellor?!"

"I am the Surgeon General, sent by Almighty Harold Himself to have your surrender or your deaths!"

Thomas had no idea what radio communications might have been passed back and forth between his three companions in their stout suits of armor, but both Rosella and Robert had raised their right arms toward the gleaming dark figure that held David. Mrs. Lifeson hovered slowly forward, edging her way almost imperceptibly down the hall.

"As the Vice Chancellor of Vigilance, I order you to release the boy!" Thomas shouted back at Packard-Dell. Whoever or whatever that was holding David, it no doubt answered to the newly-appointed Surgeon General, and so long as Thomas kept the white-robed idiot engaged in discussion, David would probably be okay. Probably.

"You have no authority, heretic! You are an outlaw, an agent of Legion and the Elder Race!" Packard-Dell proclaimed. "You will surrender now or the Lifeson boy will die!"

"You don't want to do that!" Thomas called. "Kill him, and nothing stands between you and us!"

"The Great Computer is dead! It's stuck calculating *pi*!" shouted David, struggling against the hands that held him tight.

"Enough! Enough of your blasphemy!" Packard-Dell screamed.

Then the air was filled with the ripping sounds of blazing mini-guns. Packard-Dell was shredded into pink mist. The dark gleaming figure holding David was hit in the head with a steady stream of high-velocity bullets and staggered back. It was Mrs. Lifeson who had killed the medicine-man, and now she dove under the stream of fire from Robert and Rosella. She dove and drove straight for the dark gleaming figure, hitting it low and knocking it from its feet.

The figure rolled with the impact, still holding onto David's arm with one hand. Thomas knew then, from the remarkably fluid manner in which that figure moved, that they were facing Compaq. Colonel Compaq, Bishop Compaq, now faceless metal-wrapped Compaq. There was no telling what the priests of the Red Star Medical Center had done to him now. There was no time to test his new strengths or probe for possible weaknesses. There was nothing to do but take Compaq down.

At the far end of the hall, Compaq lashed out with his free hand against the helmet of Mrs. Lifeson's armor. The blow left a sharp crease in the hardened metal and Mrs. Lifeson stumbled backward. She went airborne and rushed forward again, hitting Compaq square in the chest with both boots. It was an awkward attack, one Compaq could have dodged had he not been holding onto David's arm. But those big boots hit Compaq and he was knocked back, dragging David with him.

Rosella flew to the end of the hallway now, and Thomas ran after her. She swung her great armored fists at the fallen Compaq. He managed to knock aside her blows with his free hand, and drove his knee violently up into her mid-section, putting a clean round dent into her armor. But Rosella kept swinging.

Thomas had made it halfway down the hall when Mrs. Lifeson grabbed David by the leg and tried to pull him free from Compaq's grasp. Compaq pulled back and David began to scream. Mrs. Lifeson pulled again, and Compaq pulled back even harder. David screamed. His arm came off at the shoulder, and David screamed.

Mrs. Lifeson pulled David clear of Compaq, and tossed her son sliding across the smooth floor directly toward Thomas. David came sliding on his back, leaving a thick trail of gore behind him. His life pouring out. Thomas dropped his weapons and knelt to stop David's progress. He pressed his hands down on the open shoulder-joint but the blood kept rushing out between his fingers.

Heavy thuds of boots behind him. Thomas looked back and saw armored Robert standing there. "Crack open a couple shotgun shells, hurry," came his voice over the suit's speaker. "Spread the powder on the wound.

Thomas did as he was told, pouring the powder over and into the gaping hole.

"Now light it with your pistol," the old man told him.

Thomas drew an energy-pistol, set it to low, and fired at an angle into the wound. The powder caught and flared. David kicked and redoubled his screaming. But the wound was burnt shut. Dark blood oozed around the edges of the blackened flesh, but the torrent had stopped. "Watch him and watch this," said Robert, holding out the dark green metal ball that was a nuclear warhead.

Thomas took the bomb and watched the old man fly into the fray at the end of the hallway. With David clear, both Mrs. Lifeson and Rosella had really opened up on Compaq, firing bursts of mini-gun rounds at point-blank range whenever there was an opening, and swinging more furiously with their armored boots and fists. Compaq moved more quickly than Thomas had ever seen him move before, much more quickly than either armored woman. He dodged and blocked and kept moving to put one opponent between himself and the other, but some of their shots were still getting through. It was difficult to tell what impact the massive blows and bursts of fire were having on the newly-armored Compaq. He showed no signs of slowing, but nor did Rosella or Mrs. Lifeson, and it seemed clear that they would eventually wear him down. As Robert joined them and the odds went from two-to-one to three-to-one, Compaq's defeat seemed even more of a foregone conclusion. The four figures almost seemed to dance in the flickering red light from the flare on the floor.

Thomas was looking down at David when Compaq slipped free of the struggle. Thomas caught the slightest glimpse of movement in the corner of one eye, and by the time he looked up, Compaq was in mid-air hurtling directly toward him.

Thomas let go of the nuke and put himself between Compaq and the boy. He braced himself for Compaq's attack, but it never came. Instead, there came a rapid succession of small explosions. A barrage of micro-missiles slamming into Compaq's back, knocking him down to the floor some five meters in front of Thomas.

Compaq began to slowly rise, but another barrage of missiles knocked him down. The fluid metal in which he'd been wrapped had begun to crack and peel. Another barrage and Thomas could see bleeding flesh and flexing white plastaegis. Compaq tried once more to rise, but failed. Rosella and Robert and Mrs. Lifeson flew to where Compaq lay and tore the remaining scraps of armor from his body. Then Mrs. Lifeson knelt and pressed her big armored palm down over Compaq's beaten and blood-stained face.

The final defender of the demon called Harold bucked and struggled beneath the armored hand, but that bucking and struggling weakened and weakened, and he never moved again.

Mrs. Lifeson left Compaq's body and scooped up David, flew with him out of the Great Pyramid.

"That's fucking that," came Robert's voice over his loud-speaker. "Pick up that nuke, and let's go, Ryan."

Thomas picked up the metal ball and followed Rosella and her father to the end of the hall, where they battered down the door to that chamber where Thomas was supposed to have believed he'd felt his soul being tested before his first audience with the Great Computer. This chamber was as dark as had been the hallway before it, lit only by the flickering red flare that still burnt behind them as they proceeded to the elevator.

Rosella ripped open the elevator, and blasted a large hole in the floor of the car. She and Robert activated spot-lights on their armor. Rosella offered Thomas her arm, and he grabbed on with his free hand. Robert went down through the hole first. Rosella, carrying Thomas, followed.

The way was dark, and their spotlights cast long shadows as they descended. It was silent but for the hiss of the jets on their suits. They did not go all the way down, not immediately. First they detoured into that hidden chamber some half-way down the shaft. They walked down the short hallway to the room where Thomas had seen the copies of Cardinal Api and Father Brown, and the man who had so closely resembled Vice Chancellor Lifeson. The copies of Api and Brown were still there, laying lifeless and still beneath their plexi domes. The man who looked like a Lifeson was not.

"No fucking surprise," said Robert. "Brother Billy's gotten out while the getting was good."

They proceeded back to the elevator shaft and down to the cold and silent gray concrete hemispheric chamber of the Great Computer. The black box was quiet. No voices this time. Nothing but a single green light blinking on the console where Director Jobs had done his work before being killed by Father Brown.

"It's still functioning," said Robert, as he surveyed the panel. "But it's not doing so well. Close to locking up completely. Looks like David was right. The lights, the constructs, everything ran through these processors one way or another." He laughed. "*Pi*! Why the hell didn't I think of that? That fucking kid!"

The old man removed his helmet and gloves, and took the bomb from Thomas. Robert opened up the metal casing and twisted a dial that turned with a soft clicking sound.

"How much time will we have?" Thomas asked, taking one last look around at the chamber, and at the Great Computer that housed the demon who'd spread such tyranny and evil for so many years. He recalled how the true faithful had suffered so much for so long, and he felt not the slightest regret for the impending destruction of that machine or the monster within.

"I was thinking fifteen minutes. We can get to the surface and put a couple clicks between us and this place in that time. This room's so fucking far underground, and since we're able to plant the egg so close, I set it for a low yield. There shouldn't be much of a blast or any real fallout back up on the surface."

Thomas nodded. The old man closed the casing of the bomb and pulled his gloves back on, snapped his helmet back into place.

They left the chamber and flew quickly back to the surface. Dawn had painted the eastern sky a brilliant orange. Mrs. Lifeson was waiting with David aboard the frontier air-car, in the rear crew compartment. She had his head in her lap and sat stroking his hair. The boy was conscious but weak, and lay there with his eyes half-lidded. "Did I do it?" he asked, when he saw his uncle.

"You sure did, kid, you sure as hell did," Robert told him. The old man knelt on the deck beside the bunk. "You're making your old Uncle Robert feel like a dumbass, using that old *pi* trick, you know."

"It was Mal's idea," David told him.

Thomas went forward and cranked up the fans. Rosella shed her helmet and gloves and took the seat beside him. She placed her hand over his as he moved the throttles forward. The ship gave a momentary shudder, then left the ground. Thomas brought it up to full speed and piloted them out of the city.

07-17-2112

David stood with his mother and Mal and Uncle Robert and his strange new Uncle Billy atop the Vigilance flight deck on Level Sixty. Megadon was a dark mountain beneath them, its millions of residents still finding their ways out into the wilds beyond the wire. It had been exciting, to watch their faces as these men and women and children got their first looks at a wide open sky. The people of Xanadu had come to guide the newcomers, to show them the way, to show them how best to live off the land now ruled by trees. It would be some time before the hundreds of millions could find comfort beyond the wire, build their new lives, but they would learn and grow in ways they had never thought possible, and their lives would be their own. There would be many trials in the months and years ahead, but, for the moment, there were more pressing matters at hand.

The ships that hovered over the dead city were silver disks against the evening sky, shining with a steady inner glow. They had been holding the same position for three hours now, just hanging there over Megadon as if observing the steady leave-taking that transpired below.

"At least they're not trying to assume control," said Uncle Robert.

"Of course not," said Uncle Billy. "I wouldn't allow it in any case."

"Hey, if you can stop them from doing shit, why'd you let that shitbag Harold fuck everything up the way he did?" Mal asked.

Uncle Robert rolled his eyes. "Kid, you're just asking for a headache. I don't want to hear it again. I'll try to explain it to you later."

David looked at his new uncle. Dad's other brother. He looked more like Dad than Uncle Robert did, but he was different, very different. He'd appeared here and there over the last few days, like some kind of angel from Scripture, helping with the evacuation of the city. He'd produced provisions from thin air; he'd cured the sick and wounded; he'd even given David a new arm. One moment there had been just the throbbing stump of his shoulder, the next there had been his arm, as if it had never been torn away. Uncle Billy was different, and David supposed it was a different that was good, despite Uncle Robert's evident distrust.

"He's coming down now," Uncle Billy said now.

As if in response, one of the silver ships began to descend, directly toward the flight deck where they all stood watching. It came down slowly and silently, and it was the silence that made it seem unreal. Ships, even orbital shuttles, made noise. They buzzed or hummed or roared. But not this one. It was quiet, completely quiet, and this gave David the impression that it might not be real.

"He *who*?" asked Uncle Robert.

"You'll see."

It was a large ship, far too large to set down on the deck, but it came down to hover just meters from the surface, bathing David and his mother and everyone else in its glow.

"Hey Robert!" came a voice from behind David. "Hey, look, I'm over here!"

David spun with everyone else. He saw a stout, round but solid man standing there, smiling with teeth that were, like the rest of his body, wide but short, very deep in his broad wet gums.

Uncle Robert let out a sound that was something like a laugh or a cough and rushed the stranger, grabbing him and hugging him.

Mom put her hand on David's back. "That's your Uncle Jimmy," she said.

"Fuck, how many uncles do you have?" asked Mal.

David shook his head. He'd heard Uncle Robert's stories about Jimmy, but the sudden arrival of this long-lost relative only made him miss his father. It was unfair, that this fabled stranger should return when Dad could not. Unfair, even, that he could be granted a new arm when Dad could not be granted new life. It was wrong, so wrong, and it made David angry, not at anything or anyone in particular, but at everything. Sad and angry, the worst kind, because there was nothing to do about it, no way to stop it or change the way things were. He turned away from the happy home-coming and walked toward the edge of the flight deck. Way down below, people were moving in the early twilight. Their lanterns and torches formed divergent twinkling paths snaking slowly away from the city.

David stood there and watched the little lights below, and tried to block out the laughing and good-natured shouting behind him.

Then they were calling his name. "David! David!"

Still he kept his back to them, kept his mind fixed on his father's absence and his own loss.

Then, "Davy? Davy?" Directly behind him. The new uncle, the new old retarded uncle who somehow deserved to come back when Dad could not.

David turned around, wanting to say something spiteful, but he knew that to open his mouth would be to risk breaking into tears. He clenched his jaw tight and simply stared at the strange stout man before him.

"You look like Mikey," said the man. "Mikey was your dad, and you're Davy but you look like Mikey."

David closed his eyes and nodded.

"Mikey said I was supposed to find you, and that was the last thing he said to me. He said to find you and make sure you were safe. That's what he said. So now I found you, and that's good, because that's what he said to do. I would have found you before, but I wasn't here, so I found you now, and I need to make sure you're safe, because that's what Mikey wanted."

David opened his eyes and there was Jimmy nodding and smiling, so proud to have accomplished this last task Dad had set for him. So proud and so well-intentioned and so funny-looking with his round face and his bowl-shaped haircut and his gleaming square teeth. David burst out laughing, and with the laughter came the tears he'd been trying so hard to hold back.

"Are you alright, Davy? Are you happy or sad? I did find you, I did! And that's what he said to do! He did!" Jimmy put a thick hand on David's shoulder and squeezed, and, in a way, it was like Dad's hand, reaching from the long-gone past, Dad's hand there on David's shoulder, warm and assuring. Find him. Keep him safe.

David nodded, and kept laughing as the tears ran down his cheeks. "You found me, Uncle Jimmy. And I'm safe. Thank you."

David and his new uncle walked back to the others. The silver ships landed silently outside the city, and free thinkers and great warriors, men and women from the old world, disembarked to help build the new.

0-595-32212-3

Printed in the United States
22622LVS00005B/275

9 780595 322121